BLAST
FROM THE
PAST

JEFFREY POOLE

Jeffrey Poole's Epic Fantasy Books
Bakkian Chronicles:
The Prophecy
Insurrection
Amulet of Aria
Disneyland Debacle (short story)
Winter Wonderland (short story)

Tales of Lentari
Lost City
Something Wyverian This Way Comes
A Portal for Your Thoughts
Thoughts for a Portal
Wizard in the Woods
Close Encounters of the Magical Kind
The Hunt for Red Oskorlisk (short story)
May the Fang be With You (Pirates trilogy #1)
The Hammer is Strong with This One (Pirates #2)
These are Not the Stones You're Looking For (Pirates #3)
Blast from the Past

Dragons of Andela
Harness the Fire
Strike the Spark

Mysteries by J.M. Poole
The Corgi Case Files Series
19 delightful cozy mystery novels featuring corgi
sleuths, Sherlock and Watson

BLAST FROM THE PAST

Tales of Lentari, Book 10

JEFFREY POOLE

Secret Staircase Books

Blast From the Past
Published by Secret Staircase Books, an imprint of
Columbine Publishing Group, LLC
PO Box 416, Angel Fire, NM 87710

Book layout and design by Secret Staircase Books
First paperback edition: August, 2024
First e-book edition: August, 2024

* * *

Publisher's Cataloging-in-Publication Data

Poole, Jeffrey
Blast From the Past / by Jeffrey Poole.
p. cm.
ISBN 978-1649141873 (paperback)
ISBN 978-1649141880 (e-book)

1. Lentari (Fictitious location)—Fiction. 2. Epic fantasy fiction
3. Dragons and mythical creatures—Fiction. 4. Time travel—Fiction.
I. Title

Tales of Lentari : Book 10.
Blast From the Past
Poole, Jeffrey, Tales of Lentari epic fantasy series.

BISAC : FICTION / Fantasy/Epic.

813/.54

For Giliane —

That's it. No other words are necessary.

Acknowledgements

As always whenever I write one of my fantasies, errors surface, and let me tell you, this one had some doozies. So, without further ado, a huge hearty *thank you* goes out to my Posse members for helping me polish the story. Jason, Sharon, Robin, Louise, Diane, Caryl, Elizabeth, Wendy, and Debbie, just to name a few. You guys and gals are the best!

I'd also like to thank my second team of beta readers, from Secret Staircase Books. They are: Sandra Anderson, Susan Gross, and Paula Webb. Without everyone's help, there wouldn't be anything worth reading. :)

Table of Contents

Chapter One–Unexpected Guest

Northern Idaho was in the midst of a sweltering summer. Even though it wasn't supposed to hit temps higher than the mid-80s, much of the Idaho panhandle was seeing the thermometer climb well above ninety. At that temperature, no one really wanted to do much of anything, let alone cook. That included one couple, with a husband who had recently turned fifty, and his lovely wife, a woman in her mid-forties. The man stood six feet tall, had graying brown hair, and typically wore t-shirts, shorts, and sneakers due to his constant complaint of being warm. Walking into their favorite restaurant, a reasonable facsimile of a 1950s diner, the husband and wife were seated at a booth near the bar, and in silence, perused the menu. A commotion caused both of them to look up. There was a disturbance at the door.

"How many in your party?" he heard the hostess politely ask.

"Twelve."

The husband groaned. He could only hope that particular party was seated well away from them. Especially since the group had several youngsters under the age of three. Not that he had a problem with kids. Quite the opposite. His issues stemmed from the parents, who always seemed to go into ignore mode when the kids started misbehaving.

Breathing a sigh of relief, Steve Miller watched as the teenage hostess led the large family away, in the opposite direction.

"We dodged a bullet there," Sarah observed.

"True story."

Living in Coeur d'Alene, Idaho, for the past ten years, Steve didn't think he could be happier. They lived in a custom Tudor-style mansion just outside of town, on nearly two hundred fifty acres. The icing on the cake was the simple fact their property bordered BLM land, which meant he was never going to have to worry about someone developing the neighboring land and building a house or two.

And speaking of houses, their mansion? It was three stories of absolute perfection. Everything the two of them could've wanted was incorporated into their manor, with a few minor modifications added throughout the years. His ancestor, Luther Miller, had done an admirable job constructing the house, incorporating plenty of bathrooms, excess spare bedrooms, and his-and-her offices. Plus, the entire third story was nothing but one big primary suite, with a sitting room, observatory, terrace, and even a library.

Also, on the top floor of the house was a set of doors like none other. Leading into the suite itself, the frames were ten feet high and covered with symbols and runes. The massive double doors, when closed, depicted a single masterful carving: a countryside with seas on the east and western coasts, forests to the north and south, and mountain ranges to the north and southeast. In the top right corner, an exquisitely carved castle was seen, with multiple turrets, windows, and even a tiny drawbridge. And finally, if one looked close enough, a keyhole could be observed, masquerading as one of the castle's many windows. What did this keyhole unlock?

A doorway to another world.

That portal, Steve knew, would activate a one-way ticket to the magical Kingdom of Lentari. Creatures that only lived in fairy tales thrived there, such as malwerns, nixies, and dragons. What was the portal doing on the top floor of a house in Northern Idaho? That was easy. The mansion and the portal were built to facilitate the linking of his world to theirs. After all, it was how the two of them first stumbled their way into Lentari. To say that it had been quite an ordeal to return home would be the understatement of the century, but, thanks to Sarah's jhorun, or special power, they wouldn't have to worry about being stranded ever again.

Munching on a chip as they enjoyed their quiet time together, Steve's thoughts returned to their jhoruns. The magical abilities they acquired in Lentari also worked here, in Idaho; no one else could claim the same. Tristan, a former Lentarian soldier, and husband to Annie, Sarah's sister, couldn't use his abilities to temporarily summon a small dagger. At least, not unless he returned to Lentari. Sarah, on the other hand, could use her teleportation skills and jump them to any place she'd already been. Across the country. Around the planet. For that matter, from their world to Lentari. Sarah had done it.

For the umpteenth time, Steve wished he had a power like hers. Then again, his wasn't too shabby, either. He had a fire elemental; the strongest one anyone had ever seen. Able to deflect the fiery breath from a dragon, or stop a rampaging fire in its tracks, Steve had complete control over everything pertaining to heat and flames. Lighting barbecues, snuffing out house fires, blasting out jets of flame to incinerate a horde of huge bugs, or even to fly around like Iron Man; Steve had done it all.

He chuckled. Iron Man. He would only try that maneuver under the direst of circumstances, and even then, it scared the bejeezus out of him. He could handle the takeoffs, sure, but the landings were what worried him. He had yet to land on his feet, choosing instead, to punch his way through walls, drop through floors, or simply carry off whatever was within grabbing distance. That was the problem with his jhorun. For some inexplicable reason, it always decided to shut off too soon. He had yet to figure out why.

Iron Man needed more practice, thank you very much.

"What are you smiling about?" Sarah asked.

Steve shook his head. "Iron Man."

"You were so close last time," his wife told him, placing a patronizing hand on his, on the table. "I really thought for sure you were going to stick the landing."

"Too much momentum," Steve recalled, sighing. "Ended up ripping that poor tree I latched onto right out of the ground, roots and all. That took some explaining to the gardeners."

The waitress stopped by their table and grabbed his empty soda glass for a refill. She paused long enough to give him a querulous look.

"It's a new video game we're playing," Sarah explained. "Don't mind us."

Once the waitress had returned Steve's glass, and he had taken a healthy swig, he turned to Sarah and, taking a deep breath, decided to bring up that which had been bugging him for several months.

"Emerion."

Sarah looked up, a chip en route to her mouth. She quickly checked the nearby tables for any eavesdroppers.

"You're bringing him up? Here?"

"No one knows who he is," Steve told her. "I think it's safe."

"What about him?" Sarah wanted to know. Steve knew she was very protective over their young charge since she rescued him several years ago and brought him back to Idaho to raise. "Has he done something?"

"He's essentially full-grown. I think it might be time to see about returning him to ... to ... his home. He deserves to be with others of his kind, you know. He needs to know what it feels like to be a, uh, one of *them*."

Sarah's face fell. "I know. It's just that ... well, it'll be sad to see him go."

"It's not like we won't visit him," Steve said.

"I know we will. He's our little boy, and I'll worry about him."

"Little?" Steve scoffed, and shook his head. Lowering his voice, he leaned forward. "He's nearly twice the size of any we have ever seen, he's healthy as an ox, and I swear he has the strength of a small dragon."

"Don't forget, he's got your personality," Sarah reminded him.

"Level-headed, intelligent, and charming as hell?"

"Stubborn, impetuous, and sharp as a tack," Sarah corrected, giving him a nudge with her elbow. "You're right. I think it's time. Besides, Emerion has been dropping some not-so-subtle hints that he'd like to go exploring in Lentari. I say we let him do it."

"And so do I," a new voice added. A thin man, shorter than Steve, but dressed similarly, slid into the booth on the opposite side of them. The stranger had unkempt brown hair, a full beard, and a pair of sunglasses hooked to his bright blue shirt. There was something about his face, Steve decided, which prevented him from guessing his age. Thirty? Forty? "What's good here? I don't think I've been to this establishment before, and I've been to a great many places, believe you me."

"Excuse me?" Steve demanded, growing irritated. "What do you think you're doing? No one invited you to sit down, pal. Am-scray."

The stranger looked up and smiled. "What's the matter, Steve? You don't recognize me? What about you, Sarah?"

Steve looked at his wife. She was staring at the stranger and ready to shake her head when her eyes widened. She held a hand up to her face and shielded part of her gaze, as if she only wanted to look at a certain part of him. Her eyes widened with shock.

"Steve," Sarah whispered, "don't look at the eyes and, instead, just listen to the voice. He's right. We've met him before!"

Steve sighed and closed his eyes. "All right, you've piqued

my curiosity. Say something."

The stranger sat back in the booth and smiled. "Very well. As you Americans would say, does *Astral* ring any bells?"

Steve's eyes flew open and stared hard at the newcomer. "Eion."

Delighted, the stranger nodded. The waitress happened by just then.

"Hello, there. I didn't know you were expecting a third guest. Would you like to see a menu?"

"Oh, I wasn't planning on staying," Eion was saying.

"Nonsense," Sarah interrupted. "Yes, please bring our friend a menu. Thank you."

"What in the world are you doing here, pal?" Steve whispered. "Knowing who you are, and seeing you so nonchalantly sitting in a restaurant, is kinda freaking me out!"

Sarah's smile melted away. "Uh-oh. Is everything okay? Are you going to give us some bad news?"

The waitress returned and handed Eion a laminated menu. The young server waited a few moments, seeing if the table's newest occupant already knew what they wanted, or was going to take their time.

Steve glanced at the waitress and their eyes met.

"Will you need your order to go?"

Steve blinked a few times. "Huh?"

"Your order. I assume this is your son, and … it isn't. Oh, I'm so sorry. I'm a horrible guesser when it comes to ages."

Sarah started giggling. Eion chuckled as well, even though his nose was still in the menu.

"Do I look like I'm old enough to be a grandfather?" Steve sputtered.

"You are, you know," Sarah told him. "And in essence, you are. Mikal and Lissa are parents. Little Viv is, what, three years old now?"

"That kid's a handful," Steve agreed, nodding. "But, that doesn't mean she's my granddaughter." He glanced at Eion and saw that the Lentarian Ancient was moments away from laughing out loud. "Zip it, dude. Not funny. And you. Really? Age jokes?"

"You *are* the oldest one at the table," Sarah pointed out.

Steve hooked a thumb at Eion. "Not even close. Whatever. What'll you have, pal?"

"I'll take the Monte Cristo sandwich, please. And an iced tea."

The waitress nodded and hurried off.

"Great choice," Steve commented. "I've had them a few times here. Not quite as good as the Blue Bayou from Disneyland, but it's pretty close."

"I have yet to find a restaurant which could match the Blue Bayou's world-famous Monte Cristos," Eion said, in a companionable fashion.

Sarah gasped. "You've been to Disneyland?"

"All six of them, yes. And before you can ask, I will say that I've been to every resort Disney has to offer. What can I say? I'm a Disney fan."

"You continue to astound me," Sarah told the deity in disguise.

"You clearly get around," Steve added.

"I like to travel. Lately, I've been discovering new places to eat. There are so many to choose from!"

"You've been checking out our restaurants now?" Sarah asked, as she turned to Eion. "Is that why you're here? It's just a freakish coincidence?"

Eion shrugged. "Perhaps. Perhaps not."

"How many restaurants have you been to on this world?" Sarah asked.

Eion crossed his arms over his chest and turned pensive. "Let me think."

"Oh, come on," Steve was saying. "It can't be that many, can it? Especially if you just started."

"Thirteen thousand four hundred fifteen. This will make thirteen thousand four hundred sixteen. I hear there's a new Greek place opening up in the next few months."

Sarah sat up straighter. "There is? I haven't heard anything about it. Where will it be?"

"Off of Credenza Street," Eion immediately responded.

"I wasn't aware of a Credenza Street in Coeur d'Alene," Steve reported. "Maybe it's …?"

"… not in Coeur d'Alene?" Eion finished, continuing to

smile. "It's not. That's because it will be in a little town near London."

"England?" Steve asked. "Huh. Well, okay. England it is."

"I adore England," Eion continued. "That country has undergone so much change in the last three hundred years. I've been spending more and more time there."

Steve held up his hands in a time-out gesture. "All right, you're here, and you wanted to get our attention. Well, congrats, you got it. What's up? Is everything okay? Don't tell me ol' Captain Flinn is at it again."

"Your pirate friend is currently enjoying retirement on his private island," the Master of the Winds informed them. "He will live out the remainder of his natural life in relative comfort, so you needn't worry about him. But, enough about sailors. You mentioned you were wanting to take your griffin to Lentari? Good. You should."

"Why?" Steve wanted to know.

"Something's wrong," Sarah decided.

"Be sure Emerion is not left behind," Eion instructed.

Their orders arrived, and everyone ate in silence, with an occasional question tossed in here and there. Eion told them that, for the first time in several millennia, none of his all-powerful siblings were actively fighting with one another.

"Even Usol?" Steve asked.

"Even Usol," Eion confirmed. "Trust me, no one is more surprised than I. You were right about his stone. The wager had gone on long enough. Again, enough about me, this is more about you two. Well, you and your griffin, that is."

"What's going on with Emerion?" Sarah demanded. "You've brought him up twice now. Is he okay? Is there something we need to know?"

"I'm simply saying now would be a good time to return to Lentari. That's all. And with that, I take my leave of you. Steve, Sarah, be safe, and good luck."

There was a loud clatter in the kitchen. When the two of them returned their attention to their guest, both were shocked to see that Eion had disappeared.

"Stuck us with the bill, huh?" Steve grumped. "Fine. You owe us one, pal."

Surprisingly, a stiff breeze appeared, as though someone had propped open the front door.

"He sure has a way of getting your attention, doesn't he?" Steve said, rising to his feet. "Come on, I don't trust this. We need to head home."

Sarah gathered her purse. "Agreed."

Twenty minutes later, the two of them hurried through the side door of their enormous manor, conveniently located in the dining room. Setting his keys on the kitchen counter, Steve put his fingers in his mouth and gave a shrill whistle.

"Emerion! Are you here? Come on out, pal."

They heard a commotion from upstairs, a soft thud, followed immediately by a *THWUMP*, which was strong enough to rattle all the ceiling fans and light fixtures.

"What is it?" a strong, somewhat high voice asked, as it grew louder. "Steve? Is there something wrong with Sarah? If someone has harmed her, I will personally shred them from … oh, there you are. You scared the feathers off me. What's the matter?"

Two creatures hurried down the stairs. One was a tiny red-headed tri-colored corgi puppy, who was now yawning profusely, as though she had been in the middle of a nap and hadn't enjoyed being awoken in such an abrupt manner. As for the other, well, Emerion was the only one of his kind currently anywhere on the planet. He wasn't a rare breed of dog, nor was he an exotic pet, such as a bush baby or sugar glider. In fact, an outside observer would be hard pressed to find anything about him in any encyclopedia, book, or newspaper. What was he?

Emerion was a griffin.

Based on the loud ruckus they had just heard, Emerion and their new puppy must have been napping on the couch, something Steve had been trying to discourage. Not because he had a problem with either of them on the furniture, but because Emerion weighed in at nearly four hundred pounds. Apparently, back in Lentari, griffins might not always find enough to eat, so they fasted often. Many times, they would appear to be on the leaner side. But Emerion had two human parents who cared for him and made sure he had plenty to eat.

That, coupled with rigorous training in the air (in preparation for his return to Lentari), the tiny cub Sarah had rescued nearly six years ago was now, far and away, the largest, most muscular griffin either of them had ever seen.

And Sarah wouldn't have had it any other way.

"Emerion, are you all right?" Sarah asked, worried.

Thinking he was in trouble for getting caught sleeping on the couch upstairs, Emerion cocked his head as he stared at his foster mother. "I am fine. Why? What did you hear? Were you spying on me again?"

"I told you, I disconnected those cameras," Steve told the griffin. "And didn't I say I was sorry the last time?"

Emerion let out a trill, which was his version of laughter. "I do. Are you angry I had Zoe next to me, on the couch?"

"Only if the puppy had an accident," Steve returned.

"She did not," Emerion stated, looking fondly down at the little corgi, who was sitting next to his front foreleg.

"She takes some getting used to, doesn't she?" Sarah said, as she squatted next to the newest member of their household.

"I forget how much energy her predecessor had," Emerion admitted. "I do miss her. She was a sister to me."

"It's unfortunate," Sarah agreed. "Dogs don't live as long as we'd like them to, so the only thing we can do is cherish the time we have with them."

"And that's what I've been doing with her," Emerion confided. "I've been teaching little Zoe what is, and is not, acceptable. She's a quick learner."

It was Steve's turn to squat down low and ruffle the fur of the little black, red, and white corgi puppy.

"She's a handful, but she's worth every minute. We will always remember Peanut, and will always love her, but life goes on and we wanted to replace mourning with this highly energized bundle of fur."

The griffin looked fondly down at his new sister. "Agreed."

"Emerion, do you remember us telling you about Eion?" Steve finally asked.

"Eion, Master of the Winds," the griffin recalled, nodding. "I do."

"He joined us for dinner tonight," Sarah said.

Emerion's avian head tilted again. "Indeed? Here? Is that common?"

Both Steve and Sarah shook their heads.

"It's a first for me," Steve admitted. "So, you haven't heard or seen anything when you're flying around outside?"

"I stick low to the ground," the griffin assured him, "and only when it's dark outside. I will admit, I *am* looking forward to flying during the day."

"You will soon," Sarah promised. "We're heading to Lentari tomorrow."

"And you're coming with us," Steve added.

Emerion let out a loud, happy squawk. He dropped his nose and bumped it against the puppy's.

"Did you hear that? We're going to Lentari!"

"Zoe stays put," Sarah said, eliciting a groan from Emerion. "There's something wrong, and I can't put my finger on it. Eion kept saying we need to go to Lentari, so I'm guessing whatever's the matter will make itself known then."

"Think Annie will be able to keep an eye on Zoe for us?" Steve asked.

Sarah held up her phone. "I already asked her. She said yes. There's yet another good reason to have your family close by."

Steve nodded. "That's one way to look at it. Everyone we care about is just down the street, so to speak. Your parents, my parents, Lia and her new boyfriend. So, it's good Annie and Tristan's four kids are just around the corner. Besides, I've heard that Christopher has been hounding Annie and Tristan, hoping to get a dog, and Annie feels this would be a great way to find out just how serious he is about it. Er, pardon the pun."

Sarah wrinkled her nose. "Dogs? Sirius? That was horrible."

Steve laughed.

The following morning, Sarah found Steve in his office

on the ground floor. Both of them were wearing the leather armor given to them by their Lentarian friends years ago, although Steve did mention his cuirass was fitting a little more snugly than he remembered. Emerion and Zoe had just poked their heads into the office as well when the doorbell rang.

Zoe started barking, which came out as high-pitched yips. Emerion sighed. "I'll get it."

"Oh, no you don't," Sarah argued. "What if it's a salesman? Or someone who'll freak out if they see you?"

"It's Christopher," Emerion reported. "Here to pick up Zoe."

"Are you guessing?" Sarah asked.

"No. I can smell pepperoni."

Steve had to laugh. It certainly sounded like his nephew. Christopher was a growing boy and absolutely loved pizza.

The griffin was correct, and within ten minutes the boy had scooped up the puppy and her bag of gear—food, bowls, and toys—and headed for the door.

"Are we ready? Let me get the key and we'll be on our way." Steve entered his office and approached the statue of a griffin, standing on a pedestal. A humming started the moment he neared it, and just before he could touch it, the griffin raised its leg, revealing a button. He pressed the button and reached in to retrieve the old, rusted chest where they kept their portal keys.

The chest was empty!

"Where are the keys?" Steve straightened and held out the empty box. "Did we take them out and forget to put them back?"

"Both keys are gone?" Sarah asked, frowning. "I can understand misplacing one key, but both the green *and* the purple are missing? How can that be? No one can get in that safe but you!"

"Does this have anything to do with Eion's insistence we journey to Lentari?" Emerion asked, ruffling the feathers on his wings.

"It has to be," Sarah decided. "I'm telling you, something is wrong. Well, come on. I can still get us there."

Emerion rustled his wings. "If only I could have such a jhorun."

Steve laid a friendly hand on the griffin's tawny back. "Everyone says that, even me."

Emerion turned to face him. "You'd give up being a fire thrower so you could become a teleporter?"

Steve shrugged. "There's not much call to use my jhorun here, so yeah, I think I would."

Emerion looked over at Sarah and saw that his foster mother was shaking her head. She caught the griffin looking and mouthed *no, he wouldn't* to him.

Emerion trilled softly.

"I've got an image," Sarah announced. "I can still do it. Before we go, I think we need to get prepared. Perhaps you could pull the nohrstaf off your office wall and put it to use?"

"That's a damn good idea." Once Steve had his shapeshifting cudgel strapped to his back in its special holder, he signaled his readiness. Emerion approached. Sarah laid a hand on one of the griffin's wings and, with her other, hooked it through Steve's arm.

"Deep breath. Here we go."

The world winked out and was replaced with a beach and a panoramic view of the wide open sea. Kytes were circling overhead, with an occasional straggler dive-bombing the surface, only to emerge moments later with a struggling fish. Boats were anchored everywhere, with fishermen casting out nets, dipping poles in the water, and dropping their haul into large holds built for that purpose. The scent of brine was strong, which wasn't surprising as both husband and wife recognized the seaside village of Capily, located on the western shore.

Emerion excitedly exclaimed, "Oh, the pictures don't do it justice."

"Stick close to us," Sarah instructed. "I don't know how these people will react if they see a griffin in close proximity to their town."

Steve tapped his wife on the shoulder and pointed at a

nearby building. "There's Fensham's office. We're here, so we might as well hear what the constable has to say, right?"

"I'm sure Lissa's father has his hands full, disciplining people foolish enough to do something stupid in his town."

Heading toward the large, single-story structure located several hundred feet away, Steve took his wife's hand in his own, made sure Emerion was nearby, and ascended the short flight of steps onto the porch. Just as he was reaching for the door, it opened, allowing a middle-aged man with spiky brown hair peppered with flecks of gray, and sporting a scruffy beard, to exit. Wearing a bright blue tunic, and black trousers, he glanced at Steve. Not recognizing him, he then proceeded down the steps and headed toward town. Steve reached the door first and made to pull it open when he discovered it locked.

"Didn't that guy just come out of here?" Sarah asked.

Steve nodded. "He sure did. Hey there. Excuse me? Is the constable's office closed?"

The man who had exited the building was less than thirty feet away, and well within earshot. He turned at Steve's question and stared at him for a few moments. Deciding a closer look was needed, the stranger backtracked to the municipal building.

"The office is closed. It usually is this time of day. I refuse to work through lunch. Is there something I can do for you?"

"You work in there?" Steve asked.

The man nodded. "You could say that. At times, it feels like I live there. Constable Erik Tilsguard. You're new here? I reckon I haven't seen either of you in these parts before. And what the blazes are you doing traveling with a griffin? Wizards be damned, he has to be the biggest I've ever seen."

"Wait a moment," Steve said, holding up his hands in a time-out gesture. "Did you say you're the constable here?"

Constable Tilsguard nodded. "I am. Is there something you need?"

"Did Fensham retire?" Sarah asked.

"Who?" the constable asked, shaking his head.

"The guy who was constable before you?" Steve explained. "Remember him? How long ago did he retire?"

"I don't know what you're talking about," Constable Tilsguard insisted. "I've been serving nearly twenty years, and I took over from my father, who was Capily's constable for nearly forty before me."

"Is Lissa pranking us?" Steve asked, as he turned to the white public building behind them. "Did Mikal set this up?"

"I don't know any Lissas or Mikals," the constable said. "I think you've got me confused with someone else. Who did you say you are?"

"I didn't. Not yet, anyway. I'm Steve Miller, and this is my wife, Sarah. Over there, watching us closely, is Emerion."

"You haven't explained how you travel with a griffin," Constable Tilsguard reminded them.

"Is it a problem?" Steve asked, growing cautious. Try as he might, he couldn't shake the feeling that something was definitely wrong. "Humans and griffins are allies, so I don't see why it would be cause for alarm. Just for the record, Emerion is in our care."

"Griffins and humans are most certainly *not* allies," Constable Tilsguard spat. "Oh, I'm sorry. I shouldn't take offense. You were joking, weren't you?"

"The hell I was," Steve argued. "I was there to help broker the peace. I ended up blasting some of the griffins, and to make amends, we healed them. That one act caused the griffins to become our allies. It's ancient history, pal."

"And the weekly griffin raids are just figments of my imagination, is that it?" Constable Tilsguard demanded. "Livestock has been carried off, and houses have been destroyed. Have I just imagined it?"

"And the griffins are responsible?" Emerion asked.

"Good heavens, it speaks?" the constable stammered, looking shocked beyond words.

"Of course they do," Steve said. After a few moments, he folded his arms across his chest. "Are you sure you're not pulling our leg? This isn't some big joke?"

"I don't know who you people are," Tilsguard was saying, "but you should definitely be going. If any of my troops sees your griffin companion in town, then he's going to be attacked. I personally don't see how that would help anything, especially since he seems to be well trained, and …"

"Excuse me?" Emerion squawked. "Well trained?"

Sarah put a reassuring hand on the griffin's shoulder. "Hold on. There's something we're missing here. No need to get angry until we find out what is …"

"That's it," Tilsguard interrupted. "I've made up my mind. I simply don't trust this situation. No stranger walks into my town with a griffin in tow. You people are up to something. Guards!"

"I'm not believing any of this," Sarah confided to Steve. "Either this is some elaborate prank or else we have someone impersonating a constable."

"Agreed," Steve said, keeping his voice low. He looked at the stranger pretending to be someone he wasn't and pointed at him. "What do we do with him?"

Sarah placed a hand on his arm. "Relax, honey. I have this."

She disappeared, only to reappear moments later, standing next to the phony constable. Quick as a fox, she grabbed his arm and vanished. Ten seconds later, she was back at his side.

"Where'd you put him?" Steve asked.

"Inside his own jail. I figure we can let the proper authorities know, and then they can deal with him."

"Works for me. Umm, I think it's time to leave. There's a whole bunch of soldiers headed our way and they don't look friendly."

"We can take 'em," Emerion declared.

"You don't attack anyone without proper provocation first," Sarah told the griffin. "This might be one big misunderstanding. The last thing we want to do is to hurt an innocent, agreed?"

Their griffin companion sighed. "Agreed. I still say we could take 'em."

"I know we could, pal," Steve said, dropping his voice so he couldn't be overheard. "Sarah's right. Something is off here, and we need to figure out what. Are we heading out?"

Sarah held out her arm. Steve and Emerion moved closer.

"Yes. I'll take us to our little cabin first. It's been a while since we've been there, and I want to make sure it's still safe."

"Sounds good."

Steve felt the typical wrenching motion Sarah's jumps made, but managed to stay on his feet. Thankfully, the days of him getting nauseated after one of Sarah's transports were long over, but that didn't mean he cared for the sudden sensation that he was standing on a rug and it had been yanked out from under him.

The sounds of splashing water surrounded them on all sides. They were now standing before a small lake, fed by a tall waterfall. Runoff from the lake flowed east as a small river until it inevitably merged with the mighty Zanlu River further north.

"You gotta hand it to Shardwyn," Steve was saying, as he stared at the space their cabin should be occupying. "He knows how to conceal a house, that's for sure."

"I'll be sure to tell him you said that," Sarah returned.

She spoke the words to disable the concealment spell and waited for their tiny cabin to appear. It didn't.

"Are you sure you spoke the counterspell correctly?" Steve asked.

Sarah pulled a piece of paper from her pocket. "Just to be certain, I wrote it down, in case I couldn't remember it. Yes, it's been a while, but I still remember how to cancel the spell. Let me try it again." She tried to counter the spell hiding their cabin. Once more, nothing appeared. It was as though the cabin was truly gone.

"I don't get it," Steve complained. "Why isn't it showing up?"

"Steve, I don't think it's there to show up in the first place," Sarah said slowly, growing concerned. "First, we learn Fensham is no longer the constable of Capily. Then, the current constable claims he and his father have presided over Capily for nearly sixty years. And finally, he didn't know Lissa and Mikal's names. How could you not know the prince and princess next in line to rule the kingdom?"

"So far, I can't say I'm too impressed with this place," Emerion said.

"It's not supposed to be like this," Sarah insisted.

"Want to try someplace else?" Steve asked.

"Where, R'Tal?"

"Our portal keys are missing," Steve reminded her. "I say we head to Foronlir first. I want to find out from Maelnar what could have happened to them."

"That'll work," Sarah decided. "Emerion, stay close to us. We're headed for one of the Kla Guur cities. Borahgg was their first, and Foronlir was built later, after Borahgg grew too big."

"I've never been underground before," Emerion said. "Is it safe?"

"Stick with us and it will be," Steve promised. He held out a hand and waited for Sarah to take it. "Ready when you are."

Emerion pressed up against Sarah. "I'm ready."

"Deep breath," Sarah instructed. "Here we go."

A dark, empty cavern met their gaze. Confused, husband and wife were shocked to discover they were standing on the ledge that, at one point in time, overlooked the great cavern that would be home to nearly two thousand dwarves. Behind them, a solid, unbroken wall of rock met their eyes.

"There used to be a tunnel here," Steve said, amazed. He rapped his knuckles on the wall. "How could they have sealed it up so effectively?"

"That's what I'm trying to tell you," Sarah said. "Fensham is not the constable, Mikal and Lissa are unknowns, and now we're looking at the site where Foronlir is supposed to be, yet there's nothing here. What does that tell you?"

"I don't know," Steve admitted. "Did we somehow jump backward through time?"

"Emerion, don't react," Sarah ordered. "Understand? No matter what we find. Steve, give me your hand. We're going to Borahgg. Everyone ready? Good. Here we go."

The empty cave was gone and, instead, a much larger *illuminated* cave met their eyes.

"By the maker!" a gruff voice cried. "Brothers! To arms! We are under attack!"

Before anyone knew what was happening, Steve, Sarah, and Emerion found themselves face to face with an armed contingent of dwarves, all of whom were dressed in dark leather armor, gripping axes with both hands. Deciding he didn't like the way the dwarves were advancing on them, Steve lit both hands and blasted a jet of fire straight up.

"That'll be far enough, thank you very much. What's the matter with you people? Don't you recognize us?"

"You're no friend of ours," an angry voice shot back. The owner, a short, stout fellow wearing a set of armor inlaid with gold patterns, appeared. "Who are you and what do you want? Wizards be damned. A griffin! How did you manage to find your way here, birdbeak?"

"Birdbeak?" Emerion squawked. "I have been affronted! Prepare to defend yourself, you pathetic excuse of a ..."

"No one has affronted anyone here," Steve interjected, placing a hand on Emerion's back. "Just take it easy. Now, as for you ... you say we're not friends of yours? I beg to differ. We've been to Borahgg many times. Do you not recognize us? Don't my flames give it away?"

"Humans who have jhorun," the dwarf argued. "So what?"

Steve held up his flaming hands. "But, can any of them do this?"

"Not that I can recall," the dwarf admitted.

"Look, we just want to know where we can find Maelnar," Sarah said, exasperated. "He's probably in his office. Could you just send someone to fetch him? He'll let you know who we are."

"Maelnar?" the dwarf repeated, incredulous. Right before their very eyes, Steve could see the diminutive being deflating, as though Sarah's request had taken the wind out of his sails. "You're jesting. Tell me you're jesting."

"You obviously know who he is," Steve added. "Just go get him, would you? We're good friends with him."

"Impossible. Maelnar is dead. He died over a hundred years ago."

Chapter Two–Tangent

Yeah, right," Steve snorted, trying to contain his laughter. "Where are the cameras? Come on, you don't think we're going to fall for that, do you?"

A sea of unfriendly faces stared back at him. He felt a nudge on his shoulder. Looking over, Steve saw that his wife looked concerned and had a hand over her mouth. She was believing this nonsense?

"I think they're right," Sarah said, confirming his suspicions. "If Maelnar wasn't around to make the portal keys, it explains why they're no longer in our safe back home."

Steve held up his hands. "Okay, okay, time out. Wait a minute. There are so many things wrong with that statement that it's not even funny. First off, we saw Maelnar earlier this year. Did you catch that, guys? He was alive four months ago."

"Impossible," several dwarves scoffed.

"Second," Steve continued, "we used our portal keys at the same flippin' time, so I know they were there. Both of 'em."

"The only way you had one of our portal keys, human," one dwarf said, coming to stand beside his companion, "is if you *stole* them, which is something I wouldn't put past you insufferable bipeds. So, is it true? You have portal keys? Turn out your pockets."

Steve straightened to his full height and folded his arms across his chest. "I don't think so."

A line of six dwarf soldiers appeared.

"It wasn't a request, dolt," one of the armor-clad guards snapped.

Steve caught the warning look from Sarah and sighed. He held up his hands, in a universally accepted gesture of surrender.

"Look, I think we got off on the wrong foot. We're just here for Maelnar. If he isn't here, then we are officially wasting each other's time."

Sarah, in the meantime, had noticed the color of his hands, and had scooted behind him. Steve's hands had turned an ugly red color, which typically meant a pyrotechnical show was not far behind.

"You don't want to do this," he warned again. "We are more than capable of defending ourselves."

A commotion started behind their row of accusers. Several dwarves were rushing forward, each of them lugging the corner of a large wooden crate. Once it had been placed on the ground before the dwarven lineup, a single dwarf kicked the crate's lid off and reached inside. After fumbling for a moment or two, one of the dwarves pressed a button on the item. The cube started to shake as whatever it was appeared to wake up.

"Don't just stand there," a new voice exclaimed. "Hurl it toward them! Now! You don't want to be caught holding it!"

Steve ignited his hands and watched as the dwarf gave the cube a swift kick. The crate slid across the floor and came to a stop directly in front of Emerion.

"What is it?" the griffin asked. "I trust this not."

"You and me both," Steve said. "Emerion, get over here. We don't know what it's going to …"

The box shuddered once and a panel clinked open. Then

another, and another. Steve, Sarah, and Emerion watched — speechless — as the box unfolded itself. In less than ten seconds, the rapidly expanding box had approached the three of them, and before anyone could move out of the way, the strange contraption had expanded to *encompass* them.

In pitch blackness, Steve groaned.

"What are we going to do?" Emerion screeched.

"I can either burn my way through one of these panels," Steve began, "or…" Then he felt Sarah take his hand.

In the blink of an eye, they were outside the box, staring at a group of dwarves who, collectively, lost their smug smiles. Several reached for their axes.

"Nuh-uh," Steve told the dwarves, as his hands blazed hotter and brighter. "We came to you in peace, and this is how you behave? What the hell happened, anyway? How could the loss of one dwarf destroy an alliance between us?"

"An alliance?" one dwarf fearfully asked. "With humans? We dwarves never formed an alliance with you bipeds. Too untrustworthy."

"I could say the same about you," Sarah shot back.

"How did you get out of the bastille?" the first dwarf asked. "They have been enchanted against jhorun, and are virtually impregnable."

"You had no business putting us in it to begin with," Steve snapped.

A few of the dwarves shuffled around. There was a loud click, and suddenly, the bastille was collapsing in on itself. Within moments, it had reverted to its small cube form. One of their adversaries, in a fit of exasperation, retrieved the box and threw it at Steve.

The box made a nasty racket as it started to expand once more. This time, the container stopped in mid-air and hung, suspended, from the ground.

"I've got this one," Sarah announced. She straightened and looked up at the immobilized box and gave a quick jerk of her head. The crate shot off in the opposite direction, heading toward the same dwarf who had thrown it.

"Look out!" he cried.

The bastille made contact with the ground and

disappeared among the group of short, stout legs. Moments later, the unique prison was back, but not before ensnaring eight of the dwarves.

"So, you can escape from our bastilles," one of the dwarves said. "You think that's all we have? We can imprison you in ways not even the dragons know."

Steve looked at his wife. "Time to go?"

Sarah nodded. "It is. Emerion, we're off to the castle."

"Will they be as unfriendly as this lot?" Emerion scornfully asked.

"Let's hope not," Steve said, as several dwarves rushed to apprehend them.

The dark subterranean cavern disappeared and was replaced by bright blue skies, fluffy white clouds floating high in the sky, and a light breeze carrying scents of blooming flowers nearby. Sarah inhaled deeply and visibly relaxed.

"That's more like it."

"Where are we now?" the young griffin asked.

"This is the North Gate," Steve answered. "Across the drawbridge and through that open portcullis, you'll find the city proper. Shops and vendor booths are to the north and east, and residential areas are to the south. Do you see the castle off to the east? That's where the Kri'yans live. Kri'Entu and Ny'Callé have got to be two of the nicest monarchs we have ever met. They'll be able to tell us what's going on."

The three adventurers stepped onto the drawbridge and had only taken a few steps when they heard several crashes from the closest guard shack. A mad scrambling came next as guards, some still in the process of strapping on their armor, hurried outside to place themselves in Steve and Sarah's path. Swords were unsheathed and bows were fitted with arrows. In less time than it takes to utter a few choice profanities, husband and wife were shocked to find themselves staring at the business end of countless swords and nocked arrows.

Steve held up a hand which was still lit. "Hey, relax, guys. You know us. It's me, Steve. You remember Sarah, I'm sure. The only one I know you haven't met yet is Emerion. Granted, he's big, for a griffin, but he's harmless. We can vouch for him. Now, would you care to lower your weapons?

You're making me nervous."

"Your hand is on fire!" one guard exclaimed.

Steve nodded. "Hence the comment about you knowing me. There's only one fire thrower in the kingdom, and you're looking at him. So, what do you say we ... now what? What's the matter?"

Several of the guards had bolted back inside the guard shack. Moments later, the clang of an alarm bell began to sound. It was so loud that Steve was certain it could be heard all the way in Donlari. Plugging his ears with his fingers, he angrily turned to the guards.

"What did you do that for? You're sounding an alarm? Against us?"

"See?" Sarah exclaimed. "I told you something wasn't right."

An entire squadron of armed soldiers appeared, led by an officer Steve didn't recognize. Before he had a chance to explain anything, old-fashioned iron manacles were snapped into place on their wrists. When it looked as though the soldiers were intent on driving Emerion off, Steve took a menacing step forward, a fact not lost on the soldiers.

"He's with us," Sarah explained to the guards. "Where we go, he goes. We'll go peacefully. Just lead the way."

"Peacefully my ass," Steve muttered, under his breath.

"Yes, *peacefully*," Sarah hissed back. "Until we know what's going on, we all stick together. Emerion, you're on your best behavior, understand?"

The griffin nodded. "Aye. I stand ready to assist."

They were paraded down the street, as though they were prized prisoners of war. People stumbled out of their shops to gawk at them as they passed by. Comments were heard about Emerion's size, but everything was made in hushed tones. Gone were the frenzied vendors, who would shove anything and everything at you in an attempt to make a sale. Gone were the carts laden with colorful bolts of fabric, fresh produce, and freshly baked goods. Everywhere they looked, Steve and Sarah could see nothing but dreariness and despair.

Approaching the tall, imposing castle, Steve noticed the drawbridge was up. Frowning, he studied the castle. Windows had been covered and closed. There were no banners currently being displayed. While they waited for the drawbridge to be lowered, he cast a look at Sarah. She, too, had noticed the castle's heightened security, and gave him an unreadable look. Placing a calming hand on Emerion's head, she looked pointedly at him, then at the castle, mouthing *something's wrong*, to which Steve nodded.

Once they were across the drawbridge, and the portcullis was lifted only long enough for their party to pass through, they were led inside the castle, where a subdued and hushed environment was waiting. Chambermaids hurried by, their eyes fixed on the ground. Soldiers stood at attention every fifteen feet. The anxiety level, Steve decided, was high. He personally hadn't seen the castle like this since their run-in with Celestia all those years ago. Trying to protect the townsfolk both inside and outside the perimeter walls, the people had been ordered into the catacombs beneath the castle, while every squadron of soldiers at their disposal were called into service. The overall mood *then* rivaled what they were feeling *now*.

They reached the Great Hall and came to a stop. Looking around the familiar, and yet, not familiar chamber, Steve's growing uneasiness doubled in size. The thrones! Gone were the gilded thrones of the Kri'yans. Gone were the many tables and the welcoming fire in the huge hearth. In its place was a scattering of heavily scarred benches. And the thrones had been replaced by ugly bronze chairs.

"This has got to be the most elaborate prank I've ever seen," Steve whispered, "or else …"

"… or else this is all not a dream and something has happened," Sarah finished for him.

An unfamiliar man and woman appeared. They were older, in their sixties, and were scowling even before they had a chance to sit down. The man was balding, had a short goatee, and was dressed in a dark gray tunic and black trousers, neither of which looked as though they had been cleaned in the last week. Draped across his chest was a purple sash. His crown matched the thrones, in that it looked like it was made of iron, was bereft of any type of gold, or gems, and could probably be used as a weapon.

The queen looked to be the same age as Steve, and was nearly as tall. The female monarch had long, brown hair streaked with gray, wore an outfit similar to the king's, and looked as though she could best anyone in the room in an arm-wrestling match. Both monarchs took their seats as Steve, Sarah, and Emerion were instructed to stand before them.

Neither the king, nor queen, Steve noted, had smiled once since they had appeared.

"Who's this?" the king demanded. "And why does a griffin travel with them?"

"We caught them sneaking into the city," the guard proudly proclaimed.

The king nodded. "Excellent. Well, let's see what we have here. A man and woman, with their griffin pet? How quaint. Speak, peasants. Who are you?"

"Why do you act like you've never seen a griffin before?" Steve asked, exhibiting genuine curiosity. "They are our allies, after all."

The king snorted with amusement. "Allies? With flying beasts? What a dreadful concept. Perish the thought."

Steve stared at the stranger on the throne and couldn't hide the scowl that was forming. "Griffins, dragons, and even the dwarves. They're all our allies."

"They are nothing of the sort!" the king insisted. "What a horrible concept. Who would ever place any amount of faith in dumb animals?"

Emerion gave a warning squawk.

"Not yet, pal," Steve whispered to his griffin son. "Let's find out what we can first. So, you're calling the dragons dumb? And the dwarves? How can beings who can create such beautiful pieces of treasure be considered dumb?"

"Who are you?" the king wanted to know. "I don't recognize you at all."

"Well, who are *you*?" Steve challenged. "What happened to the rightful king and queen? Where's Kri'Entu? Did you do something to them?"

"I *am* the rightful king. You will address me as Kri'Torus.

Or Your Majesty."

Ignoring the king, Steve turned to Sarah. "Okay, I'll admit I don't get it. Who's Kri'Torus? I would've thought Mikal would have taken over, and not some stranger."

"Some stranger?" Kri'Torus sputtered. He struggled to get to his feet. "I am the *King* of *Lentari*! You will show me some respect!"

"Tell me, Kri'Torus," Steve said, as he turned to the king, who had become quite red-faced, "what's your jhorun?"

"You will cease this pointless conversation immediately!" Kri'Torus raged. "Magic has been illegal for many years. Be lucky I don't lock the three of you up just for saying that word!"

"Jhorun is illegal?" Steve repeated, amazed. He looked at Sarah. "All we need to complete this picture is to hear the theme from *Twilight Zone*."

"You dare utter the word *again*?" the king practically screamed. Flecks of spittle flew in all directions.

Sarah held up her hands in a placating gesture. "We're sorry, Your Majesty. We didn't know magic was illegal."

"How could you not know magic is illegal?" the queen asked. Her cold, gray eyes flicked from husband to wife a few times before settling on Sarah. "Where could you possibly be from? Were you living under a rock? That must be it, Torus. How utterly charming. These *keplahs* must be ignorant farmers. This is what you get when you don't seek a mate outside of your own family. Be gone, peasants. We don't have time for the likes of you."

Steve frowned. "Did she just call us inbred dunderheads?"

Sarah nodded. She was wearing her own frown. "Sure sounded that way."

"Big words, coming from someone who doesn't have any jhorun to speak of," Steve sneered.

"What are you doing?" Sarah hissed.

"Goading them on," Steve whispered back. "Look at her. She's ready to blow a gasket. What's the matter, Queenie? Cat got your tongue? It's okay. Not everyone can have a jhorun. It looks like whoever is responsible for handing them out skipped the two of you."

"We have jhorun!" the queen cried.

"Hush up, dear!" Kri'Torus commanded.

"I can change fabric colors!" the queen proudly declared. "And Torus?"

"Don't say it!" the king begged.

"He can modify the shape of flatware!"

Kri'Torus groaned and held his head in his hands.

"Change the shape of flatware?" Steve repeated. A smile formed and quickly spread from ear to ear. "You can bend spoons, is that it?"

"Like yours is any better!" the king snapped.

Steve held up a hand. He ignited it and looked pointedly at Kri'Torus.

"Whadya think? Pretty cool, huh?"

The king leapt to his feet for a second time. "A fire thrower!"

"And I'm using my jhorun," Steve said. "Oh, whoops. Said it again. Listen, I get it. Something is up. The king and queen we know are not here. No one knows who we are, and our dwarf friend died over a hundred years ago when we personally saw him at the beginning of the year. Sarah, all of these events have got to be related."

Sarah suddenly gripped his hand tightly in her own. "Do you remember when we time-traveled to the past?"

Steve nodded. "It was rather hard to forget. You fell through that portal, and I went in after you."

"Do you remember Sheriff What's-his-name?"

"Melvyn. Yeah, I remember him. He kidnapped you, so his name is kinda hard to forget. Why?"

"Do you remember the last thing he said to us?" Sarah continued. "Well, specifically, to you? He said he was going to find a way to mess up your future."

There was an angry squawk of outrage, but Steve waved a dismissive hand and returned his attention to his wife.

"I'm sorry about that," Steve said, scowling at the king. "Ignore him. So, you're saying you think Melvyn is responsible for this?"

"Think about it," Sarah urged. "Maelnar is dead. Melvyn would want to make sure we wouldn't be able to make it back here."

A steady stream of soldiers poured into the Great Hall.

"He knows you're a teleporter," Steve said, shaking his head. "What would killing Maelnar have to do with anything? You're still able to jump us from our world to here!"

There was another squawk, only this time, it was feminine in nature. The queen was now leaning forward, staring at Sarah.

"Hold on! Are you telling me you're a teleporter?"

Sarah briefly glanced at the thrones. "Yes, now be quiet, would you? We're trying to figure out what's going on here."

"Wait, wait, wait," the queen ordered, rising to her feet. "You're a teleporter, and he is a ... a ... *fire thrower*? Torus, I don't believe it! It's the prophecy!"

Torus turned to his wife. "What? What are you rambling on about?"

"The prophecy, you imbecile!"

"What prophecy are you talking about? The only one I know about is ... wait. *That* prophecy?"

Steve sighed. "Yes, we're the Nohrin. It's ancient history. Let it go, 'kay?"

"I don't think that's the prophecy they're talking about," Sarah murmured, under her breath.

The queen was on her feet. "Don't you remember what it says, Torus? If a fire thrower ever arrives, asking about the past, then we need to act!"

Kri'Torus turned pensive. He motioned to a nearby guard, who nodded and hurried away.

"What's going on?" Sarah asked. "You need to act? What do you have to do?"

The queen gave her a condescending smile. "I'd apologize, but we both know I wouldn't really mean it. I'm sorry, but we're going to have to kill the two of you."

Emerion squawked with alarm and raised both wings as he adopted a defensive stance. Both husband and wife looked at each other. Had they heard that right?

Steve nudged his wife and looked pointedly at her hands. Finally, he turned to Emerion, who nodded his readiness. Sarah took Steve's hand in hers, and then reached for Emerion.

Moments later, they were back at the waterfall, where their cabin used to be. The clanging of the alarm bells, and the hundreds of armored soldiers sprinting through the halls had mercifully fallen quiet.

"Did you hear that?" Sarah asked. "Their prophecy ... it has something to do with a fire thrower and a teleporter, only they aren't referring to the Bakkian, are they? No, they have to be talking about some warning they were given."

Steve's eyes widened with shock. "That sumbitch pulled a *Back to the Future* on us!"

Sarah blinked a few times. "Huh?"

"From the sequel," Emerion explained, nodding. "I hadn't thought of that. Very clever."

"Would someone like to explain to me what the two of you are talking about?"

Steve held out a hand, indicating he was giving Emerion permission to answer.

"In the movie," Emerion began, "a character from the future steals the mechanical time machine and encounters a version of himself from the past. The bully, named Biff."

"I know who he is," Sarah said. "What about him?"

"Old Biff gives Young Biff information which could benefit himself in the future. So, when present-day Biff suddenly sees Marty and the older human asking about the book Old Biff gave to Young Biff, he knew, since he had been warned, to not let them investigate."

Sarah nodded. "Oh, I get it. In this case, assuming Melvyn is responsible for this mess, he probably warned whomever he was helping to claim the throne that, should the two of us ever show up asking questions, then we would need to be dealt with immediately."

"Why?" Emerion wanted to know.

"Because we'd want to fix the timeline," Steve explained. "I think it's clear. We need to find a way back to the past and set things straight."

"What about the interdimensional portal?" Sarah asked. "We used it to go back in time the last time."

"Nuh-uh," Steve said, shaking his head. "You went through first, and ended up stranded in the past for six months before I showed up. We can't risk using it again. Besides, if Melvyn is the one who's responsible for all of this, and I'm fairly certain he is, he couldn't allow that portal to exist. He'd have to find some way to close it up."

Sarah nodded. "Okay, the portal is more than likely sealed, or destroyed. Zevern's portal is out."

"Zevern the Inept," Steve chuckled. "There's someone I haven't thought about in a while. All right, we know magic is forbidden. Something tells me consulting Shardwyn is no longer an option. I'm also thinking he's probably not alive in this whacked-out timeline."

Sarah sighed. "Probably not. I wonder what happened?"

"To Shardwyn? Who could say?"

"No, I mean, I wonder what happened here that made the king and queen forbid using magic. Something bad must have happened to one of them."

Emerion raised a wing, which drew a snort of amusement from Steve. "Go ahead. And put your wing down, pal."

The griffin complied. "It's my belief jhorun is the source of this catastrophe. The use of magic is clearly at fault. Why else would it be forbidden?"

"That's a pretty good theory," Steve admitted, giving the young griffin a friendly scratch between the shoulder blades. "The problem is, we don't have any way to prove it."

"The alliances are all gone," Sarah said. "Dwarves, griffins, and dragons. Dragons! What about Pryllan? Do you think she still knows you?"

Steve considered. "Well, if we assume Melvyn screwed up the past to change the future, I would say that Pryllan and I should still know each other. Granted, all the history that happened between the two of us in the present would be gone, but in the past? Those memories should still be there."

"Are you going to reach out to her?" Emerion asked.

"What do you think?" Steve asked, looking at his two companions. "Should I?"

"She might have some insight in how to get us back to the past," Sarah said.

Steve nodded. "That works for me. Okay, here we go."
Pryllan? Are you there?

There was no answer.

Come on, Pryllan. Tell me you're still alive. Tell me you and Kahvel are safe. Better yet, tell me Pravara and Pylaria are safe, too.

Who is this?

Kahvel? Is that you?

It is. How do you know me? Do I know you?

It's rather hard to explain. You and I originally met a few years ago here, in Lentari.

Impossible. I have met no humans here. How do you know my mate?

Think hard, Kahvel. Over a hundred years ago, there was a human who tried reaching out to her, asking her for help. We also located a missing dwarf child. Tell me you remember this.

Aye, I do remember this. That was you? After all this time has passed? I did not think a human could … wait. I do remember this. You had mentioned you and I were friends in the future. This is the future you were talking about?

That's right. I assume you're blocking me from Pryllan right now?

I am. How do you know this?

It's what you did to me in the past.

What is it you require?

The timeline is seriously messed up. Sarah and I need to go back to the past and fix it, otherwise life as we know it in Lentari will never be the same.

What's wrong with it now? It is as it's always been.

For you, yes. For us? No. No one knows us. Magic is forbidden. There are no alliances, and …

What alliances do you speak of?

There are three that I know about. Griffins, dwarves, and you dragons.

That was a mistake. We became allies with dwarves, and those villainous bipeds abused that peace.

Holy cow! What happened?

We were lured into several traps.

I am so sorry. Not everyone is like this. That Melvyn character? The one you helped us locate the last time we were all together? We're figuring he did something to the timeline and jacked everything up.

Can you give me an example?

Uhh, sure. We're confident he either killed Maelnar, our dwarf friend, or else he arranged his assassination.

Bold accusations. You have proof?

Our portal keys are gone, the towns no longer use portals to move around, and one can get arrested for mentioning the word 'jhorun'. Oh! We mustn't forget you!

Me? What about me? I am the exact same that I was when I spoke with you last.

Are you certain about that, Dragon Lord?

I think … excuse me?

You are Dragon Lord in my world.

Has something happened to Rinbok Intherer?

You could say that. He abdicated his position.

Whatever for?

He gave the reason, but I'm thinking I shouldn't be telling you this. You know full well how private—and cranky—he can get.

You do know the Dragon Lord.

Told you I did. Kahvel, let me ask you something. How well do you know your former allies, the dwarves?

What do you want to know?

Specifically? What's happened with them. What happened to Maelnar? Why did relations between dragons and dwarves deteriorate?

Those answers can be found within our Collective.

Can we come talk to you?

You know where to find us?

Provided you haven't moved your nest, yes.

Very well. You may come.

"Sarah? Take us to Kahvel and Pryllan's nest. They're expecting us."

"Easy enough. Emerion, we're about to visit a dragon's nest. This particular set of dragons are very good friends of ours, only in this altered timeline, not as much. You will be on your best behavior, is that understood?"

"Always with the *best behavior*," Emerion complained. "Aren't I always?"

Steve spun in place until he was facing their griffin companion. "Would you like me to weigh in here? Would you like to talk about the July 4th picnic last year?"

"Perhaps that was a poor choice of words," Emerion

hastily added. "Very well. You will only see my very best behavior."

Steve nodded. "Good. Sarah? Ready when you are."

Sounds of falling water vanished and were replaced by faint, howling winds. They were now high atop a mountain near Lake Raehón, in a cave so large that a pair of semi-trucks could have easily navigated their way around the various rock formations. Then again, that wasn't too surprising, as the two residents of this particular cave were much larger than the trucks Steve was familiar with on his world. There, directly facing them, were the two inhabitants of this cave: dragons. One was an iridescent shade of gold, and the other was a lustrous emerald green in color. Kahvel, the gold dragon, leaned down to inspect Steve up close.

"So, this is what you look like, is it? You aren't how I pictured you."

"Hello again, Kahvel."

Two reptilian eyes fixed on Sarah's. "I do not believe we have ever met, human female."

"Well, technically, in this timeline, I guess we haven't. But, in ours, we have. Many times. Where's Pravara? Is she nearby?"

"Who's Pravara?" Kahvel asked.

Movement in the far recess of the cave caught their attention.

"You, Steve, have met my mate, Pryllan. Sarah, is it? This is Pryllan. She ... you've met her, too, haven't you?"

"Several times, yes."

Pryllan approached Steve and lowered her head. "I remember you. I gave you and that dwarf girl a ride on my back, did I not?"

"You did, Pryllan. It's good to see you again."

"And you. Honestly, I had forgotten about you."

"You shouldn't have," Steve said, scowling. "That's what we need help with. Do you remember that older human we chased through the countryside? This would be after locating the missing dwarf girl?"

"Vaguely," the green dragon told him.

"We have a feeling he escaped in the past and has changed

the future to better suit him."

"Let me ask you something," Pryllan interrupted. "You mentioned a name earlier, one that I have not shared with anyone. Ever. Tell me how you came by it and I will help as much as I can."

"Are you talking about Pravara?" Steve asked.

Pryllan nodded.

"She's clearly not here, is she?"

"Who is Pravara?" Kahvel wanted to know.

Pryllan sighed and turned to Kahvel. "If we ever had offspring, and a female one at that, I always believed Pravara to be a suitable name."

Kahvel's eyes widened. "Wait. Am I to understand that Pryllan and I had offspring in this other timeline of yours?"

Steve held up a hand with two fingers displayed.

"Yep. Two of 'em."

"What's the name of the other dragonlet?" Kahvel asked.

Sarah shook her head. "We let one name slip. Let the other be a surprise, okay?"

"You may as well tell us," Kahvel argued. "If you are able to find a way to travel through time, and are able to prevent certain events from happening, then what will happen to us?"

"I would imagine a slew of new memories would suddenly appear in your head," Steve answered.

"You're basing this on, what?" Sarah asked. "More movies?"

Steve jammed his hands in his pockets and smiled. "Yeah, I guess I am."

Kahvel leaned around Steve and stared at Emerion, standing quietly nearby. "And you? Who are you, griffin?"

Sarah turned to their companion and encouraged him to answer.

"I am Emerion," the griffin began. "Son of Steve and Sarah Miller, of Coeur d'Alene, Idaho."

"Son?" Kahvel repeated, confused. "Since when could two humans produce a griffin offspring? For that matter, I did not know griffins could even exist in their world. Do dragons?"

"No," Steve said, smiling. "And neither do griffins, but

then again, this was an extenuating circumstance. We had to care for Emerion or he would have died at the hands of his flock."

"And you cared for the cub in your world? Commendable. Dangerous, but commendable."

"I owe them my life," Emerion said. "What concerns them, concerns me."

"We have two offspring, and Kahvel is Dragon Lord," Pryllan breathed, amazed. "I'm thinking we should help them return to the past."

"How?" Kahvel wanted to know. "The humans have decried magic, and there are no dragon wizards. I'm not sure how we can help."

Steve cleared his throat. "Can you answer this? What happened to the dwarves? There was a very particular dwarf by the name of Maelnar. He was known for making portal keys. I'm told he was killed over a hundred years ago. Do you know anything about it?"

Kahvel's eyes closed. "I will inquire."

"While he's asking the Collective," Pryllan said, lowering her voice, "can you tell me about Pravara? What's she like? Is she happy? Healthy?"

"She's a dark green dragon with gold-tinged scales," Steve answered, also lowering his voice to match hers. "She's bright, inquisitive, and is a close friend to Mikal, the human prince."

"There is no human prince by that name," Pryllan pointed out. "Ah. Mikal exists in your timeline, correct?"

"Correct," Steve confirmed.

Kahvel stirred. His eyes opened and he turned to Steve.

"I do have some answers for you. Ordinarily, the life of a single dwarf would be meaningless for us, but the name you mentioned is one that many of my brethren knew. You seek information on Maelnar, otherwise known as the Strathos, is that correct?"

"That's the one," Steve confirmed. "How'd he die?"

"One hundred eighteen years ago, there was a great clan war. The Kla Guur, Kla Chanus, and the Kla Snakkoth fought among themselves. The Kla Guur tried to invoke the newly created alliance with us dragons, but Rinbok Intherer wisely decided these skirmishes were none of our business. As such, all dragons were ordered to avoid the dwarf clans at all times."

"I can only imagine the dwarves didn't like that," Sarah murmured.

Kahvel nodded. "Indeed. The alliance was revoked that day, and the dwarves fought on. Your friend, Maelnar, died in the Battle of Graun, which is a city in the Chanu territory, by the way. Maelnar, and several members of the Kla Guur Council, were trying to bring the hostilities to a close, only ..."

"Only what?" Steve asked. "Were they ambushed?"

"Yes," Kahvel confirmed. "By more than one clan.

"How many live in the area?" Steve asked.

Kahvel shrugged. "Four or five."

"Does anyone know what they were fighting about?" Sarah asked.

"That is unknown, I'm afraid. Whatever the reason was, it was enough to entice a group of them Topside."

Husband and wife both groaned.

"Whatever it was," Steve groaned, "it had to be important news. I happen to know most dwarves will rarely venture into the open like that. Even more so if it's going to be a group of them."

"How many are we talking about?" Sarah asked.

"A band of ten dwarves was spotted near the southeastern border of the mountains," Kahvel reported. "They were all headed south."

"And Maelnar was one of them," Sarah said.

"Aye," Kahvel confirmed.

"Melvyn had to have told them something," Steve theorized. "I only wish I knew what was said."

"It doesn't really matter," Sarah decided, shrugging. "Whatever it was, it was enough to lure Maelnar out, which is precisely what Melvyn wanted. However he riled those clans up, we have to make certain nothing happens to Maelnar."

Steve sank down, onto the floor. Sarah joined him moments later. After a few seconds had passed, Emerion did the same.

"We have *got* to get back and prevent Melvyn from tampering with the past."

"We've got to find a way to prevent him from replacing the king and queen with someone he favors," Sarah added.

"And prevent the disruption of the alliances," Emerion said.

"This isn't going to be easy," Steve groaned. He looked up at the towering dragon. "Does anyone have any suggestions on how to jump backwards through time? I'm fresh out of gate keepers."

Surprisingly, Kahvel nodded. "An idea was suggested."

"And?" Steve prompted. "Are we going to hate it?"

"Unknown. It all depends on how well you know the shealk."

Sarah let out an exclamation of surprise and jumped to her feet. Spooked, Emerion also leapt to his feet, but adopted a protective stance next to her. Steve noticed, nodded, and gave Emerion an approving nod.

Sarah smiled. "Of course! Oh, why didn't we think about this earlier?"

"What'd I miss?" Steve wanted to know.

"The shealk!" Sarah repeated. "Of the water dragons, who do we know who just so happens to be a very powerful wizard?"

Steve nodded, and a smile appeared. "Gareth!"

"Not Gareth, the junior," Sarah said, frowning. "Actually, something tells me he was never born here. No, I'm talking about the senior Gareth. Er, Balthor."

"Obviously," Steve said. "That's who I was thinking about. With the way things are going, I'd say you're right. Gareth is more than likely not here. With that said, do you think Balthor can help us?"

"According to what I have heard," Kahvel began, "our cousins in the water have grown quite powerful. Their head wizard is purported to be unmatched and quite formidable. You would need to seek his advice, but we have no idea how to reach him. The shealk can reside at depths well below the range of any other living organism."

Steve waved a dismissive hand. "Please. It just so happens we know how to get his attention. We've watched his son do it before."

"I'm not aware of any shealk wizard producing offspring," Kahvel said.

"Well, he did," Sarah said, nodding, "only we suspect he hasn't been born here. Steve, do you remember what to do?"

"I do," Steve confirmed. "Kahvel? Pryllan? We're going to fix this."

"We need to make a list," Sarah decided.

Steve blinked a few times. "Huh?"

"A list. If we're going to do this, then we need to be certain we get it *all* right."

"Well, there are only three things worthy of your list," Steve told her. "Saving Maelnar's life is first, and that means we have to save the dragon-dwarf alliance. Then, we have to keep Melvyn's mitts off the throne. I don't know how he managed to get Kri'Calin out of power, but he clearly found a way. Assassination?"

"How horrible," Sarah whispered. "I hope that's not true."

"And finally, we need to make certain Melvyn keeps his big trap shut. I don't know how we're going to permanently silence him, but we're going to have to figure it out. The sooner we fix this, the sooner everything is back to normal and you two are back to being parents."

"And leader of the dragons," Sarah reminded him.

"Agreed," Pryllan said. "How can we help?"

Kahvel eyed her, but didn't say anything.

"Is there some standing water around here?" Steve asked.

"Standing water?" Pryllan asked. "Is that another way of asking if there's a lake nearby?" She turned to Kahvel. "The lake the humans call Raehón is nearby. Is that the closest?"

Kahvel nodded. "It is. Do you need us to take you there?"

Sarah shook her head. "No, that isn't necessary. I can get us all there. It was good to see you two. Hopefully, the next time we see you, you'll have a few more memories of us."

Steve held out his hand, Emerion crowded close, and Sarah clasped both of them. Husband and wife smiled at the dragon couple and vanished.

"Me, the Dragon Lord?" Kahvel scoffed. "They *had* to have made that up."

Chapter Three–Back to the Past

Do you think this is wise? After all, we are incredibly exposed like this." Emerion rustled his wings as he peered nervously around the quiet valley. "And you say practically every mountaintop is inhabited by a dragon?"

"There are usually two to each nest," Sarah confirmed. "Hush. We need to let Steve try and reach out to Gareth. Gareth the elder, that is."

Steve had approached the water's edge and was staring at its surface. Recalling the exact steps he had seen their young wizard friend do whenever he wanted to speak with his father, Steve scooped up a handful of water and let it trickle through his fingers and fall onto the surface.

"Balthor."

A buzzing cicada started up its loud cacophony from a nearby tree. Steve briefly glanced at Sarah before returning his attention to the water. It would seem the water dragon had not received the message.

"You're not forgetting a step, are you?" Sarah asked, from

her position next to Emerion.

"I don't think so," Steve said. "Wait. Am I?"

"Truthfully, I don't know. You sounded so sure of yourself that I let the matter drop."

"I sounded so sure of myself because I've watched Gareth call his father several times."

"Do you think he's ignoring the call?" Sarah asked. "I mean, well, so to speak."

"Hmm, that's a good question. Let me try again." He scooped up another handful of water. "Balthor. Come on, pal. I know you don't know me, but believe it or not, I know *you*. We need your help."

This time, the water shimmered once and, just like that, his reflection disappeared and he was looking at the narrow, elongated face of a water dragon.

"You're wrong, human," the image said. "I do not know you, therefore, there's no way you could know me."

"Are you sure about that?" Steve challenged. "How else would I know how to contact you?"

"There is that," the image said, nodding. The shealk's large, blue eyes narrowed as they studied him. "Who are you?"

"I'm Steve Miller. Over there is my wife, Sarah. And standing beside her would be Emerion."

"You travel with a griffin? May I ask why?"

"We're his parents," Steve said, matter-of-factly. "Listen, I know you don't believe me. I get that. But what I am going to suggest will sound very farfetched. You know what? It'd be easier if you could join us here."

"How?" the shealk demanded. "I'm a water dragon. You're a human."

"And you've traveled as a human before," Steve answered.

"You know about that?" Balthor whispered, amazed.

"I do, yes. It's how you met ... forget about that for now. Can you join us here?"

"Where are you located?" Balthor wanted to know.

"We're up at Lake Raehón right now," Steve said. "It's in the dragon valley. But, if you'd like, we can head to Capily. I know that's where you live."

Balthor let out a fierce growl. "There's no way I would

have told you that. Tell me how you know that, human."

"I will, I promise. We'll head to Capily. Meet us on shore in about ten minutes."

"How …?"

"Sarah is a teleporter. Don't worry about it. See you shortly."

Five minutes later, they were standing on the edge of the Erudian Ocean, with the seaside village of Capily spread out far enough behind them so as to not be spotted. Husband and wife, followed closely by Emerion, paced up and down the shoreline while they waited for Balthor to arrive.

Less than two minutes later, the surface of the sea turned choppy, as though a strong wind buffeted the water. Bubbles formed, suggesting the seawater was boiling hot, only it was still cool to the touch. Steve ran his hand through the water to satisfy his own curiosity. Growing larger, the bubbles lifted from the surface. One bubble, larger than the rest, rose off the surface and then touched down on the sandy beach behind them. An adult human stood perfectly at attention within the delicate, shimmering globe.

It popped.

Balthor was exactly as Steve remembered, except for a touch more gray in his hair. He was tall, slightly more so than Steve, lean, and if he wasn't mistaken, had a few more worry wrinkles around his eyes than before. The transformed shealk wizard took several steps forward and came to a halt.

"I do not know you."

"In this timeline, no, you do not," Steve confirmed.

"In this timeline?" Balthor repeated. "You're suggesting this is a … *tangent* of your own time?"

Steve nodded. "Tangent. That's a good way to describe it. Well, you're right. Our timeline has been altered."

"And you're telling me we've all met before," Balthor breathed. "Amazing. I have no memories of such an encounter. I wonder if a spell could be written which would restore them?"

Sarah stepped forward. "I doubt that. Let's bring you up to speed, okay?"

For the next twenty minutes, they filled in the wizard

about everything they had experienced, from their missing portal keys, to their run-in with the dwarves, and to the strange human monarchs currently sitting on the throne.

"Trust me when we say you're going to want to help us," Steve said, unable to hide the urgency in his voice.

"I do not think I want to become involved in this," Balthor finally said. "Before you object, listen to me, please. Yes, perhaps the events of your original timeline have been altered, but is it that bad? For these people, myself included, it's the only reality they know. How bad could it be?"

"Do it for Gareth," Steve said.

Balthor's eyes narrowed. "I *am* Gareth. How do you know that name?"

"Are you sure you want to tell him this?" Sarah asked.

"He deserves to know," Steve answered. "If this is what it takes to encourage him to help us, then so be it."

"What?" Balthor demanded. "And how do you know my true name?"

"Because it's the name you gave your son," Steve said, shrugging. "Your human son."

"In your time … I have a son … a human son?"

Sarah nodded. "Yes, he inherits your jhorun *and* your intelligence. He's the most powerful wizard I have personally ever seen."

Steve raised a hand. "That goes for me, too."

Balthor looked as though he was going to collapse. Steve scanned the area, looking for something the wizard could sit on, but before he could act, Balthor snapped his fingers and a medium-sized boulder appeared. He sat on that, instead.

"D-do you know the name of his mother?" Balthor quietly asked. "Is it … could it be … Adyna?"

Steve shared a glance with Sarah. "Actually, I think it is."

"I saw her on the beach," Balthor sighed, growing wistful. "I've watched from afar and yearned to speak with her."

"Why didn't you?" Steve wanted to know.

"I am a shealk wizard," Balthor said, shaking his head. "I use jhorun on a daily basis. Her people were forbidden from even talking about using magic. I figured it wasn't meant to be."

"Now imagine that the same circumstances happened, and this time around, there were no laws in place to prevent humans from using their jhorun. What would you have done?"

Balthor stiffened. "I would have approached her and initiated a conversation. Very well, you have convinced me. What is it you desire?"

"We need to get back to the past," Steve said. "I'm guessing it's somewhere around a hundred-eighteen years ago. We have to prevent a guy, who coincidentally happens to be from the present time, from breaking out of prison."

"He's already escaped," Sarah reminded him.

"True. So, do we focus on preventing him from escaping or else dealing with him *after* he's escaped?"

Sarah was silent as she considered. "I remember thinking Melvyn couldn't be trusted, and that we should probably bring him back with us."

"You're nicer than I am," Steve admitted. "If we want to make certain he'll never bother us again, then we need to silence him permanently."

A look of horror appeared on Sarah's face. "Are you saying ...?"

"I know what you're thinking," Steve said, sighing. "No, I'm not talking about me, but maybe turning him over to someone he has wronged."

"It's still the same thing," Sarah insisted. "Whether you do it, or we get a dragon to eat him, you're still talking about death."

"I'm just putting it out there," Steve said. "Fine. For now, let's focus on finding him and stopping him from destroying alliances and killing people who are not supposed to die."

Sarah held up a hand. "And, preventing him from replacing the existing king and queen with someone he can, what, control? Manipulate?"

"That's a tall order," Balthor observed. "Time travel. This won't be easy."

"It wasn't the last time we did it, either," Steve confided. "It took the strength of four gatekeepers to modify a portal to send someone through time."

"After all of this is over," Balthor began, as his eyes closed, "I expect you to return and tell me all about what has happened. Exploring our linear existence is something that fascinates me, and from the sounds of it, you've done more exploring than I ever will."

"You got it, pal. What do you need us to do?"

"Just be silent for a bit, while I determine what will be needed to send you back in time. Will it be just you?"

Steve shared a tender look with his wife. "Any chance you'll let me do this on my own?"

"Not a chance," Sarah said. "We're a team. Besides, you'll be needing my help getting from one end of the kingdom to the other."

"I'm going, too," Emerion declared.

Sarah was shaking her head even before the griffin had finished stating his intent.

"It's way too dangerous, Em. The last thing either of us needs is to worry about whether you're safe. Please, just go home and be safe, all right?"

"You may want to reconsider your decision to prevent him from going," Balthor murmured. The wizard's eyes were still closed.

"Why?" Steve wanted to know.

"How certain are you, once your timeline is restored, that your griffin won't be erased from existence?"

"Why would he be?" Sarah asked. "If we were protected in our world when the timeline changed the first time around, then why wouldn't Emerion be protected when it reverts back?"

"In theory, he should be," Balthor said. "However, do you really want to risk his life?"

Steve shook his head. "I certainly don't. I know you don't, either, my dear."

Sarah nodded. "No, I do not. Very well. Emerion, don't look so smug. It's incredibly dangerous to travel backward in time. The slightest wrong action on any of our parts can result in dire consequences when we return. The fact that we have to go back is proof positive that the past should be left alone."

Emerion nodded. "I understand. I will protect the two of you with my very life."

Steve approached and laid a friendly hand on the griffin's back. "Right back at you, pal."

Emerion nuzzled Steve's side before turning to Sarah and doing the same.

"We're going back to stop a human," the griffin said. "How hard could it be?"

"For this particular human?" Steve asked, scowling. "It's going to be a royal pain."

Ten minutes later, Balthor's eyes opened and he stared appraisingly at the group of three before him.

"What is it?" Steve asked, worried. "Not able to do it?"

"Oh, it can be done," Balthor explained, "but the spell is so powerful, so complex, that I'm going to need our other wizard, and my acolyte. There are just too many variables that must be modified and held in place in order to create the spell. This will be, single-handedly, the most complex, multi-layered spell I have ever created in my life."

"How long will it take you to create it?" Steve asked.

Balthor tapped the side of his head. "It's already done, but, as I said, I will need help before it can be invoked. Once the spell has been imbued with enough power, then—and only then—will it be ready to be used."

"More shealk are on the way here?" Emerion asked.

Balthor nodded. "Correct. They should be here right about …"

A dark aquamarine head rose gracefully out of the water, perched high on a long reptilian neck. The newcomer had the elongated face typical of the water dragons, was nearly forty feet long from nose to tail, and there, tucked closely to the sides of its body, were the dragon's tiny vestigial legs.

"Thank you for coming, Amentharias," Balthor told the new arrival. "Do you prefer to stay in your shealk form, or would you prefer to shift your form to that of a human?"

A soft, musical trill floated down from the water dragon's head. The chirps, clicks, and whistles sounded for a few moments before falling silent.

"This is the other shealk wizard?" Steve wanted to know.

Balthor nodded. "Allow me to introduce Amentharias, who's almost as powerful as I."

The teal shealk inclined her head.

"Where's Vass?" Balthor asked, turning to face the water dragon.

More trills and whistles. Balthor frowned. "Delayed? By what? No, I don't care if he thinks he's found some precious stone. Get a message to him. We need him at our current location. Yes, that'll do. Thank you."

Five minutes later, a dark red water dragon, with a light gray underbelly, was swaying gently next to Amentharias. This second shealk was considerably smaller in size than either of them.

A stronger set of trills and chirps sounded, as Balthor's acolyte had evidently fired off a slew of questions.

"No, I'll be constructing this one. I know you are looking for new experiences, Vass, but this one is beyond your skill. Fear not. You'll get there someday."

Sarah held up a hand. "His name is Vass?"

Balthor nodded. "That's right. My apologies for forgetting my manners. Vassilos, this is Steve and his mate, Sarah. With them is a griffin male, Emerion. And this is my apprentice, Vassilos."

The small shealk nodded politely and elected to remain quiet.

"What do you need from us?" Steve asked.

"Just your silence for the next ten minutes," Balthor answered. "Amentharias, Vass, are you ready? Good. Open your senses and calm your thoughts. I'll see you there."

Husband and wife watched closely as Balthor pulled a small item from his pocket and held it in an outstretched hand, palm facing up. Both shealk retracted their heads, vanishing completely into the water. A few moments later, they were back.

"Where'd they go?" Emerion quietly asked.

Steve tapped the side of his head. "Eyes. They dry out fairly quickly."

"How do you know?" the griffin asked.

Steve gave Emerion a grin. "Let's call it first-hand

experience."

Balthor cracked an eye. "You, fire thrower. You say you have first-hand experience? With the shealk? How is that possible?"

"We have first-hand experience because we *were* shealk for a time."

"You shifted into the body of a shealk?" Balthor asked, dumbfounded. "How were you able to do that? I thought magic was forbidden for you humans!"

"This was before the timeline was messed up, so ... wow, this story is too long. Let me sum it up: your son turned us into shealk in order to locate a missing temple. Well, your son had come up with the winning idea. We found the temple and everything turned out good."

"Simply incredible," Balthor said again. "Very well, here we go."

While their shealk friend and his two associates did whatever they had to do to make the spell work, Steve quietly led Sarah and Emerion to a nearby section of the beach that had a couple of fallen logs. Husband and wife took one, while Emerion simply settled to the ground. The young griffin nervously ruffled the feathers of his wings a few times before looking at the two of them.

"I must admit something. When I learned I would accompany you, I was thrilled. Now that I'm faced with the prospect of traveling through time..."

"Not so much?" Steve guessed. "It's okay, pal. This is actually the second time for me, and it's not fun. But at least we have a way home."

Sarah nodded. "Once Balthor gets it working, yes, we do."

Steve held up a finger. "But, if something happens, and let's say the spell is either taken, or destroyed, or flat-out doesn't work, we would still have a way home."

"How?" Emerion asked.

"Luther," Sarah said, smiling. "We could always go see Luther."

"Who is Luther?" the griffin wanted to know.

Sarah pointed at Steve. "It's his ancestor, in our world."

"In the past?" Emerion nodded with comprehension. "Ah, I understand. Wait. No, I don't. Steve's ancestor has the power to time travel?"

"It's a long story," Sarah said. "We'll explain it later. But yes, there's a way home in Idaho."

"We're ready," Balthor announced, causing the three of them to jump. He took a seat on the log next to Emerion and held out his hand. Leaning forward for a better look, husband, wife, and griffin all stared at the object: it was a seashell. Steve took it and held it between his thumb and forefinger.

"This? This is the spell? How do we …?"

Quick as a snake, Balthor laid a hand over Steve's mouth.

"Do be careful. I have yet to explain how this works, and more importantly, how to make it work. Now, the shell *is* the spell. You were about to ask how to activate it? Well, you simply hold it in your hand and say the word you were about to say. The spell is keyed in to the three of you, so regardless of where you are, you will be transported to the past."

"Do we know when?" Sarah asked.

Balthor shook his head. "All I can tell you is that you will be placed at a point where it will be possible to salvage your timeline. Once your escapee has performed certain tasks, well, it'll be too late. The spell will automatically trigger and return the three of you here."

"You've thought of everything," Sarah observed. "Thank you."

"Once there," Balthor continued, "and you have determined your mission is over, you, er, activate it a second time, and you will return here."

Steve nodded. "Got it. Anything else we need to know?"

"Be careful. And, for the record, I do hope you succeed. I believe I would enjoy having a son."

"Oh, you do," Sarah assured him.

* * *

"I cannot believe we're back here," Steve was saying, nearly an hour later.

The jump to another time had been nowhere near as

eventful as the first. There were no sparkling lights, nor any out-of-body experiences. One moment they were staring at Balthor, and the next they were standing by a very familiar waterfall.

"Are we sure we arrived where we should?" Sarah asked. "After all, everything still looks the same."

"This is the same waterfall as before," Emerion observed. "I see no differences."

Steve and Sarah watched as Emerion approached the pool, lowered his head, and took a few sips from the cool water. The griffin's avian eyes looked up at theirs and his head lifted.

"What is it?"

Steve pointed at the griffin and grinned. "You are standing at the exact spot where we first saw a griffin all those years ago."

"The *exact* same spot," Sarah confirmed. "My, how time flies."

"Where do we go from here?" Steve asked.

Sarah pointed northeast. "That way. I say we go to the castle. If that's where Melvyn has been imprisoned, then maybe they might have some idea where he headed?"

Once all three were in contact, the pristine waterfall and all its surrounding greenery vanished, replaced by an open field with a wide, gravel road running east to west in front of them. To the right, heading east, about two miles in the distance, was the West Gate, leading into the city of R'Tal. Sighing, Steve turned to his wife, but she was holding up a finger.

"No, don't complain. I dropped us here for a reason. We don't want to alarm anyone or draw any attention to ourselves."

"What about Em?" Steve wanted to know. "People are going to know something's up when we stroll through the gate with this handsome hunk of a griffin."

Emerion's eyes bulged out. "Do not even ...! Why would you ...? Eww!"

Sarah draped an arm across Em's tawny shoulders. "Pay no attention to him. He knows how to get your goat."

Emerion shook his head. "It's okay. I just wish you'd let me surprise him every once in a while. I know I could do it."

Overhearing, Steve stepped close. "Surprise me? Oh, puh-leese. You don't have a chance of scaring me."

"He does so," Sarah argued, "which is why I've expressly forbidden him from doing so."

Steve met Emerion's eyes and he smirked. "Hah. She's got my back."

"It's so you don't have a heart attack," Sarah corrected. "You're almost sixty, and we don't need you to …"

"S-sixty?" Steve sputtered. "I am *not*, thank you very much. Whose side are you on?"

"My own," Sarah giggled. "Okay, everyone ready? Let's get this party started. Steve, do you have the spell?"

"I do, yes. I've got it in my pocket. Why? Do you want to keep it?"

"No, I didn't bring my purse with me, or else I would. And why does women's clothing so rarely have pockets? Ugh. Anyway, come on. I want to see what the king and queen have to say about Melvyn's escape."

Navigating their way down the path, through the West Gate, and into the city, Steve breathed a sigh of relief. While it wasn't the version they had visited numerous times, at least the *feel* of the place was back. Vendors had jammed their carts and stalls inside the city limits, eager to make a sale. Kids were seen—and heard—as they noisily chased each other through the streets. And there, enthralling an audience of nearly twenty townsfolk, a jester juggled five balls, all without physically touching any of them.

Jhorun was no longer forbidden!

"Where now?" Emerion inquired. The griffin was starting to garner some stares, and he was becoming nervous. "The castle?"

"Yes, head toward the castle," Sarah instructed. "Before we go any further, we need to confirm Melvyn is at the heart of this."

Steve led the way to the castle, getting stopped only when attempting to cross the drawbridge. Then, a familiar face came to their aid. A tall, gaunt man in his late-forties, with shoulder length black hair, streaked with more gray than before, appeared. He was outfitted in dark maroon armor and had a single-handed sword strapped to his waist. It was Sauer, Captain of the Royal Guards, someone neither of them had planned on ever seeing again.

"You. It can't be."

"Hey there, pal. Yep, it's me. I'm back. Back from the future."

Sarah swatted his arm. "You dork. How long have you been wanting to say that?"

"Oh, ever since I knew we'd be headed back here."

"Wizards be damned!" Sauer exclaimed. "You're the fire thrower! And you? I remember you. Sarah, the teleporter. I ... a griffin? What the blazes is a griffin doing here, inside the city?"

"I wish it was under better circumstances," Steve said, sighing. "Don't worry about Emerion. He's with us. Tell me something, Sauer. Our pal, Melvyn? Did he escape?"

The captain's eyes widened. "Of course. *That* is why you're here. We had suspected it might come to this. Come with me, at once."

Steve turned to Sarah and Emerion. "Now we're getting somewhere. After you guys."

The three of them followed Sauer deep into the castle. They passed into the Great Hall, where the familiar golden thrones were present. Soon, they were standing before the Anteroom, a chamber specifically designed to repel all but the strongest jhorun. Since a sorceress was responsible for giving them their abilities, Steve and Sarah's jhoruns were classified as wizard-level or higher. Therefore, both worked inside the enchanted room.

The two guards stationed outside the room snapped to attention and pulled the doors open as they approached. Then, they caught sight of Emerion and, with looks of alarm on their faces, tried to shut the doors as quickly as possible.

"Be at ease," Sauer commanded. "The griffin is friendly, and is welcome here. Stand aside."

"Yes, sir."

"Captain?" a voice said, from inside the room. "What

is the meaning of this interruption? I thought I left explicit instructions to … you! I remember you! You're the Nohrin! What are you doing back here? Wizards be damned! I cannot believe it! To think that … Captain?"

Sauer nodded. "Aye, sir."

"Would you care to explain to me why I'm looking at the largest griffin I have ever seen, and that the aforementioned griffin is now in my private chambers?"

Kri'Calin, King of Lentari, had been sitting behind his desk, poring over a stack of documents, when they entered the room. By now, Kri'Calin was on his feet and staring—hard—at their group.

"The griffin travels with the Nohrin," Sauer explained. "They both have vouched for him."

The doors were closed and the three of them looked at the monarch who had been king the last time they had time-traveled here. Kri'Calin was older, grayer, and maybe a tiny bit thicker around the middle, but at least whatever Melvyn had planned for the king and queen hadn't occurred. Yet.

"I assume you're going to tell me why they've returned? Yes, Captain, what is it?"

Sauer cleared his throat. "They have returned due to recent events." He held out a hand. "You may recall we touched on this subject not long after the prisoner's escape?"

"What is that supposed to mean?" Steve demanded.

Sauer nodded at the king and kept his arm extended. Comprehension flooded Kri'Calin's face and he sighed.

"You are correct, Captain. It's coming back to me. We placed a wager on whether we'd see a return of our friends from the future. I had completely forgotten about that. Well, it would appear I have lost." Kri'Calin reached inside his robes, withdrew a leather pouch, and counted out several gold coins, which he passed to Sauer.

"My thanks, Your Majesty."

"I'll earn that back, mark my words. You were right. I should have seen this coming."

Steve sighed. "So, it's true. Everyone's favorite Lentarian escaped. Deep down, I was hoping we were wrong, but the evidence clearly suggested otherwise."

"How long ago?" Sarah asked.

"Nearly six weeks, I'm afraid," the king answered. "And to this day, we do not know how he escaped. One morning he was there, carrying out his daily duties, then the next, he walked, unchallenged, through the main gate and out into the city. When we investigated his absence, we noticed he hadn't taken any of his personal belongings with him."

"He just vanished," Sauer reported, his face grim. He looked across at Steve and sighed. "I seem to recall him threatening your very existence prior to his incarceration. Has he made good on any of those threats? Clearly, since you're both still here, it can't be that bad."

Emerion squawked once, annoyed.

"How bad is it?" Kri'Calin asked.

Steve spread his arms. "We're here, aren't we? It's bad. Very bad."

"What happened?" the king wanted to know. "Can you tell us?"

Steve shrugged. "I can, although I'll tell you right now, you're not going to like it. First off, Melvyn carried through with his promise to kill Maelnar."

"Maelnar," the king repeated. "He would be one of the Kla Guur dwarves, would he not?"

"Yes," Steve confirmed. "He's a master blacksmith, who is also the portal key maker. Without Maelnar, those keys are never made. If they're never made, we, the Nohrin, will never find our way here in the first place."

"So, that's bad," Sauer deduced.

Sarah nodded. "Very."

"Continuing on," Steve said, "we have … that is, we need to tell you that … wow, this is harder than I thought."

Sarah laid a hand on his. "Want me to take over?"

"Yes, please."

"Your Majesty," Sarah began, "sometime in the very near future, Melvyn does something to get you and your wife removed from the throne. I wish we could say what that was, but all we know is that there was a completely different king and queen on the throne when we went to visit yesterday, in the future."

Kri'Calin frowned. "A different king? Will you tell me he was from the same bloodline? He … you're shaking your head. You both are. That can't be good."

"I'll have the guards doubled," Captain Sauer promised. "Tripled. You and Ny'Alena will not be harmed. I will personally see to it that the two of you are protected at all times. We'll limit exposure to …"

"Just a moment, Captain," the king interrupted. "While I appreciate the added measures, I will *not* allow myself to become a prisoner in my own castle. Steve, Sarah, is it reasonable to assume once you recapture Melvyn, the threat will be neutralized?"

"We'd like to think so," Steve said, nodding. "Can you tell us how goes the search for him? I mean, if he's been on his own for six weeks, I can only assume you're doing everything you can to bring him back?"

"Every village is on high alert," Captain Sauer confirmed. "Constables have doubled patrols. Curfews have been enacted. It's only a matter of time before he's found."

"No offense, but we have to do better than that," Steve said, his face hardening. "Sitting around and waiting for him to surface isn't going to cut it. The longer he waits, the more he learns how to disrupt present day Lentari."

"What more could he possibly do?" Kri'Calin cried. "If I understand you correctly, he finds a way to replace me and does everything in his power to prevent you from returning to Lentari to undo what he's done. What more is there?"

"Alliances have been destroyed," Emerion reported, drawing gasps of alarm from both king and captain. "Dwarves, dragons, and even us griffins. None of it exists in present day Lentari now."

"And magic," Sarah reminded everyone. "Magic is forbidden."

"Active use of someone's jhorun is considered illegal?" Sauer repeated. "Whatever for?"

"Think about it," Steve urged. "Melvyn is reshaping Lentari to suit his needs alone. He doesn't care about anyone else and he certainly doesn't care if someone gets hurt, if they get in his way."

"What do you suggest we do?" Sauer asked.

"Get teams of men together. I'd say go door-to-door throughout all the villages if necessary. He's hiding somewhere, biding his time. We need to find him and do it quick."

Sarah raised a hand. "I think what we need to do is return to Borahgg. It'd be our safest move."

"Why do you think that?" Steve asked.

"Think about it, dear. What's the one thing we know for certain about Melvyn?"

"That he's a pain in the ass who must be stopped at all costs?"

Sauer snickered.

"Well, that's a close second," Sarah said, nodding. "But, what I was referring to was the fact that Melvyn intends to kill Maelnar. You heard them say he was still alive, didn't you?"

Steve's eyes widened. "Son of a …! How could I have forgotten that? They told us that both Maelnar and Breslin, er, that's his son, had been lured up to the surface by the possibility of an important archaeological discovery."

Sarah was nodding. "That's right. We need to find Maelnar, like *right now*. Melvyn has got to be waiting to ambush him somewhere along the way."

Kri'Calin looked at the two of them. "You know what to do?"

Steve nodded. "I know exactly what I'm going to do."

"Then, we'll leave you to it. You have my eternal thanks for bringing us the warning. We will be prepared. There's no way anyone will be able to sneak into R'Tal once we're done with it."

"Good for you," Sarah praised. "Em, come on. We're going back to Borahgg."

"They weren't too happy with us last time," Steve recalled. "They aren't going to welcome us back with open arms."

Sarah frowned. "I don't care. We have to help Maelnar. We can't let him be killed!"

Steve took one of Sarah's hands and pulled her in for a hug. "And we won't. I promise."

Sarah sniffed and wiped her eyes with the back of a

sleeve. "Good. Thank you."

Steve held out an arm. "Shall we? The sooner we get this over with, the sooner we can start figuring out what *else* Melvyn might have done."

Sarah hooked her arm through his and motioned for Emerion to come close. She caught sight of the king and gave him a small curtsy. "We'll keep you posted on our progress."

"How?" Kri'Calin wanted to know.

Sarah pointed at the nearby desk. "I'll drop updates there."

"Perfect. My thanks, Lady Sarah."

Steve raised a hand. "One final question, Your Majesty, for my own curiosity. Can you tell us how long it's been since we were last here in Lentari?"

Kri'Calin turned to Sauer. "Six years?"

Sauer nodded. "Aye, it's been six years, Your Majesty."

"It's the same amount of time for us," Steve observed. Noticing the confused expression on their Lentarian friends' faces, he took a breath. "We haven't seen you for six years, and you haven't seen us for the same amount of time. Somehow, I think your time and our own are progressing at the same pace."

"That makes no sense whatsoever," Sarah snorted.

Steve waved a dismissive hand. "Whatever. Not important. We'll keep you posted."

Faster than a person can blink, they were standing in the central plaza of Borahgg once more. Steve's eyes widened. He had just caught sight of a familiar face: Selwyn, the head of security, the father of little Aislinn, whom he had helped ride the back of a dragon. The dwarf's eyes widened as recognition set in. However, before either of them could say a word, guards appeared out of the shadows and immediately surrounded them.

"What, were you just waiting for us to come back?" Steve asked, exasperated.

"You could say that, human," one of the dwarven soldiers answered. "You tell us your wife be gifted with teleportation, and it becomes only a matter of time before you'll return."

"That's absurd," Steve insisted. "You had no idea we'd return."

"Of course we did," the dwarf insisted. "No one trusts humans, so why should we?"

"I will vouch for them," a voice declared. Selwyn pushed his way through the crowd until he was standing before Steve. "I will forever be in their debt. This is Steve and his wife, Sarah. Thanks to them, we have our new alliance with the dragons."

"*That* Steve and Sarah?" one of the voices cried. "Selwyn, this is the fire thrower?"

"Aye, he's the fire thrower."

Steve spoke up. "As much as I'd love to catch up, we need to talk to your Council. We have one mother of a problem, and we need to have it addressed as soon as possible."

Selwyn nodded and held out an arm. "Remember the way?"

Sarah let out a short burst of laughter. "Him? Please. Do you want to know how many times he's been lost over the years?"

Steve mouthed *way too many*, much to Emerion and Selwyn's amusement, and then followed the dwarf as he led the three of them toward the heart of the city. As they passed by various vendors, and the numerous forges, he couldn't help but think about his last excursion here, in this particular time. He never would have dreamt they'd be back, that's for certain. And that reminded him about something.

"Selwyn? How's Aislinn doing? Is she still healthy?"

"Healthy as a dragon," Selwyn quipped, giving him a smile. "She speaks of you, and Pryllan, almost daily. I feel I should let you know. My Aislinn, she's decided she wants to be an explorer when she grows up. She wants to find her own dragon, befriend it, and explore the world."

"That'd be quite an undertaking," Sarah decided. "Good for her!"

When they were finally brought before the Council, Steve had to reassure everyone that Emerion was perfectly harmless—unless either of them was threatened—and could rest assured he would be on his best behavior. Several faces, Steve noted, were familiar, and some were not.

"We meet again, fire thrower."

Steve stared at the elderly dwarf with the white robe. If possible, it had even more decorations and medals on it from the last time he had seen it.

"I remember you. Brarvur, is it? It's good to see you."

"I could say the same, human, but something tells me it's not. I was led to believe this isn't your time. It therefore begs the question ... what are you doing back here?"

Steve turned to Selwyn. "Do you remember the fugitive we were looking for the last time we were here? The one your brothers helped us with?"

"I do. You're looking for him? Again? Why?"

"He escaped, and somehow, he's doing things which will affect the future. This is critical. We need to find Maelnar. I know he's not currently here, but can someone tell me where we might find him?"

Brarvur shook his head and shrugged. "Master Maelnar, along with his son, have undertaken a journey. He did not say when they would return."

Steve felt the blood drain from his face. "What was the reason?"

Brarvur shrugged. "The only thing he told me was that new information had been brought to light, and that he was off to investigate."

"New information about what?" Sarah asked.

"Something about an archaeological expedition of extreme importance, but I paid him no mind. Who would ever believe such a far-fetched story?"

Chapter Four–Dealing With Dwarves

He can't possibly be suggesting what I *think* he's suggesting," Steve whispered. "I mean ... there's no way! It's not supposed to be discovered for over a hundred years!"

Sarah shook her head. "But, you have to admit, it's a fantastic way to lure Maelnar topside. You and I both know how fascinated he is with that city. All Melvyn had to do was dangle the carrot, and sure enough, Maelnar took the bait."

"You're talking about a dwarf?" Emerion asked. The three of them were huddled close.

"That's right," Sarah said, nodding. "Someone who has a very important role to play in Lentari's history. I don't know what Melvyn has planned for him, but whatever it is, we need to stop it."

"Do we know where?" Steve quietly asked.

Sarah shook her head. "Hang on, I'll ask. Umm, excuse me? Mr. Brarvur? Did Maelnar say where he was headed?"

The grizzled gray head nodded. "Indeed, he did, lass. He

went Topside."

"Umm, okay. Topside. It's kinda big up there. Can you give us any other clues besides that?"

"That's all he told us," the dwarf council member said. "Is there something we should be worried about?"

Steve snorted. "I'll say. I ... oof! Sarah? What'd you do that for?"

"I'm sorry, I was just stretching. I didn't see you there. It's not important, Brarvur. We just wanted to make sure he was all right. Steve? Should we get going?"

"Yeppers."

Once they were out of earshot, Steve pulled Sarah to a stop. "Why'd you sucker punch me in the gut?"

"I was trying to prevent you from telling the Kla Guur too much information. We need things to progress as they normally should, right? Well, they can't do that if they have sudden insight into what the future has in store for them."

"Yeah, okay. I'll give you that one."

"Steve!" a voice suddenly called out.

Steve turned to see Selwyn hurrying toward them. With him was a second dwarf, this one much smaller and much more slender than any other dwarf he had previously seen.

Steve stared at the girl. "Well, I'll be damned. Aislinn, is that you?"

"Hello. I didn't know if you'd remember me."

"You've no doubt noticed her beard is absent," Selwyn said. "It's her own choice. She's chosen to keep herself clean-shaven. Very un-dwarf-like, but her mother and I are just so happy she's continuing to thrive that we simply do not care. She can do whatever she wants."

"I'm happy to hear that," Steve told the dwarf. "We all are. I thank our lucky stars Pryllan and I were able to help out. Your father told us about your future plan to befriend a dragon and ride on big adventures. That's exciting."

Selwyn extended a forearm. "Good journeys to you. If you ever need anything, then you have but to ask."

Once Selwyn and Aislinn left, the three of them crowded close.

"Where to?" Steve wanted to know.

"Back to the valley," Sarah said. "I've got some ideas about where to look."

Suddenly, sunlight was streaming down on them. A stiff breeze buffeted them, bringing with it scents of wildflowers, the nearby lake, and several unidentified aromas. Animal? Plant?

They were standing just inside the ring of trees, overlooking the valley south of Lake Raehón. There, nearly a mile distant, was a scattering of large, rounded boulders. One of them, Steve knew, would be a door leading down, back to the dwarf realm. Emerion started to move out into the open, when both Steve and Sarah put a restraining hand on either shoulder.

"Not yet," Steve whispered. "Dragons are *not* our friends here. They used to be allied with dwarves, but now I'm pretty sure the alliance has been broken."

"We need to find out if that's happened yet," Sarah countered. "And if it is? It'll be just something else we have to fix. Well?"

"Well, what?"

"I'm hoping you're going to contact Pryllan."

"Oh. Absolutely. She'd be the best way to search for dwarves. In fact, maybe someone has seen them?"

Emerion squawked once. "I have wings, you know. I could start searching."

"Do you have any idea how many dragons live in this area?" Steve began. "We've covered a lot of basics, with regards to flying, but not once have we covered what to do if a dragon is on your tail."

"What should he do if one does?" Sarah wanted to know.

Steve pointed straight down. "Land, as quickly as he can. Dragons rule in the air, and granted, on the ground, they're still equally terrifying. However, at least we'd have a fighting chance of either escaping, or hiding, or …? You get the picture."

"I do," Emerion said.

"You said you've been thinking about what to do," Steve reminded her. "Care to share?"

Sarah nodded. "Of course. Listen, no one seems to know

where Maelnar and Breslin are headed, right?"

"Right," Steve confirmed.

Sarah made a circling gesture with an arm. "I'm thinking he's around here. Remember what we were told? That Maelnar dies in some type of dwarf clan war? We already know there are three or four different clans in this area. Besides, in this timeline, no one knows where Nar is located."

"Are you sure there's no way Melvyn could know?" Steve pressed.

Sarah shrugged. "Sure, I wouldn't put it past him. However, we were told Nar was nowhere around here, and that it was much farther south. That's an incredibly long way to go on foot. So, I'm thinking everything is too convenient around here, in this valley. No, I'm willing to wager Melvyn told them Nar was up here, somewhere close. Any luck contacting Pryllan?"

"I'm trying now. Let's see …"

Pryllan, are you there? It's Steve, the, er, fire thrower. We've met before, and I ended up getting you into one mother of a mess, but thankfully, it was all resolved.

You again.

Steve sighed. *Hello, Kahvel. Yes, it's me.*

What are you doing back here?

It's a long story.

He spent the next ten minutes informing Pryllan's mate everything he knew about Melvyn, and what he had done to the present-day timeline.

This same human? He is on the loose again?

He is. We need to find him ASAP. The longer we give him, the more damage he can do.

Agreed. I know you've been calling for Pryllan. My apologies. I have been blocking, since I wasn't sure who this was.

And now that you know?

I will remove my block. Do you promise to keep her safe?

With my life, pal.

Good. Very well, I have withdrawn my block. Go ahead.

Thanks. Pryllan? Are you there?

I remember you. You're the human fire thrower, aren't you? You're the one I allowed on my back.

Yep, that's me. Surprise! I'm back!

Why? Do you detest your own time so much that you'd much rather experience someone else's?

Ordinarily, no, but in this case, you could say that. Remember the older human we chased, just before I returned home?

Aye.

He's loose, and he's causing problems. We have to find him.

Kahvel has just shared with me what you told him about what has happened to your own time. We agree with you. This human should be found.

Here's my question for you two. Should we inform Rinbok?

Is it that serious? Kahvel's voice interjected.

If we don't put a stop to him, then yes.

Very well. I will inform the Dragon Lord.

Tell him we believe Melvyn is nearby. We think he's pitting the dwarf clans against each other

To what end?

To cause as much chaos as possible.

Acknowledged.

Steve, what would you have me do?

Is there any way I can get you to help me look?

Not without a verbal directive from Rinbok Intherer. Should I get it? Do you need to accompany me?

Well, that depends. Do you remember what he looks like from the last time we had to search for him?

Of course. I even remember his scent.

Perfect. I can only hope the Dragon Lord determines Melvyn is a threat and should be found.

And eliminated. Rinbok Intherer has been notified. This human must be found, and the threat neutralized.

I couldn't agree more. Melvyn is wielding some kind of power. He used to have the ability to make one forget about something that had just happened, but I'm fairly certain he can't do that anymore. The human king rendered his jhorun ineffective.

And now he wields a different jhorun?

That is our belief, yes.

We'll be careful. Excellent. Rinbok Intherer dispatched

twenty of my brethren. They are now patrolling the skies.

Wow. That was quick. Do me a favor? Tell them to ignore the two humans and griffin traveling together. We're the good guys.

A griffin? You travel with a griffin? Whatever for? Never mind. It is none of my business. I will pass the information to the Collective.

Thank you. Happy hunting, guys.

The Dragon Lord just asked a question. If this human is found, what then?

I'm going to repeat what he himself just said: neutralize the threat.

Rinbok Intherer approves of your answer.

The foreign presence in his mind faded. Steve looked at Sarah and gave her a thumbs up.

"Pryllan, Kahvel, and at least twenty other dragons are on the search. Rinbok wants Melvyn found and eliminated."

"As much as I don't want to do this, we'll be searching on our own. You, me, and Emerion."

Emerion squawked with approval.

"You're going to do your Iron Man thing, aren't you?" Sarah accused.

"Not willingly," Steve insisted.

"Hmmph. You don't fool me. I know you love flying around like that."

Steve nodded. "Flying, yes. Landing? No. You and I both know my damn jhorun seems to have a sense of humor and shuts off when it feels like it. There's no rhyme or reason to it."

"It's quite painful to watch," Emerion added.

"Thanks, Captain Obvious," Steve quipped, giving the griffin a grin. "Now, I know we haven't done this before, and if you're not comfortable with it, just let me know. Em? You always said you could carry Sarah, right?"

Emerion's eyes widened. "You're serious? It would be my honor."

Sarah turned to Steve. "Are you sure about this? I was just joking before. I know you really don't enjoy flying."

"I *am* serious and no, I do *not* like flying, but I'd classify this as extenuating circumstances."

Sarah approached the griffin. Emerion immediately

dipped a front foreleg and knelt. Once she was sitting comfortably on his back, she turned to lock eyes with Steve. "This is your last chance to back out. You broke your arm last time you tried to land, remember?"

"Ugh, what a memory," Steve groaned. "Most painful experience of my life, and that's coming from someone who's been squished flat. Twice. So, you'd better believe me when I tell you guys that I will do just about anything to avoid a repeat performance."

"Honey, look. If you think you're going to crash, give me some type of signal? That way, I can always drop you right over a lake, if necessary."

"Good idea. Thank you. As for you, my dear, if something happens, you do the same thing: get yourself to safety."

"Of course. Emerion, are you ready? Then, let's go!"

Emerion spread his wings and took to the sky. Griffin and rider rose steadily and surely to an altitude of several hundred feet and circled about in widening loops. Clearly, the two of them were waiting for him. Gulping nervously, Steve eyed his hands and frowned. What in the world was he doing? Hadn't he sworn off flying after the last time?

Melvyn's smug visage formed in his head. That was all it took.

Bracing his arms at his sides, he blasted out a jet of fire from each hand. In less than a second, he was airborne, and had streaked by Emerion and Sarah like oncoming cars on a highway. Eyeing the distant treetops, Steve grunted with effort to alter his course. With his thrust coming from his hands, and since he couldn't move his arms unless he wanted to severely alter his trajectory, his muscles became fatigued. His wrists ached, and even the simple act of making a minor adjustment ended up sending jolts of pain through his arm.

There's gotta be an easier way to do this.

I'm sorry, are you asking for advice?

Pryllan?

Aye. I assumed, since you were speaking telepathically, you were asking for help.

It was just me, alone with my thoughts. However, since you're here, do you have any advice? If I keep this up for too much longer, then I run the risk of spraining both wrists.

Describe to me your process of flying. You clearly don't have wings, correct?

That's right. I'm shooting out flames from my hands, but in order to achieve lift, I have to angle them straight down. That puts a tremendous strain on my wrists. I was hoping there'd be an easier way to do this.

These bouts of flame … can they be redirected?

What do you mean?

I may not be an expert on human physiology, but until I met you, I have never seen a human expel fire before. As of right now, that's exactly what you're doing, through your hands, correct?

Yeah, that's right.

So … redirect those flames elsewhere.

Like …?

Can you not use them in a location which does not cause you pain?

I don't see how, Pryllan. You're going to have to give me an example.

Your feet?

My feet? During the hunt with Pryllan for one of the famed oskorlisks, he made flames shoot out of Pryllan's tail. Therefore, he should be able to switch his primary propulsion from his hands to his feet.

Well, why not?

He could continue to use his hands for navigation, but if he could blast out his flames from the bottom of his feet, that *would* alleviate the pressure on his wrists. It was worth the risk.

Having a very clear picture in his mind what he wanted to do, he gave his jhorun the command to switch locations on his body and braced for the worst. After a moment, he cracked an eye and checked. Huge jets of flames were now erupting from the soles of his feet. Before he could gloat, he felt himself tipping to the left. A quick blast from his left hand restored balance. Relief! This was something he could maintain for hours, if necessary! He still might not know how to safely land, but up until that time? It was going to be a piece of cake.

Using short bursts of fire from his hands for navigational course corrections, he aimed himself toward Sarah and

Emerion and jetted by. Sarah flashed him a thumbs up.

"Pryllan suggested it," he shouted as they passed each other.

"Good for her," Sarah praised. "So, how do you want to do this?"

"Stay together, but we fly in formation. I'll take the left, Sarah, you watch the middle. Emerion, you can keep an eye on things on the right."

Sarah nodded. "Sounds like a plan."

Together, they began their sweeps of the ground. However, all three sets of eyes missed the flock of griffins they just flew over. With a series of angry squawks, griffins began taking to the air.

"We've got company," Sarah reported, after turning to locate the source of the squawks. "Emerion? Heads up!"

Steve twisted in mid-air to look behind, but that was a mistake. Off balance, his feet dipped up, dropping his head down, throwing him off. He blasted out a few jets of fire, but it was too late. Thankfully, a tree loomed in front of him, and he was able to grab a handful of branches to arrest his fall.

"Where'd he go?" Sarah asked. "I thought I saw him fly by this tree."

"The griffins are nearing," Emerion advised. "I would suggest you teleport yourself to safety."

"I will not leave you unprotected, Em. What will you do?"

"Try and reason with them."

"Not without me you aren't. Go ahead and land. Hurry!"

There wasn't much room in the tiny clearing, but it was enough for Emerion to adopt a defensive stance, wings extended and ready to return him to the sky should the need arise. As for Sarah, she had quickly spotted a fallen branch and was ready to turn it into a baseball bat should the situation call for it. Whatever these creatures wanted, she and Emerion needed to placate them as soon as possible. And *where* was Steve?

The first griffin landed and immediately turned to Emerion. Sarah studied the creature. This one looked different. At first, she couldn't put her finger on what was bothering her, but then, after a few moments of silent contemplation, it hit her: the colors. This particular griffin had lighter-colored feathers and had to be a third of the size of Emerion. Were these griffins adolescent? Then again, Sarah had seen younger griffins before, and it usually meant their wings would have a number of red feathers. These didn't, which meant they weren't young. Wait. What about young females? Sarah looked over at Emerion and smiled. Ah, that was it! From a griffin's point-of-view, Emerion must have been viewed as the ultimate catch. Young, healthy, and incredibly large for his age.

More and more of the griffins landed, filling the entire clearing with interested females. And Emerion was loving every minute of the attention. And above were at least three dozen more, all about the same size, with the same pale feathers.

"Come with me, would you?" she whispered in Emerion's ear.

Nodding, Emerion turned to follow. Sarah checked to see what the rest of the griffins were doing and almost laughed out loud. The entire flock had fallen into line and were now following Emerion like lovestruck teenagers.

"Why are they following me?" Emerion whispered.

"I think that they think you're hot stuff."

"What's that supposed to mean?"

Sarah laughed and stepped back, out of the way.

"Where are you going? You can't leave me here!"

"Oh, I'm not leaving you here, but we do need to wait a moment for Steve to signal us or to catch up. So, in the meantime, go socialize for once!"

This is exactly what Emerion needed: more exposure to his fellow griffins.

Emerion cast her a dark look, but then disappeared into the heart of the flock as the eager females surrounded him on all sides. Keeping the group squarely within her sights, Sarah slowly walked around the tiny clearing. Steve had to be around here somewhere …

Several tree limbs cracked loudly nearby. Those griffins who weren't fawning over Emerion—most likely males—

took immediate notice.

"Well, that hurt like a mother."

Sarah's head whipped around.

"Up here, my dear."

Sarah's gaze lifted. There he was, about halfway up the nearest tree. This one was a pine, and looked as though it was missing all of its branches directly above him. Steve must've tried finding something to grab on the way down.

"There you are. Are you okay?"

"I've got some splinters in a few unmentionable places, but aside from that, I'm okay. Where the hell did those griffins come from? They totally messed up my groove!"

"We flew by them earlier, Kuzco. I think they're interested in Emerion."

"Oh, yeah? How's he handling himself?"

"Poor choice of words, dear."

Steve laughed. "Yeah, I heard how it sounded the moment I said it. Sorry. What I meant was, how's he handling the attention? And would you mind getting me down from here?"

Sarah nodded. Steve vanished from his perch and appeared by her side.

"You had me worried," Sarah admitted.

"Well, *I* was worried," Steve confessed. "I'm tempted to blast everything I have when I come in for the landing, but I never know what's waiting for me down here."

"Did you break anything?"

"No, but I assure you, the first chance I get? I'm going to see about having Pryllan douse me with fire. I wasn't kidding when I said I've got bumps, bruises, and lacerations everywhere. If I don't, I'll be paying for this tomorrow. Emerion? Are you okay, pal?"

The flock parted and Emerion emerged, standing head and shoulders taller than everyone else.

"Steve! Are you well?"

"I'm good, Em. Better than you, it would seem. Are you ready to get going? Care to tell your admirers that you've got some work to do?"

A loud trilling started and it didn't sound happy. The

teenagers were apparently disappointed their newfound idol was leaving. Just then, a loud authoritative squawk silenced them all. An adult griffin, much larger than the females, but still smaller than Emerion, landed. His coloring meant he was a male, and from the way he was presenting himself, Steve guessed this was the flock leader.

"Who are you?" the griffin demanded. "What are you doing here?"

Steve pulled Sarah close and indicated Emerion should follow suit.

"We're just passing through," he told the griffin leader. "We're not causing anyone harm."

"Not causing anyone harm? Half my flock abandoned their nests and flew off! Do you really think that isn't cause for concern?"

"We didn't tell them to do that," Sarah pointed out. "I think your females are interested in Emerion."

"Emerion," the head griffin repeated, as he slowly walked around the three of them. "I've never heard of you. Which flock are you from? I will tell you that I am not looking to add any new members today."

"No flock," Sarah answered. "My husband and I raised Emerion from a cub."

The leader snorted once and then shook his head. "Impossible. No human has ever cared for a griffin cub."

"Until we did it, that was true," Sarah agreed. "Be that as it may, he's our son, and we'll protect him as such. We don't want any trouble, and with your leave, we'll do exactly that: leave."

"We all want to leave," Steve added. "There's no need for this to escalate any further."

The four griffin males appeared and started squawking out their protests. Their leader listened to them rant until finally letting out a squawk so loud that everyone, Steve and Sarah included, jumped.

"They want to challenge him," the leader reported, sighing. "They feel threatened by Emerion's presence and are eager to prove they are superior to your griffin."

"I don't need to duel anyone," Emerion said, speaking

at last. He shook his head. "I'm not interested in staying, but thanks for the offer."

The griffin males nodded, pleased, and moved off. The leader, however, turned angrily back to Emerion.

"And why not? Is there something wrong with our flock? Are our females not appealing enough?"

Steve held up his hands. "Whoa, wait a minute. Didn't you already say you weren't interested in adding anyone else to your little flock?"

"Well, yes, but ..."

"And Emerion has already indicated he's not interested, so why are we arguing?"

The leader of the griffins nodded once, barked a set of orders at his flock, and turned back to Steve. Surprisingly, he bowed. "You're right. Go, in peace."

"Thanks. Sarah? Emerion? You two get going."

"And what about you?" Sarah inquired. "How am I supposed to relax up there knowing you could be impaled by an errant branch if you fly too close to a tree? You almost did earlier!"

"Easy. Watch this."

He moved about thirty feet away and signaled his readiness. Just then, Steve's feet suddenly ignited, much like a rocket warming up its engines for takeoff. A split second later, he was airborne and rising quickly through the treetops. Below, Sarah rushed to get on Emerion's back. Once griffin and rider were high enough, he angled himself to do a flyby.

"You're going much too fast!" Sarah hollered at him, as he zipped by, leaving twin trails of smoke. "Slow it down some, will you?"

"If I go slower, I will go *lower*," Steve called out, as he circled about and passed Sarah a second time. "This is the best I can do!"

"Well, you're not crashing, so it'll work," Sarah decided. "Emerion, can you keep up with him? If you can't, it's okay to say no."

"I can, but not for long," Emerion informed her, as he dipped his left wing to place the two of them on the same course as Steve. "This speed, the one we're doing right now, is the most comfortable."

"Then, maintain this one," Sarah instructed. "Steve? Did you catch that?"

"Yep, we'll make do. Now, back to formation. I'll take left, Emerion takes right, and Sarah?"

"I've got eyes on the middle," Sarah announced.

Steve circled around for a third pass. "Perfect. Let's go find ourselves one pain in the ass, shall we?"

Keeping themselves just above the forest canopy, the three began their methodical search of the area. The more Steve thought about it, the more he was certain they were on the right path. Melvyn wouldn't want to venture too close to a human establishment or near the dragons, risking being incinerated. So, what did that leave? Either somewhere underground, which gave the advantage to the dwarf population, or else above ground, in a concealed setting. With the Bohani Mountains and Anakash forest spread out for thousands of leagues, this, then, became the logical decision.

"Like a needle in a haystack," Steve groaned.

Trees and mountains were starting to look familiar, and Steve began to wonder if they were flying in circles. Thankfully, Sarah's sense of direction was much better than his, so he assumed they were still on the correct track. He kept his eyes peeled.

Finally, four hours into it, somewhere southeast of Lake Raehón, they discovered their first clue. Or, more accurately, Emerion made a discovery that confirmed they were on the right track.

"What is it?" Steve asked, flying close to Emerion and Sarah, trying yet again to lower his flames enough to be cruising at the same speed. Almost immediately, his altitude started to drop. Cursing, he restored his flames and resigned himself to flying in circles. "Do you guys see something?"

Emerion squawked affirmatively and pointed down with one of his avian forelegs. "I see dwarves."

Steve looked down and dropped another ten feet. Hastily blasting out additional power from his hands, he popped back above the canopy before he could make contact with any of the forest's tallest occupants.

"Damn trees. Okay, where are you looking? No, wait, I see 'em. Yep, you're right. That's a dwarf. Look at all the trinkets on his belt. No wonder he's making such a racket. Wait. I can see two dwarves. Now I'm not sure. They are all dressed the same."

"There are four," Sarah corrected. "And, you'll be pleased to know one of them looks like Maelnar! We've found them! That wasn't so bad!"

"Damn glad to see he's still alive," Steve said, as he adjusted his course so that he wouldn't fly directly over them. "So, whatever is going to happen clearly hasn't yet. My question is, how is Melvyn going to get the dwarf clans to fight with one another? How do you get two …?"

Sarah looked over at him as he sped by. "What's the matter?"

"Sarah, I think I know what Melvyn is going to do."

"To make the clans fight one another?"

"Yes, and the sad part is, I'm pretty sure he's already done it. Emerion? Head south. Look around. I have a feeling we're going to discover more dwarf clans are currently on the way."

"We'll be back," Sarah promised. "Ten minutes."

Once the allotted time had passed, and the three of them were flying side-by-side once more, they compared notes.

"How did you know?" Sarah asked. "We found two additional groups less than two leagues apart and heading this way."

"Did they see you?" Steve asked.

"No," Emerion confirmed. "We were careful not to fly directly overhead."

"I found a group, too." Steve sighed. "That means they are all planning on converging somewhere around here."

"You said you figured out what Melvyn's plan was," Sarah reminded him. "Would you tell us?"

"Imagine for a moment you're a dwarf," Steve began. "You live underground, and for the most part, are peaceful toward your fellow dwarf clans. All of a sudden, news reaches you that there's something out there, waiting to be discovered, one with untold riches and, if I remember my Lentarian history, is known for some special armor. Think about it. It's every clan's dream to be the one to make this discovery."

"Nar," Sarah guessed. "You're talking about Nar."

"Right. Now, it's my belief Melvyn spread the word about Nar, and where to allegedly find it. But, you and I both know that the information is incorrect, so the only thing Melvyn is doing is …?"

"… pitting the clans against each other," Sarah finished. "Steve, we have to stop this!"

"Don't I know it. Umm, any ideas how?"

"What about scaring them away?" Emerion suggested.

"How?" Sarah wanted to know. "By attacking them? The only thing that'd do would be to sour relations between the griffins and the dwarves, not to mention how it'd make us humans look."

"Pull one of them aside and confide with them what will happen if events don't change?" Steve suggested.

"The only one we have a history with is Maelnar," Sarah said, "and that history won't happen until well over a hundred years have passed. No, I think that would only freak him out."

"Could you teleport this dwarf out of harm's way?" Emerion asked.

Sarah considered the question. "Well, I guess I could, but it still doesn't stop the rest of the clans from butting heads over this blasted Nar nonsense. No, we need to be certain that, whatever we do, we keep all the clans on speaking terms with each other."

"Can we pinpoint where they're going?" Steve suddenly asked. "Emerion, you have the best eyes. Where are they headed?"

Husband and wife watched as their griffin charge swiveled his head and then tilted it a few times, studying the ground far below. After a few moments, he let out a victorious squawk and pointed a wing.

"They appear to be headed there, to the left of that pillar of rocks."

"The one that looks like a totem pole?" Steve asked.

"Emerion, do you know what a totem pole looks like?" Sarah inquired.

"Squat, colorful carvings stacked on top of one another?" the griffin asked.

Steve nodded. "Right. I see something that looks like a rock totem pole, but I don't see what's so special about it?"

"You're looking in the wrong place," Emerion said. "It's northeast from that. Look for ... look for the sleeping hound."

"A sleeping dog?" Steve repeated, puzzled.

"I see it!" Sarah exclaimed. "I also see the totem pole. Dear, look left, and then north. They're about three hundred feet apart from one another."

"Okay, I've got it. I see a cave! Good eyes, Em! All right, if that's where they're headed, then I say we destroy that cave. Make it look like coming here was a very bad idea."

"How?" Sarah asked.

"I could probably do it with a few chasers, but more than likely, our dwarf pals won't be driven away. They'll still want to check out the area. We need to guarantee those four clans will want nothing to do with this area."

May I make a suggestion?

Pryllan? Go ahead.

I have been eavesdropping.

There's a shocker.

There are two of my brethren nearby. I have looked through your eyes and I am familiar with the area. The Dragon Lord is suggesting we stage a mock fight, and in the aftermath of the struggle, the cave is destroyed.

Steve relayed the suggestion.

"Ooo, that would work," Sarah exclaimed. "Finally, we get a bit of good news. Well, should we do it?"

"Em?" Steve called. "How soon before they all arrive?"

"Less than an hour," the griffin reported.

Pryllan? How soon can you make that happen? It has to be done in less than an hour.

It can be done in less than ten minutes.

Perfect. Please do it.

Steve? Rinbok Intherer wants to know if the human fugitive has been located.

Not by us, I'm sorry to say. We're going to keep looking.

Understood. My Lord has responded with the same response. They'll keep looking, too.

Good. Thanks, Pryllan.

"Okay, we need to find someplace to set down. I think it's about to become dangerous around here."

"There's an elevated ridge to the south," Emerion reported. "It will afford us an excellent view of the cave."

"Can we be seen?" Sarah asked.

"Highly unlikely."

"That's perfect, Emerion. Steve, we're headed over. But, I think you should attempt your landing first. That way, we'll be out of harm's way ourselves."

"Yeah, great, thanks. All right, here we go."

Steve followed the griffin and his rider over to the ridge and paled. The area Emerion had found was no bigger than their patio back home. He was expected to land there?

"You can do it," Sarah said. "Think of it like flipping off a switch. You're channeling your power through your feet, of all places. See if you can lower yourself to where you're only a few feet above the ground. Then, shut it off, like a light switch."

"Like a light switch," Steve muttered. "Sure. No problem."

Remembering all the videos of the SpaceX rocket he'd seen on the internet, where the booster flipped itself around to land neatly on the ground, Steve nodded. He should be able to do that, with a suitable amount of counterthrust. After all, if an unmanned rocket could do it, so could he!

Doing his best to forget about all the footage he'd seen of rocket crashes, Steve rose another hundred feet or so before cutting off power. Immediately, he plummeted as if a huge anvil had dropped into his arms. Flipping himself around, to fall feet first, he reapplied his jhorun, allowing the upward thrust to slow him down. However, he was simply dropping too fast.

He caught sight of a nearby tree and pointed at it. It was perfect. Hardly any small branches to impale himself on, and it was the only tree in the area. It would have to do.

The tree loomed in front of him. Steve wrapped his arms around the trunk and held on for dear life. He gave the order to cut power, only his jhorun—apparently—had other plans. Both hands suddenly tingled like crazy, and for a brief moment, he feared an explosion. His hands flared up, and he spun around the tree, much like a strip—no, it'd be best to let that one go.

Much like a *what*?

Nothing. I didn't say anything.

Yes, you did. You were about to liken your spinning to something called a stripper. What is a stripper?

Pryllan, I'm not about to explain to you what a stripper is, or what she does for a living. It was a bad analogy.

Very well.

Steve noticed that his jhorun finally extinguished all his flames, and bereft of the thrust, his spinning on the trunk finally came to a stop.

"I'll be paying for that one tomorrow, too."

"You can't get more creative than that," Sarah observed, as she and Emerion landed nearby. "How many splinters do you think you have now?"

"I have no idea. It feels like it's gonna number in the thousands. Pryllan? Where are your dragon friends?"

You should be hearing them right about ...

Twin roars erupted as two reptilian figures materialized out of thin air. A bright red dragon with blindingly white wings twisted about, looking. Once it spotted the second dragon, a magnificent black fellow with splotches of green on its chest, the two circled each other in a perfectly choreographed mock battle that appeared to put wings and limbs in mortal danger.

Stepping up their game, the dragons dropped lower to the ground and shot out blasts of fire. Flames slammed into the ground, into the trees, and the rocky surface of the nearby hills. As jets struck near the cave entrance, the stone wall began to crack. It wouldn't take much more of that to bring the entire hillside down.

Three more, actually.

Tons of stone and earth thundered as the cave collapsed. Ignoring the destruction, the battling dragons hissed and growled, rising higher into the air, eventually disappearing into the clouds.

Steve sighed with relief. "Where are the …?"

Sarah placed a finger on his lips and pointed toward what was left of the cave. Maelnar's Kla Guur had just arrived, obviously not pleased. "They probably think the cave was nothing more than a dragon lair, and count themselves lucky they hadn't gone in."

At that moment, the second clan arrived, followed almost immediately by a third. Finger-pointing ensued, followed by fist-shaking, and a few choice words directed at the sky. By the time the fourth party arrived, it was all over. The dwarves were already headed back in the opposite direction. Maelnar's group, the Kla Guur, paused only long enough to let their neighbors, the Kla Chanus, know they'd been duped. They shrugged off the chance of Nar's discovery and turned back.

"Oh, what a beautiful sight to see," Sarah said, smiling. "Sorry, Melvyn, but they're all headed home. There will be no clan war among the dwarves, thank you very much!"

Chapter Five–Melvyn's Malice

Aren't you the one who always tells me practice makes perfect? When I wanted to quit flying, who encouraged me to get out there and keep trying?"

"Yeah, yeah, that was me. This is different."

"How?" Emerion challenged.

"Easy. You're born with wings. As you can see, I am *not*. You're comfortable flying around with hundreds of feet of empty space between you and the ground. I, for one, would probably pee myself if I ever lost control up there. When I want to land, I either need to look for a body of water, or a place I won't set on fire. I don't want to hurt anyone."

Their griffin companion sobered. "I'm sorry. I hadn't thought of it that way. I guess my mistake was to take flying for granted."

Steve put a companionable arm on Emerion's fur-covered shoulders. "Hey, don't worry about it. We stick together, no matter what happens. And, for the record, you're right. I really should keep practicing. You never know when we're going to need to beat a hasty retreat."

Puzzled, Emerion looked at Sarah. "A hasty retreat? Wouldn't Sarah just teleport us to safety?"

"Well, yeah, she would. Okay, bad example. What if I really needed to get myself to safety, but Sarah wasn't there to help? What if she was helping you or some other person? I know she wouldn't want me to put myself in harm's way just because I don't like flying."

"She really wouldn't," Sarah agreed, smiling. "The point he's trying to make, Em, is that … well, sometimes we're all forced to do things we don't like. Otherwise, bad things could happen. I mean, look at us, right now. Here we are, walking through the forest in Lentari, only it's the Lentari of the past. We've been wondering how to best get you over here, and now you've been thrust in this adventure with us whether you wanted it or not."

"I wanted it," Emerion confirmed. "My place is next to you. Both of you."

"What do you think Melvyn is going to do once he realizes we've canceled his dwarf war?" Sarah asked.

"He's gonna be pissed," Steve answered.

Emerion trilled with laughter.

"Language!" Sarah scolded. "I mean, what do you think he'll *do*?"

"I really don't know," Steve confided. "There are too many unknowns."

"Like what?" Emerion asked.

They ducked under the branches of a low-hanging pine tree and skirted a boulder the size of Steve's truck.

"How was Melvyn able to manipulate four dwarf clans into coming Topside when they're much more comfortable below the ground? I mean, yes, I know everyone wants to find Nar, but how did he convince the various clans he had legitimate knowledge of the city's location?"

Sarah shrugged. "That's a good question."

"He's using some type of jhorun," Steve concluded. "He *has* to be. Whether it's a spell, or some other type of enchantment, he …"

"What about his own jhorun?" Emerion interrupted.

"He wielded the power to forget," Steve recalled. "But, it only worked for short-term memory."

"For something that just happened?" the griffin asked.

Sarah nodded. "That's right. In your case, let's say you went hunting and caught yourself something that you were planning on making your dinner. Melvyn happens by and makes you forget you caught anything."

"That's ... dastardly," Emerion decided.

"I'm not saying he actually did that," Sarah said, "but it would be something he could do. But, that's the only power he had, and even then, the king, er ...?"

"Kri'Calin," Steve supplied.

"Right. The last thing Kri'Calin told us is that their wizard, Zevern the Inept, was going to ..."

Steve burst out laughing, followed almost immediately by Emerion trilling loudly.

"That's great," Sarah complained. "You've got me doing it now. Yes, he's not the most effective wizard out there, but at least he knows his way around magic. Mostly. Fine, let's just call him Zevern. He claimed he could do something to make Melvyn forget he had jhorun. I don't know. Something has happened. Something new."

"Well, we know it's not Mikal," Steve said. "He could give jhorun to somebody who didn't have it, but we're a number of years off for that."

"And he doesn't exist in our new timeline," Sarah reminded him.

"Maybe there's someone else who has the same jhorun?" Emerion suggested. "Here, in this time?"

"I guess it's possible," Steve conceded.

"Do you feel that?" Sarah asked, several minutes later.

She came to a stop and peered around the forest. Trees were visible in all directions: evergreen, pine, a few spruce, and an ash or two.

"What are we listening for?" Steve asked.

"Not listening, but *feeling*. I swear I just felt the ground tremble."

"I felt it," Emerion reported.

"You did not," Steve mock-accused.

"Did so! Look, there it is again!"

"All right, I felt it that time. Is it an earthquake?"

Sarah shook her head. "Not coming in short, repetitive bursts like that. It's almost as if something large is moving around nearby."

"I doubt it's a dragon," Steve said.

And you'd be partially correct. But, I would advise you three to vacate the area.

Say what? Why?

They are far outside their usual territory. This can only be a bad thing.

Steve relayed the urgent message. "Emerion? Can you take off in here?"

Emerion gazed up at the thick canopy thirty feet above their heads. "Not safely."

Sarah eyed the trail. "Let's do as Pryllan suggests and head elsewhere. Just in case."

They took off at a sprint, but whatever was making the ground shake seemed to be drawing closer. Steve slid to a stop, clutching a painful stitch in his side. When he turned to look at the forest behind them, both hands ignited.

"Oh, no you don't," Sarah said, matter-of-factly. "I'm getting us all out of here, right now."

"No. Don't you want to know what's following us and *why?*"

"I'm more focused on what it could do to us and I'm not about to hang around and find out. Neither are you, so take my hand and we'll …"

"I know you can get us out of this," Steve told her. "If it turns out to be something super bad, then we'll know. However, don't you think it's too coincidental?"

Sarah blinked a few times. "Huh? The fact that there's a large invisible *something* headed our way?"

"It's coincidental, because we just nullified the threat to our dwarf friends."

"Retaliation," Emerion breathed. "You feel this is in retaliation to what we just did?"

Steve nodded. "I do. Or this is a backup option in case

the main plan fails. Sarah? Let's give it just a few moments, but I would ask you to have a safe zone or two ready, in case things go horribly wrong."

"I must be crazy to go along with this," Sarah muttered. "Stay close to me."

The trembling in the earth increased until the three of them were hard pressed to stay standing. The surface of the ground swelled into a dome, until the ground actually peeled back, revealing a spiderweb of tree roots.

Two huge claws hooked themselves into the tangle of roots and forcefully yanked them apart. The roots snapped, noisy as firecrackers. Grunting, the creature pushed its way through the opening, extricated itself from the ground, and turned to face them. Standing upright on its two hind legs, the creature's muscular forearms brushed clumps of dirt off its skin.

"A dinosaur!" Emerion breathed.

"It's a creeg," Sarah corrected. "It may look like a dinosaur, but it's actually a land dragon. I've always said you watch too many movies with Steve."

"Well, well, what have we here?" The creeg's voice was deep, booming, and powerful. Two white beady eyes fixated on Steve's. "Trespassers, eh?"

"Trespassers?" Steve scoffed. "Since when do creegs live in the forest? No one is trespassing on anyone here, okay?"

"I really don't understand what's going on," the creeg said. Its voice had become quieter and its eyes were no longer white. "What am I doing here?"

"What *are* you doing here?" Steve countered.

The voice boomed once again and the creeg took a threatening step toward them. "I'm here to remove a thorn in my side once and for all."

What was going on? It was like this creeg had dueling personalities battling for control inside its large reptilian body. Was that normal?

As Steve studied the creeg's face, the huge reptile's eyes reverted back to its regular color.

"I have no quarrel with humans," the creeg insisted, "but I don't seem to be able to control my own actions! Who are you and why are you doing this to me?"

"We're not doing anything to you," Steve argued. "You're the one telling us that … now what? Back to threatening us?" He turned to his wife. "I really don't know what his problem is. It's almost as if …"

Before Sarah could answer, the creeg's eyes closed and it groaned as if a heavy weight had just been placed on its shoulders. The skull was lowered, and in the blink of an eye, they watched the tip of the tail disappear into the earth. The ground twenty feet away swelled upward, and it began moving. Toward them.

Picking up speed, the approaching earthen ridge swerved left and right as it navigated around obstacles. It skirted around trees, stumps, boulders.

"Run!" Steve gave the others a push.

"We won't make it," Sarah panted, from atop Emerion's back. "They dig incredibly fast—through anything!"

There was a muffled roar and the ground swelled, larger than before. The creeg pushed its way back to the surface. Shaking the clumps of dirt from its body, it spied Steve and lunged forward. However, it only made it a few steps before it stopped, angrily shook its head, and then looked around the surrounding area.

"Leave me be!"

Emerion came to an abrupt halt. All three of them twisted around to look at the large, wingless dragon.

"Do as I say, and I just might, partner," the creeg spoke again.

"Partner?" Steve quietly repeated. He looked at Sarah, but she was already nodding. "Didn't that sound like …?"

"Melvyn," Sarah whispered. "How in the world did he take control of a creeg?"

"Get after them," the creeg said. Then, after a few moments, the voice seemingly changed pitch. "But, I have no quarrel with them!"

"This is weird," Emerion decided. "Seeing a creature arguing with itself?"

The creeg shook its head again and, unfortunately, when it turned to look at Steve, everyone could see that the small, beady eyes had turned white once more. "You will meet your doom."

Steve crossed his arms over his chest. "Sounds rather ominous, doesn't it?"

The creeg seemingly sank into the earth and disappeared. Moments later, the raised ridge on the ground began to move toward him, picking up speed.

"Can I get us all out of here yet?" Sarah asked, from her position on Emerion's back. "There may be tons of roots slowing him up, but he's still moving toward you."

Steve was jogging at a healthy clip. "Not yet. Look. He's stopped again."

"… then stay above ground."

The creeg emerged from the earth a third time, gave itself a few shakes, and then stomped forward.

"Are you able to respond to me?" Steve asked, as both hands ignited.

The creeg didn't break stride. "Yes."

"Are you under some sort of spell?" Sarah asked.

"Yes."

"I knew it!" Steve exclaimed. "Can you tell us who cast it?"

"I do not know," the creeg admitted.

"It doesn't matter," Steve said. "We are ninety-nine percent certain it was Melvyn, a degenerate human who has a problem with authority."

Steve altered course and abandoned the game trail. The creeg hesitated about following him deeper into the forest. It turned to Sarah and Emerion.

Steve blasted a jet of fire at the creeg. The flames bounced harmlessly off the walking reptile's chest, but they *did* get its attention.

"You're going to need more than that," the land dragon told him, using the deeper, threatening voice. It took the first tentative step toward him. "Are you going to flee? It's the only thing you're capable of doing."

"What kind of power is Melvyn wielding that would allow him to take over a creeg?" Sarah wondered aloud. "Excuse me? Can you go back to the poor creeg you've taken over?

We'd like to talk to him, please."

The land dragon paused in its advance toward Steve. The white eyes faded and the creeg shook its head in an attempt to think straight.

"I am not liking this," the creeg reported. "Who are you lot? Why am I trying to kill you?"

"We have our suspicions, but I'm hoping you'll confirm," Sarah told the creature. "Can you describe who cast the spell on you?"

"I was napping," the creeg recalled. "Suddenly, I smelled someone in front of me. By the time I opened my eyes to look, this person's mind was in my own. I cannot explain it. As for what he looked like, well, he was like you."

"Human," Steve guessed.

"Brilliant, Sherlock," Sarah snorted.

Emerion trilled with laughter.

"Smaller, more irritable, and …? I'm sorry, I don't know how to describe humans. You all look alike to me."

Steve tapped his hair. "Was it white up here? Older, meaning, more wrinkles? Did he have hair growing above his mouth? Right here?" Steve traced a finger along his face, outlining where a moustache would be.

"Yes. What does this tell you?"

"It tells us that our suspicions are confirmed," Sarah sighed. "Melvyn knows we've returned."

Steve's hands formed a time-out. "Wait a minute. How in the world is Melvyn taking over something as large as a creeg? He didn't have that jhorun before. How does he have it now?"

Sarah held up her hands. "I don't *know*."

The creeg shook his head again. "He heard you. He's angry. He's trying to regain control. I don't know how much longer I can fight him."

"Don't worry," Sarah assured the dragon. "If we leave, then he'll probably leave you alone, too. Is everyone ready? I'm getting us out of here."

"Wait a minute," Steve interjected. "What about him? What if our departure doesn't persuade Melvyn to leave him alone? That would mean he'd be at Melvyn's beck and call until he's released. We can't leave the poor fellow like that."

"Can you really extricate him from my mind?" the creeg hopefully asked. "I cannot live like this."

"We'll start working on this," Sarah promised. "In the meantime, try to stay in this area, okay?"

"If you can rid me of this enchantment, I will forever be in your debt. I will try to remain here, but I make no guarantees. My body seemingly answers to someone else at the moment."

Steve hurried to Sarah's side, just as the creeg started shaking his head again. Melvyn, trying to reestablish control. Steve leaned against Emerion and took Sarah's hand in his.

"We're all here. Fire away."

"I don't think we're too far from the valley," Sarah said. "I'll put us back at the edge of the forest."

The familiar wrenching returned, but only for a brief moment. They were now standing in the exact spot as earlier today, facing the valley and the distant lake. Sarah sighed and sank down to the ground.

"I don't understand how Melvyn has all this power."

Steve joined her, followed immediately by Emerion. "However the creeg was chosen for Melvyn's machinations, he needs to be *unchosen*."

Sarah smiled and clapped her hands. "Machinations? Ooo, good word, hon."

"Every so often," Steve said, smiling at her. "Now that we're here, what's the plan? How do we, er, *evict* Melvyn from that creeg? There's gotta be a way."

Sarah sighed wistfully. "We need Gareth."

"I couldn't agree more. However, we both know that's not going to happen."

"All right, let's think about this. A creeg is a land dragon. What would shock a land dragon?"

"A land dragon is just another way to say earth dragon, right?"

Sarah shrugged. "I guess so. Where are you going with this?"

"Earth," Steve said, scuffing a toe on the ground. "Earth is an element, as is fire. We know fire's opposite is water, so what would that make earth's?"

Sarah shared a look with Emerion. "Uh, I don't know. Water? After all, wouldn't water dissolve earth?"

"Not really," Steve decided. "It'll turn earth to mud, but it doesn't dissolve it."

"Okay, fine. Water can erode earth, right? Let's think about this, using your logic. What would we get if we match up air and earth?"

Steve was silent as he considered.

"Nothing," Emerion decided, once it became apparent Steve didn't have an answer.

Sarah nodded. "Exactly. Now, what about fire and earth?"

"I would say earth would smother fire, so that wouldn't be the way to go," Steve said.

"Too true," Sarah continued. "Now, what does that leave us? Water. And, as mentioned earlier, water can erode earth. I say we splash some water on him. That ought to wake him up, don't you think?"

"It's as good of a plan as any. You're the teleporter. Can you wiggle your nose and take care of that?"

"Wiggle my nose? Are you looking to get soaked as well?"

"All right, all right, there's no need to get testy. I think you're right. Water ought to wake the creeg up. So, how easy is it for you to do exactly that?"

Sarah held out a hand. "Let's go find out."

Back at the clearing, Sarah held a finger to her lips and then tapped her ear. Steve nodded. She wanted to listen.

Emerion, having a more acute sense of hearing, cocked his head and immediately pointed a wing east. After a few moments of silence, they heard the creeg moving about. Steve cringed. From the roar it had just let out, it sounded as though the poor fellow was in pain!

Steve looked at his wife. "Are you ready to do this?"

"What are you going to do?"

"Get his attention. That ought to bring him back here, where you'll then soak him with water."

Sarah nodded. "Got it. And … I'm ready."

"Oh, woe is me!" Steve cried, as he stepped from behind the cover of several trees. "I'm so lost and I just don't know what I'm going to do! I should just put myself out of my misery and offer myself to the first creeg I see. Oh, the horrors of it all."

Sarah and Emerion snickered from somewhere behind him.

They all felt the ground tremble more violently. The creeg would be in visual range in less than twenty seconds.

"Heads up," Steve cautioned. "He's on his way back. Hey, there he is, my favorite low-life degenerate. It's been a long time, Melvyn."

"You can call me *sheriff*, partner."

"I'm no partner of yours, pal," Steve returned.

"How are you even here?" the creeg's deepened voice asked. "You're supposed to be dead, or better yet, non-existent."

Steve spread his arms. "And yet, here we are. I'd say better luck next time, but guess what? This is your end of the line."

"We'll see about that, partner," the creeg replied, lurching forward.

"Now!" Steve exclaimed.

A large, shimmering mass of water formed directly above the land dragon's head; it hovered in place for a few seconds before Sarah withdrew her jhorun. The water crashed down, knocking the creeg off its feet, leaving it in a muddy mess on the ground. The huge bipedal reptile rose to its feet with a roar of anger. The eyes, Steve noted, were still white.

"You were a peon before, but are even more so now," Melvyn's voice announced. "I'm going to enjoy tearing you limb from limb!"

"Plan B!" Sarah called.

Steve turned. "Which is?"

Suddenly, they were back at the forest's edge, staring at the wide valley before them.

"So, water didn't work," Steve said, throwing in a healthy pinch of sarcasm. "Now what? Should we just try the others? Fire? Air? Earth?"

Sarah shook her head. "I don't see those having any better chances than water. No, there *must* be something else we can do."

A distant rumble pulled their attention to the distant ring of mountains across the valley. A dark thundercloud was visible, hovering low in the sky. A flash of lightning illuminated the interior of the cloud. In unison, the three travelers turned to stare at each other.

"Electricity!" Sarah exclaimed. "Of course! I'll wager it'll do a much better job of … of … what do you call it? Exorcising? I'll bet a lightning strike will force Melvyn to leave."

The cloud flashed again. Ten seconds later, they heard the crack of thunder. Steve held up his hands. "Wait a minute. Are you suggesting we need to hit the creeg with a lightning bolt? And how, pray tell, are we supposed to do that?"

Sarah shrugged. "I don't know. Teleport it?"

"Uh huh. Have you ever teleported a lightning bolt before?"

"Well, no, but how hard could it be?"

"A lightning bolt?" Emerion repeated. "Those are the terrifying flashes of light that you've told me mean certain death if one ever touches us?"

Sarah fidgeted uncomfortably. "Well, yes."

"And these flashes of light," Emerion continued, "they occur infrequently, and only exist for a fraction of a second?"

"Umm, yes."

"Steve? You're okay with this?"

"Not really, Em," Steve confessed. "But, I do see the logic of her argument. I think she's right: a jolt of electricity should wake him up. However, I'm … *confused*."

"About how I'm planning on teleporting a bolt of lightning?" Sarah finished for him. Steve nodded. "Believe it or not, I have a plan. Em? Stay here. No, don't argue. There is nothing but dragons over there. The last thing we want to do is draw attention to ourselves."

"Fine. Promise me you'll be careful." When Sarah didn't say anything, the griffin extended a wing and tapped her on her shoulder. "Say it. Promise me."

Sarah smiled at the young griffin. "You've been hanging around Steve for so long you've picked up his mannerisms."

"It's not a bad thing," Steve remarked, holding up his

fist. Emerion noticed and bumped it with his front claw. "All right, let's hear your plan."

"You know how I am able to partially freeze something in the air?" Sarah began.

"When you essentially tell your jhorun to move the item from point A to point B just as slowly as possible?" Steve asked.

Sarah nodded. "Exactly. I say we head over to that storm and wait for a lightning bolt to strike. When it does, I freeze it, then teleport us back to wherever the creeg happens to be."

"What if the creeg isn't where you left him?" Emerion asked.

Coming to Sarah's defense, Steve cleared his throat. "Well, we'll have to teleport over there and verify he's still there. Once we know that, then we'll go after the bolt."

Sarah held out her hand. "There's no time like the present. Ready?"

Steve nodded. "Let's bring it, lady."

"You two be careful," Emerion cautioned, pointing a wing first at Steve, then Sarah. "Don't make me have to fly all the way out there to rescue you."

Steve nodded at the griffin. "Not a chance. We'll be back."

The forest returned. There, resting on the ground nearly a hundred feet away, with its back to them, was the strangely quiet land dragon. Sarah held a finger to her lips and immediately held out a hand. Steve nodded, and placed his hand over hers. Moments later, they were on the other side of the valley, with Lake Raehón spread out before them. Rain was steadily falling and the thundercloud they had seen in the distance was now directly over their heads.

"Now what?" Steve inquired. "We wait for a lightning bolt?"

"Do you have a better idea?"

"I don't. How fast can you freeze this thing and then teleport the two of us back to the creeg?"

"Hopefully not long at all," Sarah said. "Lightning bolts are so terrifyingly fast that I'm starting to think that maybe this isn't the best idea in the world."

"Hey, if anyone can do it, it'd be you," Steve assured her.

"Strongest teleporter that's ever been reported, remember?"

"I know. I just don't want to put you in danger. Even if we … Steve, look out!"

A white-hot bolt of pure electricity shot out from beneath the cloud and struck the ground with a billion volts of electricity. Even a quarter of a mile away, up the side of a mountain, Steve swore he could feel a shock wave coming from it. Less than a second later, the resulting peal of thunder was so loud that it dropped him to his knees. Once the ringing in his ears passed, he looked over at his wife, who was in the same position, kneeling on the ground.

"Are you sure we aren't going to kill the creeg by hitting him with this?" Steve asked.

Sarah held up her hands. "Who can say? Tell you what. Let's do this. With the first bolt that I'm able to teleport, I'll let it strike nearby, and not physically touch him. Maybe the resulting blast of power will be able to break Melvyn's hold?"

"It's a plan. Let's get this over with."

"Agreed. All right, here we go."

They ended up waiting nearly three minutes for the next blast to strike. When it did, it was so sudden that it was over before either of them could blink. Steve immediately plugged his ears with his fingers, as did Sarah. Once the rumbling after-effects had passed, Steve looked at the distant strike zone and shook his head.

"I had no idea those things were so damn fast. It's like … blink and you'll miss it."

"I *have* missed it," Sarah said, frowning. "Twice. All right, third time's the charm. Here we go. Stay close, 'kay?"

"Always," Steve reported, as he stared up at the belly of the cloud.

This time, it took nearly five minutes of waiting before they saw a few flashes of light. Sarah tensed and ordered her jhorun to stay on high alert. But, before she could complete the thought, a bright bolt of light was snaking down to the ground, only it was further away than the previous two.

Sarah didn't care. This was a lightning bolt, and it would do quite nicely, thank you very much. She ordered the electrical bolt to slow as much as she was able.

The downward strike of the bolt slowed considerably, but since most lightning strikes travel at a speed in excess of two hundred fifty thousand miles per hour, they could still easily watch its progress down.

"Omigod, it's moving so fast!" Sarah exclaimed. She thrust out her hand. "Take my hand! Hurry!"

Steve leapt forward and took his wife's hand, just in time to be placed in the middle of the same forest. There, sitting in the midst of the trees, was the creeg. Steve blinked with surprise. The trees! How was a lightning bolt supposed to strike the ground when so many trees were in the way?

Sarah looked up at the sky and saw, to her horror, the bolt streaking straight down. They had less than two seconds before it struck. Hoping beyond hope that the poor creeg was out of harm's way, she flung herself at her husband and, together, they toppled to the ground.

The lightning bolt struck the forest canopy and ripped through it, with no more resistance than a sheet of paper. The white bolt struck the ground less than fifty feet from the creeg. It flew head-over-tail backwards. The booming thunder bounced around the enclosed clearing and rendered Sarah temporarily deaf. Steve screamed and all went black.

He came to as Sarah gently pulled him to a sitting position. He had a loud ringing in his ears, and a pounding headache, but aside from that, seemed to be okay.

"I know where I don't want to be," he remarked, as he climbed to his feet. "You don't screw around with Mother Nature, no doubt about it." He felt a heavy weight on his back, threatening to tip him over, and reached an arm behind to investigate.

"You have a huge shield on your back," Sarah said, as she knocked a knuckle on the surface. "I think the nohrstaf was trying to protect you."

That explained the weight.

"Uhh, I'm okay," Steve announced. "Danger's over." The shield vanished. "Are you hurt?"

"I can't hear you," Sarah yelled.

Instantly concerned, Steve approached, but not before he felt a nudge on his shoulder. Turning, he saw Emerion, looking relieved both of them were alive.

"That was so powerful, it ruffled my feathers," Emerion admitted.

"It knocked me out," Steve told the griffin. "When did you get here?"

"When neither of you returned, and I heard the thunder come from this area, I knew something had happened. I made my way over here myself. You two should be more careful."

Steve shook his head and winced at the pain. "I think it temporarily deafened Sarah."

She read Steve's lips and responded. "I think it's only temporary."

They heard a loud groaning nearby. Steve ignited his hands and hurried over to the creeg, which was only now regaining its feet.

"How are you doing there, pal? Tell me it's you, and only you."

"He's gone," the creeg said, as it rose to its full height. "I have to say, that was most unpleasant. I thank you for removing that parasite. Humans. I never would have imagined I'd ever make the acquaintance. I am Chuber."

Steve nodded. "Hello, Chuber. I'm Steve, this is my wife, Sarah, and the griffin is Emerion.

"Ah. I …"

"What is it?" Sarah asked, as Chuber trailed off. A look of surprise appeared on its large reptilian face. "Are you okay? He's not trying to regain control, is he?"

"No," Chuber reported. "But, I can feel his anger. Whatever you did to eradicate him has infuriated him to no end." The creeg fell silent as it observed the scorched ground at its feet. "Lightning struck the ground here, alarmingly close to my feet. *Oh*. This is what drove away that maniacal biped, is it not? Er, no offense, human."

Steve waved him off. "Trust me, none is taken. The only thing we wanted to be certain of was that he's gone and will leave you alone."

Chuber nodded his head. "Most thoughtful. Very well, I take my leave of you. Thank you. All of you."

The creeg sank into the ground, as though the large

dragon had just wandered into a patch of quicksand.

Husband and wife gave each other a high-five.

"That's twice!" Steve happily exclaimed.

Sarah nodded. "True, but the problem is, Melvyn is more powerful than we thought. Where did he get this extra power?"

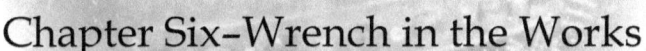

Chapter Six–Wrench in the Works

"That's two down," Steve said, rather smugly. "Two times Melvyn has attempted to mess with our future, and twice now he's been rebuffed."

"The problem is," Sarah said, shaking her head, "we don't know how many more problems he might have created. I just don't have any idea how we're going to know if we've found them all."

Steve held out his hands in a helpless manner. "That would make two of us. Emerion? What's the matter?"

Their griffin companion had become so agitated that he had started to pace.

"I don't like this," Emerion began. "This human. This Melvyn person. If I find him, I'm going to rip him to shreds."

"Join the club, pal," Steve said, adopting a jovial tone. "You won't hear any qualms from me."

"Time after time, this human has attempted to inflict bodily harm on you two," Emerion continued. "Thankfully, you both were able to remove yourselves from harm's way. However, this human has indicated he will not stop. When will it end?"

"When we feed him to the dragons," Steve replied, dropping his voice to the barest of whispers.

Sarah elbowed Steve in the gut. "Oh, no you won't. We're better than that."

"What if a dragon tosses him down the hatch on their own free will?" Steve suggested.

"That's not any better."

"It's better in the sense that we'd have nothing to do with it."

"There has to be another way," Sarah insisted.

"And I'm all for looking for that way," Steve told her. "However, you need to consider the option that we may not have any choice."

"You're okay with … with …?"

"Doing what needs to be done?" Steve nodded. "Absolutely. When it comes to your safety, and Em's, and for that matter, the rest of Lentari? Yes, I will do what has to be done and I *won't* lose any sleep over it."

"Can't we just leave him someplace where he won't get into trouble?" Sarah asked.

"And, what, allow him to plot out yet another revenge?" Steve argued. "I think we need to accept the fact that as long as Melvyn is alive, he's a threat to our very existence. I, for one, will not allow either of you to be placed in harm's way. So, if that means I need to make an uncomfortable decision, then so be it."

Sarah patted his hand. "I know you won't. And I also know you don't want to cross that bridge unless you absolutely have to. You're right, of course. I just don't want to think about it."

Steve gave her a hug. "And you won't. I'll deal with this, not you."

Nodding appreciatively, Sarah held out her hand. "All of you who are going back to R'Tal, give me your hand and wing. We need to give the king an update."

The forest winked out and they were back in front of the West Gate, only the gate was closed.

"No more visitors!" a guard shouted at them, from behind the portcullis.

Sarah extended her hand again. "All right, one more time. This time around, we're headed for the castle."

"Inside, right?" Steve asked. "If this gate is closed, then more than likely, the drawbridge will be the same."

"Got it. Inside the castle. Here we go!"

The gate disappeared. What appeared in its place was a darkened hallway, stretching off in both directions. Servants were seen hurrying along, carrying bundles of linen, trays of food, and a slew of other things. Guards clunked noisily by as they patrolled the corridors. Sarah pointed left.

"The Great Hall is that way. Come on."

They had only taken a few steps when one of the four guards they were following came to an abrupt stop. Slowly pivoting on his heel, he turned to look down the hall, directly at them. The armed soldier pulled his sword and rushed straight at them.

"Is he gonna welcome us or run us through?" Steve quietly asked.

Emerion deliberately stepped in front of them. Squawking a challenge, the griffin adopted an offensive stance and waited for the human soldier to arrive. Before he could lunge forward, however, he was physically yanked backward by an invisible force.

"No, you don't," Sarah scolded. "We can handle this."

The attacking guard arrived a few moments later. With a cry of rage, the soldier leapt through the air, intent on delivering a crippling blow. Thankfully, Sarah was ready for him.

A split second before he arrived, the soldier mysteriously slowed to a snail's pace—in mid-air—and stayed there. No amount of yelling, or thrusting with his sword made any difference. Steve looked at the wild-eyed young guard, who couldn't have been older than twenty, and the weapon he was brandishing. When it became apparent Sarah was holding the guard's arms still, Steve gently pulled the sword free from his grip.

"Let me down! I will kill you all!"

"Not much incentive to let you down, is it?" Sarah countered.

Steve studied the young soldier and grunted. "Do you think he always looks like this, or could it be that Melvyn somehow got his hooks into this guy, too?"

Sarah's eyes widened. "I hadn't thought of that. Do you really think so? What do we do?"

"We need a way to drive Melvyn out," Steve said. "We have to do to him what we did with Chuber. However, I don't think we'll be able to find a bolt of lightning in here."

"We need to give him a jolt of something," Sarah decided. "I just don't know how to do it. Ordinarily, I'd say one of us could go home and purchase a taser. However, that won't become an option for many years to come."

Something fell to the ground with a loud *thump*.

"What was that?" Sarah wanted to know.

Steve turned to look. "Beats me. I ... wait. What the hell? It looks like a TV remote. Hold on, it has the same coloring as ... is that the nohrstaf?"

There, laying on the cobbled stones inside the hallway, was something that looked like ... well, it looked like a white futuristic weapon from a very popular television show. What was going on? Since when could the magical gizmo adopt a shape never seen before in Lentari?

Steve gingerly picked the device up and studied it. Just like the nohrstaf's default form, it still retained the smudges and tarnished finish, making it resemble nothing more than a piece of junk. Holding the nohrstaf as he would if it was a remote control, his fingers felt a raised button on the left side, right about where his thumb was resting. A trigger?

A notion dawned. Hadn't they just been talking about finding a way to deal with a potentially-possessed guard? Looking down at the strange device, Steve started to smile. It couldn't be. Could something Shardwyn have made really work as well as he thought? Walking over to the thrashing soldier, still suspended in mid-air, Steve held the device up to the young man's arm and pressed the button. They all heard a loud buzz, and just like that, the soldier was twitching uncontrollably

Taking several steps back, Steve waited for the soldier to regain control over his faculties.

"P-please tell me he's gone! I c-couldn't do anything but watch from afar. I don't ever want to ...? What's this? Why can't I move?"

Steve held up a hand. "I guess that answers that question. Wait a moment. Before we let you go, can you confirm that the guy who took control of you is no longer there?"

"How'd you know about that?" the soldier whispered, in awe.

"We've dealt with him before," Sarah told the young soldier. "Is he gone?"

A smile appeared on the soldier's face. "Yes, it would seem so! Thank you! Thank you very much! Er, would you please let me down?"

Sarah lowered the guard to the ground and released him.

"Thank you. Who ...? Wizards be damned! A griffin! What is a griffin doing in here?"

"This is Emerion," Sarah interjected. "He's harmless. He's with us, and is very protective. Remember that."

"Yes, ma'am."

The guard hurried off.

"I'm not liking this at all," Steve decided. "I think that was another aspect of Melvyn's contingency plan. He's clearly smarter than we've given him credit. First a creeg, and now a soldier? Inside the castle? Where does it stop?"

Sarah shook her head and pointed left. She wanted to keep going. Once they emerged into the large chamber, they could see that the gilded thrones were occupied, and that the king and queen were in the middle of some type of conference with a large group of villagers. Nearby, Captain Sauer could be seen, giving orders to a number of his men.

"Concentrate your efforts on all exits," the captain was saying. "Double the guards everywhere. If someone tries to ...? What are you doing? Get back here at once!"

The guard Sauer had been talking to suddenly locked eyes with Sarah, let out a cry, and bolted toward her.

"Here we go again," Steve muttered. He gripped the nohrstaf, still in taser form, and readied himself. "My dear, if you'll do the honors?"

The soldier rose into the air just as he leapt for Steve, with his sword drawn. Acting as though he was supremely bored, Steve ducked under the exposed blade, held the nohrstaf against the soldier's right leg and then pressed the button. The shock threw the poor soldier backward by nearly ten feet. Sauer arrived first and irritably pulled the man to his feet. The poor fellow teetered on wobbly legs and went down again.

"Just what do you think you were doing, soldier?"

The young guard blinked his eyes a few times as he stared into his commanding officer's angry face.

"Captain, I … I'm sorry, I really don't know what to say. It's like … it's like I couldn't control myself!"

"What are you talking about?" Sauer snapped. "Unable to control yourself? What nonsense is this?"

"It's Melvyn's nonsense," Steve announced, as he hooked an arm under the soldier's and, nodding at Sauer, the two of them helped the man to his feet a second time. "We now know Melvyn is aware of our presence. He's sent one land dragon and two of your soldiers after us."

Sauer's eyes widened. "It cannot be."

"It is, I'm afraid," Sarah confirmed. "He knows we're here, and he has some type of contingency plan in place. Your guards see us, and if they've been compromised by Melvyn, they attack. The only way we've discovered to snap them out of it is to zap them with a bit of electricity."

Steve held up the nohrstaf and waggled it. "That's what this is for. I never would've imagined it would be so useful here."

"Electricity," Sauer repeated. "I'm not familiar with the word."

"Oh, umm …?" Steve turned to Sarah, who shrugged, indicating she didn't know how to adequately define the term, either.

"All right. Have you ever taken your shoes off and, wearing only, er, stockings on your feet, walked around on various rugs?"

Sauer nodded, "On a few occasions. What does this have

to do with anything?"

"Have you ever touched a piece of metal afterwards and felt a shock? Like a dagger, or a sword, or even a fork?"

Sauer's eyes widened. "I have. You're talking about spectral energy."

"Spectral?" Sarah repeated.

"Aye. We cannot see what conjures it, only its effects. Therefore, specters must have created it."

"Not even close," Steve said, but waved a dismissive hand. "It's not important right now. There must be more of Melvyn's lackeys in here. We have to find a way to ferret them out."

Sauer turned to find both the king and queen staring at him. Kri'Calin waved him over.

"What was the meaning of that?" the king asked. "Did one of your men actually attack the Nohrin?"

"Yes," Captain Sauer admitted. "We believe the fugitive known as Melvyn has enchanted a number of our men and the hapless fool was just doing his bidding. As for why the guard chose that exact moment to attack, we can only theorize it was because of the presence of the Nohrin."

"They weren't attacked the last time they were here, were they?" the queen's smooth voice asked, speaking for the first time since they arrived. "What has changed?"

"We've foiled several of his plans," Steve answered. "In essence, we've confirmed what has to be his worst fears: we've returned here, from, er, our home, and have started to unravel all the damage he's done."

"How many more of your men have been affected?" the king asked Sauer, using a low tone.

"I have no idea," the captain answered, his face hardening. "I do believe we need to find out as soon as possible."

"Agreed, Captain. I will task Zevern with resolving this dilemma."

"A wise decision, Your Majesty."

Kri'Calin looked at the three of them. "You are all well? None of you have been injured?"

"Well, it's not for a lack of trying," Steve said, chuckling. "You haven't lived until you've had a creeg on your tail."

"A creeg on your ... how in the world did your fugitive manage to possess a creature the size of a creeg?"

Steve, Sarah, and Emerion all shrugged.

"Who knows," Steve sighed. "But, it's all good. We gave the poor fellow a jolt, and that seemed to wake him up."

"Creegs are enormous!" the king proclaimed. "How were you able to escape?"

Steve hooked a thumb at Sarah. "Oh, it was easy. Sarah teleported a bolt of lightning, and dropped it pretty close to the creeg. Thankfully, it shocked him senseless. When he woke, he was back to normal. And Melvyn, it would seem, was officially kicked out, which didn't make him happy."

"Hey! You lot! Stay right there!"

King, queen, and captain turned to see four soldiers rushing toward them. Swords were unsheathed. Sauer hurried to put himself in the attacking men's way.

"You will stay where you are. Cease! Desist!"

Steve tossed the nohrstaf taser to Sarah and joined Sauer. He ignited his hands and blasted out a wall of flames. Three of the guards immediately slid to a stop. The fourth made it another four steps before being yanked upside down and brought close. Sarah then used the nohrstaf to wake him up.

One at a time, the guards attacked. Each one was distracted by the pyrotechnical show Steve generated, which was more than enough time for Sarah to immobilize them and apply the remedy. Once the four men were unconscious, lying flat on their backs in the middle of the Great Room, the king sent word for the castle's wizard to join them.

"How the blazes did so many of our men fall victim to that ... that ... vagabond?"

"He's had to have access to them at one point in time," Sarah said. "When he was prisoner here, did he have many visitors?"

Sauer shook his head. "No. And besides, Melvyn's jhorun was the ability to tamper with short term memory. How is he able to persuade these people to do his bidding?"

"I don't know," Steve admitted, "but I'd sure like to find out."

Sarah snapped her fingers. "I think I have an answer to the

question of how many men Melvyn might have influenced, and how to possibly find them."

Kri'Calin perked up, as did Captain Sauer.

"Indeed?" the king exclaimed, pleased. "Very well, let's hear it."

Sarah turned to Sauer. "How meticulous are your records?"

The captain folded his arms over his chest. "Elaborate."

"Your guards? Do you keep track of which soldier was assigned to which position, or task?"

"Of course. Why?"

"I'd check your records and find out which guards were stationed in the dungeons at any point in time when Melvyn was there," Sarah urged. "That way, you can find out who Melvyn might have had access to, and see for yourself whether or not they're compromised."

"And how would we know?" the king wanted to know.

"It's easy," Steve explained. "Line 'em up, and then you can parade them in front of us. If one of them is still working for Melvyn, then …?"

"They'll attack," Sauer finished. "Very well. I will start working on this."

"At least that will be one more problem solved," Sarah decided. "This will make the third we've dealt with. I do hope there won't be any more."

"Three *what*?" Kri'Calin asked, as they watched Captain Sauer hurry away.

"Three facets of Melvyn's master plan," Steve answered. "The first involved stopping a skirmish among the dwarves.

"What about the second?" Kri'Calin wanted to know.

"Survival," Steve said. "Remember the creeg we were telling you about? That was Melvyn's retaliation for solving the first problem."

The king was nodding. "Amazing. And the third?"

Steve pointed at a group of nearby soldiers. "You've just experienced the third. We've figured out that a threat exists inside this castle. Somehow, Melvyn has managed to influence your men. We don't know how many have been infected, but we should soon."

"What else do you think he's done?" Kri'Calin asked.

Steve shrugged. "Anything and everything which would help benefit him in the future. Logic suggests his prime target would be Luther, in our world, but thankfully, he's safely out of reach."

"He is, isn't he?" Sarah asked, growing concerned. "You cannot reach him here, can you?"

"There is no key here which can activate his portal," the king confirmed. "If memory serves, you, Steve, were the one who stressed the importance of that point."

"The interdimensional portal!" Sarah exclaimed, as she reached out and gripped Steve's hand. "He could always use that!"

"It's unstable," Steve recalled. "There's no guarantee whoever uses it would come through, unscathed, on the other side. For all we know, it'd take you back another hundred years, or even longer."

"Couldn't he use it if there were no other options?" Emerion asked. "If he was fleeing his pursuers, and he was desperate to escape, couldn't he use it?"

"He could," Steve groaned.

Kri'Calin scowled. "Not if I have any say in the matter. Leave it to me. I will make sure that portal is sealed off."

Steve held up his hands. "Wait. If you do that, then you run the risk of messing with the future, too. That portal has to be open in my time in order for my future to play out as it should."

The king sighed. "What would you have me do?"

Sarah thought for a moment. "Seal it, in this time."

"Now wait," Steve began.

Sarah laid a finger on his lips. "Just a moment. Hear me out, okay? Your Majesty, seal the portal in this time. Make absolutely certain there's no way anyone could access it. I'd say post guards, whatever, but we know Melvyn is wielding some kind of super mind-control power, so I won't."

"But, you just said you didn't want to mess up your own timeline," the king protested.

Sarah nodded. "That's right. It won't. Once we deal with Melvyn, and, using Steve's words, neutralize the threat, then we'll reopen the portal, which will allow our timeline to run its natural course."

Kri'Calin nodded thoughtfully. "I understand. *Temporarily* seal the portal. Once your fugitive is dealt with, we then restore it."

"Exactly."

"Consider it done."

Kri'Calin turned on his heel and headed toward the hall Steve and Sarah knew would eventually lead to the Antechamber. Entering the enchanted room, the king sat at his desk, composed a list of instructions, and handed it to a young page. Ordering the boy to place the message into the hands of one of his generals, the king returned his attention to his guests.

"What else do I need to worry about? Please, have a seat. You all look exhausted. Emerion, is it? Feel free to lie wherever you like."

Emerion flopped down, directly in front of the burning hearth.

"You can't tell me you're cold, pal," Steve told the griffin. "It's warm out there."

"To you, yes," Emerion replied, as he folded his wings tightly against his back. He inched closer to the hearth and stretched. "For us normal folk? This feels very nice."

Sarah beamed her approval and patted Emerion on the head. "And that's why we love you so much."

"Brown noser," Steve snorted, which made Emerion trill with laughter.

Once everyone was comfortable, and had taken some refreshment from the provisions the king had delivered, Steve sat back in his chair and let out a heavy sigh.

"I gotta tell you, Your Majesty," he began, "if you had told me last week that I'd be back here, in the past, I would have labeled you a lunatic."

"The feeling is mutual," the king assured him, with a smile. "I would like to offer you my apologies."

Sarah sat up straight in her chair. "For what, Your Majesty?"

"For not taking Melvyn's escape seriously. I should have

devoted all the resources at my disposal into his immediate apprehension. I didn't, and this is the result. How badly did that affect your timeline?"

Steve spread his hands. "We're here, so that ought to let you know."

"A valid point."

"We underestimated him," Sarah said.

Steve nodded. "I think we all did. He's clearly had time to think things through. I mean, he even anticipated our return! Makes you wonder what else he's thought of, doesn't it?"

"Where did he get this power?" Kri'Calin demanded. "The jhorun he now wields is vastly superior to what he formerly possessed. How has he achieved this?"

"I wish I knew," Steve admitted. "We've all been asking that same question for a while now."

"I think that should be next on our *to do* list," Sarah said. "Find out what type of power Melvyn now has, and who gave it to him. We need to make certain that, once this is all said and done, he doesn't do it again."

"I'm hoping he'll somehow let it slip," Steve said. "Whether intentionally or unintentionally, I hope the old fool drops a few clues. I'm not saying it'll be that much of a help, but at least it might give us a direction to go."

"First things first," Kri'Calin said, rising to his feet. "I want to know just how many of my people are loyal to *him*."

Steve held up a hand. "Minor correction. You're not looking for disloyal people. You're looking for those who have been compromised, or influenced, or …"

"Possessed," Emerion suggested.

Steve cringed. "Well, that's one way to put it. No, these people aren't traitors. They're those who have no control over what they're doing. I hope you remember that, Your Majesty."

Kri'Calin laid a fatherly hand on Steve's shoulder, even though they were probably the same age. "You're a good man, Steve. Yes, I won't forget."

An hour and a half later, Captain Sauer was ready. After reviewing the logs of soldiers, and the location of their posts, three dozen soldiers had been rounded up and were waiting to be paraded by the Antechamber, where Steve, Sarah,

Emerion, and the king were waiting. Steve lent the nohrstaf-taser to Sauer and demonstrated how to use it. Nodding his thanks, the captain instructed one of his lieutenants to begin the inspection.

Eleven other compromised men were revealed as each came into visual contact with the guests from another time. Eleven different times, the soldier in question would leap out of formation and try to draw his weapon. Thankfully, Sauer was there and proved he was worthy of holding his rank of captain. Not one of the possessed men made it into the Antechamber.

"You're sure these are the only men who came into contact with the prisoner?"

"They are the only ones who've worked the dungeons since Melvyn became our prisoner," Captain Sauer replied.

The king nodded, pleased. "Excellent. Send for Zevern. We have much to discuss."

When the castle wizard finally appeared, nearly an hour later, it was without much of the flourish from their first visit. Zevern had previously insisted on heralding his arrival with trumpets, fanfare, and about any other loud source of noise he could procure during their first meeting. This time, when he entered the Antechamber, Zevern had a handful of assistants with him, fawning over every move he made. Just as before, his outfits hadn't changed much, except for the color. Wearing the brightest yellow costume Steve had ever seen, Zevern appeared and strutted his way toward the king. The wizard was still bald, had even less red hair above his ears than he did last time, and had to be at least thirty pounds heavier.

Zevern was wearing a yellow poet shirt with balloon sleeves, banana-yellow trousers, and a dark yellow belt which held all manner of trinkets, gadgets, pouches, and so on. His footwear reminded Steve of Persian genie shoes, complete with the toes curling up at the very end. Finishing his outfit was a blood-red sash, hung from his right shoulder to his left hip.

Zevern finally lowered his nose, aimed his smug smile at the king, and then noticed they weren't alone. His arrogant expression vanished the moment he locked eyes on Steve.

"You."

"Yep. Miss me?"

"I ... I ... er ...?"

Kri'Calin held out an arm in invitation and indicated Zevern should take the seat next to Steve. Swallowing noisily, the wizard headed toward the hearth, intent on complying, when he froze in place. Without saying a word, he started patting down his pockets. He reached inside a hidden pocket on the underside of his sash and retrieved two small vials. He held them up, as though he were going to present them to Steve, when he let out a very uncharacteristic yell and lunged forward. Unfortunately for everyone present, no one had anticipated Zevern as being one of the influenced, and were completely caught off guard.

Zevern began chanting in a low tone and uncorked the vial, throwing it at Emerion. A blinding flash of light rendered them all temporarily blind. Emerion, unfortunately, froze in place, resembling nothing more than a statue.

The king lurched backward, rubbing his eyes. He stumbled into one of the plush armchairs and landed hard. Vigorously rubbing his eyes to restore his vision, Kri'Calin was about to call for guards when he noticed the friendly griffin. Emerion had been in the midst of rising to his feet, but had only made it about halfway up. With his head down low, his rear-end up high, and a look of concern on his face, Emerion was now frozen in place.

"Em?" Sarah called, concerned. "Speak to me! Are you all right? Emerion?"

There was no answer.

Steve rounded on Zevern and ignited his hands. "You have precisely two seconds to restore him before I personally turn you into a charcoal briquette. What'd you do to him?"

Zevern turned to look at him and suddenly, Steve got the chills.

"I gotta admit, partner, you're the last person I wanted to see here."

"And I gotta hand it to you, Melvyn," Steve returned, not missing a beat, "you're a bigger pain in the ass than I thought possible. We should've fed you to the dragons when we had the chance."

"Yes, you should have. Well, partner, you're here, which means you've had a taste of your new future. How'd you like Lentari of the future now? *My* future. Find it to your liking?"

"Gloat while you still can," Steve said. "We'll see who has the last laugh."

"Be gone, fire thrower," Melvyn's raspy voice said, coming out of Zevern's mouth. "Your dragon pet isn't here to save you this time."

"Who says I need Pryllan to save me?" Steve countered. "And besides, who's the one hiding behind harmless citizens?"

"What's the matter, fire thrower?" Zevern/Melvyn taunted. "Can't find me? That's too bad for you, 'cause I'm having a fantastic time."

"Where'd you get the power to control these people?" Steve asked, as he and Zevern began circling each other in the small chamber. Sarah and the king had taken refuge by the desk. "Come on, you smug dillholes are always looking for ways to show off. Tell me, how'd you do it?"

"Wouldn't you like to know?" Zevern sneered. "Long have I waited for this day, fire thrower. Let's see what you do with this, shall we?"

The second vial was uncorked and its contents were flung away from them in a wide arc. A fine mist of tiny water drops materialized. It quickly coalesced into a thick jet of water, which then surged toward Steve.

"Been there, done that," Steve yawned, as he effortlessly shot out a blast of fire to counteract it.

Fire slammed into water, and huge bouts of steam erupted, blanketing everything in a dense cloud of mist.

"Sarah, get Em and the king out of here, now!"

"I couldn't agree more," Sauer's voice said, from somewhere to his left.

"Steam?" Zevern's voice sneered. "Really, fire thrower? Do you think I cannot handle a little mist?"

"What's he doing now?" Sauer asked. "I can't see a blasted thing."

Just then, something began stinging his eyes. The steam,

Steve noted, rapidly disappeared, to be replaced by swirling columns of … sand!

"Have a taste of this, partner," Zevern gloated. "Let's see how well you can see and hear when there's so much … hey!"

The sand abruptly vanished, leaving the Antechamber clear, if not soggy. Sarah was there, standing next to him, and she wore the biggest, haughtiest grin he had ever seen.

"The thing about sand," Sarah began, using her stern lecturing voice, "is that it's something you can see. If I can see it, guess what? I can teleport it, too."

"Blast you to hell and back," Zevern swore. "You're not getting him back. The wizard is *mine*."

Husband and wife watched as the fake wizard reached into a pocket, pulled out a handful of objects, selected one, and threw it on the ground. There was a flash of light, and right before their eyes, a shimmering portal opened. It wasn't big, not by a long shot, nor did it appear to be too stable. However, it gave Zevern the escape route he so desperately needed.

"Until next time, partner," Zevern called, as he waddled as fast as he could toward the portal.

Steve and Sauer bolted for the portal. Sauer dove through first, with Steve hot on his heels.

"Find me!" he shouted to Sarah, as he disappeared through.

About ready to go follow Steve through, Sarah cursed as the shaky portal collapsed on itself and disappeared.

"What happened?" Kri'Calin demanded, as he strode into the room. "Where are they?"

"Zevern activated some type of portal. He made it through, with Steve and Captain Sauer going after him."

"You're the teleporter," the king pointed out. "How are they supposed to find their way back?"

Sarah smiled. "Please. I can find my husband anywhere. I'll get them both back."

* * *

"Where are we?" Sauer whispered.

Steve glanced around the wide, green valley and noticed a large body of water in the distance. He pointed at it.

"Is that north?"

Sauer looked up to note the position of the sun. "Aye. Wait. Is that Lake Raehón?"

"Yes. That means we're in the dragons' valley."

"You'd better believe it, partner!" Zevern's voice cried. "And they don't like intruders! Let's see you get out of this one!"

"What's the matter, Melly?" Steve taunted. "Afraid of dragons?"

"Everyone is afraid of dragons," Zevern raged. "And *don't* call me Melly! I swear to you, I'm gonna enjoy watching those nightmares feed on your carcasses!"

What a horrible image.

Hi, Pryllan. Sorry to intrude, but we didn't have a choice. We followed ...

Is that your fugitive? Do you require assistance? Rinbok Intherer would dispatch every dragon to your aid if we learned it is.

I wish it was. However, it's just a hapless human who has been possessed by Melvyn.

How can we assist?

I don't think you can, unless you can somehow get a lightning bolt to fall nearby, thereby eradicating Melvyn from this fool of a wizard.

Lightning? You need a bolt of lightning?

Since when do dragons generate lightning bolts?

I have relayed your request to the Dragon Lord. He just informed me that Omri has been dispatched, and will be there momentarily.

Omri? I've never heard of him.

She. Omri is Rinbok's mate.

Really? I never knew Rinbok was mated.

Indeed?

Stop making me talk! Just tell me how this Omri dragon is going to help me.

Omri is a rare maelstrom dragon who can summon lightning.

Tell her to look for the human wearing bright yellow. Don't strike him, but target something nearby.

Acknowledged.

"... don't know you, and I don't care to know you," Zevern was saying. "That *kelpah* has foiled me for the last time. I promise you here and now I'm going to enjoy watching him get eaten by a dragon."

Be at ease. No dragon will harm you, by order of Rinbok Intherer.

Thank you, Pryllan.

Steve turned to see Zevern and Sauer hurling insults at one another. Why wouldn't Melvyn simply use part of Zevern's jhorun to take care of Sauer?

The roar of a dragon sounded in the distance. Steve's eyes widened. *That* was Melvyn's plan. He was going to sacrifice Zevern to the dragons! With his next insult, the portly wizard wheezed. Zevern looked utterly exhausted. Yes, he was out of shape, but someone who was used to carrying around that much weight should have more stamina. It was almost as if ...

Steve's eyes widened. He recognized the signs of overextended jhorun. Creating that portal must have drained Zevern's power. No wonder he hadn't cast any spells. He couldn't! Not until his jhorun had a chance to recharge!

"You're looking a little tired there, buddy," Steve observed. He glanced over to Sauer, while speaking to the wizard. "Well, I've got some bad news for you. These dragons, the ones you're waiting for are friends of mine, and they already know not to attack us."

"Impossible," Zevern/Melvyn gasped.

"Believe it, don't believe it, I don't care. But, I should warn you, if you don't surrender now, and return the wizard to us *unharmed*, then you're going to be forcibly expelled just like at the castle."

"I told you, partner," Melvyn's voice snapped. "This wizard is too useful. He's mine, and I won't be releasing him anytime soon."

Another roar sounded, much closer. Steve looked up and saw the sleek form of a dragon flying toward them

Zevern laughed maniacally. "There you go. One dragon ought to do it. You don't look so smug now, fire thrower. Any last words?"

Steve watched as the dragon drew closer. This special dragon had to be the richest, darkest metallic blue color he had ever seen. Omri's scales sparkled in the sunlight. Steve nudged Sauer's shoulder.

"How fast can you run?"

"Excuse me?" Sauer sputtered.

"Trust me." Steve looked up. Omri was directly overhead. "Run, now!"

The two men took off, sprinting for a group of trees fifty feet away. When they were halfway there, they ran out of time.

A brilliant bolt of pure blue lanced straight down. It struck the ground less than twenty feet from Zevern and created a crater thirty feet in diameter. When the smoke cleared, Omri was gone, Zevern was flat on the ground, unconscious, and the two men were unharmed, face-down in the soft grass.

"What just happened?" Sauer wanted to know, rolling to his feet and spitting out a few blades of grass.

"The dragons just assisted us in removing Melvyn from Zevern's body."

"What? How?"

"I'll have to explain it later," Steve admitted. "For now, we both need to let it go."

They hurried over to Zevern and sighed with relief as they saw the obese wizard take a few ragged breaths.

"Roll him over," Steve suggested. "Onto his back. We might be able to pull him up to a sitting position."

"Agreed."

Once Zevern was sitting upright, his eyes fluttered open. When Sarah appeared Steve flashed her a smile and, once he was certain the wizard wasn't going to topple over, gave his wife a hug.

"Good to see you. Took you long enough."

Sarah slugged him on the arm. "Please. I wanted a challenge this time, so I gave you a head start."

"Oh. Really?"

"No, you goof. Believe it or not, locating someone without knowing where they were teleported in the first place isn't exactly easy. Hey, look at that. Your BFF is awake."

"Wh-what happened? Where am I?"

"We're south of Lake Raehón," Sauer answered, as he hooked his arm through Zevern's and held him steady. "Can you walk? We need to make it to Verdayn by nightfall."

"Puh-lease," Sarah scoffed. "I can have all of us back in R'Tal in just a few seconds."

Sauer nodded. "Excellent."

Steve approached Zevern and looked him squarely in the eye. "Tell me you're all alone in there."

"I can only imagine what you must think of me," the wizard began, growing distant. "I know you already think I'm incapable, but I swear to you, I had no control over my actions. Please, you have to believe me!"

"Oh, we believe you, all right," Sarah assured him. "Can you feel his presence? Is he gone?"

"I can ... I don't know, *sense* someone beyond the fringe of my consciousness. I can't feel much, but what I do feel is ... *anger*. This person clearly didn't want to let me go, which does nothing to dispel my unease."

Steve grunted once. "You're the wizard. Can you tell me how someone like Melvyn managed to acquire this power?"

A breeze skimmed lazily along the treetops. Picking up loose leaves, pine needles, and various other bits of debris, the wind dropped lower, until the leaves were seemingly dancing in the air between them. After a few minutes of watching the swirling leaves, the winds pulled together and formed a small dust devil. A form began to take shape as the winds condensed. When the dust devil sprouted arms and legs, and the winds disappeared altogether, the humanoid form took a step. Then another.

"Eion," Steve breathed.

The Master of the Winds nodded once before turning to look at Zevern. The overweight wizard took one look at the Ancient and fainted dead-away. Eion switched his gaze to Sauer.

"Are you who I think you are?" the captain of the guard

carefully asked. "Are you really Eion?"

"I am." Eion turned to Steve. "Steve, come with me. We have much to discuss."

"Can you tell us what's going on?" Steve asked. He pointed at Zevern. "Do you know how Melvyn got his power?"

"I do. It was given to him by one of us, I'm sorry to say."

Chapter Seven–Ancient Assumptions

O f course!" Steve groaned. "Why didn't I see this coming? I mean, who else would be able to give someone that much power? No wonder Melvyn has become so strong."

"It's not you, is it?" Sarah asked, turning to Eion. "Tell me you're not the one who gave someone like that an ability he can so easily abuse."

"I am not responsible," Eion confirmed.

"Then, who is?" Steve wanted to know.

"My sister. Aura."

"The fire chick," Steve breathed. "I'll be damned."

"Aura?" Sauer repeated. "I thought there were only four Ancients: Usol, Eion, Oros, and Aeus. I have not heard of Aura."

"When she wants people to believe she's male, she goes by Oros," Steve explained. "We were confused about that, too."

"You're really an Ancient," Captain Sauer breathed,

impressed. "I don't know what to say."

Eion turned his pupil-less white eyes toward the captain and then shrugged. "Then don't. We really have more pressing matters to deal with, starting with your favorite time traveler." The Ancient looked over at Steve. "I think we should …"

A loud groan sounded. Everyone turned to look as Zevern struggled to sit.

"… in the presence of an Ancient, and I look terrible! I need a bath. I need a manicure. I need …"

"… to go elsewhere," Eion sighed. He waved a hand and a swirl of air appeared around Zevern. Before the wizard could protest, he was gone. "Now, I think the four of us need to go somewhere quiet and talk."

Steve shrugged. "What about Astral? It's not as though we haven't been there before, and from what I remember you telling us about it, there's no chance anyone could be eavesdropping on us."

Eion nodded. "Astral it is."

There was no wrenching sensation, or loss of balance, or anything to indicate they had just been teleported. One moment they were in the wide-open valley south of Lake Raehón, and the next? A very familiar setting in an open glade appeared, ringed by trees and mountains.

Steve took Sarah's hand and started to look for a place to sit down when they heard a squawk of surprise. Turning, they saw Emerion staring around the glade with wonder in his eyes.

"Nice to have you back, pal," Steve said, as he approached the griffin and scratched the area between Emerion's wings, a known favorite. "I'll be honest and say you had me worried. Eion? Thanks for bringing him here."

The Ancient nodded. "You're welcome."

"I don't know what happened," the griffin said. "One minute I was rising, to come to your aid, and the next? The danger was gone and everyone appeared in different locations. It's like I … hmm. I do not know how to best describe it."

"It's like you lost a chunk of time," Sarah offered.

"Yes, exactly. Thank you. It's just like that."

"It *is* just like that," Sarah clarified. "Melvyn had taken over Zevern and did something that immobilized you. Eion, I'm assuming you had something to do with breaking the spell?"

"That was me," Eion said. "It was nothing more than a temporary stasis spell, and not a very good one, if you must know."

"That's Zevern for you," Steve chuckled. "Always seems to be half-assing things."

"Half-assing things," Eion repeated, chuckling. "I like it. I might have to borrow that phrase and use it on my siblings."

Steve wandered over to a section of thick grass and was preparing to lower himself to the ground when he stopped. There, in front of him, was a depression. Bent blades and irregular shapes outlined an area that was nearly fifteen feet long, by no more than two feet wide. The strange shape was also slightly curved, as though a group of people were sitting in the grass, in a slight semi-circular formation. Noticing someone silently approach on his left, he turned to see Captain Sauer regarding the grass-covered ground, too.

"We aren't the only ones here," the captain observed.

"Fairly recently?" Steve wanted to know, lowering his voice to a whisper.

"Aye."

"Who was here?" Steve asked, as he pointed at the ground. "Do you see this? And this? Someone was sitting here. I'd say, what, no more than ten minutes ago?"

Sauer nodded once. Eion appeared by Steve's side and briefly glanced at the ground.

"Oh, that. Well, that'd be you, wouldn't it?"

"Huh? We just got here," Steve insisted. "None of us have sat down yet. That's certainly not from us."

Eion started pointing. "You were there, and Sarah was there. The blonde woman from your world was there, on the other side of Sarah. The two dwarves were there, and the young wizard and his guur were there."

"That happened years ago," Steve pointed out. "No, wait. Scratch that. The point in time you're talking about won't happen for over a hundred years."

"Point of fact, you and your friends were here, at this

very spot, just ten minutes ago," Eion insisted.

"Not possible," Steve argued, shaking his head. "There are a couple of things wrong with that statement. First and foremost, we were here when we were battling Flinn and the pirates. You brought us here to give us some help, which was very much appreciated. However, that was years ago."

"At least six," Sarah quietly added.

Steve nodded. "See? There you have it."

A flat stone appeared. Eion smiled and casually sat down. "You said you had more than one objection. Let's hear it. I do enjoy proving you humans wrong."

Steve snapped his fingers. "Right. Moving on. Putting the part about it being in our past, and we're talking years, let's not forget one simple thing: we're here, in the Lentari of the past. Yes, we've jumped backwards in time, but that was much longer than it's been since we were here. The point in time you're referring to happens to be known as *When Pigs Fly*. Your indentation in the grass? It had to have been made by some animal."

"I see your objections," Eion began, giving Steve an appraising smile, "and raise you one non-linear experience."

Steve blinked a few times. "Huh?"

"The way humans live their lives can be described as ... let's do this." Eion rose to his feet and faced his audience. He traced an imaginary line through the air. Inexplicably, a white line appeared, as though the Ancient was drawing on a glass pane. Eion tapped the far-left end point. The beginning of the line now had a larger, more noticeable initial point and glowed brighter. "Now, let's see if I can describe this in a manner in which you'll understand. You're here, living in the present day. Tomorrow comes, and it can be represented by another point on the line." Eion tapped the line again, and a second dot began glowing, inches from the first. "You are now here. Hypothetical question: what happens if you want to go back here, to the first point?"

"You don't," Sarah said. "Not even if you wanted to. Well, I mean, not unless some serious magic is involved."

The Ancient nodded. "Correct. A typical human will not ever be able to visit a previous point, because that's in the past. Are we all agreed on this?"

Heads were nodding.

"Good. Now, let me see."

Eion started gesturing in mid-air. Lines, curves, arrows, tangents, and more lines appeared. He then added a variety of dots, directional arrows, and a few unknown symbols. Stepping back, he studied his creation and then grunted once.

"It doesn't do it justice, but that's about as simplistic as I can get it."

"What are we looking at?" Steve wanted to know.

"My timeline," Eion answered. "My existence is *not* linear. I can revisit any point, at any time, at a moment's notice. Quite frankly, this is what fascinated me about your species. I didn't think anyone could live in such a way, so I've entertained myself for … well, a very long time, just in observing you humans."

"You're saying you can revisit any period of time you want?" Steve asked, amazed. "Even a few thousand years?"

"I can," Eion confirmed. "Haven't you wondered why I'm not the Eion from the past? Where, by your reasoning, I shouldn't even know you? Yet here I am, conversing with you, when earlier today we were in Coeur d'Alene, having lunch. And, if I really want to boggle your human minds, I can tell that three of your hours ago, I *was* at a point in time several thousand years ago. So, when I tell you that you were here just a little while ago, rest assured, you *were*."

"I have no idea how to process that," Sarah admitted.

"Nor do I," Emerion added.

"He truly is an Ancient," Sauer said, stunned. "How can someone live in such a manner?"

Eion waved a dismissive hand. "It's easy. Don't fret about it. All you have to do is just realize time doesn't work the same for us. Accept that, and all will be well. Now, can we move on?"

Steve shrugged. "Uh, sure. About Aura … what can you tell us? Why would she be willing to give Melvyn the power to screw up our future?"

"You're not going to like the answer to that," Eion said, sighing. "All right, here it goes. It's because of you, Steve."

"Me?" Steve scoffed. "Why?"

"She's holding a grudge against you."

"Say what? Why? I've never met her!"

Eion nodded. "That's true, only …?"

"Only what?" Steve wanted to know.

"You gave Usol back his powers," Eion said, shaking his head. "Do you remember me telling you that this would more than likely not go over well with my sisters? This …" the Ancient patted the air, palms facing down. "… is the result of that."

"Usol was already using his powers!" Steve insisted. "Giving him back his stone was the right thing to do!"

Sarah placed a restraining hand on his shoulder. "No one is saying you did the wrong thing. Right, Eion?"

"I've come to terms with it," Eion said, nodding. "Aura, on the other hand, has not. She's angry, and she can be very vindictive, as you have now learned."

"What about Aeia?" Sarah asked. "Did you ever give her back her stone?"

"The Essence of the Sea," Eion recalled. "Yes, I finally found her, and made my peace with her. We are back on speaking terms, thanks to you. Why do you think I'm offering my help now? Your abilities may be more than a match for any of your fellow humans, but against my sister? You are hilariously outmatched."

Emerion nuzzled Steve's side before looking up at Eion. "I stand with him. He will not have to face your sister alone."

"Of course he won't," Sarah vowed.

"That goes for me, too," Sauer announced.

"Thanks, guys," Steve said, giving Sarah a hug and then leaning forward to give the griffin a few back scratches. "However, something tells me that making peace with Aura won't be an easy task. So, Eion, hit me with your best. How can I get your sister to drop her grudge against me? Let me guess. She wants to see me humiliated in some way?"

"I think she's already plotted her revenge," Sarah said. "The only question I have is, how did Aura know she could cause that many problems for Steve by helping Melvyn?"

"Because she knew of the feud between the two of

them," Eion answered. "While I strongly advised against it, citing my refusal to interfere with human affairs, my sister disregarded my advice and bestowed enhanced jhorun unto Melvyn."

"What do we know about his new jhorun?" Steve asked. "What is he capable of doing?"

Eion chuckled. "Haven't you figured it out yet? Your friend, the former sheriff of Coeur d'Alene, now has the powers of persuasion. Melvyn utters a command, and it is followed."

"I'm not liking that at all," Steve decided. "That kind of power with that type of person?"

"It's a recipe for disaster," Sarah agreed, sighing. "All right, tell us. Aura gave it to him, so I'm guessing she can take it back?"

"Convincing her won't be easy," Eion said.

"Maybe not, but what other choice do we have?" Steve asked. "Eion, you know your sister better than us, obviously. Can we make all of this go away? And, for that matter, does the other sister, Aeia, hold a grudge against me, too?"

"No. She has her stone back. I don't believe she knows who you are."

"Good," Steve said. "I hereby promise you that I'm going to try and keep it that way. Now, do you have any suggestions on what I should do?"

Eion turned pensive and fell silent. After nearly a full minute, the Ancient suddenly smiled, looked over at Steve, and gave him an apologetic smile. Steve took one look at the omnipotent being's face and paled.

"I'm going to hate this, aren't I?"

Eion shrugged. "That all depends."

"On?"

The Ancient focused his attention on Sarah. "How is he at finding lost items?"

Sarah laughed. "Not great, I'm afraid. Why? Has Aura lost something?"

"She has, aye. It's something she covets so strongly that, should it be returned, I'd wager she'd be willing to forget any type of grudge."

Steve sighed. "Let's hear it. What's she missing?"

"Her tiara."

Sauer scoffed once and shook his head.

Steve blinked and stared at the Master of Winds. "A tiara? Oh, you've *got* to be kidding me. I didn't know you Ancients wore such jewelry and accoutrements."

"We don't," Eion confirmed. "Well, I don't, nor does Usol or Aeia, that I'm aware."

"Just her, then?" Steve groaned. "Figures. Wait. Does it? Why does Aura wear a tiara?"

For the first time, Eion appeared hesitant. "Well, it's like this. She's ... ? Let me put it this way, using an analogy you'd be familiar with. Aura is my sister, and she just so happens to be ... bat crap crazy."

Steve snickered, and Sarah giggled. Sauer snorted once. Then, they heard Emerion's trill of laughter.

"I really shouldn't say that," Eion backtracked. "Just a moment. I'll search your memories and see if I can come up with a better explanation."

"Search our memories?" Steve repeated, frowning. "What does that entail?"

"Done. I have another reference, one that was created last month. Steve and Sarah, you took a road trip through Oregon, and were driving through a small town when you stopped for lunch. You, Steve, went inside while Sarah remained in your vehicle. Now, think of the waitress. Do you know the one I'm talking about?"

"A waitress from Oregon?" Steve repeated. He looked at Sarah, who was nodding. "No, I sure don't."

"Yes, you do," Sarah chided. "I believe we stopped at a place called Casa de Joe's. One of the regulars recommended we should try their asada burritos, so you ordered two to go. You told me the girl behind the counter was a complete ditz, seeing how she messed up the order, couldn't give the right change, and then wrote your name wrong."

"The blonde teenager," Steve groaned. "I stand corrected. I *do* remember her."

Sarah nodded. "Exactly. You said she was probably seventeen, and acted every bit like the spoiled, entitled teenager?"

"It's coming back to me. Yeah, what a pain. Oh, I see where this is going. Aura is like this?"

"Very much so," Eion agreed. "All I'm trying to point out is that she may be the same age as the rest of us, but like many humans, doesn't act her age. Therefore, Aura has what I call a *skewed* sense of priorities. I believe the phrase you people would use is mid-life crisis. She's been acting like a ... pardon me for borrowing yet another saying from your world, but my sister has become a whiny teenybopper."

"Suggesting she's currently acting immature," Sarah said. "I get it. Well, for whatever the reason, if Aura really wants this tiara, and it will appease her anger at Steve, then it sounds like we're going to have to suck it up and find it for her. Eion, what can you tell us about it? How big? What does it look like? When was it last seen?"

"The answers to your questions," Eion began, "are very little, bigger than a crown, gaudy, and three years, four months, and eighteen days ago."

"That's a very precise number," Emerion said, drawing the Ancient's attention. The griffin squawked nervously and sidled closer to Steve. "I only mention it to bring attention to how quickly you answered."

Eion bowed. "Well done, griffin. Well done. You've noticed what these two have not."

"What have we missed?" Steve curiously asked. "So, you know the exact moment you saw that tiara last. What's the big deal?"

"Three years, four months, and eighteen days," Sarah repeated, thinking hard. "By any chance, would that be the exact time Usol's power was returned?"

Eion shook his head. "No."

Steve was relieved. "Oh, good."

Sarah frowned. "I can't be that far off. Do you know how long it's been since we were here? By that, I mean, from our point of view."

Eion nodded. "Three years, four months, and seventeen days."

Husband, wife, griffin, and Lentarian soldier all shared a look. That couldn't have been a coincidence, could it?

"We were here," Steve began, "fought the pirates—and won—and then returned Usol's emerald. You're telling us the day after we did that, and left Lentari, Aura's tiara was stolen?"

"Technically, we were here the day after all that happened," Sarah clarified. "We spent the night at our cabin, remember? We were all so exhausted that we elected to rest. It was our first night with Emerion."

"It was?" the griffin asked. "I have no memory of that."

"It's not surprising," Steve said. "You were just a tiny cub."

Eion snapped his fingers. "I had forgotten about that night, too. Very well. In that case, yes, your leaving, and the last day I saw Aura's tiara, are one and the same."

"It vanished on the same day," Steve mused thoughtfully. "Did Aura misplace it?"

"No."

"Did she give it to someone?" Sarah asked.

"No."

"It was taken," Sauer deduced.

The corners of Eion's mouth turned upward. "You could say that."

Sarah's eyes widened and a look of enlightenment appeared on her face. "Usol. Usol's powers were returned, the Alchos stone was given to Steve, and then what? He confronted Aura and stole her tiara?"

"He confronted the three of us," Eion corrected, "and then stole the tiara the moment Aura turned her back."

"Why?" Sarah wanted to know. "Payback?"

"Something like that," Eion admitted.

Steve pointed at the Ancient. "Wait, didn't you say that you're the one who took Usol's power from him?"

"I am."

"Why isn't she mad at Usol? Aura shouldn't be mad at me. After all, I didn't do anything to her."

"Except give Usol his powers back," Sarah said, sighing. "I think I'm starting to understand Aura's grudge. Steve, we've *got* to find that tiara. Quite honestly, I'm tired of Ancients holding grudges against you."

"I'll second that," Steve grumbled.

"As you humans would say, you just can't seem to stay off our radar, can you?" a new voice chimed in.

The five of them whirled around. A black-haired, bearded man was there, arms crossed, sporting an exasperated smirk on his face. He had a full beard, was heavily muscled, and reminded Steve of what he had envisioned the Greek hero, Hercules, would look like.

The figure turned to Steve. "Hercules. I love it. You're starting to grow on me, fire thrower."

Steve's eyes widened. "Usol."

"The one and only."

Sauer started to point, but Sarah caught the arm and gently pushed it down.

"Isn't that ...?" Sauer began.

"Yes," Sarah said.

"Both of them? At the same time?"

"Let it go, dude," Steve advised.

Eion's face was twisted into a menacing scowl. "You dare to step foot on my isle?" Tornadoes sprang into existence and touched down on either side of the figure leaning against a nearby tree. "You have until the count of three to vacate before I allow my elementals to attack."

"Hear me out, brother," Usol pleaded, holding up a hand. "I didn't come here to quarrel. If you want me to leave, then say so, and I'll do just that. However, I think your guests might want to hear what I have to say."

"Don't you think you've caused enough problems?" Eion demanded.

Usol pointed at Steve. "At ease, brother. I came to talk to him."

"You want to talk to Steve?" Sarah asked. "Why?"

"He's probably having second thoughts about giving me his emerald," Steve guessed. "If you want ... What the ...? Hey! Ouch!"

"What is it?" Emerion asked, worried.

Steve reached into his right trouser pocket and struggled for a few moments to extricate an object that had just appeared. Since the pocket had been designed to hold a much smaller item, the foreign object refused to budge until Steve gave it a mighty yank. Turning, he held out a sparkling dark green emerald in the shape of a tetrahedron.

"That's definitely gonna leave a mark," Steve said, sighing. "I actually thought I'd be safe here, yet here it is."

"If it helps, I didn't think it would make it all the way here, either," Sarah added.

"What is that?" Sauer wanted to know.

Steve held up the jewel. "Umm, let's call it my jhorun-infused good luck charm."

"And it teleported itself directly to your pocket?"

Steve shrugged. "It has a nasty habit of appearing at the most inopportune times. Like now, for example. I don't want it here, and I certainly don't need it here, but it came, just the same." Recognizing a popular rhyme from a well-known Christmas animated classic, he groaned. "Not a word, dear. Eion? Let me guess. These stones don't follow the normal timeline, either?" Both Eion and Usol nodded. Steve held the emerald up and waited for Usol to take it. "Here you go. I kept it safe for you."

The Earth Guardian shook his head. "And I told you that it is yours now. I don't need it."

Dejected, Steve stared at the unique gem in his hand. "Fine. As for you, go away, would you? I really don't want to carry you around."

The green stone ignored him.

"You're talking to that jewel as though it can understand you," Sauer quietly observed.

"There are times when I think it can," Steve whispered back. Grunting irritably, he slipped the gem into a larger inside pocket. "Have it your way."

"What's the matter, fire thrower?" Usol teased, using a surprisingly good-natured tone of voice. "Can't handle the power of the stone?"

"Oh, I've got it under control," Steve assured the Ancient. He then tapped his head. "Kinda. It's all up here. I just have to watch what I say, that's all. I've since learned that, if I so much as mention an animal's name, then I become that animal until I can get my thoughts under control. It's not the easiest thing to do when you suddenly find yourself in another form."

"Please," Usol scoffed. "I've had the power of shifting mastered for many thousands of your years."

"You're also an Ancient," Steve pointed out. "You're used to dealing with all this power. But, that's neither here nor there. You wanted to talk to me? About what?"

Usol's unsettling white eyes fixed on Steve's and he shrugged.

"I thought I might be able to shed some light on the matter, but if you don't need me, it's fine. I'll leave."

"He's up to something," Steve decided, as he turned to Sarah and waved Emerion and Sauer over. "I think our past history speaks for itself."

"I cannot believe I'm here," Sauer confessed.

Steve laid a friendly hand on the captain's shoulder. "Well, table that for now. We have a bigger issue to address. Do we believe anything Usol has to say?"

"And why wouldn't we?" Sauer countered. "He's an Ancient, isn't he? He would never lead us astray."

Husband and wife glanced briefly at the bearded Ancient before turning to Sauer. Such was the look of disgust on Steve's face that Sauer immediately backpedaled.

"You people clearly know something I don't. I apologize."

Steve shook his head. "Don't sweat it. As for you, Usol, I'm with Sauer. You've caused us so much grief that I know you're up to something. Out with it. What's your angle?"

"My angle," Usol began, as a smile formed on his face, "as you so eloquently put it, is that while I still harbor some resentment toward my siblings for what they did to me, I have no intention to put any of them in harm's way."

"And for us humans?" Steve asked.

Usol shrugged. "Your species simply provides too much entertainment to ignore."

"I knew it," Sarah sighed.

"I think we all did," Steve said, nodding. "Okay, pal. You admit you're not out to harm any of your siblings, but for us it sounds like you're all for a little comic relief. What do you have planned? After all, we know you're the one who stole Aura's crown in the first place."

Usol nodded. Those unsettling white eyes stared at him, unblinking. "So, who best to offer some insight on how to retrieve the crown than the person who saw it last?"

"You could just give it to us," Steve suggested.

Usol let out a loud bark of laughter. "And where's the fun in that?"

"Why isn't Aura going after you for stealing her crown?" Sarah suddenly asked. "Doesn't she know you're the one responsible for its disappearance?"

When the Ancient remained silent, Sarah let out a groan. "You've insinuated Steve is to blame for the crown."

"Oh, that's just peachy," Steve groaned.

"For what purpose?" Sauer asked.

A loud squawk sounded from behind them. Turning, Steve looked into Emerion's surprised eyes. "I had no idea that'd be so loud. I'm sorry."

"You have something to say, griffin?" Usol asked. "Out with it. You need not fear any repercussion from me."

Emerion turned his frightened eyes on Steve. "Well, I think it's obvious."

"What is?" Steve asked.

Emerion nervously rustled his wings and faced Steve. "According to what you've told me about Usol, he's put you through the wrecker. He knows what you're capable of, and he ... what is it?"

Steve was laughing. "I think you meant to say, he's put me through the *wringer*."

The griffin cocked his head. "Does that not mean the same thing?"

"Well, a wrecker is ... you know what? It's close enough. Yes, Usol has put me through hell, but I'll be honest and say that I brought a lot of that on myself."

"You surprise me, fire thrower," Usol said, smiling.

Steve held up a finger. "You didn't let me finish. What I *will* say is that, throughout our history together, you've turned me into a very cautious person and proven you Ancients are adept at holding grudges."

Usol shrugged. "Fair point. Now, do you want my help or not?"

"Seeing how you've indicated you won't be willing to return the tiara anytime soon, yes, I would appreciate any help you can throw my way."

"You heard my brother. Aura is very immature. She holds you personally responsible for the theft of her crown."

"Thanks for that," Steve murmured

"Because of that, Aura has taken it upon herself to exact her revenge on you," Usol continued.

Sighing, Steve sank down on the closest item that could be construed as a seat, which was the ground, seeing how there were no suitable boulders or logs. Sarah and Emerion quickly joined him. After a few moments of hesitation, so did Sauer.

"That jewel," the dark-haired deity explained, "is your … what do you call it on your world?"

"A pain in my ass," Steve murmured.

Emerion trilled.

"I think you mean *saving grace*, if I used the phrase right. The only way you're going to defeat my sister is by using my old stone."

Steve retrieved the sparkling emerald from his pocket and held it aloft. "This allows me to change forms. I'm not aware of it having any other powers. Usol, am I wrong?"

"Without a doubt," the Ancient informed him.

"I thought Alchos Stones only had one magical property," Sarah protested. "Invisibility for Aeia's, and shapeshifting for yours. What did we miss?"

Steve scoffed. "It's more like, what weren't we told?"

Husband and wife turned to regard Eion. Steve crossed his arms over his chest. "Care to add anything to that?"

"Yeah, about that. I might've left a few things out."

"I'm all ears, pal."

"To fully appreciate the stone's power, you'll have to discover that for yourself."

Incredulous, Steve turned to Usol. "You're not going to tell me how to use your stone?"

"I leave you with one word, fire thrower: practice."

Usol vanished. Eion smiled sheepishly and started to sit down. Emerion, noting that there was nothing for the

Ancient to sit on, opened his beak, but Sarah gently pushed it closed. Holding a finger to her lips, she pointed at the Master of Winds.

A flat rock appeared, just before Eion would have tumbled to the ground.

"I've got such a headache," Steve confessed. "We've got to find a crown that Usol stole."

"And hid," Sarah added.

"Right. Stole and hid. This isn't going to be easy."

"Perhaps you should learn more about the crown?" Eion idly suggested.

"What's that supposed to mean?" Steve wanted to know. When there was no answer, he glanced over at Sarah, who shrugged. Looking back at the Ancient, intent on asking for help, he was startled to see they were now alone. "Did he just ditch us? On Astral?"

"He knows full well I can get us out of here," Sarah said. "He wants us to learn more about Aura's crown? Fine. Who should we ask?"

Sauer rose effortlessly to his feet. "First things first. I say we return to the castle."

Steve tried his best to replicate Sauer's success, however, his joints cracked and popped as he carefully rose to his feet. Sarah gave him a concerned look.

"Are you all right?"

"Getting old sucks."

"You keep saying that. I'm going to tattoo that to your forehead."

Steve grunted, but stayed silent.

Once they had been returned to the castle, and were standing outside the open drawbridge, Sauer motioned them to follow. Falling into step behind him, Steve came to an abrupt halt when he noticed Sarah hadn't joined him. Turning, he saw her at the water's edge, looking down at the moat.

"What is it?" he asked, dropping his voice in case Sarah didn't want the others to overhear.

"I think I know what we have to do next."

"Oh? I'm all ears, my dear."

Sarah pointed at the water. "Would you do me a favor

and call Balthor?"

"You realize he won't know us here, right?" Steve reminded her. He dropped to his knees, reached down to scoop up a handful of water, and then let the water trickle out, through his fingers. "Balthor, er, Gareth. Or whatever other name you go by."

The reflections of their images on the water's surface disappeared. A shealk's head appeared. It rotated as it looked first at Steve, and then at Sarah. When it didn't bother shifting to its human form, Steve let out the breath he had been holding.

"Before you think I have the wrong number," he began, offering the water dragon a smile, "let me just say that I do know you. Just not the *you* from right now."

The shealk was silent as it gazed at him. After a few moments, the image rippled and became a younger version of the human man they had met at Mikal's wedding.

"I do not know you, human," Balthor began.

Steve held up his hands in a time-out gesture. "I know, I know. Please hear me out. My name is Steve, and this is my wife, Sarah. We aren't from this time."

The image of Gareth's father frowned before he crossed his arms over his chest. "You've come this far, don't stop now. And what time am I supposed to believe you're from? The future?"

Steve nodded. "Well, yeah. One hundred eighteen years, to be exact."

"Are you wizards?" Balthor asked, still frowning.

"No."

"Your mate is a wizard?"

"No."

"The spell necessary to transport a being through time could only be handled by the most gifted of wizards."

Sarah nodded. "You're correct, Balthor. That's precisely what you told us."

For the first time, the shealk wizard's composure faltered. "What are you saying? *I* am the one who sent you back?"

Steve retrieved the shell he had been given and held it up. "You gave me this. It brought us here, and when we, uh, set it off, it'll take us back. You told us it was single-handedly the most complex spell you had ever created."

Balthor was silent as he studied the shell.

"You are holding my personal marisk shell. How did you …? Ah, I see what I must have done. My future self must have predicted you'd need help now, in this time, and if you approached me, I would need some way to verify your legitimacy. Using a personal item for the spell was an intelligent move, if I do say so myself. Very well. You've piqued my curiosity. Do you require assistance? What do you seek?"

Steve stepped back, out of the way, and watched as his wife took his place.

"Balthor? What can you tell us about Aura's crown?"

The shealk wizard's eyes shot open. "You never fail to impress. A moment, if you please."

Five minutes later, Balthor was walking alongside the four of them. Sauer guided them to a quiet section of the inner keep, where relatively few people were seen wandering about.

"First, I have to ask what your interest is in that particular crown," Balthor said.

"The only interest we have is finding it and returning it to its rightful owner," Steve answered.

"Its rightful owner," Balthor slowly repeated. "You're referring to Oros himself?"

"Make that, Aura herself," Sarah corrected.

"Be that as it may, no one has laid eyes on that particular crown for many centuries."

"It was stolen three years, four months, and eighteen days ago," Sarah said.

"By none other than Usol," Steve added.

"We need to locate this crown so that we might appease Aura and take back the power she bestowed upon Melvyn, the fugitive," Sauer finished.

They approached several large logs that had been carved into benches and sat. Emerion settled on the ground, closest to Sarah.

"Very well. I wish you luck on your quest. I can tell you what I know of it."

"Please do," Sarah urged.

"It is known as the Flaming Crown, crusted with jewels, and the most valuable part of the piece is a large ruby." Balthor paused to meet their eyes. "Granted, I have never seen it, and this may be the stuff of legend."

"Sounds like way too much bling for me," Steve decided.

Looking at his wife, he chuckled. Tiaras? Jewels? As gaudy as it probably was, Sarah would most definitely be willing to try it on. For posterity's sake, of course.

"Tell me about the ruby," Sarah instructed. "How big is it?"

Balthor shrugged. "I'm sorry, I do not know. I have not personally seen it. But, you will know you've found it once you see the ruby."

"And why's that?" Steve asked.

"Because, this ruby? It's the only one like this in the entire world."

Steve sighed. "Full of bling and now we learn there's a one-of-a-kind ruby associated with it. No wonder Aura wants it back so bad."

Sarah nodded. "That means this tiara is unique. I'm hoping that it'll make it easier to find. Wait. Balthor? What makes this ruby so unique?"

The shealk wizard smiled. "This particular gemstone was cut into the shape of a flower."

Chapter Eight–Power Problems

Don't you think we've found a remote enough location to do this? I mean, look around you. There's no one for miles. Donlari is that way about, what, fifty miles away? And to the west? Not a darn thing."

It was just past dawn the following day. Steve, Sarah, and Emerion were standing in the middle of a group of low, rolling hills. A slow-moving river snaked its way through grass-covered mounds. Schools of small fish could be seen darting here and there in the clear water.

"Good. I don't want to hurt anyone doing this, yourself included."

"Yes, yes, I know. If something strange happens, I'm to take Em back to the castle."

"Something strange?" Steve scoffed. "Please. I'm about to use something that is infinitely stronger than a jorii, is easily more powerful than the Amulet of Aria, and stronger than Mikal's jhorun. You remember what happened when he accidentally boosted my power, don't you?"

"You burnt down half the city," Sarah wistfully recalled. "Don't worry. We won't let that happen here."

Steve stretched his back, which was still angry with him for sleeping on the straw mattress at the inn they found in Donlari. "We really need to remember to bring some ibuprofen with us at all times."

"I don't know what you're complaining about. I slept like a baby."

"As did I," Emerion added.

"Yeah, yeah." Steve held out an empty, open hand. "All right, you pyramidal pain in the butt. I may have left you back on Astral, but all I gotta do is think about holding you in my … yep, there you are." The green tetrahedron glittered invitingly on his open palm. "We already know about shape shifting," Steve said, as he stared at the many sparkling facets cut into the huge emerald, "so I'm not exactly sure how to make you do something different."

"You've always said that you don't specifically request to change into another form, isn't that right?" Sarah asked.

Steve nodded. "It picks up on things I say, that's for sure."

"Can you change at will?" Emerion asked.

"Yeah, you've seen me do it. Remember last month? When we went out to the small lake near our house and we had a picnic? We were literally attacked by ants. I was ready to torch the whole stinkin' lot of them, but instead, I made the mistake of cracking a joke."

"I do not remember this," Emerion admitted.

"Remember when Steve became the squat, hairy animal with the long snout? And we had to pull him away from the ant hill?"

Emerion let out an excited squawk and trilled happily.

"I'll take that as a yes," Sarah giggled. "Anyway, he had become what's known in our world as an anteater, and he was ready to do just that: have lunch."

"If you're trying to make me barf, you're doing an admirable job," Steve groaned. "The point I'm trying to make is that I didn't order myself to change form. I merely *thought* about it, and that damn jewel did the rest."

"Could you change form now?" Emerion asked. "If you

wanted — or needed — to change into, say, one of those funny black waddling birds, could you do it?"

"A penguin? Probably."

Steve vanished, and in his place stood a banded penguin. It turned until it was facing Emerion, and then a loud call sounded, like the bray of a donkey. Sarah was laughing so hard, tears were squeezing out of her eyes. Sarah's laughter, and Emerion's trill, only made the penguin glare that much harder at the two of them before it was able to close its eyes and revert back to human form.

"You did that on purpose," Steve accused. "Snot."

"He really didn't," Sarah wheezed out, between laughs.

Ignoring the constant stream of giggles coming from his wife, Steve turned to Emerion. "What was the question? Can I switch forms without thinking about it? I guess so, seeing how I apparently just have to say the word and presto, I become it."

"Wonder Twin powers, activate!" Sarah snickered.

"Hardy har har. Can we get serious, please?"

"Can anyone else use the green stone?" Emerion asked.

Steve instantly forgot his annoyance and stared at his wife.

"What a good question," Sarah praised. "Should one of us try it?"

"What happens if it changes you into something, and you don't know how to change back?" Steve asked, worried.

"Wouldn't you like to know if the power extends to someone besides you?" Sarah countered.

Steve held up the Alchos stone. "Just be careful with it."

Sarah took the pyramidal emerald and stared deep into the heart of the jewel. "I've always wanted to be a unicorn."

Steve cringed, and automatically closed his eyes. This time, though, when he opened them and scanned the area, there were no one-horned horses staring back at him. Sarah was still standing next to him, holding the stone, and looking at him as though he was the one responsible for keeping her from changing forms.

"That's disappointing."

"You actually *wanted* to change into something else?"

Steve asked, incredulous. "Need I remind you how much you *didn't* enjoy being me when Gareth switched you, me, and Pryllan around?"

"That's right, I didn't. Here. Take this back."

"Wait. Before you do, try shifting into something that actually exists. We both know that unicorns don't."

"They might here," Sarah said, sighing.

"Doubtful, and not helping. What else do you want to try?"

"Oh, I know! I'd love to be a fairy and fly wherever I wanted to go. We know those exist in Lentari."

The three of them waited, in silence, for something to happen. Sadly, nothing did.

"So, only I can use it," Steve observed, as he hefted the large gem in his hand. "That's good to know, right? The last thing I want to do is abuse an Alchos stone. I already have one Ancient mad at me. Again. I don't need any others."

"An Alchos stone," Sarah repeated, using a soft tone. "I wonder ...?"

"You wonder *what*?" Steve wanted to know.

"Remember the temples?" Sarah asked, referring to the three Alchos temples they had to locate during their skirmish with a band of invading pirates. "The one that was underwater?"

"Kinda hard to forget," Steve chuckled. "That was temple number two. Gareth turned us all into water dragons in order to swim down to it. What about it?"

Sarah pointed at Steve's emerald. "Do you remember all those little statues with the open arms? We had to figure out which ones held the replicas of the four stones?"

Steve slowly nodded. "It's coming back to me. You're asking about this ... why?"

"Those smaller jewels were replicas of the real thing," Sarah explained, growing excited. "And, I seem to recall that one of the stones was a ruby, and that it just so happened to be in the shape of a flowering rose."

Steve snapped his fingers. "Aura's crown? Er, tiara? The ruby on it? Oh, of course! It's her stone! No wonder she wants it back so damn bad."

"My thoughts exactly."

"If I was her, I'd be mad at Usol," Steve said.

Sarah nodded. "Understandable. After all, he's the one who took it. But, that doesn't do us any good now. Aura has directed her anger at you. To her, this happened because of you. She gave Melvyn these new abilities, and then all of this happened."

"If she gave him new powers because she lost her crown …" Steve began, "then …"

"Tiara," Emerion and Sarah corrected, at the same time.

"… and since her stone is on her crown …"

"Tiara," the two of them corrected again.

"… then logic suggests she'd take back the power from Melvyn, making him fair game for the rest of us."

Emerion clicked his beak a few times. "That works for me."

"As if we don't have enough to do around here," Steve said, sighing. "Not only do we have to be on the lookout for our pal, Melvyn, who knows we're here and bent on stopping us, now we have to track down—and locate—this missing cr—, er, tiara, that just so happens to have one of the Alchos stones on it? Yeah, sure. No pressure there."

"What about what Eion said?" Sarah suddenly asked. "We were originally told there was another Alchos stone in Lentari. We all thought it simply referred to Usol's stone. So, the tiara? I don't think it's in Lentari."

"What about Ylani?" Steve suggested. "Or … Damn, what's the name of the country to the south?"

"Straosia," Sarah volunteered.

"Right. How do you remember that, anyway?" Steve wanted to know.

"Because my memory is better than yours?" Sarah answered, batting her eyes at him.

"Walked into that one. Okay, so, I guess that means we'll need to head either north or south. Sarah, we've been to Ylani before, so I think we should start there. Earth to Sarah, Earth to Sarah, are you there? Anyone home?"

Sarah had a faraway look on her face when she suddenly blinked, and a smile formed.

"No, it's here, in Lentari."

"Didn't you just hear what I said? It can't be here. Eion said that there were only two Alchos stones in the kingdom, and they're both accounted for."

"Non-linear."

Steve stared. "What was that?"

"Non-linear. Remember how Eion described himself, and his own timeline?"

"I do, and I remember him saying that. How does that apply here?"

"Points in time," Emerion exclaimed, letting out a soft squawk. "The ancient human said he could return to any previous point in time. Would that not suggest the same holds true for the ancient female?"

Steve's eyes widened. "Of course. Aura had her crown, and then jumped backward to a previous point in time. So, at this exact moment, there very well could be *three* stones in Lentari."

"Which means the Ancients are right," Sarah deduced. "Again. If Aura's tiara is somewhere in Lentari, then that validates our decision to believe him."

Steve held up the emerald. "You're talking about this, aren't you? Meaning, I need to practice using it. Well, there's no time like the present. Where do you think I should start? I'm all ears."

The green jewel flashed, and just like that, it was now being held in the trunk of a very large African elephant. Emerion squawked with alarm and leapt backward. Sarah, on the other hand, slapped a hand over her mouth and tried valiantly to keep the giggles from escaping.

A look of disgust swept over the elephant's features. The massive ears flapped a few times, and the trunk lifted until he was glaring at the green gemstone sparkling invitingly at the tip.

"What happened?" Emerion asked. "I've seen this type of creature before, haven't I? It's a, uh, it's a … I seem to have forgotten the species."

"Elephant," Sarah answered. "The funny thing is, I didn't hear Steve say *elephant* at all, so it must have been the *ears* comment. My, my, that stone is sensitive, isn't it?"

Steve dropped the tetrahedron and trumpeted angrily, causing Emerion to jump back in alarm a second time. The two large eyes closed and, moments later, Steve appeared, on his hands and knees.

"That sucked some major rocks," he grumbled, as he rose to his feet. "I can see it changing me into a creature that I say aloud, but I didn't on that one."

"You were thinking about it," Sarah guessed.

Steve scuffed a toe in the dirt. "Maybe. Damn thing. I have to watch what I'm thinking now? Oh, sure. Piece of cake."

"You always tell me you can empty your mind on a moment's notice," Sarah reminded him. "Now's the time to put your money where your mouth is. Think you can do it?"

"I'm sure as hell gonna try. All right, let's give this another shot."

"What is he doing now?" Steve heard Emerion whisper.

"He's trying to clear his mind to see about getting Usol's stone to do something else."

Steve took several deep breaths, holding each nearly thirty seconds, before slowly exhaling. He did this a few more times and, when he was certain there were no more thoughts bouncing around inside his head, he looked at the glittering gem in his hand. It was a tetrahedron, a triangular pyramid. The corners were gently rounded, and unlike many gemstones, there weren't many facets cut into the four-sided jewel. It was a dark forest green color, and it was roughly the same mass as a baseball.

And apparently, the gem had a wicked sense of humor.

Humor … could that be the key to unlocking other capabilities the stone might have? What *else* might a prankster enjoy doing to someone? Steve was silent as he considered. Having played practical jokes on friends throughout the years, he thought back to some of his better attempts.

One of his favorites, during his childhood, was scaring his mother whenever she walked into a room. Bonnie Miller was not known for watching where she was going, and, as a result, would focus on whatever was directly in front of her.

What was the result? Getting the bejesus scared out of her more times than either of them could count.

As the memory faded, Steve's eyes snapped open. The gem was warm! Was it like that before?

"What the hell!?" Sarah suddenly exclaimed.

Steve ignited his hands and sprang forward. He and Emerion both arrived by Sarah's side at the same time.

"What is it?" Steve asked.

"Are you well?" Emerion asked. The fur along his back was sticking straight up, and his wings were partially extended.

Wordlessly, Sarah pointed at a spot directly behind him. Turning, Steve's eyes shot open. There, not ten feet away, was a second Steve! He had turned, too, and was looking in the other direction.

Steve held up his right arm. His twin did the same. Steve spun in place and watched his twin do the same.

Emerion edged closer. "How are you doing this?"

Steve hefted the gemstone. His copy did the same, although his hand was empty.

"Well, there's something you don't see every day."

Sarah timidly approached and stared at the emerald. "How'd you do it?" Sarah asked.

"I asked myself what would a prankster do? The first thing I thought of was a memory from my childhood, scaring my mom."

"You've told me about that," Sarah said, nodding. Then she giggled. "You were a mean son."

"Pssht. Anyway, that's when the stone grew warm. A split second later, you must have seen the doppelganger ..."

"... ooo, good word," Sarah praised.

"... and got the two of us to turn around. Go touch him, would you? I'd be curious to know if he's an apparition, or maybe something else?"

Sarah shook her head, and then looked at Emerion. "You do it, would you?"

Nodding, the griffin cautiously approached Steve's twin and swiped one of his wings across the second Steve's face. Encountering no resistance, the wing spun Emerion around.

"You're not there. You're here."

Husband and wife eyed each other. Steve chuckled. "Good to know I'm not over there, too." He turned to Emerion. "You didn't feel anything at all? Your wings felt ... *squawk!!*"

Sarah glanced up. "A griffin now, huh? Stop fooling around, dear. We have work to do."

An angry tirade of squawks and shrieks sounded. Simply uttering the word *wing* had prompted Usol's stone to change his form to that of a griffin. Emerion sidled closer and he let out a long string of chirps, whistles, and clicks.

"No, I don't want to stay this way," Steve told the griffin, using the same set of vocalizations. "But, I am glad you approve."

Two minutes later, Steve was back. He draped an arm around Emerion's tawny shoulders.

Steve held up the stone. "I think this thing was telling me that it has more power than me, and unless I treat it nice, it's gonna make my life hell. Moral of the story? Don't disrespect the stone. Got it."

"Could it be sentient?" Sarah asked, amazed.

Steve shrugged. "It's been with Usol for so long that who knows what powers it could have absorbed. Fine. Mr. Gemstone? I'll play nice if you do. I'm sorry if I insulted you. Are we all better now?"

"You're talking to that gem as though it is listening to you," Emerion said, trilling.

"It just became cool," Steve reported, as he gave the griffin a smile. "One problem out of the way. Hopefully. Now, let's see what else this can do. You two had better stay over there."

Bringing back up the emotions he felt whenever he was feeling particularly playful, Steve thought back to the times he played harmless jokes on Sarah, and then remembered her retaliation when she wrote obscene words on his skin, and drew moustaches on his face when he was asleep. As expected, the stone grew warm. Steve swallowed nervously. Now, it was a waiting game. If something was going to happen, it should be soon.

He wasn't disappointed.

"Omigod, what is that? Make it go away!"

Steve appeared next to his troubled wife in a flash.

"What is it? What's the matter?"

Sarah lifted a shaky finger and pointed at the ground. He and Emerion peered intently. Once Steve's eyes focused, and he saw what Sarah had noticed, all thoughts about the emerald vanished. Sitting on the ground, waving its antennae at them, was the biggest, fattest cockroach anyone had ever seen. The ground trembled, and before anyone knew what was happening, several dozen more of the large roaches magically appeared. Whether or not they had tunneled their way to the surface, or the power of the stone had simply conjured them, Steve didn't know. What he *did* know was that bugs and Sarah were the equivalent of oil and water: they didn't mix. Sarah was already backpedaling, choosing to hide behind Emerion's much larger form.

"You've got to be kidding me! Why are they here? Honey, make them go away! Please!"

Steve ignited his hands and was preparing a blast when he remembered the stone. Had he called them? Was this a facet of the stone's power? Steve eyed the large bugs and sent an order.

Stop.

"Is this right?" Steve whispered, more to himself than to anyone. "It controls bugs? What in the world for?"

During Steve's hesitation, several of the insects broke free and scuttled toward Sarah, who immediately screamed and leapt up, onto Emerion's back. Ever the protective son, Emerion extended his wings and readied his forelegs.

I said stop.

The bugs halted again.

Get back here.

The roaches hurried back to Steve and fell silent.

"Are you doing this?" Sarah whispered.

"It would appear so," Steve answered. "Now I'm telling them to collect on that tree over there. Now, I want them to line up in rows of four. Look at that! Those are some impressively straight lines. Alright, now I'm having them march toward that patch of sunlight. Perfect. See? I just released them and let them scatter."

"Why in the world would that emerald give you power over bugs?" Sarah asked.

Steve shrugged. "Usol was known for his mischief. Imagine the dastardly things he could do with those bugs. Torment his sisters. Hell, imagine the torment he could do to us humans."

"The ability to create a copy of yourself," Emerion was saying, "and now the power to control insects. Both are aspects of Usol's power, using that emerald?"

Steve nodded. "It would appear so."

"Is that all it can do?" Sarah cautiously asked.

"I have no idea," Steve admitted. "I actually thought back to several pranks I've pulled over the years. That was when things started happening. So, I thought I'd give it another few minutes and see if anything else happens."

"Like what?" Sarah wanted to know, only the voice that came out was not her own. Surprised, her eyes widened and she clapped a hand over her mouth. Her voice had deepened and had become somewhat stuffy, as though she now had a cold. "What happened? Did I suddenly swallow a frog?"

Concerned, Steve took his wife's hand. "What happened to your voice?"

Sarah stared at him. "Your voice sounds just like mine!"

"Oh, *hell* no," Steve grumped. "Why am I using your voice? Give me mine back!"

"I never took it in the first place."

A loud trill sounded from nearby. As one, husband and wife turned to the griffin. Emerion was rolling on the ground, laughing his furry tail off.

"We didn't do this on purpose," Steve snapped, using Sarah's much higher voice. He retrieved the emerald. "It's this damn thing. It's messing with us."

"Thereby answering the question about what else that stone can do," Sarah said.

"Is that what I really sound like?" Steve demanded. "Gruff and nasally? I swear, I'm not stuffed up, but I sure as hell sound like I have a cold."

"It's your allergies," Sarah told him.

"I don't *have* allergies," Steve corrected.

"And I'm living proof you do," Sarah argued. "Forget about that for now. Clearly, this stone's purpose is to prank other people. I think it's good that you're practicing with it. Do you think you could switch our voices back?"

Steve gave the emerald an angry shake. "Give it back. I don't want to sound like her, and she sure doesn't want to sound like me. You've made your point. You're a very powerful talisman." Thinking it might be wise to get on the stone's good side, provided it had some sense of sentience, Steve continued on. "Tell you what. I think this would be a helluva prank to pull on some unsuspecting Lentarians. Give us our voices back and we'll see about using it some more on some unsuspecting people. Do we have a deal?"

Just like that, his voice was back.

"We really need to watch what we say," Sarah was saying.

"I'd say this thing enjoys causing mayhem," Steve said. "If we play along, I'm getting a feeling we'll get more cooperation from it. Hey, look at that! Usol's emerald is getting warm. I think it agrees with me!"

"Think you have a handle on its powers?" Sarah asked, in all seriousness.

Steve eyed the gem. "Believe it or not, I think so. I think the key is respect. This stone wields a tremendous amount of power. Respect it and I do believe I can wield it." The stone grew warm for a second time. "Oh, it likes that. It's warm again."

Sarah nodded. "Good. Now, we need to determine where to go to find Aura's tiara. Does anyone have any ideas?"

"Ordinarily," Steve began, "I'd ask young Gareth to come up with some type of spell. The kid never fails. I know he'd be able to find it."

"But, he isn't here," Sarah reminded him. "On top of which, we've determined that Aura's stone is part of her tiara. Gareth has already said his spells are ineffective against it."

Steve nodded. "True. Well, what if we find the foremost expert on tiaras and ask them?"

"Who do you have in mind?" Sarah wanted to know.

Steve shrugged. "Well, we have the dwarves, of course.

And then there are the dragons. Everyone knows dragons covet treasure. Maybe one of them has the tiara we're looking for? It might explain why no one has seen it for centuries."

"There are hundreds of dragons, each with their own horde. I doubt very much they'd give it up, or even acknowledge they have it, let alone let us anywhere near their treasure."

"We might be able to get Pryllan working on that if we don't have any other leads," Steve said. "I'd rather not, though. She's already done enough."

"What about the shealk wizard?" Emerion asked. "He's powerful. He has helped us before. Could he help us again?"

"If Gareth couldn't get a reading on the Alchos stones, then I doubt very much his father could," Steve said, sighing.

Sarah was silent for a few moments. "I think Em is right. We should contact Balthor."

"Why?" Steve asked.

"He's used to dealing with complex spells. Plus, there is more than one shealk wizard here, so if he needs help, he has it."

"He's not going to be able to track an Alchos stone," Steve insisted.

"What if we don't need him to?" Sarah asked. "What if we can get him to track down the rest of the tiara?"

"Hmm, you make a good point. He might be able to locate a tiara with a ruby as its centerpiece. Good thinking, my dear. Let's see. Take us to a source of water, would you?"

Sarah nodded, and held out a hand. Once Steve and Emerion were in physical contact, they vanished, reappearing leagues away by a very familiar waterfall and pond. Nodding appreciatively, Steve headed for the pond and scooped up a handful. Letting the liquid fall through his fingers, he called for the wizard. Once Balthor had arrived, and heard their request, the shealk wizard sank down on the nearest log to consider.

"What you're asking won't be easy," the transformed wizard began. "But, if I organize the spell into layers, and assign each layer a task, then I should be able to accomplish that which you've asked."

"I can definitely see where your son gets it," Steve quipped, as he grinned at Balthor.

"Tell me, fire thrower," Balthor implored, "my son is a wizard? Like me?"

"The two of you have the exact same jhorun," Sarah confirmed. "He can see the inner workings of a spell inside his head. What he can do puts even Shardwyn to shame."

"Shardwyn needs to retire," Steve scoffed. "I've been pushing Mikal for some time to let Gareth take his place."

"My son? He's to become the castle wizard for you humans?"

"It hasn't been made official," Steve began, "but I do know the king and queen are considering it. Then again, it's all a moot point if we can't get the timeline repaired."

Balthor nodded. "Give me some time. I will create the spell you require."

"You got it, pal. Er, how much time do you need?"

"Half an hour. I will return."

Just like that, Balthor was gone.

"We're awfully lucky he's on our side," Sarah said.

"We're awfully lucky that having kids is something he's thought about," Steve pointed out. "Think about it. If he never wanted kids in the first place, he'd be less inclined to help us, wouldn't he?"

Sarah's eyes widened. "Ooo, I hadn't even considered that. Good point."

Steve took his wife's hand and, with Emerion trailing behind, approached the water's edge and studied the waterfall.

"To think that it's back there, waiting to be discovered," Steve said.

"Push that thought out of your head," Sarah instructed. "We can't do anything to mess up our future, remember?"

"What are you staring at?" the griffin inquired.

Steve pointed. "On the other side of that waterfall is a hidden cave. Inside it is something that has remained undiscovered for hundreds of years."

"What's in there?" Emerion asked.

"Oh, just a broken piece of jewelry, once owned by a sorceress."

Emerion rustled his wings. "Fascinating. Is that what Sarah meant? We mustn't interfere with our future?"

Steve nodded. "Exactly. Think about it. If I go back there, find what I know is there, and then take it, what'll happen to the future me?"

"Your broken piece of jewelry won't be there for you to claim it," Emerion deduced.

"Right. And, seeing how we desperately needed it to defeat a very powerful foe, we would risk losing that battle."

Twenty minutes later, Balthor was back. He held out a small, iridescent conch shell.

"What's this?" Steve asked, as he studied the tiny, glittering spire on the vacant snail shell. When the shealk wizard opened his mouth to explain, Steve barreled on. "Oh, I get it. This is a marker, isn't it? We need to put it on a map and then it'll move to wherever this tiara is, won't it?"

Balthor blinked a few times, evidently surprised. "As a matter of fact, yes. Have you experienced many spells such as this? I thought I was being clever."

"As a matter of fact, we have," Sarah confirmed.

"My son has used similar spells, hasn't he?" Balthor guessed. A smile was threatening to form. "I must say, I do hope you three are successful in restoring the timeline. I find the idea of having a human son most intriguing."

"Well, prepare for fatherhood, pal," Steve said, slapping a friendly hand on the wizard's shoulder. "This is going to work. We're going to put things back to the way they were."

Balthor bowed. "Since you are familiar with the workings of the spell, I will take my leave of you. Good luck on your quest."

"Can we call upon you again, should the need arise?" Sarah hesitantly asked.

Balthor nodded. "Of course. If it is within my power, I will help."

Once the shealk had gone, Steve held out a hand and waited for Sarah and Emerion to take hold. "Ready to head back to the castle?"

Sarah nodded. "Allow me to venture a guess. The Archives?"

"We know there are maps there," Steve confirmed. "I say it's a good place to start. This thing should work with one of them."

"Agreed. Em? Ready?"

"Aye."

The sounds of falling water vanished, replaced by the low murmur of a dozen different conversations. They were now standing before the entrance to the castle's records department. Everything, from tax laws to census reports, was kept in the large chamber directly in front of them. But, in order to cross the threshold, the three of them had to walk past the archivist's desk. Try as they might, there was simply no way that two humans, followed by a larger-than-normal griffin, would go unnoticed.

A young blond woman, with her hair pulled up in a tight bun, and wearing a thin set of spectacles perched on her nose, looked up from the book she was reading. She frowned at the intrusion and held up a hand.

"That will be far enough. Who are you? What are you doing here? And what is a griffin doing inside the castle?"

Steve made the introductions. "We need to, er, check out a map. I know you guys have a large, antique map that shows the entire kingdom, and even a bit of Ylani and ... and ...?" Shaking his head, he gave Sarah a helpless look.

"Straosia," Sarah supplied.

Steve hooked a thumb in her direction. "Right, what she said. May we borrow it?"

"Castle resources are *not* to leave the Archives," the archivist haughtily informed them. "Maps are located in Section Three, rows one through five. Topographical maps are on rows four and five. Your griffin? He will behave himself?

Sarah nodded. "Of course."

The records keeper waved them through. "You may proceed."

Sarah and Emerion walked past the desk just as the woman returned to her book. "Thank you." She waited until they were out of earshot, in Section Three, before turning to Steve. "I wonder if she's related to Andra?"

"I'm wondering if she *is* Andra Alwyn," Steve said, using a dead pan voice.

Sarah swatted his arm. "Oh, come on. There's no way she and Andra are the same person. Yes, Andra from our time is old …"

"… ancient," Steve interrupted, disguising it as a cough.

"Shush. Yes, Andra is old, but you have to remember, we're over a hundred years in the past. She hasn't even been born yet."

Steve glanced back at the blond woman and shook his head. "I don't know. She might be a hundred-twenty. Who can tell?"

"You're terrible," Sarah said, giggling. "All right. There are the maps. Know the one you want?"

"Yes. I think we ought to use the same one as last time, that big old one. I see it there, all the way to the right."

Sarah walked around the bookcase to view the opposite side. Several seconds later, she was back, clutching a long, cardboard tube. Gesturing at a nearby empty table, Sarah opened the tube and unfurled the map. Steve grunted once and fetched two goblets, one decorative rock, and a carved figure of a dragon from another table.

"Careful," a faint voice warned.

Steve, Sarah, and Emerion turned. The archivist was there, in the distance, still seated at her desk. Her head was down, looking at her book. As they were staring at her, the archivist lifted her head and stared straight at them. A few seconds of silence passed before she returned her gaze to her book.

Grunting irritably, Steve set the first goblet on the map's top left corner and had just placed the second in the top right when he felt a presence behind him.

"That map is at least a hundred years old," the curator explained, frowning. "Please show it the respect it deserves."

"We just need something to hold it down," Steve explained. "We'll be extra careful, and we'll put everything back where we found it. We promise."

Mollified, the librarian drifted off.

"For one so young, she certainly appears dedicated,"

Emerion quietly observed.

"I still maintain she's Andra, in a younger form."

"Don't be silly," Sarah scolded. "Now, do we put Balthor's marker on our current location?"

Steve nodded. "That's what Gareth did last time, when he … I mean, it's what he's going to do when we get back, only he's already done it, so …? I have no idea what I'm trying to say. I'll shut up now."

Pulling the shimmering seashell from his pocket, he nervously eyed his companions before placing it on the tiny drawing of a castle, representing R'Tal. After a few moments, when nothing apparent was happening, Steve looked at Sarah and was about to ask a question when the marker began to move. It slowly inched north, to settle in an area of the Bohani Mountains above the Lentari-Ylani border.

"That's not right," Steve said, tapping the map. "It shouldn't be picking up the, uh, you-know-*whats*."

"I don't know what you're talking about," Emerion admitted.

"Sarah does, and it's not something we should talk about in the open. But, I will say I'm impressed that Balthor's spell is picking them up. He must have found a way to search for … let's call them lucky charms."

"Or found a way to search for objects around the lucky charms," Sarah suggested. "Either way, we already know what's there, so let's try again."

Several minutes later, Balthor's seashell ended up in the exact same spot.

"Could it be up there?" Steve asked.

Sarah shook her head. "I strongly doubt it."

"Is all well here?" a new voice asked.

Husband and wife looked up to see Sauer leaning over the table.

"So far, so good," Steve reported. He pointed at the marker. "We're getting some help looking for a certain something, and …"

"…we're getting the wrong results," Sarah interjected. "Something tells me that, no matter how many times we start over, it's always going to head north."

Noticing Captain Sauer was wearing a large medallion around his neck, Steve cleared his throat and pointed at it.

"Hey, is there any way we can borrow that for a second?"

"My medallion? Whatever for?"

"I want to test a hunch."

Sauer slipped the gold chain from his neck and handed it over, curious. Indiana Jones couldn't have been prouder as Steve snatched the marker and deftly replaced it with Sauer's medallion. Handing the shell to Sarah, he nodded.

"Let's try it again, shall we?"

"It'll just push the medallion out of the way," Sarah said, frowning.

"Well, let's see how strong it is. With the medallion blocking where we know one of *them* happens to be, let's see where else we can look. Fire away."

"Okay, it's moving," Sarah reported.

"Why is there a seashell moving along the map?" Sauer wanted to know. Sensing it was a sensitive subject, he dropped his voice. "It's enchanted? To do what?"

Steve grinned and pointed at the map. "To do *that*! Check it out! It worked! The shell is moving east, toward the Great Sea. That's gotta be where … no, wait. Aww, man! It stopped over the Seven Kingdoms."

"There's nothing over there but empty land," Captain Sauer insisted.

Steve held a finger to his lips. "No, it isn't. However, this is also the location of the other, er, item we know about, so this doesn't help us, either."

Sarah took her own medallion from her neck and handed it to him. "Here, do your thing again. Let's block both locations."

"Done. Start 'er over, would you?"

Sarah reset the conch shell and, together, the four of them waited to see what happened. Sadly, nothing did.

"Well, that's depressing," Steve groaned.

"It moved," Emerion said.

"No, it didn't," Steve argued. "It started on R'Tal, and it's still there. If there's nothing to find, then …"

"It moved," Emerion insisted.

Sarah moved next to the griffin and leaned over the table. "Are you sure, Em?"

"It trembled, and barely moved, but it *did* move."

"The griffin is right," Sauer said. "I watched it move, too. It made the tiniest wobble."

"Well, then, it didn't go far," Steve observed. "What does that tell us?"

Sarah was silent as she studied the map. "We know the spell is working. The shell has already located two. It's trying to locate the third, but either it is encountering resistance, or ... wait! What if ... what if the location is here? Somewhere in R'Tal? That might explain why it didn't move."

"Because it didn't have to!" Steve exclaimed. He hurried around the shelves to start searching the maps. "Somewhere in here has gotta be a map of the city. I mean, it ... yes! I found one! Okay, roll that one up and let's try this one."

Once the maps had been switched out, and promptly secured on the table, Sarah set the seashell down, directly over the castle. After a few moments, the marker began to move, but it only made tiny circular motions around the castle. Around and around it went, without stopping. After five minutes or so, Sarah snatched the shell, and eyed her companions.

"No luck with this thing. But that doesn't mean it's *not* here in the castle. We'll need more information."

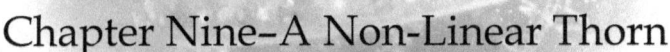

Chapter Nine–A Non-Linear Thorn

All right, if Aura's trinket *might be* somewhere in the castle, then we can split up and cover a lot more ground. So, what do you say we … what?" Steve questioned, looking between Sauer and Sarah cautiously.

Sarah sighed and shook her head for a second time. "Dear, I'm going to say something, and I'm sorry to say that you're not going to like it."

Steve crossed his arms. "Hit me with your best shot."

"Non-linear existence."

"You're talking about the Ancients. What about them?"

"Don't you remember what Eion said? They said going back thousands of years is nothing more than a blink of an eye to them."

Steve shared a look with Emerion. "Do you know what she's going on about?"

The griffin squawked with alarm. "This trinket could've been hidden anywhere and at any point in time!"

"I mean, it could have been hidden in the castle, but I've

heard the castle is nearly a thousand years old," Sarah added. "Then again, who's to say Usol didn't hide it somewhere else, *before* the castle was even built?"

"That adds a whole new degree of difficulty, doesn't it?" Steve groaned.

"It gets better, I'm afraid," Sarah said, giving him an apologetic smile. "What if Usol concealed Aura's stone within a, well, another stone? Then, by definition, that'd mean Aura's stone could be anywhere."

Steve pulled out a chair and plopped himself down. Sarah did the same.

"That's discouraging as hell," he decided. "Where do we go from here? I mean, this makes it worse, not better."

"Not necessarily," Sarah argued. "I've been thinking about this. Look, Usol took the tiara from Aura and fled. Logic suggests Aura would've pursued. Now, if we were the ones who stole the tiara, what's the first thing we'd do? Well, since we wouldn't want to be caught with the incriminating evidence, we'd hide it. It sounds like no one, not even the Ancients, would want to cross another Ancient. However, he has more powers at his disposal. One of those powers is the ability to jump through time. It's logical to assume that's what Usol did, but we still have to discover *where* he hid it."

Steve raised a hand. "I think it's safe to say Usol's hiding place shouldn't be too complex."

"Why do you say that?" Emerion asked.

"Aura. You said it yourself. Usol took the tiara from his sister and immediately fled. Like any quarreling siblings, if one takes something belonging to the other, then you're gonna have one pissed off member of the family coming after you. Aura has the same powers as the rest of them. She would have wanted her crown back."

"I like where you're going with this," Sarah told him, nodding her approval. "All right, if he didn't have much time, then it's safe to say finding a complicated and safe hiding place is out."

"Meaning it's probably hidden in plain sight," Steve guessed. "That's what I'm thinking, too."

"Sarcasm?" Sarah wanted to know.

"Not this time. For all we know, we could be looking right at it and not know it. So, let's go with what you said: if we wanted to know more about crowns and tiaras, who would we ask? I mean, do you think they could have an exhibit somewhere?"

"This isn't the Tower of London," Sarah pointed out. "I don't think they have any museums here. In this case, I think we should start small."

"I thought that's what we were trying to do," Steve argued.

"Appearances," Emerion said, ruffling his feathers. "Agreed. What's your idea? Where do we start?"

Sarah pointed at Steve. "Actually, I think we follow *his* idea."

Steve looked up. "Hmm. I don't see any."

Sarah and Emerion both checked the sky.

"What are you looking for?" his wife wanted to know.

"Flying pigs. You agreed with me? Wow. I think … ouch! Okay, okay, you didn't have to slug me. You know I love you."

"Mm-hmm. As I was saying, I think your idea is sound. That means we should …"

"… find someone who knows something about them?" Steve asked, after she trailed off.

"Yes. I don't suppose you have any ideas?"

Steve snapped his fingers. "Dragons. Who better to ask about a piece of treasure than a dragon?"

"Just because they could have something like that in their hoard, doesn't mean they'd know much about it," Sarah decided. "What about the dwarves?"

Steve nodded. "I like that. They were probably the ones who made the crazy thing in the first place. However, which clan do we focus on? I don't think I've ever heard of a dwarf who made an ugly piece of treasure. I think they're all experts."

Sarah suddenly nodded, as if coming to a decision, and indicated they should follow her. Soon, much to Steve's dismay, they were back in the Archives. The same young woman was there, still manning the front desk, but at least she ignored them as they passed by.

"Here," Sarah said, nearly fifteen minutes later, as she

looked up from a stack of books she had retrieved.

Steve looked at the title. *Masons of the North.* The book was nearly eighteen inches wide and two feet in length, with a thickness of a few inches. The text, Steve could see, was not printed, but handwritten in a thick, angular script. To Steve, he could easily see the words carved into stone. Whoever wrote this particular book had to have had a steady hand, as all the letters were the same size and perfectly straight.

"I take it that book talks about the clans?" Steve asked. "Does it say how many there are?"

"The title may indicate this book is all about stone workers, but it's not. Instead, this book seems to be about the known clans who live in the area. Check it out. The first section is about the Kla Guur. There's one about the Chanus. Here's one about a clan that started in the Bohanis, but eventually relocated to the south. Wait, this is interesting."

"What is it?" Emerion asked.

Sarah tapped the page. "Has anyone heard of the Kla Snakkoth?"

"Wow, that's a mouthful," Steve commented. "And no, I haven't."

"Wait, *we* have heard of them," Sarah insisted. "While I will admit we've never met any of them, we've seen them before. Check out this illustration and tell me if it looks familiar to you."

Steve leaned over his wife's shoulder. It was an illustration of a dwarf male. Aside from the bushy eyebrows, and long braided beard, nothing else could be seen of the dwarf's physique because every square inch of the small figure was covered with what looked like thick plate armor. If ever someone wanted to hide their appearance in broad daylight, *that* particular outfit would be the way to go.

"I can only imagine they must make quite a ruckus whenever they try walking in that getup," Steve said, chuckling.

Sarah nodded. "That's precisely what I remember about them. They were noisy. Steve, it says here that Kla Snakkoth were master goldsmiths. They're the ones who are usually commissioned to make a piece of treasure, like …?"

"… a crown?" Steve finished for her.

"Precisely."

Steve smiled. "Okay, where can we find this Snakkoth clan?"

Sarah returned to the map of R'Tal, rolled it up, and handed it to Steve as she walked by him.

"Where's she going?" Emerion asked, in a soft voice.

Steve shrugged. "I'm not sure. I think she's looking for a book that might help her, although I can't imagine … hello, what have we here? She's on her way back already, and she's holding two books. Em? Grab that other map. Let's put them back on the shelf."

"I think I have it," Sarah announced, nearly twenty minutes later. "Now, look at this. Kla Snakkoth has two cities: Dymer and Korn."

"Corn?" Steve scoffed. "That's a silly name for a city."

"It's spelled with a *K*," Sarah clarified. "And, from what little I've been able to find about it, I'm thinking that's the city we want."

"Why?" Emerion asked.

Sarah tapped the book. "The author mentions there is a steady source of gold nearby."

Steve nodded. "Their own gold mine. Smart. All right, they've got my vote. How do we get there? You've never been there before, so it's not like we can jump straight there, without …? What's that look for? Wait. Are you saying we *can*?"

"It's something I've been practicing," Sarah explained. She placed the two books into a nearby bin and then sank onto the chair.

With bated breath, Steve watched his wife take a deep breath and hold it. After a few moments, her features visibly relaxed, and she slowly exhaled. Sensing movement on his right, Steve noticed his griffin son open his beak in preparation of asking a question. Holding a finger to his lips, Steve nudged Emerion and shook his head no. Whatever Sarah was trying to do, she'd be allowed to do it in peace.

"Last month," Sarah began, using a soft voice, "I started thinking about how I was able to teleport us all to that strange city in Ylani. Do you remember?"

"I do," Steve said, nodding.

With her eyes still closed, Sarah smiled. "It's always bothered me, so I took it upon myself to figure out how. I wanted to see if I could do it again, but this time I'd pick a place in *this* country."

"And?" Steve prompted. "What happened? What place did you choose, and, did it work?"

"Yes and no. I chose Giza Plateau, in Egypt."

"Where?" Emerion asked, confused.

"It's where you can find the pyramids," Steve explained. "Well? Did you make it?"

"I did, yes. Before I knew what was happening, I was standing in downtown Cairo, and in the distance I could see the great pyramids."

Steve frowned. "Is that a good test? I'm sure you've seen pictures of Cairo before, haven't you?"

Sarah nodded. "I have, that was the *yes* part. So, I looked up the name of the largest city in Siberia."

"Russia?" Steve sputtered. "You wanted to go to Russia?"

"Absolutely not," Sarah argued. "And that's my point. I don't know a single thing about any Russian city, so for me, it's the perfect test."

Steve visibly relaxed. "Ah, I get it. Go on."

"The largest city in Siberia, just so you know, is a place called Novobirsk. It's the third largest in all of Russia, after Moscow and St. Petersburg. I've never been there, and I've never seen any pictures. So, I decided to try my luck."

"And it worked," Steve guessed.

"Not even close," Sarah laughed. "Do you remember Gareth explaining to us how multi-layered spells work?"

Steve groaned. "I get a headache every time I do, so thanks for that."

"I don't," Emerion announced. "A multi-layered spell? Is it what it sounds like?"

"Long story short," Sarah said, "it's a spell with more than one component. The second part is contingent on what happens when the first part is triggered, and the third goes off the second. Are you with me?"

Emerion nodded. "I believe so. I think."

"Right. Anyway, I learned either my teleportation skills behave in the same way, or …?"

"… your power is growing," Steve guessed, after she trailed off.

"Right. So, I ended up telling my jhorun not only what I wanted to do, but I made it as specific as I could: where to go, what type of locale to drop me, while making sure the space isn't currently occupied."

"Or in an unsafe situation," Emerion added, "such as a body of water, or a stone wall, or in front of a wild beast, or …"

"I get it," Steve said, interrupting. "I just want to know: did it work?"

Sarah looked up and met his eyes. A few seconds later, she was smiling. "It *did*. I ended up somewhere I've never been, and was looking at things I've never seen before."

"So, how do you know it was Novobotnik?"

Sarah sighed. "Novobirsk. Because, I took a picture on my cell. Then, I checked to see where it said the photo had been taken."

"Gotta love satellite GPS," Steve said. "Sarah, this is fantastic news! The ramifications of this are monumental! You can now go wherever you want, regardless of past experiences!"

"I can," Sarah said, nodding. "However, the caveat is that it takes a bit longer for the first time. Once I'm there, obviously, I can create one of my safe zones. But for the first, I'll need a couple of minutes of prep time."

"You got it. Em? Let's head over here. Sarah? Let us know when you're ready."

"I will. Thanks."

"She can teleport to places she's never been to now?" Emerion asked, as his eyes widened. "That's … that's …"

"… amazing," Steve finished. "Makes me wonder if it's due to her power growing stronger, or her understanding more of how it works."

"I say her power is increasing," Emerion decided.

"Let's hope so, pal. If it is, then that means mine could possibly be growing stronger, too."

"I think I have it," Sarah announced a few minutes later.

"I really hope this works, 'cause I think I'm getting the hang of it."

"You already know how to teleport," Steve pointed out. "This shouldn't be too tough, right?"

"It's just a different way to do things." She held out a hand. "All right, Steve, Em."

Once they were all in physical contact with one another, Sarah ordered her jhorun to move her, Steve, and Emerion to Korn, wherever that may be. The pristine, quiet insides of the castle's records room vanished.

In its place was a huge, brightly lit cavern stretching hundreds of feet to the left and right. This cave, Steve noted, was rectangular and was probably a few hundred feet across at its widest point. The opposite wall of the cavern was practically flat, as though it had been carved out of solid stone by hand. Openings were visible everywhere, with many of them illuminated.

Steve blinked a few times and then looked at his wife.

"They're dwellings! I think this has to be where all of the Kla Snakkoth live. Looks like a big apartment building, doesn't it?"

"Interesting," Sarah decided. "I wonder why they chose to live in such a fashion?"

Steve shrugged. "It's probably what was readily available. My guess is there was some type of cave system, and the Snakkoth adapted it for their purposes. Remember what Maelnar told us about the Kla Guur? That entire cavern was already hollowed out, and had tunnels branching off in all directions."

"That's because it was nothing more than a large ant hive," Sarah recalled, shuddering.

Distant voices sounded from the mouth of the empty tunnel behind them. Turning, Steve studied the large passageway and then eyed his companions.

"Looks like we've got someone behind us. I don't see one of those round announcement plates like the Kla Guur have. I'm not sure I want to be caught like this, out in the open."

"What would you have us do?" Sarah asked, growing concerned.

Steve took Sarah's hand and, once he was sure Emerion was following, hurried to the edge of the tunnel's mouth. Crouching in such a way that they were hidden from inside the tunnel, the three of them anxiously awaited the arrival of whoever it was who was rapidly approaching.

"We have to consider our future," one voice was saying.

"We have, Master Balon," another insisted. "Why do you think the four of us are here? To get some exercise?"

"There's no need to be rude," Bael's voice grumped.

"Dwarves," Steve quietly reported.

Sarah rolled her eyes. "Really? You think?"

"Hush, you two," Emerion scolded.

The approaching procession halted.

"Who goes there?" a new voice demanded.

Sighing, Steve stepped away from Sarah and Emerion and turned to look inside the tunnel. Four dwarves were standing less than a dozen feet away, each with a look of bewilderment on their faces. Each dwarf, Steve noted, was dressed in dark clothing: tunics, trousers, and boots. Each of the four, he also noted, were wearing dark leather gauntlets.

"You're Kla Guur," Steve guessed. "You're here from Borahgg?"

"How do you know of our city?" the lead dwarf snapped. It was the first voice they had heard, making this one Master Balon. "No human has ever been there."

Steve nodded. "Yes, that's true. I'm sorry, there's no way to explain how I know what I know. Listen, you're on your way to meet with the Snakkoth? I know I don't have any business asking this, but may we tag along? We need to ask them a favor, too."

"We're not asking for favors," Balon said, as he patted his breast pocket. "We're here to hammer out a few changes to our trade agreement. Who are you and what do you want of them?"

Sarah appeared. "Don't mind my husband. We're here to, uh, research a book about the masterful treasures Kla Snakkoth have created. We were hoping to see some examples of their finest work."

"Treasures?" one of the dark-clad dwarves scoffed. "And

you come to Kla Snakkoth? Please. You should be talking to us. We're the unequivocable masters of all things treasure."

"I thought you didn't want any humans in Borahgg?" Steve asked, throwing as much innocence into his question as possible.

Bael grunted, turned to the companion who had made the suggestion, and smacked him upside his head.

"The human has a point. Let the Snakkoth deal with humans. We don't need anyone learning about our skills. Now, one side. We have business to attend to."

"That's far enough," a new voice ordered.

With all the finesse of a dragon tiptoeing through a fully stocked armory, six heavily armed Kla Snakkoth guards appeared before them. These dwarves were dressed from head to toe in thick, clunky plate armor, revealing only noses and eyebrows. Axes were drawn and arrows were fitted to bows.

Steve's hands went up. "That really isn't necessary, guys. We're harmless. So are they. They want to talk about their trade deal."

"Kla Guur?" one of the Snakkoth asked.

Eager to put distance between themselves and the human intruders, the Kla Guur stepped forward.

"We are. We come to speak with the Council."

"You are expected. Kraghak will escort you."

The Kla Guur delegation bowed.

"We thank the Snakkoth for their hospitality," Bael intoned, in a formal voice.

The first Kla Snakkoth dwarf shrugged, as if all this formality was boring him. Once they had gone, he returned his attention to Steve and frowned.

"Now, as for you two. Eh? What's this? What the devil is a griffin doing in our tunnels? You three are *not* expected. Lock the humans in the dungeon and kill the griffin intruder."

"We come in peace," Steve insisted. "Put the weapons away. We just want to talk. Then, we'll be on our way and leave you guys alone."

"What do you want?" the lead Snakkoth demanded. "What are two humans and a griffin doing here? Speak now, lest you incur the wrath of Firnik Trollforge."

"Who is Firnik Trollforge?" Emerion asked. When no one answered, the griffin turned to look at his adoptive parents. "Perhaps it's *him*?"

"Of course it's me, you blathering ninny," the dwarf exclaimed. "What are the lot of you doing here? You don't wish to be thrown in the dungeon? Convince me."

"You couldn't throw us in the dungeon even if you wanted to," Emerion returned, growing angry.

Steve stepped between dwarf and griffin and held up his hands. "We mean you no harm. We're here because we need to talk to someone who knows a thing or two about tiaras. Or crowns, I guess."

"Crowns? Tiaras? You're here because your human rulers want new crowns? If so, then they can go through the proper channels, just like everyone else. Now, begone."

Forgetting Firnik would have no idea what the gesture meant, Steve held up his hands in a time-out. "Wait, we said nothing of the sort. We need some info, pal, and we're hoping you'll be able to help us. Everyone knows the only treasure worth owning is made by the Kla Snakkoth, so are you really that surprised we're here?"

"Nice," Sarah quietly murmured.

Firnik drummed his fingers on the hilt of his axe. "Well, for humans, you have good manners. You want us to help you? May I ask in what capacity?"

Steve shared a look with Sarah. "With, umm, with …"

Sarah placed her hand over Steve's and gave it a few pats. "All right, I'll level with you. My birthday is coming up, and my husband knows how much I love jewelry. I've always mentioned I'd like a tiara, and Steve is just trying to make that happen."

"You are hoping to commission a tiara from one of our goldsmiths, is that it? Tell you what. I'll escort you to Master Vael. You may run your request by him. If he agrees to talk with you, then so be it. But, if he refrains, then you leave. Agreed?"

Steve nodded. "You have a deal, pal."

"Good. Follow me."

"What can you tell us about Master Vael?" Sarah asked after a few minutes had passed. They had come to a set of stairs leading down to the cavern floor below. "Why take us to him?"

"Master Vael is an instructor," Firnik explained. He reached the bottom step and immediately set out for the huge arched doorway leading into the massive multi-storied structure everyone seemed to live in. "He is a retired instructor. His workshop is four levels up."

"If he's retired, then why does he have a workshop?" Steve asked.

"I do not understand the question. Every Snakkoth has a workshop."

"They all do?" Sarah asked, amazed. "How big is this level?"

Steve, Sarah, and Emerion followed their dwarf guide through the huge entrance. Staircases angled off in all directions. Kla Snakkoths were everywhere, doing every manner of task imaginable.

They passed a series of gatherings on the first floor. Firnik explained this was where their children were educated about everything they needed to know in order to succeed. Blacksmithing, metallurgy, tempering, smelting, and so on. Also on this level, Firnik continued, were large spaces commonly used as meeting places. Councilors, governors, and elected officials met regularly to ensure the nearly fifteen-hundred members of their community were cared for properly.

The three visitors passed by a large group of children in the midst of discussing self-defense techniques, in case they were ever faced with mortal peril. Youngsters grappled, adults pointed out where their hands should be for maximum effectiveness, and sparring matches were held. However, all that came to an abrupt halt as Emerion was noticed.

"Firnik? What is this? Why bring a griffin here? By Usol, look at the size of it!"

"The griffin is a guest," Firnik explained. "It accompanies the humans. They vouch for its behavior."

"The griffin has a name," Steve mumbled angrily. Before

he could say anything else, Emerion nudged him with a wing and shook his head. It wasn't worth it. "You're a better person than me, Em."

They proceeded the rest of the way through the demonstrations in complete silence. No one moved, and no one said a word. Smiling at the quiet throng of people, Sarah and Steve guided Emerion deeper into the hallways.

"How much farther is it?" Sarah wanted to know.

"Not far," Firnik reported. "Master Vael's workshop is part of the Mire. Er, that's what we call our distinguished elders, who have retired from public office. I believe five others also regularly use the space for their various projects. You ask about tiaras and crowns? Collectively, members belonging to the Mire have fashioned hundreds. Anything you want to know, they can tell you."

Sarah clapped her hands excitedly. "Oh, I'm so glad to hear that. I have such a specific vision in mind for my birthday. I just hope they'll be able to pull it off."

"We're here," Firnik announced, as they climbed the last step and arrived on the fourth floor.

The telltale scent of burning fires, and the incessant clanging from numerous hammers pounding away on anvils hit their senses. Steve whistled. How they were able to mask the activities on this level from the other floors was beyond him. Then again, with so many people living in such close proximity, and as a clan who specialized in goldsmithing, the concept of soundproofing must have been something they mastered long ago.

Firnik guided them past several lit forges, row upon row of anvils, racks of every conceivable tool, including numerous bins which contained devices whose shapes Steve had no chance of guessing. They had been told that these workshops only accommodated six dwarves, but there were easily four times that number milling about. Every single one of them stopped what they were doing as they caught sight of their little group. It probably had to do with Emerion's presence.

"There he is," Firnik reported, as he drew to a stop next to a long table that had a single elderly dwarf seated at the head of it, poring over some schematics. The dwarf looked up, saw the four of them, and quickly dropped the utensils. "Master Vael, do pardon my interruption. I have guests here who would like to speak with you. Will you listen to them?"

"I will, based on the fact that griffins typically do not accompany humans, or any other species, in such a docile manner," Vael exclaimed. He indicated the chairs at his table. "Do sit down. As for you …?"

"Emerion," Steve offered. "I'm Steve, and this is my wife, Sarah."

"Steve. Sarah. And …?"

"Emerion," Sarah reminded him.

"Ah, yes. Emerion, you are the first griffin I have ever encountered. I am honored."

"It is I who am honored," Emerion returned. "Thank you for agreeing to meet with us."

Nodding, Firnik spun on his heel and departed.

"I just have one question," Vael said, holding up a finger. "How is it you travel with two humans?"

"Those two humans are my parents."

The dwarf's eyes widened with surprise.

"It's a long story," Steve said, waving a dismissive hand. "We were told you could help us."

Vael shrugged. "Perhaps. What is it you require?"

"Do you know much about tiaras?"

Vael sat back in his chair, grinned, and then tapped the top of his head. "Well, I know they're typically worn here. I might have crafted … oh, let me see. A few thousand, I guess. If you're trying to get me to make another, then I'm afraid you have made this trip for naught. I have served in my official capacity for long enough." He tapped the designs on the table. "*This* is what interests me now. Mechanical contraptions. I'm absolutely fascinated by them."

"Can we at least describe the tiara we were hoping to get made?" Sarah asked the dwarf. "Maybe you'd be able to tell us who would be able to help us? Please, we know the Kla Snakkoth are masters. We're hoping there's at least someone out there who can make it."

"There are no finer goldsmiths in the land," Vael stated.

"We know this," Steve said. "That's why we're here."

"Very well. I will listen to this description."

Sarah cleared her throat. "I'm hoping this can be made of gold, obviously."

"Obviously," Vael agreed.

"It'll be of a design that no one has ever used before, or has since," Sarah continued.

"Harder to guarantee, but not impossible," Vael observed.

"And gemstones," Sarah said. "The more the merrier. Red is my favorite color. My favorite stone, rubies. I've seen some specially cut rubies before …"

"… extremely rare, and very expensive," Vael muttered.

"… so what I was hoping to have done is to get a ruby cut into the shape of my favorite flower and have it set with rows of diamonds, sapphires, and … what is it?"

"What you're asking for, and I will admit that it is theoretically possible, is something that would take years to make properly. And the price? You could buy your own kingdom for such detailed work."

"Oh, I was hoping you knew of something similar to use as inspiration," Sarah said, sighing heavily.

"I do not, I'm afraid. Now, if you're serious about pursuing something of this caliber, I might be able to put you in touch with some qualified masters."

"When you say this will be pricey," Steve began, "are you exaggerating or are you serious?"

"No exaggerations are necessary for an order of this magnitude," Vael was saying.

"Can we think about it?"

"Take all the time you require. I will leave word with the Guild of Monitors, who patrol our tunnels. Should you wish to pursue this project, then simply mention my name to any of them and I will refer you to the appropriate craftsmen."

Steve nodded. "Thank you. Now, how do we get out of here?"

The retired dwarf issued a set of instructions that would take them back to the Citadel's front entrance. From there, they could make their way back to the tunnel, and once they were away from prying eyes, Sarah would be able to teleport them back to the surface.

"I really thought they'd be able to help us," Steve said, nearly thirty minutes later.

Sarah had just returned them topside, and once there, taken them back to R'Tal. "If our dwarf friends don't know anything about this, who else can we ask?"

Steve shrugged. "I don't think we have very many choices left. My vote is we should go talk to the dragons."

"They're experts at treasure," Emerion agreed.

Sarah nodded. "Fine. You're the dragon expert. I take it you'll ask Pryllan?"

You'll ask me what?

Hi, Pryllan. We're having absolutely no luck trying to track down something we're trying to find, namely a tiara.

"You went quiet," Sarah observed. "Are you talking with Pryllan?"

"Yes. I'm telling her what we're looking for."

"Remember, we must proceed carefully."

Steve had just shut his eyes to return to his conversation when they both snapped open. "Huh? Why?"

"The dragons here are not all our friends," Sarah pointed out. "Nor are they our allies."

"So? I won't be reaching out to anyone I don't know, if that's what you're trying to say."

Sarah fell silent.

"Is something the matter?" their griffin companion gently asked.

"We're not due to meet Kahvel until much later," Sarah pointed out. "Steve, you may have talked to Kahvel of the past before, but you haven't met him yet. We know it doesn't take much to mess things up. What you're proposing is going to further screw up our timeline. Therefore, I'd really prefer to keep contact to an absolute minimum."

"With Pryllan and Kahvel? My dear, you have nothing to worry about. I trust both of them with my life. *Our* lives, if necessary."

"Do you think they each feel the same way?" Sarah countered.

"Probably not," Steve admitted. "At least, not yet."

True. However, I can see how you and I would

become good friends. I do hope you're successful in restoring the balance to your timeline.

That's a good way to look at it, Pryllan. Trust me when I say that, locating this missing tiara would go a long way to put things back in order.

You've claimed before you know where our nest is, is that so?

Hello, Kahvel. And yes, we do. May we approach?

You may. We are here. I would actually prefer this method, since the alternate would mean physically traveling to our valley, in full sight of everyone here.

"I have permission," Steve announced. "Sarah? If you would, please take us to Pryllan and Kahvel's nest."

"Am I going, too?" Emerion asked.

"Of course. No one gets left behind. Sarah, whenever you're ready."

R'Tal disappeared, as did the bright sunshine, the chirping of hundreds of birds, and the quiet murmurings of hundreds of conversations. Once more, they were gazing at the huge expanse of their dragon friends' cave.

Emerion squawked with alarm. Standing before them were Kahvel and Pryllan, who were staring at them with unmistakable curiosity visible on their faces. Each were now a hundred years younger, which meant they were slightly smaller from the previous versions they had met earlier, in the altered timeline.

"So, you are the insufferable biped who's been accosting my mate."

Steve stared up, into Kahvel's slitted reptilian eyes and nodded. "It's interesting, don't you think?"

Kahvel blinked. "What is?"

"The two of you. I met you back when Sarah and I first arrived in Lentari. The same goes for Pryllan. I became lost, and she found me. Now? Those are *my* memories of meeting you guys for the first time, but not for either of you."

"We've communicated before," Kahvel pointed out.

"But, never met," Pryllan agreed. "I certainly didn't think I'd see you this soon. And this? You mentioned you traveled with a griffin." The green dragon approached Emerion and lowered her head to within a few feet of Emerion's. "What is your name?"

"Em-Emerion," the poor griffin squawked.

"You have nothing to fear from us," Pryllan said.

Sarah turned to their griffin companion and laid a protective arm on his tawny shoulders. "It's okay, Em. You've met them before."

"No, he hasn't," Kahvel argued.

"Er, back in our time," Steve tried to explain. "Umm, make that the timeline that was messed up."

Kahvel nodded. "Ah."

"Trust me when I say you have nothing to fear from these two," Steve told Emerion. "We know them well. I mean, we will."

Kahvel nodded once, as though that settled the matter, and focused his attention on Steve. "So, what is it you wish from us? You seek something?"

"A tiara …" Steve began.

"I have seen many," the gold dragon pointed out.

"… with a large ruby," Sarah added.

Kahvel shrugged. "Again, not that uncommon."

"… that is shaped like an opening flower," Steve finished. "A rose, if memory serves, provided you have those here."

"A piece of human jewelry with a uniquely-shaped ruby?" Kahvel repeated, frowning. "I can safely say that I have never encountered a jewel such as this."

"Nor have I," Pryllan added. "And you wish to verify if anyone using the Collective has?"

"That's right," Steve nodded. "Got it in one, Pryllan. Kahvel, I'll level with you. We need to find out where this particular tiara is so that it can be returned to its rightful owner. It was taken from her, and she's adamant about getting it returned. The human fugitive everyone is looking for is using a new jhorun. Well, it turns out that, if we can produce this *piece of jewelry*, as you put it, and return it to its rightful owner, then our pal Melvyn will lose his newfound abilities and then we can deal with him. Permanently. What do you think? Will you ask?"

"The simple act of restoring ownership to this item will

remove the human fugitive's jhorun?"

"Yes."

"How? Is this item cursed?"

Steve looked at Sarah and shrugged. "Well, not in the literal sense, but seeing who its owner is, then I suppose it wouldn't be a stretch to call it that."

"Who is the owner?" Kahvel wanted to know.

"Aura," Steve sighed. "Otherwise known as the Fire Ancient."

Kahvel's eyes widened. "You had me at *Ancient*."

The giant golden head lowered to the ground and his eyes closed. Steve took Sarah's hand and, together, they headed for Pryllan.

"I'll bet you didn't expect to see us back here, did you?"

"I was honest before when I said I had forgotten about you. No offense, of course."

Steve nodded. "Of course. Dragons and humans don't typically interact. Think Kahvel will find anything out?"

Pryllan shrugged. "As you just stated, wyverians and humans aren't usually known to be in close proximity with one another. I have to believe no one will know anything about this on the Collective."

"I have some news," Kahvel announced, a few minutes later. His eyes were still closed and he had softened his voice. "There are reports several of my brethren remembered seeing something similar several hundred years ago. I have also informed the Dragon Lord about the importance of finding this item. He is eager to strip the puny biped of his jhorun and confront him. Oh. No offense to you humans, of course."

Steve grinned. "Of course. You know what? There is nothing that I'd like more than to be a fly on the wall when that meeting happens."

Pryllan looked his way. "A fly on the wall? I do not understand the reference."

"He'd love to watch the meeting without anyone knowing he was there," Sarah translated.

"Ah. Understood."

"Finally," Kahvel breathed. His eyes opened and his head

lifted. "I believe I have an answer for you. And a correction. You do not search for a tiara. You search for a crown."

"A crown?" Sarah repeated. "That suggests that one of you saw the tiara being worn by a sovereign?"

"Crown," Kahvel corrected. "And that is true."

"Who was wearing it?" Steve wanted to know.

"We do not know," Kahvel admitted. "What I can tell you is nearly five centuries have passed since this person ruled."

Sarah turned to Steve and held up her hand, ready to give him a high-five. When Steve didn't return the gesture, she sighed.

"Fine. Leave me hanging. What are you moping on about? This is great news! We should be able to figure out who was ruling at that time and determine what happened to the crown. Honey, we finally have a lead!"

Chapter Ten–Griffin Quest

Well, I'm glad you're so very upbeat about this," Steve was saying, after they had bid their farewells to Kahvel and Pryllan. Sarah had decided to teleport the three of them to the southern edge of the valley so that they could have a few moments among themselves. "I don't think you realize how hard it's going to be to identify the queen who was wearing the crown."

"I've seen their Archives," Sarah reminded them. "Past or present, they have meticulous records. I'm sure we can narrow down the possibilities with minimal effort. Then, it'll just be a matter of digging up some information about her, and voila! Instant crown. Easy peasy."

Steve frowned. "I don't know. I guess I'd feel better if we knew what her name was. That way, we could ..."

Ny'Bardonne.

Excuse me? You have her name?

Kahvel just learned it, so I'm passing it on to you.

That's awesome, Pryllan. Thank you!

You're welcome.

"And ... now you're smiling," Sarah noted. "Care to share? What's going on?"

"We're looking for a human queen by the name of Bardonne. Ny'Bardonne."

"There, see? There's absolutely nothing to worry about. I do believe fortune is finally smiling upon us."

The three of them turned, eager to head farther into the forest before teleporting back to the castle, when they came face to face with no fewer than twenty griffins. No one moved or breathed while each group stared at the other. Steve finally let out a massive sigh and playfully smacked Sarah on the arm.

"That's what you get when you make a statement like that. *Fortune is finally smiling on us.* Seriously? You couldn't have executed a better jinx for us."

"This is *not* my fault. How was I supposed to know that a bunch of griffins would be waiting for us inside the forest? Besides, what are you worried about? We can handle ourselves."

Emerion placed himself between the griffins and his parents. He extended a wing and pointed at one griffin in particular.

"We've encountered these griffins before. That one, I do believe, is their leader. What they're doing here is anyone's guess."

"We're here because of *you*, Emerion," the prime stated, squawking irritably. "You're the reason for all of this. I should rip you limb from limb!"

Steve ignited his hands and stepped in front of Emerion. "Not a chance, pal. You'll have to go through me first. And, let me just say that, unfortunately, I have plenty of experience fighting griffins." His hands flared and expanded to his arms. "Don't make me do this."

A fallen tree, one with a six- or seven-foot diameter trunk, shuddered, and lifted into the air. It floated over to the prime and rested in midair, less than two feet from the head griffin.

"You heard me say that Emerion is my son," Sarah began. "If I so much as *think* you're planning on hurting him, then

I'll launch you all into next week."

The prime let out a few nervous squawks. "I think … I think we got off on the wrong foot. No one is attacking anyone. It was a poor choice of words on my part."

Steve pointed an accusatory finger, which just so happened to be presently engulfed in fire. "What are you doing here? What's happened?"

"A dozen of my flock, nothing more than young females, have disappeared."

"And what does this have to do with Emerion?" Sarah asked. "Would these be the same griffins who were fawning over him earlier?"

The prime nodded. "They would."

"I didn't have anything to do with that," Emerion insisted.

"I know you didn't, Em," Sarah told him. "He seems to think you did. I just need to know why."

The griffin leader irritably rustled his wings. "They all left, intending to search for *him* and plead his case to me so that I'd let him join."

"What do we call you?" Sarah wanted to know.

"You may address me as Prime."

"That's a title, not a name," Steve pointed out. "And you're not our prime. Do you think I like to be called *fire thrower* all the time?"

"Very well. You may call me Phaethon."

"Thank you, Phaethon," Sarah began. "What happened to your flock? They left to search for Emerion?"

"It was Chante," Phaethon said. "She fancies herself the most beautiful, the most appealing. All the other females obediently follow along in her wake. So, when Chante set her sights on bringing Emerion to our flock, her followers joined her."

Steve's flames snuffed themselves out. "Okay, you're worried about members of your flock. Young members. What do you say we go find out who took them, or else find out what's preventing them from returning, and why don't we do it together?"

"Ceraon is with them."

"And Ceraon is …?" Sarah prompted.

"My offspring. My only offspring."

"Your daughter," Steve translated.

"Aye. She is like me. Acts first, thinks second. She's …"

"… forthright?" Steve suggested.

"Yes. Something has happened to my daughter, or she would have returned by now. I have all able-bodied griffins searching for signs, but nothing has been found. It's like they've disappeared from the surface."

"Do you really think we can find them?" Steve asked.

Phaethon was silent for a few moments before reluctantly shaking his head. "You're right. I know your griffin isn't to blame. I am worried. Forgive me. This doesn't concern you. We will deal with this ourselves."

Sarah's arm shot out and she pulled the head griffin to a stop. "We have a few tricks up our sleeves that you might find useful. We'll help you search."

"I'm all ears, my dear," Steve told her. "I don't see any way we can help out. That is, unless we happen to stumble across a bloodhound."

Steve vanished. In his place was a russet-colored, floppy-eared hound dog. The canine tilted his head as he stared at Sarah, before turning to look at Emerion, who had approached and was lowering his neck for a closer look. Then, the hound's head dropped to the ground as he stared at his own front paws. A loud baying was heard as the dog howled with frustration.

"What just happened?" Phaethon asked, growing nervous. "Where is your mate? Is he now that slobbery, oddly wrinkled creature?"

"That's him," Sarah admitted. "It's a long story. Give him a few moments to shift back to a human."

It took nearly thirty seconds of angry pacing before the dog disappeared and Steve took its place.

"Serves me right. I know better than to mention the name of a creature. Damn that stone. You-know-who certainly knew what he was doing when he gave that thing to me."

Thunder suddenly rumbled high above their heads in a blue cloudless sky. Steve sighed, shook his head, and then flashed the sky a thumbs-up. Sarah was laughing hysterically.

"Keep it up, Chuckles."

"A dog. Oh, that's priceless. You looked great with wrinkles!"

"Hardy har har. Can we move on, please? Phaethon needs our help. We need to figure out … wait a moment. Maybe I should try going back to that previous form? After all, as a D-O-G, I could probably follow any scent."

Sarah sobered. "What an interesting thought. The problem is, we don't have time to wait for a dog to cover that much ground. So, unless you know of a winged variety, I'm not sure how that helps."

Steve snapped his fingers. "Wings. Of course. I'll change myself into, you know, one of *them*."

Sarah looked up. "Really? You want to change to one of them, here? Is that wise?"

"Why not? I've been one before."

"Gareth isn't here in case something goes wrong," Sarah pointed out.

In response, Steve held up a hand and waited for the green tetrahedron to appear. He gave Sarah a grin and, holding the gem tightly in his hand, closed his eyes. That was all it took. A few moments later, Steve vanished, and was replaced by a form so massive that he could have easily held Emerion in the palm of his hand.

Steve was now a dragon.

He eyed the wyverian body Usol's stone had given him and rose to his feet. Higher and higher he rose, as his body lifted from the ground. Feeling the urge to stretch his back, he watched as two jet black wings unfolded themselves, flapped a few times, and then were returned to lay against his back. His neck, now over twenty feet long, swung gently to the left and right as he took stock of his surroundings. The griffins, squawking with alarm, retreated to the safety of the trees.

Steve sighed contentedly. This was more like it! He surveyed his new form, which was resting on all four legs. Shiny black scales covered his torso and abdomen, a long serpentine tail was coiled by the trunk of a nearby tree, and the tail wing at the tip was currently extended, as though his body thought it might need to make a quick departure.

"How is this possible?" Phaethon demanded. "Are you a wizard?"

"Not really," Steve's deep voice rumbled. The great black head shifted and then lowered until it was less than a dozen feet from the surface. "Let's just say I happen to have a good luck charm."

Emerion approached and gazed up at Steve with awe written all over the griffin's face. "Steve, is that really you?"

The dragon nodded. "None other. Guess you weren't expecting to see this, were you?"

"You're a dragon!"

"It's only temporary," Steve assured him. "And that reminds me about something."

Pryllan?

Yes?

Just to let you know, and in case Rinbok Intherer figures it out, I'm currently in the form of a dragon.

Indeed? May I ask *how*?

It's a long story. I can change to pretty much any form.

Have you always had this ability?

Umm, let's just say that it was a gift I was given.

Very well. I'll inform the Dragon Lord if the call goes out.

Thank you.

"You went quiet," Sarah accused. Her face brightened. "Oh. You were letting Pryllan know, weren't you?"

"I was. Just in case."

"Ah. Gotcha. Are you ready to get going?"

"Yeppers. We help them locate their missing griffins, and presto, we're on our way. Come on, the sooner we get moving, the sooner we can return to our own search. Now, let's see what … oh, I know. Phaethon, can you please come here? The quickest way for me to find someone is to sniff them out," Steve explained. "Dragons have the sharpest olfactory senses of any creature I've ever encountered, and that included the dog you saw before. If I can smell you, then I should be able to track that scent and find whoever took them."

"Aye," Phaethon said, nodding. "Very well. Learn my

scent. Tell me who took my daughter and I promise you I *will* have my revenge."

Several other squawks sounded from all around them.

"It's all of you, isn't it?" Sarah asked, as Steve leaned forward to sniff the griffin. "You've all lost someone, and that's why you're here? Fear not. We'll get to the bottom of this."

"We'll follow you," Phaethon vowed. He turned to his fellow griffin and squawked out orders. "Please. Take the lead."

Steve eyed Sarah and Emerion. "And you two?"

"I'll be okay," Sarah insisted.

"I'll keep her safe," Emerion promised.

Steve nodded. He unfolded his wings and took to the sky, rising steadily and surely. It had been a few years since he had been inside a wyverian's body, but he did remember the basics: don't over analyze the situation and don't underestimate what this reptilian form already knows.

At an altitude of several hundred feet, Steve banked his wings and began a gentle pass of the surrounding landscape and vegetation. Spiraling outward in increasingly larger rotations, he searched for some sign of the missing griffins. Had they interpreted this wrong? He knew Pryllan could detect the tiniest trace, days after their prey had wandered through the area.

On his third pass, his nostrils flared. He had just picked up the scent! And like before, the scent was so strong, and so powerful, that he could actually *see* the scent particles in the air. Faint, shimmering lines appeared before his vision and, acting like mile markers on the roads, told him which way to go.

"I've got something," he reported.

Phaethon was by his side in a flash. "What do you see? Can you tell where they went?"

"You must really know your wyverians," Steve said. "You're right. I can actually see which way they went. For the record, it's *that way.*"

"East," Sarah said, from Emerion's back. They flew in silence for a quarter of an hour before she turned to look at her husband. "Steve, how are you holding up?"

"I'm okay. I remembered more than I thought I did. Remind me to thank Gareth once we get back to our own time. Hey, I've been meaning to ask you something."

Emerion flapped his wings a few times and appeared next to Steve, being careful to avoid the occasional flapping of dragon wings.

"What is it?" Sarah asked.

"These missing griffins, and the one who is acting as their leader. Do you think Melvyn could be responsible?"

"I wouldn't put it past him," Sarah decided. "If he can bend a creeg's will to do his bidding, what's to stop him from trying his luck on a griffin? He knows Emerion travels with us, and is quite an asset. What better way to distract us than by throwing a handful of airborne obstacles our way?"

"Why?" Steve asked. "What good can come of this?"

"Time," a new voice added. Phaethon appeared, flying on Emerion's right. "If what you said is true, and this human wizard is determined to cause mischief, perhaps he already has something in mind and needs more time to implement it?"

"I don't like the sounds of that," Sarah decided.

"Right there with you," Steve added. "Okay, the trail has started descending. Whoever has them is using the trees for cover. There's nowhere for me to land."

"What will you do?" the leader of the griffins asked.

"That's easy. I'll change to something smaller."

"For a human, you have a very impressive jhorun," Phaethon decided.

Steve shrugged. Suddenly, his eyes opened wide.

"Griffins. I'm smelling multiple griffins. They're not moving. Hang on, let me see if I can find out where they're at."

"The canopy is too thick," Emerion said. "We can't see the ground."

"I was told before that a dragon's gaze can pierce many things, and one of them was vegetation. I should be able to see all the way to the forest floor."

"You hope," Sarah smiled.

"Yeah, roger that." Steve turned his attention on the passing treetops. He tried relaxing his eyes and pretended he was looking *through* the many branches, but to no avail. Growling with frustration, he blinked his eyes and was ready to try again when his body took over. The passing scenery suddenly rushed toward him, almost causing him to flinch. Leaves, twigs, and tree trunks rushed by his vision until he was looking at the leaf-strewn forest floor. A breeze appeared inside the forest canopy; his gaze shifted as he automatically started flying in circles high above.

"Do you see something?" Sarah asked, as she and Emerion flew close.

"Maybe. I'm looking at the ground. Something tells me that ... oh, you've gotta be kidding. What in the actual eff?"

"What is it?" Phaethon asked, overhearing.

Steve lifted a muscular foreleg and pointed down and slightly east. "Right there. One, two, three ... six. I see six cages, each holding two griffins."

"Can you tell who's taken them?" Sarah asked.

"I'm looking. I ... there's someone. Human. He's ... no, there's another. And another. Okay, I see about six or seven people milling about. Looks like a camp of some sort, and not a very nice one at that."

"Are they being mistreated?" Sarah asked, horrified.

"That's not what I meant," Steve said, shaking his head. "Their camp. It's dirty. Unclean. Like these people are nothing more than scavengers."

Sarah suddenly slapped both hands over her mouth. "Tell me they don't plan on ...?"

"Eating them?" Steve finished. "No, I don't think so. Hang on a second. Let me see if I can hear what they're saying."

Phaethon and several other griffins passed over Steve's head.

"Using jhorun?" the prime asked.

"No, it's something dragons can do. I did it once before. Everyone be quiet. Let's see if I can hear what ... wow, okay. That was easy. They're talking about silver."

"Silver?" Sarah repeated. "Why?"

Steve's reptilian head shook. "I don't know. The men aren't happy. They claim they aren't getting their fair share of silver. All right, now we've got some fighting. Lots of name-calling. Ooo, that's gonna leave a mark. One guy just smashed something over the head of another dude. Guys? I think they're planning on selling the griffins."

"I will personally rip them to shreds before they're given that chance," Phaethon vowed.

"And I'll help you do it," Steve promised. "That's no way to treat another creature."

"You're human," the griffin leader said. "Well, you *were*. And, Sarah, you still are. Perhaps you can tell me the consequences if I order my griffins to attack. I do not wish to incur the wrath of the human king."

"This attack on the griffins was not sanctioned by Kri'Calin," Steve said.

"Or any other person," Sarah agreed. "These are crimes committed by humans who have allegiance to no one. They're renegades. I say we … look out!"

A spinning bola suddenly punched through the forest canopy and came dangerously close to hitting Phaethon. The leader of the griffins squawked angrily and spun out of the way. He snapped out orders and the griffins dipped below the tree line and vanished. Muffled squawks and cries of alarm sounded from below.

Steve tucked his wings to drop through the trees, when two more sets of the spinning weapons appeared directly in his path. He tensed. The first bola hit one of his front legs and quickly tangled itself up. The second wrapped around his tail, mercifully avoiding his tail wing.

"Steve, are you all right?" Sarah called out.

He held up one of his heavily muscled black forelegs and inspected the damage.

"Whatever this thing is, it's wrapped on there good."

"Do you need to land?" his wife asked.

"No, I've got this. Watch."

Under his gaze, Steve ordered his jhorun to ignite the ropes. Moments later, tiny flakes of ash fluttered down to the forest below, all that was left of the rope. A quick glance at his tail had that rope engulfed in flames, too.

Sarah shouted, "Em, watch out!"

A volley of arrows streaked upward. Emerion froze. Sarah cried out in alarm. Seconds before the arrows could strike, they both vanished. Steve, also in the line of fire, watched as the arrows struck his scaled hide and bounced harmlessly away. A second volley appeared. This time, Steve directed his anger at the threat and unleashed his jhorun.

The arrows detonated and a one hundred square foot section of leaves and twigs was suddenly incinerated, revealing the grass-covered forest floor. Steve could see—without the use of his wyverian senses—the small handful of humans trying furtively to throw up a defense. There, using her jhorun to hold up a large fallen tree trunk, was Sarah. The trunk was swinging wildly about, its sheer size persuading the humans to abandon this foolish attempt at making some quick cash.

Phaethon landed, and a quick swipe from his front claws made short work of the crude cages. Relieved screeches and trills sounded as the newly freed griffins took to the air.

"Let 'em go!" one of the men shouted. "Look at 'im! He's worth his weight in gold, lads. Don't let 'im get away!"

"But, what about the tree, boss? She's wieldin' that thing like a club!"

"She can't fight off all of us. You two, head north. Circle around. You and Grayson try to distract her. She …"

CRACK!

There was a scream, followed by a sound of an object hurtling through the tree branches at high velocity.

"Better forget about Grayson, boss."

"Blast it all to hell! Forget her! Get that griffin! No, the big one! He'll bring in a handsome reward! Get the net shooter! Get all of 'em! Bring that big boy down *now*!"

Intent on reaching Sarah's side, Emerion squawked challenge after challenge at the bad humans. Now they seemed to be firing more projectiles his way. Nets shot out of large, bulky weapons, but the humans were terrible shots. Not one of their nets touched him.

He landed and immediately swiped at a human with one of his avian forelegs. The man's weapon was reduced to splinters. Sarah shouted and he whipped around. The humans had regrouped, aiming bows nocked with arrows. In slow motion, they were released.

Sarah motioned with her hands, and all arrows froze in place. Confused, the humans began to reload, but an instant later one very angry black dragon swooped over the ground.

Steve dodged trees and swooped over uneven terrain, approaching the temporarily frozen arrows and using a wing to swat them all aside. He targeted the first ruffian he spotted and prepared a blast of fire.

"Nuh-uh," the thug warned, as he watched Steve circle about overhead. "Kindly direct your attention to the cage you failed to destroy. What do you see?"

"My daughter," Phaethon seethed, landing beside Emerion. "For this, I will gut you like a fish, you ungainly biped. Oh. Er, no offense, human."

"None taken," Sarah assured them. "Wait, what's that contraption next to the cage?"

"Our crossbow?" the leader sneered. "I had a feeling … so we made certain we were prepared. Like it? See the hanging bag of sand? You'll notice it's already emptying. Once enough weight has been lost, the bag will lift, and the bolt will be released."

"You dare harm my offspring?" Phaethon squawked, outraged.

"I will if you don't let my men go," the leader returned. "*With* our current quota. And don't worry, big boy. We'll be back for you. Our contacts will be dying to get their mitts onto you."

"How much time is left?" Steve's deep voice rumbled.

The scraggly thug looked up at the dragon flying overhead. "Oh, so it speaks? Looks like … about fifteen seconds. You had better decide soon or else there'll be griffin shish kebab on the menu tonight. Stop that growling, beastie. If you don't want anythin' to happen to her, you'd best be …"

The nervous griffin inside the last cage suddenly vanished.

"… wh-what? What just happened? Where did she go?"

Every griffin suddenly landed and hurried to join their leader. Phaethon looked over at Sarah, who nodded, before turning to the trembling human thug.

"You're looking a little worried. Things not going your way?"

TWANG!

The last of the sand flittered to the ground, and the two-foot-long wooden bolt shot out of the weapon, encountered no resistance within the cage, and shot through the other side. It was headed straight for their small group.

Steve's dragon body reacted before he could give it the command. One moment he was circling effortlessly in the sky, trying to figure out how to fire off a safe shot; a split second later, he was dropping like a stone, on a desperate course to intercept the arrow before it could reach his companions.

Sarah was waiting. She saw the arrow heading for them and pushed it away, redirecting it to their right. The bolt, unfortunately, struck a rock on the ground and ricocheted up, slamming into Steve's chest. His wings tucked close to his body and his tail coiled itself around his abdomen.

The dragon's impact with the ground was so strong that it knocked everyone, including the outlaws, off their feet. Surrounding trees were blown backwards, and a large plume of dust and debris filled the air.

"Steve?" Sarah called out. "I am so sorry! I didn't know you were here. Are you all right? Is anything hurt?"

"Just my pride." Steve's voice came from the thick of the dirt cloud. "I just got dumped on my ass. I don't want to know what size of an imprint I just left."

"What about the arrow?" Sarah asked. "What happened to it?"

"It struck me in my stomach, but I'm covered with scales, so no harm done. Are you and Em okay?"

"We're good. We can't see anything, so we're staying put."

"It's not safe," Steve decided. "Stay put. I'm gonna clear the air."

"How?" But in that moment, a brief—but violent—thunderclap sounded from all directions. A blast of wind scattered the dust cloud like a puff of smoke. There was dragon-Steve, crouched in the section of downed trees. All around him were the outlaws, who were trying to beat a hasty retreat.

Steve lowered his neck and stared at the closest person. "I'd suggest dropping that if I were you. You just watched that arrow bounce off my chest. Want to see what happens when I use you as a baseball and knock you into the next county?"

A couple of them turned to defend their companion—until Steve sat back on his haunches and picked his teeth with one of his talons.

"Choose your next actions wisely. I'm getting hungry."

The seven thieves looked at Steve, back at the empty cages, and then at the angry griffins that were lining up next to the dragon. They all screamed like little girls. Then, as one, they all bolted, disappearing into the trees as fast as their legs could carry them.

As one, the griffins turned to look at their prime. Phaethon nodded once in his direction, and again at Sarah. Then, he turned to his flock.

"Go easy on them," Steve urged. Gone was the huge dragon. He was just now taking a few uneasy steps on human legs. "When you get that many humans traveling together, they're bound to do some stupid things. I'd like to think that they didn't know what they were doing."

Phaethon turned to Steve and bowed. "Thank you for your help. It will not be forgotten. Where is your griffin? I don't see him anywhere."

Confused, Steve turned to see for himself. Sarah was there, heading toward him now.

"Where's Emerion? He should be here," Sarah was saying. "Once I saw the griffin in the cage about to be skewered, I teleported Phaethon's daughter out of harm's way."

"And where did you put her?" Phaethon asked. "Where is my daughter?"

"They were both just here," Sarah explained. "I told Em to take care of her. They should both be close. Em? Emerion? Where are you?"

Steve held out a hand and watched as the green emerald appeared. "Okay, I need the form of another tracker. This time let's pick something that's not as big as a dragon, 'kay?"

"I don't get it," Sarah was saying. "They should be here.

Something must have spooked them!"

"And if it was the sheriff?" Steve asked.

Sarah's face paled. "Oh, no! I hadn't thought of that."

Phaethon let out a series of squawks and trills. Griffins began organizing themselves, lining up in rows of four. Less than a minute later, every griffin present, including the females, were waiting quietly in their formations.

Sarah turned to Steve. He was once more a dragon, but nearly one third as big as the black form he had adopted before. This species of dragon was thin, wingless, and red. Steve's head lifted and he turned north.

"See anything?" Sarah asked.

"I'm watching the jerks who were just here. It's just them. I can see all seven. They're sticking together, which makes them easier to spot."

"What about Em?" Sarah asked.

Steve slowly swung his neck in a circle. "I can smell them. Two griffins, both around the same age. They're together. I haven't located them yet."

"Are they moving?" Phaethon asked.

Steve was silent as he shifted his eyes and tried to get them to focus on distant objects. "Yes. Away from us."

"Something *has* to be pursuing them," Sarah insisted, "but what?"

"Everyone be quiet," Steve ordered. "I'm trying to see if I can hear anything besides the two of them. If something is chasing them, then I should be able to hear *something*."

"This is not a good idea," Steve suddenly heard Emerion whisper. "What if we're caught?"

"No one will even know we're gone," the second griffin was saying. This one was definitely a female. "Would you relax? We're almost there. See? There's the stone! What we're looking for is buried inside. Come, come, you're big and strong. Break this boulder open."

"I hear them both," Steve whispered. "The girl griffin …"

"… my daughter," Phaethon haughtily corrected. "Ceraon."

"Right. Ceraon. She's trying to get Emerion to smash a boulder."

"She wants him to do *what?*" Sarah asked, certain she had heard him wrong.

"That makes no sense," Phaethon said, at the same time.

Steve shook his head. "They're talking again. Sounds like there's something buried inside the rock. Ceralon says ..."

"... Ceraon," Phaethon corrected.

"... she discovered it while flying through the area, weeks ago. She investigated, tried to get whatever this thing is *out,* but only succeeded in rolling the stone over. She lacks the strength to roll it back. She ... okay, Em just did that. Now he's kicking the snot out of it with his back legs. I really don't think that will ... I'll be a monkey's uncle. It just broke. They found something red. That's all I can see. Okay, okay, they're headed back here. Do we let them know we watched the whole thing?"

"I'll deal with this," Phaethon declared. "I will find out what is going on without arousing suspicion. Mark my words."

Several minutes later, the two griffins arrived. Steve was back in his human form, and he was pretending to talk with Sarah. Emerion hurried over to Sarah's side and nuzzled her arm.

"There you are," Sarah said, letting out a genuine sigh of relief. "I was worried, Em. What happened to you? Where'd you go?"

"Well, I ... that is to say, we ...?"

"We just went for a walk," the second griffin said, growing defensive. "We didn't do anything wrong! Why are you hassling us?"

Steve glanced at Sarah, who then shot Phaethon a look which said if he didn't deal with his daughter, then she would.

"Let's see it," the prime stated.

"See what?" Ceraon asked.

"This object you pulled out of the stone. I will take it now."

"I don't know what you're talking about," Ceraon sighed, throwing in an exasperated squawk for good measure.

"And the boulder you had Emerion break?" Steve casually asked, eliciting a squawk of surprise from the prime's daughter.

Emerion automatically hung his head, but Ceraon tried to defend herself.

"You had no right to spy on me! That's rude!"

A loud, piercing squawk made everyone jump. Phaethon approached his offspring and indicated the ground.

"Place it there. *Now.*"

Steve had to suppress a smile. Phaethon's daughter looked like she had every intention of rebelling, but then again, the look on the prime's face dared her to try. She reluctantly retrieved the object from somewhere under a wing and let the item fall to the ground. Her nose lifted and she stormed away. Phaethon glanced at two of his fellow griffins. Both nodded and hurried after her.

"What is it?" Steve asked, as he leaned down to see for himself what was concealed within the stone. "It's red, so it could be ... wait a moment. Sarah? We've seen one of these things before. Why, it's one of those twisted rubies! You know, the kind that is powering Breslin's magical hammer? Sarah? What's the matter?"

Sarah was staring at the stone with a look of horror on her face. "Steve, if that's what I think it is, then I think Melvyn just messed with our timeline. Again!"

Steve shook his head. "No, I think it's just a fluke. I seem to recall the original ruby was found by Dirgath and Tirgath, one of the zweigelans. This can't possibly be the same."

"Do we know this for certain?" Sarah asked. "What if ... what if this ruby was supposed to be found in a certain place at a certain time, and now thanks to us, it won't happen?"

Steve groaned. "Someone remind me to feed the sheriff to the next dragon we see, huh?"

Chapter Eleven–A Jeweled Twist

When we find him, I'm gonna pound him into the ground," Steve vowed, as he paced in front of his wife. "Do I even want to know just how many more of these unpleasant messes are waiting for us to fix? Every time I think we're gaining some ground, we're thrown another curve ball."

"It'll be all the more satisfying to tell him in person he's been thwarted at every turn," Sarah countered.

"What are we supposed to do?" Steve asked. He pointed at the spiraled ruby. "That thing isn't supposed to be discovered for another hundred years!"

Sarah held up a finger. "Not necessarily true. That particular gem *has* been discovered, just not by us."

"It looks like a peculiar ruby," Phaethon decided. "I'm confused. Does it mean something more than that?"

Steve nodded. "Way more, I'm afraid. But, it's nothing for you guys to worry about. We can handle this. Phaethon? I do believe you've got some hunting to do, don't you?"

"Hunting?" Phaethon repeated, tilting his head. "I don't think … oh. Oh! As a matter of fact, I do." He turned and squawked out a set of instructions. A dozen adult griffins immediately sprinted into the heart of the forest. Not one of them, Steve noted, made a sound as they were running. "Ceraon!"

The young griffin that had accompanied Emerion approached. Her head hung low as she kept her eyes on the ground. Emerion rustled his feathers and moved to intercept, but not before Sarah placed a hand on his shoulder.

"Stay here, Em. This isn't for you."

"But, I accompanied her. I should be by her side. She doesn't deserve to be reprimanded for actions that I …"

The griffin leader suddenly turned to Emerion. "Was it your suggestion she follow you into the forest?"

"Er, no."

"Did you, perhaps, insinuate bad things would happen to her if she didn't accompany you?"

"Huh? Of course not."

"Ceraon? Speak."

"I have nothing to say to you," the adolescent female snapped. "I had to get away, at least for a little while. I needed to be *me*. I needed to be *free*. I just can't with …"

"Enough!" Phaethon snapped. His daughter fell silent. He looked at Steve and then angled his beak at his offspring. "Is there anything you wish to ask her?"

Steve nodded. "As a matter of fact, there is. Ask her how she knew where to look for that ruby? How did she know it was there?"

Phaethon turned to his daughter. "Answer the question."

"I don't want to."

"I wasn't giving you a choice, youngling. Answer the question!"

"Fine! I knew it was there because I overheard a human saying he had lost it somewhere in the area. So, I looked."

"And when you saw you couldn't get into the boulder, you enlisted Emerion's help, is that it?" Sarah asked.

Ceraon nodded her head. "*I* found that gemstone. Father, I want it *back*."

"You do realize you were led there, right?" Steve asked.

"That biped lost it, I found it," Ceraon repeated. "It's mine and I'd like it back now."

"A human lost it?" Sarah repeated. "Inside a boulder?"

The young griffin female fell silent. "Well …"

"That ruby has been there for many years," Steve told the griffin. "I'm sorry, but it has to be returned to the owner."

Phaethon nodded, pleased. "Good riddance. Now, we will be returning to our nests. Go in peace."

Steve, Sarah, and Emerion gave the prime a curt nod. Then, in a frantic flapping of wings, the griffins were airborne. As they flew away, they could hear Phaethon's daughter squawk her outrage at having to give up her precious ruby.

"How are we going to make sure this stone falls into the right hands?" Emerion asked. "Who does it belong to?"

"Tirgath and Dirgath," Steve answered. "They live to the south, in a nest high up the side of a mountain."

"Dragons?" Emerion asked.

Sarah held up a finger. "Just one. They are zweigelan: a two-headed dragon."

"Oh. I didn't know they existed."

"You've got a lot of catch-up to do, pal," Steve told the griffin. He looked at Sarah. "What are we supposed to do, stop by and hand it to them?"

Sarah shook her head. "We can't. I think we need to keep to the original timeline as much as possible. They need to discover it for themselves."

"And how are we supposed to ensure that happens?" Steve wanted to know. "Where could we hide it that we'd know for certain the zweigelan would find it?"

"I'm working on that," Sarah admitted.

"What does it matter whether or not the two-headed dragon finds this jewel?" Emerion asked. "It's rather fetching. I can see why Ceraon fancies it."

Sarah hefted the jewel in her hand. "This ruby plays a very important part of Lentarian history. It powers our friend's Narian hammer. Breslin obtains this jewel by outsmarting the zweigelan many years from now. If that doesn't happen, Nar will never be discovered, and it will create a mess that, quite frankly, I'm not sure we'd be able to solve."

"What's so important about that hammer?" Emerion asked.

"It can pulverize stone with just a few swings," Steve said. "It will remain light in the hands of its wielder. And, it only responds to those who have Narian blood. Now, this might not sound like a big deal to you or me, but to the dwarves it's priceless."

"Don't forget the armor," Sarah reminded him. "Nar is known far and wide for their armor. Impenetrable and uncrushable, it can protect its owner from practically all weapons. Every dwarf clan in existence wants to get their hands on that technology."

Emerion's head tilted as he looked at the ground. "And that gemstone is capable of disrupting, what, its discovery?"

Steve patted the griffin on his shoulder. "Precisely. That's not to say Nar wouldn't be discovered somewhere down the line, but it's just something else that will make our lives, the *present*, more difficult."

Sarah picked up the ruby whorl. "I don't suppose there's any way to tell if this is the actual gem that belonged to Tirgath and Dirgath, is there?"

"Not unless we ask them," Steve answered, shrugging. "And even then, I doubt they'd tell us, since at the moment, they hate all dragons and pretty much everything that isn't a zweigelan."

"What if we do nothing and simply put the ruby back where it was found?"

Steve shook his head. "It was busted out of a boulder, remember? If we somehow conceal this inside another boulder, how would we know it would be noticed? We have no idea how the zweigelan singled out that particular boulder. As much as I'd like to ignore this whole mess, we can't."

"How in the world did Melvyn find this?" Sarah demanded, growing angry. "How could he be so effective in creating problems for us?"

"You heard Eion. He's got the power of persuasion. And, he's been on the loose for at least six weeks. No, this isn't something we can ignore. We have to act."

Sarah sat down on a nearby rock. Emerion lowered himself to the grass-covered ground and watched her.

"All is not lost. Let's think about this. We know Breslin found that gem in Dirgath and Tirgath's nest several years ago."

Steve nodded. "That's right. He's told me he was part of some group following a map on a boy's back."

"A map on a boy's back?" Emerion repeated, amazed. "Is this normal?"

"Far from it," Steve told the griffin. "I won't go into details, but the boy's mark was intentionally put there. In essence, the mark was nothing more than a map to Nar."

Emerion rustled his feathers. "Wait. I'm confused. If the mark is a map to Nar, then why are you worried about whether or not the city would be found? It sounds to me as though the steps were already set in motion to discover the city. How could a misplaced jewel disrupt that?"

Out of answers, Steve looked at his wife for help.

"I see where you're going with this," Sarah began. "And trust me, I like your line of thinking, Em."

"What do we do?" Steve wanted to know. "Is Emerion right? Can we just ignore this?"

"No. This may not be as bad as we originally thought. Emerion has brought up a good point. The mark? The map? It points to various places to find the components of the hammer. Breslin was led to the nest, so all we really have to do is get the gem in zweigelan hands and I think we're good to go."

"Can you just teleport it straight to them?" Steve asked. "We don't need to be seen, do we?"

"We could, but since we don't know whether the manner the gem was discovered plays a part or not, we probably need to stick to the original method of discovery as much as possible. In this case, we need to make sure Dirgath and Tirgath discover the ruby inside a rock."

"Can you teleport it inside?" Steve asked. "That shouldn't be a problem, right?"

"I've been thinking about that. I believe we can make them *think* it was found within a stone."

"How?"

Sarah held out a hand. "I'll tell you when we get there. Em, latch on. Good. Now, is everyone ready? Deep breaths. We're heading south."

Steve felt a slight jerk, as if he had stumbled, and just like that, Lake Raehón and the large grass-covered valley disappeared, replaced by a veritable mountain of solid rock directly on their right. Tall pine trees surrounded them on three sides, with a small clearing visible to the east. Sarah automatically held a finger to her lips and motioned the others forward. At the edge of the clearing, she hesitated and then pointed up the side of the mountain.

"There. Do you see it?"

"What am I looking for?" Emerion wanted to know.

"The zweigelan's nest. It's there, about two-thirds of the way up. At least, that's where it is in our time."

"Do we know if Dirgath and Tirgath are living there now?" Steve asked.

Sarah shrugged. "Dragons live for such a long time that I just assumed they would be. Hey, here's an idea. Switch back to that bloodhound. See if you can smell it."

"I don't want to be a dog again," Steve complained.

That's all it took. Steve vanished, and a dog appeared, only this time, it wasn't a bloodhound, but a frilly white poodle. Steve's new form yapped angrily before lifting its nose and turning to look at the distant mountaintop. The fluffy white pooch gave Sarah another glare before switching back to his human form.

"Would you stop that?"

"No one forced you to pick a poodle," Sarah said, between giggles.

"I don't know how you're doing it, but that's gotta be on you. Do you really think I'd want to look like that? You made me say ... oh, no you don't. Not again. I'm not falling for that. Fine, you win. Yes, they're still up there. I could smell them. Well, let me rephrase. *Something* is living up there.

"How do we know which one?" Emerion asked. "The face of the cliff looks like it's riddled with caves."

"We don't have to know which one," Sarah countered.

"We're not planning on going up there. We're going to get it to come to us."

"Er, do we know how?" Steve asked. "And how will we make it look for that ruby?"

"That'll be the easy part," Sarah promised. "Right now, spread out and look for a couple of large rocks that are next to each other."

Steve looked up. "Huh? What for?"

"Trust me. I have an idea."

"How large must these stones be?" Emerion asked.

Sarah shrugged. "They need to be heavier than most people can lift. Why? Do you see some?"

"I do," Emerion confirmed. "Look north, about twenty meters away. I see four large boulders within close proximity to each other."

Sarah shook her head. "No, I think these stones will have to be inside the forest. Otherwise, why wouldn't the zweigelan have discovered it before now? No, we need some stones that look as though they could have broken off each other."

"So that the dragon will think it was embedded in the stone," Steve realized. "I think that'll totally work. In that case, come on. Let's check the area."

"And stay quiet," Sarah urged. "No talking. We already know dragons have excellent hearing."

The three of them tip-toed away from the clearing and headed into the forest. Keeping mostly together, they started to search for a suitable place for the zweigelan to 'discover' its new favorite jewel.

"What about this?" Emerion asked, twenty minutes later.

"What did you find?" Steve asked, as he joined the griffin.

Emerion extended a wing and pointed at a jumble of large rocks. "Maybe it was some type of formation? Perhaps a pillar?"

"I think that's perfect. Let's ask the boss, shall we?"

"Oh, that'll do nicely," Sarah said, as she inspected the mass of stones. "Em is right. I think this was once a larger pillar of some type, and it has since broken."

Steve pointed at the closest chunk of rock. "Okey dokey, put the ruby there, we'll draw out Tirgath and Dirgath, and lead them over here. They find the gem, and presto, problem solved. Er, right?"

"We're not that far away from their nest," Sarah said. "In order to sell this, I think we need to break up one of these larger ones. Chances are, Dirgath and Tirgath have seen this before. Wouldn't you be suspicious if a gemstone suddenly shows up out of the blue? No, we have to make sure we don't give them any excuse to *not* pick this up."

"My flames are strong," Steve said, as he eyed the five-hundred-pound boulder, "but they're not that strong. How are we going to break it?"

Sarah closed her eyes and steadied her breathing. A few seconds later, one of the broken pieces lifted from the ground.

"Good, I can lift it if I have to."

"What's your plan?" Steve asked.

Sarah leveled a look at her two companions. "Emerion, you're going to battle Steve."

Steve's eyes widened. "Say *what*?"

"Not for real, of course. You guys are going to make enough noise to draw out the zweigelan. They are going to watch you guys battle, and during all the fighting, one of the stones will be broken."

"I already told you that my flames aren't strong enough to break open rocks," Steve pointed out.

"Which is why you'll be a griffin."

"This stone is much larger than the one I broke before," Emerion said, as he rustled his wings. "Plus, it doesn't appear to be limestone, so I don't think it'll readily break."

"It does look like granite," Sarah conceded. "Hmm."

Steve cleared his throat. "Look, let's make this as easy as possible. I'm going to be a … wow, almost said it. I'm not ready to change just yet. So, I'll become one of *him*. Let's make the fight over the jewel. Give it to Em. We can battle away, or pretend to, and during the fight, whomever is holding the ruby can 'accidentally' drop it."

"That'll work," Sarah said, nodding. "Perfect. Emerion, are you ready? Steve, Wonder Twin powers *activate*! Form of a …?"

Steve sighed. "Not funny, woman. One griffin coming … *squawk!*"

An adult griffin appeared in Steve's place. It looked at Emerion, squawked a second time, and then took to the air.

"Here, Em," Sarah said, presenting the spiraled jewel to the griffin, "take good care of this thing. Use your best guess when it comes to dropping it. We want the zweigelan to see it."

"I will."

For the next ten minutes, Emerion and Steve each let loose with a barrage of insults. Emerion, being the largest and most adept flyer, kept taunting Steve by performing barrel rolls around him. Steve, for his part, would pretend to be outraged and give chase. The two of them occasionally dipped below the treetops, only to emerge moments later, both squawking like crazy.

"Come on, you big lug!" Steve squawked out. "I thought you were a decent flyer! Don't be such a crybaby. Come get me! Whoa!"

Emerion tucked his wings and dropped like a rock. A split second later, he hurtled past Steve, but not before both his wings made contact with Steve's beak.

"Oh, no you didn't," Steve said, more shocked than anything. He didn't know if a griffin could smile, but he was certainly giving it his best effort. "Did you just bitch-slap me?"

"What are you going to do about it?" Emerion teased.

Sensing the game just shifted into a competition to see who was the better flyer, Steve pumped his wings in an attempt to catch his adopted son. However, what became painfully obvious was that he was severely outmatched in the air. It was no wonder, since Emerion had been flying for nearly five years.

Movement in his peripheral vision caught his attention. Sarah was waving at him, so Steve decided it was time to take the battle to the ground. He caught Emerion's eye and pointed a wing straight down.

"The next round is on the ground. I think Sarah has something to tell us. Keep up the aerobatics, Em. You're doing great!"

Emerion squawked appreciatively and hurtled by Steve a second time. As before, the tips of his feathers made contact with his beak.

"Go ahead, you little showoff," Steve scowled. "I dare you try that again."

Emerion complied. The much larger griffin twisted about in the air and before Steve knew what was happening, Emerion was zipping by him again. This time, he felt a slight sting on his hind quarters.

"Booger. All right, here we go. You know what to do?"

Emerion spun through the air above him. "I'm ready."

The two bickering griffins continued to squawk and screech at each other as they raced along, barely higher than the treetops. However, before they could reach the area where they knew the two-headed dragon was hiding, a new voice brought both of them up short.

"Fighting is never the answer. Cease this frivolous behavior at once."

Steve was so surprised he pulled up and pumped his wings in an attempt to stop. Emerion had already circled about and was staring, beak agape, at the newcomer. When Steve finally located the speaker, his eyes widened with shock.

It was another griffin, one so unique neither he nor Emerion had ever seen the like before. The newest flyer was the same size as Steve's griffin form, but that's where the similarities ended: there was not one set of wings, but *two*. The primary wings were located somewhat closer to the shoulders, the smaller secondary wings were near the flank, and each set was flapping independently from the other.

Steve whistled with amazement, which came out as a high trill in his griffin body. Having four wings wasn't even the most shocking aspect, either. The four-winged griffin was gold, and not just a gold color, but looked like it was made of solid, twenty-four karat gold. Its lustrous golden complexion was so shiny in the sunlight that Steve had to look away.

"Griffins should never fight among themselves," the gold griffin declared, giving Steve a scornful look. It twisted its neck and it gave Emerion the same admonishing look. "What could possibly be worth fighting over?"

Sensing an opportunity to stick with the plan, Steve pointed a wing at Emerion and screeched an insult at him. "He took my ruby. I want it back!"

Emerion's eyes widened. His head tilted, as if Steve had grown his own second set of wings. Then, realization dawned and the much larger griffin nodded. "I did no such thing. I found it, therefore it's mine."

"You took it from me," Steve continued, raising his voice. "You say you found it? Hah! You broke into my home, er, nest, and took it!"

"I only borrowed it," Emerion complained, throwing a sneer into his voice.

"When you borrow something, and you don't tell anyone about it, well, that's stealing," Steve sighed, warming up to the game.

"Whatever this gemstone is, or whatever it means to you two," the golden griffin replied, "is it worth ruining such a beautiful friendship over? No, of course not."

"Who are you?" Emerion asked.

"You may call me Zieth."

"Zieth," Steve repeated. "Have you always looked like that?"

"What's wrong with my appearance?" Zieth asked, as he looked down at himself. "Is there something wrong?"

"I've never seen a griffin such as you before," Emerion decided, telling the truth.

"I resemble you two, but am not a griffin. I am a graeus."

"Graeus?" Steve repeated. "I don't think I've heard of the term before. Sorry."

"How can you, a griffin, not have heard of a graeus?" Zieth asked. "Never mind. It's none of my concern. You two are done fighting?"

"What about my ruby?" Steve complained.

"What about it? Could you not let your companion have it?"

"If I can't have it, then no one should," Steve decided.

"Fine," Emerion grumped. He produced the ruby, from a location Steve couldn't determine, and held it up in the air.

"No one gets it."

The ruby was dropped. It disappeared through the treetops and moments later, they heard a soft *thump* as it struck the ground.

"You owe me a ruby," Steve squawked, as he turned to fly away.

"In your dreams," Emerion shot back.

Zieth sighed and pumped his wings, gaining altitude. He disappeared into the clouds and was no more.

* * *

"How'd we do?" Steve asked. He was back in human form and had doubled back once he was certain he was no longer visible from the ground. "Think Tirgath and Dirgath will fall for it?"

Emerion chose that moment to touch down. He approached Steve and nuzzled his side. "I do apologize for slapping you in the face with my feathers."

Steve laughed. "It's okay. I know you're a better flyer than I am. You didn't have to make it look so easy to outperform me. That smack on the ass? Hmm. You'd better watch yourself, boyo."

Emerion trilled with laughter. Steve felt a tap on his arm and looked at his wife.

"You asked about the zweigelan? Would you be happy to learn that you and Emerion did such a great job that Tirgath and Dirgath already have the ruby?"

"What? Really? What did they do, wait for the moment we left the area?"

"That's exactly what they did," Sarah confirmed. "They heard the ruby hit the ground and it was all they could do to contain themselves. Let me ask you something. Who were you two talking to out there?"

Steve and Emerion shared a look before turning to Sarah.

"You didn't see him?" Steve asked.

"He was rather hard to miss," Emerion added.

Sarah shook her head. "I didn't see anyone but you two. Then again, the sun was in my eyes most of the time. Why?

Who was it?"

"He said his name was Zieth," Steve said. "Sarah, this was a gold griffin!"

"Like a golden statue come to life," Emerion added.

"Really? I didn't see anything like that down here. A gold griffin. How about that?"

"He said he wasn't a griffin," Steve recalled. "Em, what did he call himself?"

"Graeus."

Sarah shook her head. "I've never heard the word before. Wait. Could that have been Eion in disguise?"

A breeze appeared. It whipped along the ground and picked up leaves and twigs. Twirling about high in the air, the swirling detritus formed letters: N-O.

"Was that one of your siblings?"

N-O.

"Was that something else in disguise?" Sarah asked.

N-O.

"Was it really a four-winged griffin?" Steve wanted to know.

Y-E-S.

"Four wings?" Sarah repeated. "A four-winged *golden* griffin?"

"Apparently called a graeus," Steve said. "Well, whatever it was, we'll worry about it later. I say we head back to the castle. I'd like to see if the king and queen can shed any light on Ny'Bardonne."

Sarah nodded. She held out a hand and waited for the others to take hold. "The R'Tal Express is heading out. First stop, the castle."

The Great Hall appeared. Typically, Sarah wouldn't choose a busy locale for one of her safe zones. But, Sarah had wisely chosen the corner farthest from the two golden thrones as the destination for her teleportative jump. Steve breathed a sigh of relief.

That particular area might have been vacant, but the rest of the hall couldn't say the same. More than a hundred peasants were seated in semi-circular rows facing the thrones. It seemed the king and queen had been hosting a public gathering, trying to quell the growing uneasiness among the villagers about an alarming number of raids, carried out by … griffins. The townsfolk wanted the Kri'yans to do a better job of keeping their skies clear.

When Emerion accidentally backed into a stack of chairs and knocked them over, pandemonium ensued.

"It's a griffin!" one villager exclaimed, rising to his feet. "And in the castle! I knew it! I knew they were after me!"

"Oh, hush!" the man's wife said. "You know nothing of the sort."

"Run fer yer lives!" an older fellow screamed. "Them beasties will rip us to shreds!"

The citizens ignored the frantic orders of the guards and abandoned the Great Hall. Guards herded the throng of townsfolk to various castle exits and watched, bemused, as the frightened villagers disappeared from sight.

"You three," Sauer said, shaking his head. "I had forgotten you travel with a griffin now. Lousy timing that you appeared in our midst just as the king was to address everyone's concerns."

Steve eyed the king and shrugged. "I'm so very sorry, Your Majesty."

Kri'Calin waved a dismissive hand. "How is your mission? Making much progress?"

Sarah nodded. "As a matter of fact, we are. What can you tell us about Ny'Bardonne?"

"Ny'Bardonne?" the queen repeated, confused. She rose from her throne and approached. "Why do you say that name? What do you want to know about her?"

Husband and wife turned their full attention to the queen.

"Everything you can tell us about her reign," Steve implored.

"It's odd you should mention that name," Ny'Alena said. "Perhaps we should continue this in the Antechamber?"

Kri'Calin nodded. "As you wish, beloved."

Once everyone was seated in the king's private chambers, the queen took off her crown and rubbed her temples.

"Ny'Bardonne is a name that isn't often brought up in our history."

"Why?" Sarah wanted to know. "I mean, are we allowed to ask?"

Kri'Calin nodded. "Of course. It's just that … you might not like the answer. Ny'Bardonne was kidnapped and married, against her will."

"What?" Steve demanded.

Emerion squawked with alarm.

"You heard me," the king said, nodding. "She was taken, hidden from her people, and when war became inevitable, implored her husband …"

"You mean her kidnapper," Sarah interrupted.

"… to step in to keep the peace. You see, by that time, much to her surprise, Bardonne had fallen in love with her captor. She had come to love the land, the people, and the responsibilities she had been given as queen."

"Whoa, are you saying the king was the one responsible for kidnapping this woman?"

"I am, Steve," Kri'Calin confirmed. "Only, at the time of her kidnapping, he was but a prince."

"Oh, because that makes it better," Sarah scowled. "Men. Why do they always think they can get away with everything?"

Ny 'Alena snorted with amusement and had to look away.

"Her people? Who were they?" Emerion suddenly asked.

Kri'Calin smiled. "Well done, Emerion. Her people were the Fae."

It was Sarah's turn to gasp with shock. "Wait. By any chance was Ny'Bardonne a princess?"

Kri'Calin nodded. "Aye. Only daughter of King … King … blast, I can't remember his name. Bardonne was their only daughter, so you can imagine things did not sit well with the Fae king. He demanded her return, but by the time the Fae learned of her location, the princess had fallen for the prince."

Sarah smiled. "How sweet! It … no! No way, not sweet! It's kidnapping, plain and simple."

"How do you know of this story?" Ny'Alena asked. "It has been stricken from our history. The Fae no longer want anything to do with us, and have essentially disappeared from the kingdom."

"We know more than we should," Sarah admitted. She turned to Steve. "They never told us her name, did they?"

Steve shook his head. "Nope."

"Who are you talking about?" the king wanted to know.

Steve held a finger to his lips. "Mum's the word, I'm sorry to say."

Kri'Calin sighed. "Very well. Now you know who she is, and how she ended up one of our past queens. Can I ask why you need to know?"

Sarah took a deep breath and pointed at the queen's crown, sitting on a side table next to her chair.

"Your Majesty, what do you know about the history of crowns worn by the kings and queens of old? For example, would that crown have been worn by Ny'Bardonne?"

"I can answer this," Kri'Calin said, eliciting an appreciative nod from the queen. "I cannot speak for other kingdoms, but in Lentari, reigning monarchs are given the option to keep their crowns, thus paving the way for a new one to be created for the next ruler, or passing it on as a way of honoring the next in line."

"And do we know what Ny'Bardonne did?" Steve asked, growing excited.

"I'll answer your question if you answer one for me," the king stated. When Steve nodded, Kri'Calin continued. "Ny'Bardonne never considered herself a true queen. She viewed herself as nothing more than a consort, so when it came time for their successors to take over the throne, she gave up her crown willingly."

Sarah asked. "She wasn't allowed the opportunity to keep it?"

"She was," Ny'Alena confirmed. "And, as Kri'Calin said, she refused."

"Did she return to her people?" Emerion asked.

The queen shook her head. "That was the belief of many, but Ny'Bardonne surprised them all by remaining by her husband's side. After all, she bore him five sons and loved her family more than anything."

"We were told she didn't keep her crown," Emerion reminded them. "Would we then have to know which queen served next? Did she use that crown, or perhaps craft one of her own? And would the crown have been buried with one of these future queens, wherever that is?"

As one, Steve and Sarah turned back to the king and queen. Ny'Alena, it would seem, didn't know, as she was staring at her husband. Kri'Calin finally smiled.

"First, let me answer the question of where we bury …? Past kings and queens are in the Royal Vault. And, since I know you'll be asking me where that is, it's directly beneath our feet."

"How far beneath our feet?" Steve wanted to know.

Ny 'Alena captured—and held—Kri'Calin's eyes. "Thirty or forty meters, isn't it, my love?"

"Aye. Every king or queen who has ever ruled has their own place to rest for eternity."

"And what happens if their, er, casket has to be opened?"

"Expressly forbidden," Kri'Calin reported. "The Royal Family will never be disturbed during their long slumbers."

Steve's hopes fell. "That means no one has opened a casket—ever?"

"Not once," Kri'Calin confirmed. After a few moments, he smiled again.

"Is there something I'm missing?" Steve asked.

"There is."

Sarah's face lit up. "Wait! You know, don't you? You know where to find this crown!"

"Your theory was quite good," the king said, as he took off his own crown and studied it. "Many of our kings and queens are, in fact, buried with their crowns. However, as of late, many believed being buried with a priceless piece of treasure, inlaid with diamonds, rubies, and pearls, and fashioned out of gold and other precious metals, might be too tempting for a grave robber to pass up. No, what Lentarian monarchs have been doing for a while now is simply making some type of addition to the existing crown. Maybe it's just a jewel, or perhaps the addition of a symbol on the band? Perhaps replace the cap's material with something else? The possibilities are endless."

"How does this help us?" Steve asked.

Kri'Calin chuckled. "Haven't I mentioned it yet? I'm sorry, it must've slipped my mind. The crown Ny'Bardonne wore during her reign is right there. My own lovely wife has worn it for over twenty years now."

Chapter Twelve–Aura's Crown?

You're kidding. Are you suggesting that what we've been looking for has literally been staring at us all this time?"

"It certainly sounds like something Usol would do," Sarah said. She leaned forward in her chair to study the crown. "It just doesn't look like what I expected."

"Do continue," Ny'Alena urged. "You thought my crown would be different? Is it not beautiful? Are you suggesting it's ... *ugly*?"

Steve watched the color drain from his wife's face. "Good god, no. She wasn't implying that at all, Your Majesty. She simply meant ..."

"I've seen some other crowns before," Sarah continued, after he trailed off, "and ... Steve? Do you want to help me out here?"

"What's she's trying to say is that all crowns are different," Steve began, striving for a diplomatic approach. "If this is what we think it is, then that means our search is over.

Only … Sarah? Look at it. I don't see any rubies on it."

"Of course, there aren't," the queen laughed. "There haven't been any rubies on it since, oh, way before my time."

"It's gotta be enchanted," Steve decided. "That's the only explanation. Usol must've cast some type of spell on it."

"Provided we have the right one, I'm inclined to agree," Sarah decided.

Kri'Calin pointed at the crown. "What's so special about this one? Why do you seek it?"

"You're familiar with the four Ancients?" Steve asked.

Sarah reached out to pluck the queen's crown off the table when she hesitated. "May I?" Ny'Alena nodded her permission. "If we're right, this crown was once worn by Aura, the Fire Ancient."

"Oros," Kri'Calin said.

"Aura," Sarah corrected. "But, she's gone by both names." She held up the bejeweled iron band that was Ny'Alena's crown. "The problem is, there's supposed to be a flower-shaped jewel on this, and I don't see anything of the sort."

"Perhaps it fell off?" Emerion suggested.

Steve shook his head. "Off a crown? And one that belonged to an Ancient? I doubt it."

Sarah rotated the circlet in her hands. "If it fell off, there'd be an empty place for it. Or, let's say you're right, and the Alchos stone was once on here but fell off. You'd think they would try and replace it, but no. Look at this. Every inch or so, there's a gem. They're all equidistant from one another. Look, this one's a diamond, and the next, a sapphire. Then, the pattern repeats until it makes it all the way around, and they're all roughly the same size. There's no place to fit the ruby. It'd throw off the symmetry."

"Maybe a piece of the crown fell off?" Steve suggested. "And that piece held the gem?"

"More than likely, your first theory is right," Sarah told him. "There must be some type of spell on it. Steve, let me ask you something." She held up the crown. "Do you remember the current queen wearing this?"

Steve nodded. "I do."

"No, not *that* queen, but the current Kri'yans. I'm not

talking about the ones who were sitting on the thrones the last time we were in the castle in our time."

"Oh. You know what? Now that you mention it, I seem to recall more color. And it was, I don't know, poofier, if that's a word."

"Poofier?" Ny'Alena repeated. "I do not know what you mean by that."

Sarah held up her hands and held them a foot apart. "It was higher. I remember more designs up here, on the top. There were more gemstones, and a purple cap, here. You know, it was shaped like an imperial crown, but had more bling on it."

"I'm not familiar with …"

Steve held up a hand. "It's okay, we get it. The only thing you need to understand is that the present-day queen, the one before the timeline was messed up, did *not* have that crown."

"Then, this must be what you're looking for," Kri'Calin said, growing excited. "Obviously, you can take this crown with you to appease the Ancient, and then we will commission new crowns."

Sarah smiled. "That's why you haven't protested the possibility of losing your crown. You're hoping to get another."

"Guilty as charged," Ny'Alena murmured, eliciting a smile from Sarah.

"What if," Emerion began, "the interference from the Ancients influenced the design of the crown? Maybe it changed *because* of them?"

Everyone in the room stared at the circle of iron Sarah was still holding. The king gently placed his own crown on the table.

"These are a matching set. Clearly, anyone can see that. What interference do you speak of?"

"It's rather hard to explain," Steve said. "Um, these guys can jump through time." Steve spent the next ten minutes describing how the Ancients were living a non-linear existence, and what that meant.

"Mind boggling," Kri'Calin decided.

"Right there with you," Steve agreed.

Sarah moved to place the queen's crown back on the table, next to the king's, but Ny'Alena held out a hand, indicating she wanted it back. "To think this was worn by one of the all-powerful Ancients."

"This *has* to be enchanted," Steve insisted. "I mean, look at it. It's made out of iron, there are, what, only about a dozen small-ish gems on it, and … ouch! Sarah, why did you hit me? What's the … oh."

"That's right, Einstein. You're insulting our hosts. You just insinuated their crowns are ugly."

Steve sighed. "Oh, man. I'm sorry, Your Majesties. I …"

"He's not wrong," Kri'Calin said, slapping Steve on the back. He rapped his knuckles on the side of his crown and listened as a few dull notes rang out. "The arse-end of a troll looks better than this."

Steve snorted with laughter. Emerion trilled.

"Kri'Calin!" Ny'Alena exclaimed. "Language!"

"My apologies. My wife is right. I have no problem giving up these in exchange for something new."

Sarah slowly stood, prompting the others to follow suit. "Right now, we need to find a way to verify this is, in fact, the crown Ny'Bardonne wore during her reign."

"How do we do that?" Emerion asked.

"Where's Zevern?" Kri'Calin asked. "He should be involved. He is, after all, the castle wizard. You there. Send for Zevern immediately."

Standing by the Anteroom's door, the guard nodded. "At once, Your Majesty."

"So what if it is?" Steve suddenly asked. "We learn Aura's crown is somehow concealed within the queen's. How do we break the spell?"

"I'll trust Zevern to solve that particular problem," the king said.

"No offense, Your Majesty," Steve said, "but you can't possibly think Zevern's name and the word *trust* belongs in the same sentence, do you?"

Kri'Calin made the mistake of reaching for a nearby goblet and taking a drink of water when he heard Steve's reply. He snorted with laughter and nearly choked on his drink. The queen smiled fleetingly before turning at the sound of the door opening.

The entrance of R'Tal's wizard's clothing was much less extravagant today. His outfit had gone from a clean, albeit wrinkled, robe to a stained tunic, mismatched trousers, and black sensible shoes. The small tufts of orange hair behind his ears were sticking straight up or bent at unnatural angles, suggesting he had woken that way. The person who presented himself before the king and queen was a changed man.

"You sent for me, Your Majesty?"

"I did, Zevern. Might I say that you appear rested."

"Didn't sleep a wink," the rotund wizard argued.

Kri'Calin pointed at the smaller of the iron circlets. "What can you tell us about that?"

"Her Majesty's crown? What do you wish to know?"

Kri'Calin looked over at Sarah and inclined his head.

"Can you tell us if it has a spell cast over it?" Sarah asked.

"Of course not. Why would you say such a thing?"

"You didn't even look at it, pal," Steve scowled.

"There's no need to," Zevern insisted. "I've seen it many times. That crown has been worn by Lentarian royalty for hundreds of years."

Sarah rested her hands on her hips. "And you're telling us it hasn't changed? At all?"

"Of course not."

"And when this diamond and sapphire pair were knocked loose?" Ny'Alena asked, tapping on two separate gems. "Or what about when the gold inlays here and here were added?"

"Oh, that. Well, nothing major, Your Majesty."

Steve took a breath, intent on replying to the wizard's nonchalant attitude, when Kri'Calin placed a restraining hand on his shoulder.

"Zevern," the king slowly began, "we need your help. We'll need you to focus all your attention on the following matter. We believe this crown to be enchanted."

"Enchanted *how*, Your Majesty?" Zevern inquired, curious despite the circumstances.

"Does it matter?" Ny'Alena asked.

"Believe it or not, it does, Your Majesty. If there's a spell on your crown, then in order to detect it, I'd need to know what to look for. Counter spells for fortification, for example, are completely different than those for shifting."

Sarah looked at Steve, who shrugged.

"I can't believe I'm saying this," he began, "but I think I can agree with him. In this instance, it's probably illusion. We think it might look like something completely different."

More confused than ever, Zevern stretched out a pudgy hand, but hesitated before he made contact with the crown. When the queen nodded her permission, Zevern picked it up and gently ran his hands over it.

"It feels just like it looks."

"Why wouldn't it?" Steve inquired.

"Tactile sensations are *very* difficult to mask," Zevern explained. "If what you say is true, the person who cast this spell was an absolute master. I can feel every indentation, every jewel, and even a few scratches that …"

"*I beg your pardon*," Ny'Alena interrupted. "There are no scratches on my crown."

Steve leaned over Zevern's shoulder and looked for himself. Without thinking, and without waiting for the queen's permission, Steve plucked the crown out of Zevern's hands and ran his fingers along the inside of the band. Zevern was right. There were several deep scratches present.

"No, he's right. They're there, all right. Your Majesty? Look, right there. Is that something you've seen before?"

Ny 'Alena's eyes widened. "No, I haven't. It wasn't there this morning, I swear!"

Sarah looked at Steve. "What does this tell us? How could scratches appear in less than a day without her noticing?"

Steve glanced at Emerion and nodded. "I think we're back to non-linear. Let's call this a sign. My guess is that the queen is correct. Those scratches weren't there this morning. That means something happened to this crown *today*."

Kri'Calin nudged Zevern toward Steve. "There's your proof. The crown is bewitched. I need you to find out how to break it."

"What's that noise?" Emerion suddenly asked.

Suddenly, it was so still in the room that Steve could hear

the king breathing.

"I don't hear anything."

"It's coming from that way," the griffin said, extending a wing and pointing toward the door, where two guards stood at attention.

Steve took a few steps toward the exit, passing his wife and the queen, when he hesitated. He cocked his head, listened for a few moments, and then retraced his steps. Frowning, he moved toward the door once more when he stopped.

"Okay, I heard it back there, like a … I don't know, a buzzing noise? Once I make it to here, then it's gone. Good ears, Em. Let's see. Sarah? I don't suppose you've got your phone on you, do you? It sounds like one of your silent text messages."

"I didn't bring my phone here, silly man," Sarah mock-scolded. "But, you're right. I hear it, too. Let me … what's that? What the …?"

Detecting the alarm in her voice, Steve's hands ignited as he rushed to her side. "What's the problem? Is something attacking you?"

"I just heard it," Sarah reported. "You're right. Something is buzzing. Is it something I'm carrying? I … no, it can't be. I don't have any pockets, and I certainly didn't bring my purse with me."

"Then, what could it be?" Steve asked.

Sarah returned his frank stare. "I think it's you, my dear. Walk by me again, slowly this time."

When he did as he was asked, Sarah reached and pulled him to a stop. "It's you, Steve. There's something you … your pocket! There's something in your pocket that's vibrating."

A smirk formed on his face. Sarah hit him on the arm. Hard.

"Get your mind out of the gutter, you nincompoop. Now, empty out your pockets. I want to see what … well, what do you know? I think we found the culprit."

They were staring at a small, light blue seashell. It was the spell that Balthor had created in order to move them through time. At the moment, it was gently vibrating. However, once Steve stepped away from the table, and on his way to the room's exit, the buzzing stopped.

Steve held the shell out and spun in place. The shell remained inert until it came within a few feet of the queen's crown. When it did, everyone present could see it tremble in Steve's hand.

Kri'Calin presented his crown to Steve. "Would you check to see if you get the same reaction from this?"

Steve held his hand near the larger iron crown. When nothing happened, he slowly moved his hand over to Ny'Alena's. The shell's trembling began anew.

"I'd say that confirms something's up with it," Steve decided. He looked over at Zevern, who only had eyes for the shell. "What? Haven't you ever seen a seashell before?"

Kri'Calin pointed a finger. "It's a vessel, isn't it? Someone has imbued a spell within it, haven't they?"

"They have," Sarah confirmed, "which is why we are going to be super careful around it."

"Well, I wasn't suggesting we …"

"It's okay, Your Majesty," Steve interrupted. He returned the shell to his pocket. "Forget about it. She was talking about me, not you."

"Oh. Of course."

"My gosh," Ny'Alena exclaimed, as she looked at her crown with reverence. "If my crown was once worn by the Fire Ancient, does that mean it has some type of power?"

Everyone stopped to look at the crown.

"What an excellent question," Kri'Calin praised. "I don't know how to answer that."

"Has anything peculiar ever happened to you while wearing it?" Steve asked.

"Not once, I'm afraid," Ny'Alena confessed. "Wouldn't that suggest that it doesn't?"

"The scratches," Sarah reminded everyone. "The scratches suggest that the crown changed its nature sometime today. So, the proper question would be to ask whether or not you noticed something happen today."

The queen fell silent as she considered. After a few moments, she shook her head. "There's nothing I can recall."

"And that's probably because Aura's crown is currently

disguised as your crown," Steve said. "For all we know, this thing's power has been stripped away while it's … I don't know, in disguise?"

Sarah nodded. "I can buy that."

Steve let out an exclamation of surprise. "I guess we can try to stop figuring out what we can do to break the enchantment."

"Why?" Sarah wanted to know.

"Usol. Usol is the one who stole the crown from Aura, which means he's the one who cast the spell. We, as lowly bipeds …"

Emerion trilled with laughter.

"… have no chance whatsoever to defeat an enchantment made by an Ancient."

"What will you do?" Kri'Calin wanted to know.

"Exactly what we're supposed to do," Steve proclaimed. He pointed at the door. "It's time we return this to the rightful owner, don't you think?"

"How?" Sarah demanded. "It's not like you can just say her name three times and then give it back to her when she appears."

Steve smiled. "It just might be that simple." He reached over and took the smaller crown. "Your Majesty, may I?"

"I can't wait to order my new one," Ny'Alena exclaimed, pleased. "With my express permission, Steve, you may take it."

A faint breeze appeared inside the Antechamber and gently circled around the room, causing both burning hearths to flicker. Steve noticed almost immediately, as did Sarah. Husband and wife smiled conspiratorially at each other before heading for the door.

"How do you plan on doing this?" Sarah asked.

Steve glanced behind him and saw that both the king and queen, along with Zevern, were following.

"I don't know. Maybe just call out to her?"

"Where are you going?"

They walked past the kitchen and into the Great Hall. Steve immediately angled for a smaller arched doorway in the southwestern corner of the room.

"Right through there is the inner keep. That ought to do. I figure if we're successful, and we can get Aura to put in an appearance, and seeing how she's the Ancient of Fire, doing so *outside* would be in everyone's best interests."

"Appreciated," Kri'Calin said, as he strode by Steve and made it to the door first.

It was a partly cloudy day in the northeastern corner of the kingdom. The wind was blowing, but only enough to sway a few branches of the nearby trees. Kytes were chirping away, and numerous mammals could be seen skittering through the upper branches of the treetops. Steve chose a spot near the middle of the keep and stopped. Looking down at the crown, and then at the sky, he took a hesitant step forward.

"Aura? You and I have never met, but you know who I am. I also know you are quite angry with me. Look at what I have here. I know you want this. I'm here to return it to you. All you need to do is show up and claim it. What do you say?"

A few crickets chirped obligingly.

"Maybe try Eion?" Sarah suggested.

They heard a small gasp of surprise from somewhere behind. Turning, Steve saw the king and queen in a hushed, animated discussion. Perhaps they were overwhelmed at the thought of not one, but *two* of the omniscient beings putting in an appearance?

"Eion?" Steve called, raising his voice. "Would you mind coming here for a moment?" Nothing happened. No subtle breezes, no swirling debris to spell out letters, nothing. "Listen, we could use some help. What do you say?"

"I don't think he's coming," Sarah said, growing despondent after several minutes passed.

"Come on, pal. We've got the crown. Let's get it back to your sister and put everything back the way it should be. Wouldn't that be a good thing? Still nothing? You're not gonna say anything? All right, good talk."

"Now what?" Sarah wanted to know.

"We know they're capable of hearing us," Steve said. "Usol, or Eion, they have always indicated they're watching. Clearly, he's choosing not to respond. Begs the question *why*? About Aura. What if … what if she isn't listening?"

"Suggesting we have to get her attention," Emerion said.

Steve rounded on the griffin. "Exactly. We need to get the attention of someone who has the ability to watch and listen from afar. How do you think we can go about getting this particular Ancient's attention?"

Emerion thought for a moment before rustling his feathers. "Flames. She is the Ancient of Fire. I would say that you, Steve, will have to do it."

"You're talking about creating a pyrotechnical performance specifically for her?"

Sarah nodded. "Em, that's perfect. Steve, this is on you."

"Fine. All right, everyone step back. Your Majesties, that includes the two of you, too."

Once everyone was watching from the safety of the castle's entryway, Steve cracked his knuckles and thought about what to do. In this case, it didn't take long.

Steve's hands ignited. Then, the flames expanded to encompass his entire body. He lifted both arms and blasted huge jets of fire up into the sky. A dozen chasers appeared next. They zoomed around the keep, one after the other. They darted by windows, ducked under trees, and even spiraled up a nearby flag pole, being careful to avoid touching the pennants.

Once the chasers had been snuffed out, Steve blasted out a jet of fire from each hand, creating fire whips. He twirled them above his head before giving a performance that one thrill-seeking, fedora-wearing adventurer would have envied.

Finally, he redirected the jets of fire to his feet and blasted up, from the ground. He rose a few hundred feet before zooming around the castle, leaving a long trail of flames and smoke behind him as he flew. Reducing his speed, he returned to the keep and tried to position himself for a safe landing. Then, his flames suddenly snuffed out. Steve hovered in midair a few moments before he fell like the two-hundred-fifty pound sack of potatoes he resembled and tumbled to the ground.

Sarah was there first. "Omigod! Are you all right?"

Steve rolled to his knees, massaging his right ankle. "That's about all the fun I can take for one day. Oh, man.

That hurts."

"It looks like you've sprained your ankle," Sarah told him. "That's just great. Now what are you going to do?"

"Hobble my way back to the Anteroom and use its hearth to fix myself," Steve grumped.

Emerion appeared on Steve's left. "I don't know what to say. That landing? Well, it was …"

"Ungraceful," Steve finished. "You don't have to tell me twice. I've never had my flames cut out before. Why the hell did they do it now?"

"Ahem, ahem."

Kri'Calin cleared this throat. Steve glanced over at the monarch. Before he could ask the king anything, Sarah was tapping his shoulder.

"Sarah, what's the matter?"

"Steve, *listen!* Do you hear that?"

"No. I don't hear anything."

"Exactly. Everything has gone quiet!"

Steve looked around the castle courtyard. "So? That probably happened when my ass created the crater I'm currently sitting in."

Sarah still had her finger against her mouth. She turned to Kri'Calin and Ny'Alena, but saw that they had noticed, too. "When was the last time you've heard everything get this quiet?"

"Never," the king confirmed. "There's something …"

Kri'Calin trailed off as his eyes glazed over and a vacant expression appeared on his face. The queen appeared similarly dazed. Steve turned to see what they were looking at when he uttered an exclamation of surprise.

They were no longer alone.

A blonde woman was standing twenty feet away, with her hands on her hips, looking supremely annoyed. She stood no more than five and a half feet tall, wore her thick, luxurious hair halfway down her back in a braid, and was wearing a gold bikini straight out of a very popular sci-fi movie. A hot pink sarong completed the picture.

Steve stared at the woman who didn't look old enough to be out of her teens. "No. Tell me you're not …?"

"You may call me Your Excellency," the girl told him, lifting her nose. "I know who you are, fire thrower. Be thankful I don't have you drop to your knees and worship the very ground I walk on."

"You're Aura?" Sarah asked, after she managed to get her voice.

"None other. I know you as well, teleporter. Be gone. My business is with *him*."

"He didn't do anything to you," Sarah protested. "He didn't steal your crown."

"Crown? Do I look like I wear a crown? Only the finest craftsmanship will touch this skin. I want my tiara." She sashayed over to Steve and held out a hand. Uncertain of her motives, Steve took it and gave it a friendly shake. "Unhand me, you pathetic mortal! I want my diadem. You said you had it. Give it back this instant!"

Steve held up the iron circlet he was holding. "I've got it right here. I'm hoping we can end this today, all right?"

"That's not mine," Aura snapped. "I wouldn't be caught dead wearing something as hideous as that."

"She sure doesn't sound like an Ancient," Steve heard Emerion whisper to Sarah, who immediately hushed him.

"We know it's yours," Steve insisted. "Granted, it might look a little different, but …"

"But nothing!" Aura suddenly shrieked. The perfectly clear sky was suddenly filled with dark thunderclouds. "You call me here and dash my hopes? My dreams?"

"Your dreams?" Steve repeated, confused. "That's a bit melodramatic, don't you think? You're one of the Ancients. I would think you could do anything you wanted. Hey, whatever. That's neither here nor there. I want you to know I didn't steal this thing."

"You have it, you're holding it, and you're giving it back to me," Aura responded. "What else am I supposed to think? And besides, I'm not accepting that back until it's returned to me in the exact same condition it was when it was stolen."

Steve shrugged. "That's beyond me. You know me. You said it yourself: I'm a fire thrower. Do I look like a spellcaster? Am I capable of creating something that can disguise a piece of treasure owned by one of you guys?"

Aura was silent as she studied him. "Hmm. You might have a point. If you didn't steal it, who did?"

Steve shared a look with Sarah. The last thing he wanted was to throw Usol under the bus and make him angry again. What was he supposed to tell her? Should he just suck it up and accept blame? After all, they had managed to recover Aura's crown. Er, tiara. Finally. The problem was, they just had to convince Aura of that, all while leaving Usol's name out of it.

"Who stole it isn't important," Steve said. He held the crown out, as if it was a peace offering. "Its return *is*. So, with that being said, I hereby return this crown to its rightful owner."

The teenager in disguise stared at the proffered crown with undisguised disgust on her lovely features. She crossed her arms over her chest and pouted.

"I will *not* touch it. Not until it has been returned to its glorious state."

"Isn't that something you can do?" Steve asked. "Can't you look at this, wiggle your nose, and restore it?"

"I shouldn't have to," Aura pouted. "And are you implying I'm a witch?"

Steve sighed. "Figures. I should've known you were well traveled, too."

"I have been *everywhere*," Aura proudly declared. She refolded her arms and lifted her nose.

Steve eyed his companions. The king and queen hurried over.

"Now what?" he wanted to know. "She wants it returned, and I have to admit, I can see her point. It was taken from her, transformed into *that*, and now she just wants the original back. There's gotta be a way we can do that for her. We need her cooperation, otherwise she'll never take back the power she gave Melvyn."

"If you're not going to give me my tiara in its natural form," Aura cut in with a sigh, "then I'm leaving. I don't have time for this. I'm a busy woman. Er, girl."

"Would you stop with the theatrics?" a new voice

bellowed. A gust of wind appeared in their midst and became a mini tornado. In seconds, the swirling winds condensed into a humanoid figure. Eion took a few steps toward his sister when he stopped. "You've got your trinket back. End this."

"Eion," Aura returned. "This is none of your concern."

The Master of the Winds strode angrily over to Aura and locked eyes on her. "What affects one, affects all. Do you really think that a human is responsible for your precious stone's theft?"

A clap of thunder rumbled angrily from the sky.

"What do you know of it?" Aura demanded. "If I find out you were involved, then …"

"… then what?" Eion sighed. "We quarrel? Fight? All of us are evenly matched, my dear sibling. And, as I've mentioned before, there is no quarrel between the two of us."

"Good. Then, step away. I'll pry the information out of that smug human's mind, even if I have to pull it out through his nose."

Steve clapped a hand over his face. "That sounds unpleasant. Thanks for that particular visual."

Eion pointed at Steve. "Him? You think a human pulled off this brazen theft? Aura, think about it, would you? You're suggesting he snuck onto Shria and plucked your precious diadem out from under your nose? I think you give the humans too much credit."

"Shria?" Steve repeated. "Is that your version of Astral?"

"It is," Aura confirmed.

Steve shrugged. "I guess I could take offense at that jab from Eion, but do you know what? He's right."

Aura scowled. "Just … persuade him to give it back."

"Think about it," Eion urged. "Just this once. Consider what has happened, and see if you truly think this human is responsible."

"Hmm. You have a point."

"To further hammer home this point," Eion continued, "you're accusing a human of being able to jump through time and hide your tiara in the past. The humans aren't capable of time travel."

"Excuse me?" Steve sputtered. "Are we, or are we not,

currently in the past?"

"You're not helping your case," Eion told him. "Please be silent for a moment."

"Sorry."

"If he didn't do it, then who did?" Aura asked. Her attractive face scrunched up into a frown as she considered. Just then, a triumphant look washed over her features. "Oh, I knew it. This has Aeia written all over it."

Eion slapped his forehead and ran his hand down his face. "Come on, sis. You're smarter than this. You know you are. Put it together."

"If it's not you, and it's not Aeia," Aura began, "then …?"

Steve held his breath. Was she going to do it? Was she going to piece this together without him saying anything?

The sky rumbled again. Ironically, no one paid it any attention.

"Who's left?" Eion asked, rolling his eyes.

"Usol? That doesn't make any sense. Why would he … the wager! He's sore because his powers were stripped from him and he didn't have his stone! And my own stone is now missing! Why that two-timing, conniving, deceitful …"

"Bingo," Steve quietly breathed. "We have liftoff."

"Told you I didn't need your help," Eion whispered back.

"… cowardly, sneaky, mischievous …"

"I can't believe this is happening," a voice whispered from behind them.

Kri'Calin and NyAlena were staring, in undisguised shock, at the two figures who were circling each other.

"Now, I can't speak for him," Eion was saying, in an attempt to calm Aura down, "but I …

"… despicable, disgusting, sleazy …"

Eion leaned forward to tap Aura on the top of her head. "Take a breath, would you? The last thing I need right now is for you to burst out of that outfit and cause these poor humans to lose their sight."

"Aura?" Steve began, as he held up a hand. "Can I say something?"

The blonde woman's angry glare settled on Steve. "What?"

"First off, I just wanted to say that ever since I learned there was a Fire Ancient, I've always wanted to meet you. And as for this crown? Are you able to tell if your tiara is hiding beneath some type of spell? Did we, or did we not, find the right one?"

Aura surprised him by holding out her hand. Steve wordlessly passed her the crown.

"I see what he's done," Aura seethed, growing angry once more. "Concealment, illusion, false history. There must be a dozen false layers here."

"Can you break the enchantment?" Sarah asked.

Aura scoffed once. A series of tiny red rivulets appeared on her arm and grew steadily brighter. Sensing what was about to come, Steve spun Sarah in the opposite direction and immediate twirled his finger so that the king and queen, along with Emerion, could do the same.

An intense, brief flash of heat appeared behind him. Checking to make sure none of his companions but himself had felt the blast, Steve turned to see Aura holding up a glittering tiara made of solid gold. Set into the center of the top ornament was a red jewel shaped like no other: an open rose.

"Aura's diadem," Sarah whispered. "Oh, thank goodness. This nightmare is finally over."

"Not yet it isn't," Steve groaned.

Sarah took his arm and spun him around. "What do you mean?"

Steve quietly pointed at Aura and held a finger to his lips.

Aura, holding her newly revealed tiara in all its glory, was staring — while frowning — at the large ruby set into the center of the extravagant piece of jewelry. She caught Steve's eyes and deliberately passed her beloved tiara over to him. Confused, Steve stared at the item in his hands before giving the Ancient a confused look.

"Does that look like my ruby to you?" Aura snapped.

Steve turned to his wife. "Refresh my memory. Rubies are red, right?"

"Right," Sarah confirmed.

"Is that not what's on here?" Steve asked. "One large

ruby, shaped like a flower?"

"That isn't mine," Aura reiterated. Quick as a snake, her arm jetted out and plucked the ruby from its place on the crown. "This isn't emanating any of my essence. You've found a fake."

Chapter Thirteen–A Crowning Achievement

"Oh snap," Sarah groaned. "How is this possible? This isn't supposed to happen. We find her crown, she'll take back Melvyn's power, then everything will go back to what they were before. And now? We're in trouble."

"No, we're *screwed*," Steve corrected, letting out a heavy sigh.

"As they would say in your world, don't throw in the towel yet," Eion instructed. He reached out. "Hand me that, would you? There must be a simple explanation for this. Now, let's see. Is this Aura's tiara? Yes, there we are. I can feel faint traces of her power within. But, this is … odd. My sister is right. This isn't her stone."

"And I don't suppose you can determine what happened to it, can you?" Steve asked, hopeful. "This is really the last thing we need right about now."

Eion ran his hands along the surface of the tiara, which earned him a scowl from Aura. "Fear not," he told her. "I have no designs upon this. Quite the contrary, I'd like to see this returned to you—intact—as much as they do."

"Where is it?" Aura demanded. "Where's my stone?"

"It's not here," Eion said, after he spent nearly two minutes going over every square inch of the tiara. "I can't feel its power anywhere."

"That's just great," Steve scowled.

Eion held up a finger. "Let me finish. What I said before is correct. There are no traces of the stone here. But, that means …? Anyone?"

"The Alchos stone was never on that crown," Emerion answered.

"Diadem," Aura crossly corrected.

Steve looked up. "Wait a minute. If it was never on the crown, then that would mean …"

"Usol never hid the stone with the tiara in the first place," Sarah finished.

Aura vanished and instantly reappeared next to Eion. She snatched her tiara back and studied its surface. Frowning, Steve watched as a series of thin, spidery red lines appeared on Aura's arms. Starting at her fingertips, they quickly spread up her arms and onto her chest. Realizing what was going to happen, Steve barely had enough time to turn away and shield everyone from the blast of power he knew was coming.

With his back tingling like mad, he returned his attention to the female Ancient and saw that she was now holding a much smaller version of her tiara. She had broken it? What had she done, thrown a temper tantrum?

Eion snorted, but disguised it as a cough.

"Where's the rest of it?" Steve wanted to know.

Aura regarded him as though he had just accused her of being unable to light a match.

"There is no more of it, simpleton," Aura stated. "It was a ruse. A trick. That is soooo Usol."

"You don't talk like an Ancient," Steve decided. "You sound more like … well, you kinda sound like a human."

"So? Humans have more fun than we do."

Eion's head popped up. "Excuse me? They most certainly do *not*. They can only exist in this moment, in this place. They can't spontaneously jump to a random location to … well, Sarah can, I suppose. But all the others? No, it's not possible. Why do you say that? That's why you sound like a petulant child? Because you want to sound like one of them?"

"It suits me. So, human, I may sound like one of you, but rest assured, I am not."

"You defeated Usol's enchantment, and did so fairly easily," Steve recalled. "That's impressive. I don't care who you are."

For the first time, Aura flashed him a smile. Then, her eyes dropped to her tiara and she scowled. "This? You say this is broken? That's because it is."

"Broken by you," Eion murmured.

"Only because it's missing my stone!" Aura protested. "How's a girl supposed to have fun without her stone? I must have it back!"

"Let me make a deal with you."

The keep fell quiet. All eyes turned to Steve.

"You'd better know what you're doing," Sarah whispered.

"Aura? If I can get your stone back to you, let this be over. Remove the powers you gave Melvyn. He's caused enough headaches, and until he is stripped of his newfound power, we won't be able to stop him. What do you say? Your stone for one powerless human?"

Aura strode forward, swinging her hips with every step. Steve's eyebrows shot up, but thankfully, he managed to slap a neutral expression on his face before Sarah noticed.

"Very well, fire thrower. A favor for a favor. You return my stone and I'll remove the jhorun I bestowed upon the older human. You have my word."

A smile split Steve's face. "You have no idea how much I needed to hear that."

"Oh, there's just one other thing," Aura cooed.

Steve's smile vanished. "And what's that?"

"I grow tired of waiting. You have an hour to return it, starting now."

"Wh-what? Only an hour? I need longer than that!"

"An hour only, you stud muffin."

"What did you call him?" Sarah asked.

"You heard me. Your hunk of a husband had better get going."

"Stud muffin, and hunk of a husband. Are you hitting on Steve?"

"Of course not. I'm just trying to rile the two of you up. What do I care about humans?"

Steve nodded. "Roger that, just checking. Once I find it, where can I find you?"

Aura pointed straight down. "Right here will do. Don't disappoint me. You really think you can find it?"

"Believe it or not, this will be the third stone we've searched for, having returned the first two."

Aura's mouth gaped open. "No way."

"We returned the Essence of the Sea, and Usol's stone, as you're aware."

"It's true," Eion confirmed.

Aura shrugged once and then vanished.

"What in the world possessed you to make a deal with her?" Eion demanded. "Do you really think you can find her stone? Usol could have hidden it anywhere!" Thunder rumbled overhead. Eion glanced up, sighed, and then returned his attention to Steve. "To coin a phrase from your world, I think you might have bitten off more than you can chew."

"I know, pal. We've got a good group of people here. I'm thinking we'll be able to find it."

"I hope so. Good luck."

With that, the second Ancient vanished. Emerion wandered close.

"I stand ready to assist."

Steve draped an arm around the griffin. "Thanks, Em. It's appreciated."

Kri'Calin and Ny'Alena approached. "We overheard your deal," the king began. "It sounds like you're going to need some help."

"Lots of help," Sarah said. She smacked Steve's arm. "I'm with Eion. Why in the world would you make a deal with *her*?"

"We want her as an ally," Steve insisted. "Look, we need her cooperation. Do you want to put everything back the way it should be? Do you want to go home? The one thing which will guarantee that is the return of Aura's stone. So, it looks like we're going to look for number three." The emerald tetrahedron appeared in his hand. "Oh, come on! I wasn't even talking about you. Go away, would you?"

The sparkling green gem vanished.

"This shouldn't be too hard," Emerion said. "You have your magic shell in your pocket. It should be able to detect the stone, isn't that right? After all, it detected the tiara."

Kri'Calin held out a hand. "Come. Let us continue this in the Antechamber. I don't need anyone to know who was just here."

"Would they freak out?" Steve asked.

"Freak?" Kri'Calin repeated, puzzled.

"Would they be able to cope with the knowledge two Ancients were here?" Sarah translated.

"Absolutely not," Ny'Alena answered.

"Nice textbook answer," Steve chuckled.

They headed indoors. Once they were back in the king's private chambers, Kri'Calin began summoning pages and guards. He relayed instructions on what to look for and sent every available guard and able-bodied person to begin the search.

"You think the stone is in the castle," Sarah guessed. "You know what? I think so, too. However, I can pretty much guarantee it won't look like its usual self. Usol will have disguised it in some fashion."

Steve retrieved the spell Balthor had given him and studied the shell. It was no longer vibrating.

"We have less than an hour. We really need to get moving. Sarah, how certain are you the stone is somewhere around here?"

"One hundred percent, without a doubt."

"Why?" Emerion asked. "How?"

"It's based on what we already know," Sarah explained. "Look, we know Usol made off with Aura's tiara right around the same time his powers were returned."

"One of the Ancients lost their powers?" Ny'Alena repeated. "How is that possible?"

"Just accept it as fact," Sarah told the queen. "Usol was

given his powers, he took out his anger on his sister, and stole her tiara. Now, we know each of the Ancients is an even match for the other, so Usol knows he has to ditch the tiara and do it quickly. We thought it would end there, but apparently, Usol took the stone and hid it in a separate place from the diadem."

Steve nodded. "Makes sense. He had to know she was hot on his tail, so yeah, he'd want to get rid of it as quickly as he could."

"Whether he hid the stone first or second, I don't think we'll ever know," Sarah continued. "So …"

Gripping Balthor's spell in his hand, Steve rose to his feet. "I get it, I'll start searching. We've only got so much time before Aura will be back. I can start in the …"

"Hold up," Sarah interrupted. "We need to be smart about this. We don't have the time to search the entire castle. And, let's face it. That spell didn't find the stone after all."

"What? Sure it did. You saw it vibrating. We know it was working."

"The stone wasn't on the tiara," Kri'Calin reminded him. "Your shell spell couldn't have picked up on Aura's stone."

Steve closed his mouth and grunted. "Good one. I didn't think of that. Okay, well, why did it vibrate when it got close to the queen's crown? If the stone wasn't there, what was setting it off?"

"Usol," Emerion announced. "You called him a prankster. He probably did it just to fool us into thinking the shell had extra powers when it did not."

Steve let out a heavy sigh and returned the shell to his pocket. "Well, that blew my theory out of the water. Great. Now what? How do we find this stone? How do we know Usol, being the trickster that he is, won't simply move the stone to a more secure location?"

"Oh, I didn't think of that," Sarah lamented. "If he wanted to, he could make certain that stone was never found."

There was a knock on the door.

"Enter," Kri'Calin called.

A guard poked his head into the room. He held out a folded piece of paper. "My apologies, Your Majesty, but I was just asked to give you this."

"A message?" Kri'Calin asked, puzzled. "Just now? Who gave it to you?"

"I … don't remember," the guard stammered. "I am so sorry."

The king unfolded the paper and read a single sentence, written in an elegant hand. He gasped aloud and leveled a gaze at Sarah.

"You have some powerful friends. This would appear to be from Eion."

Steve looked up. "Huh? Since when does he write his responses on a piece of paper?"

"Since it'd be considered rude to blast wind in here and spell out letters," Sarah said. "That was exceptionally thoughtful of him. What'd he say?"

The king flipped the paper around so that everyone could see it.

He's constantly being watched, so you're good to go.

"Usol is being watched," Steve read. "Of course! He dare not interfere now, unless he wants to attract unwanted attention for himself. Eion was right. All the Ancients are evenly matched. It would seem that Usol is hiding from Aura."

Emerion squawked appreciatively.

"So, if the location of the stone won't be changing anytime soon," Sarah began, thinking hard, "we should be able to figure out where he stashed Aura's ruby."

"It's another damn puzzle," Steve complained.

"One that we're more than capable of working out," Sarah reminded him.

"What's the purpose of the puzzle?" Emerion wanted to know.

"I was going to ask the same question," Kri'Calin added. "Why the puzzle? What does he hope to accomplish?"

"Worthiness," Emerion said. He rustled his feathers. "Only he who is meant to decipher the meaning *will* decipher the meaning."

"Okay, you watch way too much television," Sarah told the griffin. "This isn't the movies, and we're not talking about a certain hammer that only certain people can lift."

"Great movie by the way," Steve whispered to Emerion.

"The first is my favorite," the griffin confided.

"How many have you seen, Em?" Sarah asked.

Emerion suddenly decided it was time for a full inspection on his wings, and extended both so that he could verify all his feathers were undamaged. In doing so, he promptly shielded himself from Sarah's view.

"You're as bad as Steve," Sarah sighed. "He's always watching one of his slapstick comedies, so … wait. Usol is a prankster."

"We know this already," Steve pointed out.

"Knowing that he loves to joke around, what can we determine?" Sarah asked.

"He may be one of the four Ancients," Ny'Alena began, "but for all intents and purposes, he's a person. I believe his actions are predictable."

"You bring up a tantalizing notion," Steve told the queen, as he started to pace. "Let's think about this. Everyone's favorite Earth Ancient gets his powers back. He's bitter, and he wants retribution. What does he do? He torments the first person to cross his path, and in this case, it must've been Aura. He steals her tiara, which has her stone. Knowing full well he'll be pursued, he chooses a time and location. He hides the tiara in the castle, but doesn't really have time to choose another location for the stone, so what does he do?"

"He picks a spot next to the queen's crown?" Sarah asked.

"M-my crown?" Kri'Calin sputtered. "I sincerely doubt it."

Steve rubbed his hands together. "And we just have to think like an Ancient. Oh, I've got a good feeling about this. We can figure out what he did with it."

"What's your plan?" Kri'Calin asked.

"Let me set the scene. You're hustling, you've just stolen your sibling's favorite toy, and now that sibling — who's quite capable of knocking the stuffing out of you — is close to catching you. Being the trickster he is, I also believe he wants us to spend time looking for it, and that means the object is out in the open for all to see."

"Where?" the king demanded.

"I estimate we have about forty minutes left," Sarah said.

Steve sighed and pulled out the shell. "I say we start in the Great Hall. There's no time to lose. Your Majesty? If you'll …"

"We've been through this," Sarah interrupted. "Put it away, Steve. Balthor's spell is not going to help us. The stones are beyond any wizarding spells that could be crafted."

Steve was unmoved. "Fine. All we have to do is to find whatever is *holding* the stone. I know Gareth was able to look beyond the stone and focus on the surrounding areas. I think that's what we need to do here."

"Know your adversary," Emerion said.

Husband and wife both turned to their griffin son.

"What was that?" Sarah asked.

"Huh?" Steve said, at the same time.

"Use what you've learned about Usol to figure out what he's done," Emerion suggested.

"Care to give me an example?" Steve asked.

"What's important to Usol?" Emerion countered. "What does he like?"

"I think I see where he's going with this," Sarah said. She rose to her feet and headed for the king's table. "May I borrow a piece of paper?"

Kri'Calin pointed at a tray. "There's some there, in the corner. You'll find a quill and a bottle of ink next to it."

"Thank you. Now, let's start a list."

"We barely have more than a half an hour left to search," Steve complained. "Do we really have time for this?"

"You know how big this castle is," Sarah returned. "Trust me, the only way we're going to find that stone in time is if we figure out this puzzle, as you and Emerion call it. For the record, I think you're both right. We need to narrow down our search. Steve, think! What does Usol like?"

"Playing jokes," Steve grumbled. "Meddling in human affairs. Riling up his siblings."

"Hold on," Sarah instructed. "I'm writing as fast as I can."

"Green," Steve said, after considering for a few moments. Sarah looked up. "Green?"

"Remember when he and Eion were fighting with each other as we were battling the pirates?"

"They kept changing forms," Sarah recalled.

"Exactly. Eion always chose white, and Usol's had some type of green in it. Plus, his stone? It's green."

The emerald obligingly appeared in Steve's hand. "Nope, don't need you. Maybe later."

The Alchos stone vanished.

Sarah added the color to her list. "Okay, this is good. What else?"

Steve suddenly pointed at Emerion. "Griffins. He's always been fond of griffins."

"Ooo, good one," Sarah praised. "Green, and griffins. Hmm. I don't know how that helps us. It's not like we're going to find any griffins in this castle. At least, not yet."

Kri'Calin looked up. "You'll find griffins in the castle from your time?"

"Only if we can find that damn stone," Steve returned. "And you didn't hear that from me."

Sarah looked at the queen. "Aside from Emerion, we know there are no live griffins in this castle. But, what about fake ones?"

"I don't follow," Ny'Alena said, frowning.

"That makes two of us," Steve admitted.

Sarah rose from the desk and started to pace. She stopped at the nearest painting. "What about pictures? Paintings? Er, how about tapestries?"

Ny 'Alena placed her hands on her head and massaged her temples. "Let me think. Griffins. Griffins. No, I can't think of any, I'm sorry."

It was the king's turn to stand and pace. He fell into place behind Steve and Sarah and, together, the three walked along the perimeter walls together.

"Carvings?" Steve asked.

"I've never seen any in the castle," Sarah reported.

"Because there aren't any," Kri'Calin announced. "That is, unless that changes in the future?"

"I was referencing the castle I remember," Sarah told the king. "So, that would be our future."

"Ah."

"Kri'Calin, what about statues?" the queen asked. "Surely, there must be some representation of a griffin somewhere inside this place."

"I'm sorry, my love. I cannot think of a single example of anything I've seen."

Sarah suddenly froze. She spun on her heel and looked at the wall behind the king's desk. "What about *that* one?"

Kri'Calin looked up. "What one? There aren't any griffins over there."

Steve perked up. "Don't you have a safe behind that wall? I'd say that qualifies as a griffin."

"I had completely forgotten about that," the king said, as he hurried to his desk. "I did not know you were aware of its existence."

"Believe it or not, I've got a similar one back home," Steve explained. "And, I've seen the king, er, the present-day one, open it a number of times."

Kri'Calin looked around the room. Everyone, including Emerion, was now standing before the wall concealing the safe. He chuckled.

"This is supposed to be my private safe, yet everyone seems to know not only that it exists, but where to find it. Oh, well."

Kri'Calin pressed a specific spot on the wall and it slid aside, revealing a lifelike statue of a griffin. The sculpture faced outward, and was perched on a large stone pedestal. Kri'Calin approached the stationary griffin and, once he was standing in front of it, waited for the griffin's leg to lift up. Once it did, he pressed the recessed button that had been concealed underneath. The pedestal opened. Kri'Calin gently pulled the door open and peered inside.

"See anything good?" Steve asked, eager for some good news.

"Nothing that shouldn't be here," the king reported. "This was opened just a few days ago. I didn't see anything out of the ordinary in it then, so I fail to see how it could possibly have an all-powerful gem now."

"The scratches on my old crown appeared only earlier today," Ny'Alena reminded him. "If I understand the explanation correctly, about how an Ancient can move through time, then if something was to happen, it would have done so earlier today."

Steve gave the queen a bow. "Nicely done, Your Majesty. I think you understand what's going on better than I do."

Ny 'Alena nodded politely at Steve before turning to watch Kri'Calin pull various items from within the safe.

"Let's see. Obviously, there's nothing to be seen in the latest treasury reports. My love? Would you put that on the desk?"

Ny 'Alena nodded. "Of course."

Kri'Calin retrieved a large velvet bag with a cinch-string closure. He opened the sack and gently tipped it over. A pearl the size of Steve's fist appeared in Kri'Calin's hand.

"Capily's Tear. I had forgotten that was there."

The pearl was returned to the bag and placed on the desk. Several sacks of coins — gold grifs — joined the rest on the desk.

"There's something we didn't consider," Steve observed. When everyone looked his way, he continued. He pointed at the bags. "Lentari's gold coins. They have a griffin on one side. Relevant?"

The queen reached inside one of the bags and pulled out a few of the golden disks. She studied the image for a few moments before handing one to Steve.

"I don't see how."

"That'd make two of us," Steve groaned. "Nothing to see here, I guess."

Shrugging, Kri'Calin returned to the safe. He pulled out another sack, but this time, it was filled with small smoky spheres. Steve automatically stepped away from the desk, which earned him a smile from the king.

"You are clearly familiar with the jorii."

"I am. I've seen what it can do to my jhorun, and let's just say I'm not eager to see a repeat performance."

Sarah looked at the queen and mouthed *disaster!* The

queen chuckled. Emerion wandered close.

"What are these? Marbles?"

Sarah took a few moments to explain what the jhorun-enhancing spheres could do, and why they were coveted so much. The young griffin's eyes widened with alarm, and, like Steve, moved away from the table.

Kri'Calin grunted once and deposited an ancient, pewter box roughly the size of a shoebox on the table. He then reached in with his hand and felt along the insides of the safe.

"That's all there is, I'm afraid."

"What's that?" Emerion asked, as he studied the box. "What's in it?"

The king nodded at Sarah, who was already smiling. "Would you?"

"Of course. Em, that's the Bakkian. It's what holds the prophecy about the arrival of the Nohrin, which is us. Anyway, it's a crystal shield about the same size as that pearl you saw earlier. It has a ... Steve! The Bakkian! It has a picture of a griffin on it!"

Kri'Calin opened the chest and inspected the object nestled inside.

"I've only seen this once. I've always wondered how ..."

"You mean like this?" Steve asked. He reached inside and placed a finger on the surface of the crystal. When nothing happened, he gave a sheepish grin and then motioned for Sarah to join him. The instant both of them were in physical contact, the voice began.

Many years from now, it will come to pass ...

They withdrew their fingers and the message immediately ceased.

"Simply incredible," Kri'Calin breathed.

Sarah looked at the crystal and frowned. Then, her eyes widened with shock. Her mouth opened, but nothing came out. She grabbed Steve's arm and pointed at the box.

"What is it?" he asked.

"Look! The griffin is different! The last time we saw this, it was of a griffin with one leg raised, as if it was taking a step.

Now? The wings are extended. Something—or someone—changed this!"

"And this couldn't be just a coincidence?" Steve looked at the king and tilted his head. "Can I take a closer look?"

"Permission granted," Kri'Calin said, nodding. "I've opened that container a few times, and I have not seen anything untoward before. You say the griffin symbol has changed? I … Len, I know I've showed you the Bakkian before. Do you remember the wings looking like that?"

Ny 'Alena only needed a brief glance to confirm Sarah's suspicions. "Sarah is correct. The wings were not extended before."

Steve took the crystal object from its resting place and ran a finger along the wings. Just as before, the image felt as though it had been etched onto the surface of the object.

Many years from now, it will come to pass …

"Oh, for Pete's sake," Steve grumbled. He gripped the shield in both hands and applied a secret move Maelnar had taught him years ago. The prophecy instantly fell silent. "That's better. Now, the question is, did this symbol change as a result of something that has been messed up?"

"No," Sarah answered. Based on the speed of her response, Steve guessed she had been thinking about the answer. "Do you remember what Maelnar told us? He created the shield hundreds of years ago. Caladonia, the sorceress who made the prophecy, lived hundreds of years ago. No, whatever happened to this, did so today."

Steve nodded. "I like how your mind works, dear. Okay, what do we have to do?"

Sarah interrupted. "Wait a minute. The first time we saw that thing, and we heard the prophecy, nothing happened until we both touched it."

Steve shrugged. "So?"

"And just now? It waited until the both of us were touching it again before we heard anything."

"What's your point?" Steve asked.

"You just touched it, and it started talking. Steve, I'm over here. I'm obviously not touching it. So, why's it telling us the prophecy now? This is just another example of something that has changed. It must be relevant!"

About to argue, Steve closed his mouth. She had a point. Then, a notion occurred. Steve looked at his wife, then the king and queen, and finally, poked his finger at the shield. Once contact was made, the voice started again.

Many years from now, it will come to pass,
An elemental will come, a pain in my ass.
Looking for something, belongs to them not,
Broke into Astral, should've been shot.

Forgave him I did when he returned my stone,
Bet was broken, siblings did they moan.
Not all was happy, vengeance they vowed,
But only one was mad, because she was plowed.

Crown was stolen when she looked the other way,
Hid the blessed thing on a previous day.
Sister was upset, plans were forsaken,
Ire was misdirected, and steps were taken.

Now future is rewritten to suit a man,
One that has long been plotting a master plan.
You better get moving, cast aside all doubts,
Only ten minutes remain until your time runs out!

"Did Usol write this?" Steve demanded. "What is he, a frat brother now? And how did he manage to get Caladonia to change her prediction?"

"He's an Ancient," Sarah reminded him. "He can probably do whatever he wants."

"And I'm a pain in the ass?"

Emerion trilled with laughter.

"To him, you probably were," Sarah told him, using as gentle a voice as she could muster. "Right now, we need to focus. You heard Usol. We only have ten minutes before Aura returns."

"It was a recording," Steve insisted. "He couldn't possibly have the time right, could he?"

"It's been close to an hour," Kri'Calin admitted. "My guess is that your Ancient friend could tailor the prophecy as he saw fit."

"Makes me think that, if we had been able to get to the Bakkian in our time, we could've figured this whole mess out a lot sooner," Steve sighed. "All right. Ten minutes. I don't know, guys. We're no closer to finding Aura's stone than we were when we last saw her."

Sarah pointed at the crystal shield Steve was still holding. "It must have something to do with that. Could Usol have disguised the stone for the Bakkian?"

"The Bakkian is still around in our time," Steve recalled. "And we already know Aura's stone wasn't, so I don't think that could be the case. What ... wait. Why isn't it talking anymore?"

"You didn't silence it, like you did before, did you?" Sarah asked.

"No. Every time I left it alone for a few minutes, and then touched it again, the prophecy would start. As for now, well, watch this." Steve set the shield on the desk and stepped away. He waited a few moments before scooping it back up in his hand. "See? No more talking."

"What about the griffin?" Sarah asked. "Are the wings still extended?"

"They are," Steve confirmed.

Sarah joined him and together, they studied the crystal. "What if we both touch it at the same time?"

"We've already done that," Steve pointed out.

"This is the part where I remind you we're dealing with an all-powerful Ancient with a sense of humor."

Steve shrugged and held the stone out. Once both husband and wife came into physical contact with the crystal, there was a brief flash of light. When the spots cleared from Steve's vision, he could see something red on the floor before him. As for the Bakkian? The symbol of the griffin etched into the crystal had returned to the one-leg-raised version they were familiar with. The outstretched wings were gone!

"My, my, what have we here?" Kri'Calin exclaimed.

Sarah stooped to pick up the red object. It was a ruby, and it was shaped like a perfect rose, just beginning to open.

Steve whooped aloud. "Now we're talking!"

Chapter Fourteen–Righting A Wrong

"Ten minutes must have passed by now, right?" Steve asked. He, Sarah, Emerion, and the king and queen had returned to the inner keep. "I seriously miss my phone."

"You spend too much time on it," Sarah accused.

"Do not. You spend more time than I do."

"I'm more popular," Sarah sniffed, before giving him a smile. "Unlike *you*, people actually enjoy hearing from me."

"Keep it up, lady," Steve grinned, enjoying the game. "I'm not afraid of you."

"You should be," Sarah said, giggling. "Who else can dangle you upside down dozens of feet in the air for an extended period of time?"

"You can," Steve laughed. "And I wasn't laughing at you at the restaurant, I was laughing *with* you."

"Mm-hmm. Think Eion is here?"

Emerion squawked once. "There is a breeze blowing.

Does that mean he is?"

"Eion?" Steve asked, addressing the open air. "Is that you?"

This time, there were no gusts of debris, or peculiar jets of air twisting about mid-air.

"It doesn't appear to be," Sarah reported. "If he's here, he doesn't seem to be making his presence known."

Steve looked up. "Usol? What about you? Are you hanging around, too?"

They were no overhead rumblings, and certainly no thunder. The skies were clear, the sun was shining, and the temperature was comfortable. There was no sign any of the Ancients were there.

"If I didn't know any better," Steve began, "I'd say they were all afraid of Aura. I mean, what does she have over them, I wonder."

"I'm the oldest," Aura's voice snapped.

The five of them gasped with alarm and spun in place. There, standing in the castle doorway they had just exited from, was the Fire Ancient. She was wearing a sparkling blue bikini this time, and had her hair arranged in a shag haircut with curtain bangs. Clearly, Aura was aware of the popular trends with human females. The problem was, this particular style was popular among teenage girls.

"You're only as old as you feel," Aura said, shrugging. "Time's up, fire thrower. Do you have my stone or not?"

Steve held out the delicate flower-shaped ruby. "I've got it right here. I'd like to hereby return this to its rightful owner."

"Oh, no you don't," Aura argued, as her nose lifted. "I'm not taking that."

At a loss, Steve turned to Sarah and held up his hands. "I give up. She wanted this stone, we find the blasted thing, and now she won't take it?"

Sarah stared at the female Ancient and suddenly smiled. She knew what to do.

"Steve, I do believe she wants her crown …"

"… diadem," Aura corrected.

"… back in the same condition as when it was taken."

"And what would that be?" Steve wanted to know. "I

have no idea what condition it was in when Usol stole it."

The skies chose that time to rumble angrily.

Steve looked up. "Well, it's true. You stole it, and we're expected to clean up your mess? How screwed up is that?"

Thunder boomed overhead.

"Usol, I've got this," Sarah said, patting the air. "I'll knock some sense into him."

The rumblings ceased.

"You'll knock some sense into me?" Steve repeated.

Sarah pointed at Aura. "For goodness sake, we're trying to make things right with *her*. We don't need to aggravate *him* while doing it. Anger him again and you might just find yourself visiting the moat."

Kri'Calin snorted with laughter.

"Fine," Steve sighed. "You win. Well? Can someone tell me what we need to do? We don't even have the crown anymore. She took it."

Aura groaned aloud, waved her hand, and then crossed her arms over her chest. That was when Steve caught sight of a flash of yellow on the ground. The crown was back. Looking over at Aura, and waiting for her permission to touch it, Steve took the golden circlet in one hand, with Aura's stone in the other, and held them close together.

Right before his eyes, the two inanimate objects reacted to each other. Aura's ruby flashed once and then started to glow a deep red color. The crown, held tightly in Steve's left hand, vibrated softly. The golden piece of treasure began to grow, like a germinated seed. New arms, arches, and a top ornament formed, with a very clear depression in the center.

Steve held the ruby next to the tiara and the large jewel jerked out of his hand to land snugly in its setting within the tiara. The gold bands continued to grow and weave themselves into a symmetrical pattern until, once completed, the ruby pulsed twice, giving off bursts of red light each time. Steve watched in silence for a few more moments to be certain Aura's headpiece had finished merging, or growing, or metamorpho—he shook his head. Whatever the term was, it appeared to be done.

He turned to Aura and formally held out the crown,

although he realized it should no longer be called that. It was a circlet no more, but an actual tiara. Granted, the thing looked ridiculously top-heavy, and he could only hope Aura didn't have any need to look down. But, that was neither here nor there.

"I do believe this is yours."

All smiles, Aura gracefully reclaimed her tiara and set it upon her head. "How do I look?"

Steve smiled. He had been married for far too long to screw up that particular answer.

"You look fantastic. It suits you."

"Why thank you, kind sir."

Steve's eyebrows lifted. This was definitely a plus. Aura was being polite and cordial to him now? Could that mean he was officially out of the doghouse?

"Yes, fire thrower, I hereby acknowledge the return of my stone. We can now ... Usol! I know you're there. Come here."

"I don't think he's listening," Steve started to say.

Usol appeared. His eyes were on the ground, and for the first time that Steve could remember, the Earth Ancient appeared nervous.

"Er, did you call my name?"

"What have I told you about eavesdropping?" Aura asked. Her voice was calm, there was no malice, and she was gazing at her sibling with a neutral expression. "It's rude. You did this, didn't you? I want to hear it straight from you."

Usol cringed. "Maybe."

"Maybe? You'll do better than that."

Usol sighed. "Yes, this was me."

"And you tried to pin blame on the humans."

"Not exactly. I was only trying ..."

"What's going on?" Sarah whispered in his ear.

"I think Usol is being told off by his sister," Steve whispered back. "His *big* sister."

Aura turned to Sarah and nodded. "That's one way to put it. Sarah, is it? I apologize for putting you and your husband through all of this. I should have trusted my instincts. There was simply no way humans could have pulled this off. No offense, of course."

"Of course," Steve returned. "Can I ask you something? You now sound like a normal person. Er, I guess I should say an adult. I pegged you as someone stuck as an angry teenager. And now, it's like you've dropped the angry youngster façade. Can I ask why?"

Aura glanced down at herself and seemingly noticed for the first time she was wearing a very revealing swimsuit. She frowned. Color sprouted up and down her body as a professionally pressed and tailored black pant suit appeared. Her long blonde hair suddenly straightened and tied itself into a knot on the back of her head. She clasped her hands behind her back.

"Would you prefer I looked like this?"

"I should think you would wear whatever was the most comfortable for you," Steve said, "and to hell with anyone else's opinion."

The Fire Ancient stared at him for a few moments before her clothes shimmered once and switched back to the swimsuit.

"Thank you. This is far and away the most comfortable outfit to wear. You asked why I acted the way I did? The best answer I can come up with is, why not? When you've lived as long as I have, you tend to try new things just so you don't become bored. I have been fascinated with adolescent human females for many of your centuries. They always appeared to be having so much fun, I thought it'd be a perfect way to cheer myself up. A great change of pace, if you will. Then what happens? My dolt of a brother takes the one thing I treasure more than anything."

"Are you not all evenly matched?" Steve asked. "Why's he so scared of you?"

"I am *not* scared of her," Usol scowled.

"No one asked you," Aura said, as if she was a full-blooded human and addressing an annoying younger sibling, which in this case, she was.

Usol's face fell. "My apologies."

"You *are* scared of her," Steve said, amazed. "You guys are no different than us!"

"Spoken like someone who has siblings," Aura said.

"Actually, I'm an only child. I said that to bring attention to the fact that you sound like a human when you talk like that."

"You aren't offering offense by that, so none will be taken, fire thrower."

Steve smiled. "Uh, thanks, I think. Listen, I gotta ask you something. Melvyn. Er, he's the guy you gave powers to in order to mess up my timeline."

"You want to know why I did it?" Aura asked. A red wave of energy rippled through her. "I thought I covered this."

"No, um, I mean yes, you did. That wasn't what I was going to ask. I need to restore the future to what it was prior to Melvyn gaining new powers. Will you do that for me?"

"It's already done," Aura reported. "The human known as Melvyn has been stripped of his gift."

Steve let out a whoop and grabbed Sarah to give her a twirl. "Yes! Thank you so much, Aura! You have no idea how happy that makes us."

Emerion approached and went down on one knee. "You have my eternal thanks. I would do anything for my parents."

Steve grinned. He watched a look of confusion spread across the Ancient's face before she turned to him. "You … are the griffin's father?"

"He's adopted," Steve said, by way of explanation. "It's a long story. The gist of it is Emerion wouldn't have survived if we hadn't intervened. So, as a promise to his mother, we took over parental responsibilities."

Aura nodded. "Commendable. I think that's …"

The gentlest of breezes appeared.

"… commendable. You two are incorrigible."

Steve looked up, confused. "I'm sorry? We're what?"

Aura ignored him and turned to a nearby tree. "Do you really think I can't tell when you're here? Stop being a pest, Eion, and show yourself, or else I'll do it for you."

Several fallen leaves, strewn across the grass, suddenly swirled together. The winds increased until every scrap of detritus in the area was airborne. The outline of a face appeared. It rotated until it faced Aura.

"Did you call, sister?"

Aura's eyes flashed fire. Literally. "Don't act coy with me. You were spying. You have five seconds."

The face disappeared so quickly that the bits of grass and leaves comprising Eion's face fell to the ground, bereft of the air currents that held them aloft.

"I apologize," the Master of the Winds said, from behind them. Eion walked around Steve and Sarah and faced his sister. "Yes?"

"State your interest in this. Why were you eavesdropping?"

"I consider these three my friends."

Aura crossed her arms. "So?"

"That means I do not want to see any harm befall them."

The Fire Ancient frowned. "You've been hanging around the humans for too long."

"See?" Usol said, becoming more animated by the second. "Haven't I been saying that for the last millennia?"

"No one asked you, brother," Aura stated. "I haven't yet decided what consequences you will face for pulling that stunt of yours."

Usol's face fell. Steve was amazed. He thought for certain, based on their experiences with the Earth Guardian, that Usol would show defiance, even anger. No, Sarah was right. He was nothing more than a younger sibling cowering under the disapproving stare of his kin. Perhaps he would give up being the prankster?

"One can only hope," Aura sighed. "These matters do not pertain to you humans. May I offer one piece of advice?"

"I'll take anything you are willing to give us," Steve responded, earning him a soft trill of approval from Emerion.

"What you seek lies underground."

Steve shared a look with Sarah. They needed to go underground? Is that where Melvyn was hiding? Just then, Sarah clutched his arm.

"Melvyn. He's going after Maelnar again!"

Steve frowned. "He wouldn't dare."

"Listen to her," Aura urged.

"You mean she's right?" Steve asked, frowning harder. "We manage to save Maelnar's life, but that idiot still goes after him? How are we supposed to find him?"

"This is the part where I'd point them in the right direction," Eion suggested to Aura, using a quiet—but firm—tone of voice.

The Fire Ancient regarded her brother for a moment before turning north. Her eyes closed, and when they opened, they could all see that her eyes had become completely white.

Steve murmured to Sarah, "That still creeps me out."

"Don't knock it til you've tried it," Aura said, as if she was scolding a child. "There he is."

"You see him?" Steve asked, growing excited. "Where is he?"

"I may have lived for thousands of your years," Aura began, "and have seen so many sights that it would pickle your mind to think about it for too long, but this? I will admit I have not spent much time underground."

Usol looked up. "You've always said you prefer to stay away from ... how should I describe this? The *creepy-crawlies*?"

Aura shrugged. "Guilty as charged." After a few moments, she held out an arm. "I'm only nice once or twice every few centuries, so don't get used to this. You, fire thrower. Take my hand. I will share my senses."

Steve pointed at Sarah. "Can she see it, too? Her sense of direction is much better than my own."

"Fine. Be quick about it. Wait. What are you two doing?"

Eion and Usol eyed each other, and then—in perfect unison—they both shrugged.

"To satisfy my own curiosity, I'd like to see, please," Eion said.

"You're allowed."

"What about me?" Usol asked.

"Clairvoyance still giving you troubles?" Aura asked. Her tone was neutral, she didn't raise her voice, or throw in any sarcasm, but the meaning came through loud and clear. "You may."

"I'll find him myself," Usol grumbled. "Why are you letting *him*?"

"There's not much wind beneath the surface," Aura said, exasperated. "For an earth guardian, you don't know much about geology."

Usol scowled and clamped his mouth shut. His eyes had gone white, like Aura's, and he slowly spun in place as he searched. Facing slightly northwest, he stopped and nodded. "I see him now."

"Will someone please tell me where this is?" Steve pleaded. His eyes were closed. "I see him, all right, but I have no idea what I'm looking at. It's dark, not much light, but I ... wait. Do you hear that?"

"Water," Sarah said. "I just heard the splashing of water."

Husband and wife studied the scene. Melvyn was definitely underground, and in a large cavern. A soft glow smeared on the walls and ceiling gave enough illumination to see that, whatever cavern this was, it was enormous.

They both heard a distinctive splash.

"It sounds like something fell in," Steve added. "A rock, perhaps? Or maybe a jumping fish? And wherever this is, it looks like he's by himself. Man, I can't wait to wipe that smug smile from his face. The sooner we figure out where he is, the better."

"Maybe we can get you and Usol the same tutor?" Sarah teased. "I know exactly where he is. It makes perfect sense."

"You do?"

"Where is this human?" Emerion demanded. "I will shred him from limb to limb."

Sarah scratched the griffin's back, between his wings. "Take it down a notch, okay? Steve, what comes to mind when you consider all the facts? Consider: it's dark, we know there's water nearby, and the person we're looking for is Melvyn."

"I know you know," Steve began, "and I know you know I *don't* know, so could we just skip the part where I don't know, and you just tell me what you know?"

"I didn't follow a word of that," Emerion said.

Sarah smiled. "Borahgg. Melvyn is in Borahgg."

"How do you know it's not some other big cavern with a body of water? Are you sure?"

"One-hundred percent."

"How in the world did he manage to make it past the guards?" Steve demanded.

"I'm guessing he still had his powers then," Sarah said. She frowned. "Now that they're gone, it means he's stuck underground, with no foreseeable way to escape."

"It also means he knows who's responsible," Steve reminded her. "That right there makes him dangerous. Come on. Let's end this. After all, we don't know how many more of these situations we'll have to defuse before we can safely head home."

"This is the last," Aura stated, matter-of-factly.

Husband and wife rounded on the Ancient.

"How do you know this?" Sarah asked. "Are you certain?"

"As certain as someone who can see anything and everything can be," Aura returned, shrugging. "Consider it my way of offering an apology for everything I've put you through. You have very efficiently neutralized every threat your anachronistic friend has concocted, therefore he has returned to the dwarven realm."

Steve looked over at Eion and Usol, who were both standing motionless and silent. "Would either of you like to give us a hand?"

"Usol and I are going to have a little chat," Aura announced. "He'll be indisposed for, let's say, an *indeterminate* amount of time."

Both she and the Earth Guardian vanished into thin air. As one, the rest of them turned to Eion, who shrugged.

"This is a task you must perform yourselves."

Then he vanished.

Sarah turned to Emerion. "Is there any chance you'd wait here for us to return?"

Their griffin companion rustled his feathers irritably. "No."

Sarah sighed. "Fine. I figured you'd respond that way. Your Majesties? We'll be back as soon as we can."

Kri'Calin rose to his feet, prompting Ny'Alena to do the same. "Good luck to you. Please let me know the moment this threat is neutralized."

Steve nodded. "Count on it."

* * *

"It sure is quiet in here," Sarah observed, as she and Steve peered nervously out the tunnel's exit and studied the city before them. "I thought for certain this place would be on high alert."

"That's only if they know he's here," Steve corrected. "Or if they even know he's on the way. For that matter, how do we know Melvyn hasn't bewitched anyone who lives here?"

A group of armed dwarves, wearing the traditional dark leather armor soldiers of Borahgg were known for, rapidly assembled in front of them. Judging by the speed in which they appeared, and the fact they were all fully armed, Steve figured they'd been waiting just out of sight. Thankfully, Steve spotted a friendly face at the head of the group and his face broke out in a grin.

"Selwyn! It's good to see you, buddy. We thought the worst. Listen, has there …"

"You're all under arrest!" the head of security snapped. "Prepare to be detained. Bring the manacles!"

Steve stepped forward and stared hard at their dwarf friend. "Tell me something, pal. Who am I?"

"An annoying pest who doesn't deserve to live," the dwarf snarled. He was holding a small axe in one hand, a double-headed hammer in the other. "Put up some resistance. Please. I implore you."

"Methinks we be a smidge too late," Steve sighed. "Come on, Selwyn. I know you're in there. You've obviously had a run-in with Melvyn. He's here, hiding. We're pretty sure he's planning on …"

A thousand gallons of water suddenly appeared, suspended over Selwyn's and every other dwarf's head. None of them bothered to look up.

"Last chance to snap out of it," Sarah told them.

Selwyn took a menacing step forward. Gallons and gallons of water fell from overhead, as if the mass of water were motion activated. The dwarves were knocked off their feet and swept downhill, tumbling, yelling, and cursing their displeasure. After a few moments, when the water had disappeared, Steve watched Selwyn scramble to his feet and hurry over, wringing his beard out in the process.

"What the blazes just happened? Where did that water come from? And how did I make it back to the city?"

Sarah waved. "The water was my fault. I figured you and your men needed a way to wake up. Only ... wait. Steve, why did the water work this time, and not when we were trying to wake up the creeg?"

"What made you choose water?" Steve wanted to know.

"I have no idea," Sarah admitted. "It was the first thing to pop in my head, and for some reason, I didn't question it."

"If you ever figure it out, please let me know," Steve implored. He turned to Selwyn. "What's the last thing you remember?"

"Patrolling the tunnels. My squadron and I were investigating a guur sighting, and ... and ... then I was here. Soaked."

"Melvyn is here," Sarah told the dwarf. "The human we're looking for managed to sneak into your city, and my guess is you encountered him in one of those tunnels."

"Your fugitive? You're suggesting *I* brought him here?"

"You didn't know what you were doing, pal," Steve told him. "He's got the power of persuasion, and knowing him, made you forget the two of you ever met."

"We already know he's responsible for your actions here," Sarah added. "However, we can safely say it won't happen again. His jhorun was taken away. However, that will probably make him even more dangerous."

"Why?" Selwyn wanted to know. "What have we to fear?"

"A cornered animal will almost always fight back," Sarah said.

"Why's he here?" Selwyn wanted to know.

"To cause more problems, what else?" Steve replied. "Forget about that for now. We have it on good authority that he's somewhere near a water source."

Selwyn sighed. "The most readily available is obviously Thammut Lake. That body of water has nearly a thousand meters of shoreline. Finding him will be no easy task."

"Actually," Sarah contradicted, "I think it very well could be. Look what just happened here. Melvyn is obviously worried about us coming after him. He set you guys to watch the entrance, and should we arrive, take us all into custody without asking any questions. I think the same thing will happen again. I believe the closer we get to his hiding place, the more obstacles we're going to discover in our path."

"I will have every available guard searching," Selwyn promised.

"Make sure they go in teams," Steve reminded him. "Just in case."

Selwyn nodded toward one of his guards. "Understood. You. Alert the Council. We search for the human fugitive. Every searcher is to bring water, in case we encounter anyone suffering from one of his enchantments."

Steve, Sarah, and Emerion followed Borahgg's head of security toward the city.

"You say you were able to see him?" Selwyn was saying.

"With some help," Steve admitted. "We know he's near water, and it was dark. This is the only place I could think of, and since we've already foiled one of his plans regarding our dwarf allies, logic suggests he's back to try again."

"He will not succeed," Selwyn vowed. "Wait. You said it was dark? Wizards be damned. I'll bet I know exactly where that *kelpah* is hiding, and it's not good."

Selwyn hurried to the middle of the cobbled street. Muttering to himself, he squatted, pulled a tool off his belt, and pried something up from the street.

A glowing blue disc was revealed.

"I'll be damned," Steve muttered. "It's one of those announcement disks."

"We call them harken stones."

Selwyn pulled his axe from its holder. "Cover your ears."

A single blow to the stone brought everyone in a two-hundred-foot radius from their shops and homes.

"Get to higher ground!" Selwyn ordered. "This goes for *everyone!* This is a Rookhivian alert! Rookhivian River feeds our lake," Selwyn explained. "To prevent flooding in the city, it has been sealed behind a very ingenious seal, which can control the amount of water being fed while ensuring the pressure never dips too low."

Steve paled. "And if something happened to that seal?"

"The city would be doomed."

Steve groaned. "Sarah, we've got to stop him. Selwyn, can you take us there as quickly as possible?"

Selwyn nodded, but not before he struck the harken stone with his axe hand in three short, successive bursts. This time, soldiers appeared.

"You're all with me. We have reason to suspect the human we're looking for will try and find a way to destroy the Rookhivian seal!"

Several soldiers cursed with disgust. Ignoring them, Selwyn pointed east and urged them to hurry.

"The sooner we get there, the sooner we can make sure nothing happens."

"What if something does?" Sarah asked, as they sprinted down streets and alleys. Selwyn ducked through a particular narrow alley and hesitated only long enough to verify Emerion was able to follow. "Is there a contingency plan in place for emergencies?"

"Aye, there is," Selwyn confirmed. They emerged from between two three-story structures and slowed down. Marginally. "It's known as the calamity gate."

"Catchy," Steve said. "Where's it at?"

Selwyn pointed at a natural split in the rock wall on the southern border of the huge lake that was visible in the distance. "Through there you'll find a tunnel leading down. The gate is nearly three-hundred feet below ground."

"How complicated are the controls?" Steve asked. "You say it's how more water is added to the lake. Can someone like Melvyn figure out how to work it?"

Selwyn shook his head. "Not unless you're familiar with dwarf engineering."

Steve sighed. "Good."

Sarah smacked his arm. "Good? He doesn't need to know how to run it, or open it. All he has to do is figure out how to ..."

BOOM!

A plume of smoke and dust burst through the crack and rapidly expanded.

"Oh, no!" Sarah cried. "We're too late!"

"He destroyed the gate!" Selwyn shouted. A loud rumbling had begun and was growing steadily louder. "He's doomed us all!"

Emerion immediately stepped in front of them and herded them away from the gate. "We must flee!"

"And let all these people die?" Sarah wailed. "I can't do that!"

"There's nothing we can do!" Steve argued, raising his voice to be heard. "Your powers are strong, but they're no match for …"

The side of the cliff wall exploded outward as a huge wall of water punched through the rock. Hundreds of thousands of gallons of water poured through the jagged opening and headed straight for them, rapidly filling the cavern with water.

"I can't believe this is happening!" Sarah shouted. "What do we do?"

"We get the hell out of here!" Steve shouted back. "Sarah, there's nothing we can do to stop this! We have to leave!"

With tears streaming down her face, Sarah reached for Steve's hand and then placed her other on Emerion's head. But, before she ordered her jhorun to make the jump, a strange thing happened. The rushing water, now less than five hundred feet from them, suddenly froze in place, gently undulating back and forth.

"Eion, tell me this is you," Sarah pleaded, addressing the open air.

There was no answer.

"What about you, Aura?" Steve asked.

They were still met with silence.

"What's going on?" Selwyn demanded. "How long can you hold back that water? It might be enough to …"

"It's not us!" Steve interrupted.

"Then how …?"

"*I am.*"

The four of them, including Selwyn, whirled around. The owner of the voice was female, and may have sounded human, but that's where the similarities stopped. What was standing before them was a twenty-foot-tall humanoid comprised of nothing but water. And the eyes! They were glowing blue.

This definitely wasn't Aura, and it certainly wasn't Usol or Eion, so that could only mean it was ...

"Aeia!" Steve breathed. "What are you doing here?"

The watery figured turned at the sound of her name and looked down, as if noticing for the first time she wasn't alone.

"Settling a debt. I cannot abide favors."

Aeia's voice was light and airy, but absolutely emanated power. The Water Ancient flicked her wrist and the mind-numbingly gigantic wave of water pushed backward. Without moving, her form shifted forward, sliding along the ground.

"You owed a favor to someone?" Steve asked. "Can you tell us who?"

"You, who else?" Aeia said. Her hands made a tiny motion and the huge wave rushed back to the subterranean aquifer. "This will absolve my debt."

"How is it you owe me a favor?"

Aeia held out a hand. A very familiar blue stone appeared.

"It's your Alchos Stone," Emerion said.

Aeia turned to the griffin and nodded. "Exactly. You returned this to Eion, who in turn, returned it to me. I am grateful. I have been rendering assistance for a while now," Aeia remarked. "Perhaps you noticed?"

Sarah's face lit up. "Just now! When Selwyn snapped out of his trance when I splashed water on him. That was you?"

"Aye, and the lightning bolt. You're a gifted teleporter, for a human, but there is no way—"

"You know about that, too?" Steve asked, amazed.

"Who do you think slowed down the bolt long enough for her to teleport it?" Aeia asked, shrugging. "You needed some help. I provided it."

Sarah sidled close. "Excuse me, Aeia? Can you tell me if the person responsible for this mess is still in the area?"

She was ignored. Aeia surveyed her work, looked at the ceiling, and whistled once. Almost immediately, the ground beneath their feet began trembling.

Usol appeared moments later. The Earth Guardian was wearing his customary green robes and appeared a little more disheveled than usual. His thick black hair was standing on end, his robes looked dirty, and he didn't seem too happy about being summoned.

"Yes? Did you need something?"

Aeia pointed at the wall. "That needs to be sealed up. We can't have that water causing any more damage than it already has."

"You're meddling with human affairs?" Usol asked, incredulous. "Miss Goody Two-Shoes is breaking her own …"

"I'm rectifying a situation *you* had a hand in causing," Aeia snapped. The waters comprising her form rippled and condensed. Suddenly, she was the same size as Usol. "Anytime now, brother."

Usol frowned and crossed his arms. "And if I don't want to?"

"I'm sorry, but did I preface that with a *by your leave*?"

Usol's defensive stance vanished, but his scowl remained. "Why not have Aura do this? She's the one who …"

A huge ball of flames spun into existence next to Aeia. It rapidly expanded into human form.

"Would you care to finish that statement?" Aura challenged. "She's the one who … *what*? Created this mess?"

Usol dropped his gaze to the ground and shuffled off. Once he was hard at work restoring the stones to the broken wall, one sister looked at the other and laughed.

"He pouts like a baby," Aeia observed.

"You haven't been around for millennia," Aura returned. "And don't forget, he's still the youngest."

"Excuse me?" Steve asked, raising a hand.

Both female Ancients turned to give him neutral looks.

"I'm sorry to ask, but can either of you tell me if the idiot who broke that gate is somewhere close?"

Aeia shared a look with Aura and then sighed. Her blue eyes pulsed several times before she closed them. When they opened ten seconds later, they fixed on Steve.

"May I assume you two are the only humans who are supposed to be here?"

Sarah nodded. "That's right."

"A third is currently fleeing."

Aura nodded. "He would appear to be trying to return to

the surface."

"Where's he at right now?" Steve asked.

"A cavern smaller than this one," Aeia answered.

"But not by much," Aura added.

Sarah clutched Steve's hand. "I know where he is! He's currently in the big cave at the end of the first flight of stairs from the valley! Remember the one with the unfinished tunnel?"

Steve nodded. "I sure do."

They nodded their thanks to the two Ancients before disappearing. Aura looked at the empty space the trio had just occupied and raised a sultry eyebrow.

"Should we have told them he's not alone?"

Aeia shrugged. "He'll figure it out sooner or later. Usol? Where do you think you're going? Have you no skill? It looks like a pack of humans did that work. Have a little pride, would you?"

Usol grumbled a response before turning back to the broken wall.

Chapter Fifteen–Showdown

How many times have we been here now?" Steve whispered, as the three of them crouched behind a bulky stalagmite. The pillar of rock stretched nearly twenty feet high before tapering to a point. "Actually, I think this is the same stalagmite I climbed when I was that huge centipede fighting the pirates."

"I wish I could have seen that," Emerion said, dropping his voice to match Steve's.

"No, you don't," Sarah argued. "He was a nightmare on legs. He was so big that you could actually ride him. Ugh. What a memory. Now, where do you think Melvyn is?"

"How do we know he hasn't already made for the stairs?" Steve asked.

In response, Sarah turned to their griffin companion. "You have nocturnal vision, Em. What do you see?"

Emerion crouched low and peered around the stone column. "One moment. I am scanning for movement."

Steve tapped a finger and pointed north. "Search that way

first. That's where the tunnel is that'll take you up and out of here."

Emerion's eyes widened. "Hush, both of you. I hear something."

Husband and wife waited, silently, for their griffin son to report his findings.

"I see him," Emerion declared, growing excited. "There's an elderly human against the far wall. He's crouching on the ground, fumbling with … I'm not sure, a package? Every few seconds he stops what he's doing and goes quiet. I think he's checking to see if he's being watched."

"Makes sense," Sarah decided. "This package. Can you tell what it is?"

"I'm waiting for him to … what's this? The package just stood up! There's another person!"

Steve looked worriedly at Sarah. "An accomplice? That can't be right. Since when does Melvyn actually trust someone enough to take them along?"

"It has to be someone he's bewitched," Sarah decided.

Steve cleared his throat. "Or, I'm thinking there's a third option: he's taken someone hostage."

Sarah was silent as she stared at the distant wall. Unfortunately, it was much too far away to see anything clearly.

"Keep watching the second person," she ordered. "We need to know if it's someone we have to watch out for, of if it's someone who needs rescuing."

Emerion was silent as he studied the two images. The larger, older human kept his smaller companion in front of him and together, they explored the area. Melvyn, true to his paranoid form, kept looking over his shoulder, as if he expected them to pop out of the darkness at any moment.

"They're on the move. Melvyn is following the smaller human. They appear to be …"

"Wait a moment," Steve interrupted. "Smaller? Just how small are we talking?"

The griffin grunted. "Less than half the size of Melvyn. Slight. Facing away, so I cannot say for certain."

"Child-sized?" Steve pressed.

"The companion stands mid-chest to your fugitive."

"Tiny," Sarah said. She looked at Steve. "What are you thinking?"

"Either he's got a kid with him, or …?"

"He's taken a dwarf prisoner," Sarah groaned. "Of course. It makes perfect sense. Damn that man!"

"Do we know who it is?" Emerion asked.

Steve shook his head. "It doesn't really matter. We have to get whomever away from him. Sarah? Can you do your thing and teleport him out of there?"

"Not without being able to see what I'm doing," Sarah said. "They're too far away, and it's not bright enough in here. We have to get closer."

Steve held out a hand. "Fine. Let's get closer. Em, are you ready? Beautiful. Sarah, whenever you're ready."

Just like that, they jumped closer by several hundred meters. That was the good news. The bad news was that they were still easily a thousand meters away. And, judging from the look on Sarah's face, Steve guessed that she was still too far away to use her jhorun.

"Anything?" Steve asked.

"No. I'm sorry."

"They're having an argument," Emerion announced.

"Can you hear them?" Sarah asked, hopeful.

"A moment, if you please. I'll see if … maybe … oh, no."

Steve flinched, almost igniting his hands in the process. Sarah was beside him in a flash.

"No, you don't. No lighting anything on fire. Not yet. Em? What'd you see?"

"The hood slipped off the face of the prisoner. I can now see who she is."

"She?" Steve repeated. "Something tells me I'm going to hate this, aren't I?"

"You are," the griffin confirmed. "It's the dwarf female, Aislinn."

"Damn it to hell!" Steve swore. "How? How did Melvyn know to take her?"

"He either saw us with her or asked someone who she was. After all, the daughter of the security chief would make a good hostage."

"Can you get her out of there?" Steve asked, as he dropped his voice so low that Sarah could barely hear it.

"Emerion? Is she still the one in front?"

"Aye. Melvyn just gave her a vicious shove, and she stumbled. She managed to stay upright, though."

Two jumps later, Sarah was within visual range.

"I've got this," Sarah quietly murmured. "I'm going to escort Aislinn back to Borahgg. Don't go anywhere."

She blew him a kiss before disappearing. Up ahead, they all heard a cry of outrage as the tiny figure trudging ahead of Melvyn suddenly vanished into thin air.

"Fire Thrower!" Melvyn shrieked. "I know it's you! Care to come out and play?"

"I trust this not," Emerion said. "Let me challenge him. He'll be no match for me."

"I don't trust this, either," Steve confided. "Stay in the shadows. Don't let him know you're here. I'll stall him long enough for Sarah to return."

"Sarah is not going to like it," Emerion said.

"That's why we're going to keep it to ourselves. Besides, I've got an idea. Just keep quiet. You have my back?"

"Say the word, and I will engage," Emerion promised.

Nodding, Steve stepped into view and ignited both hands. "Hey, pal. I'd say nice to see you, but we both know I'd be lying."

The former sheriff jerked upright. "You've been a thorn in my side for long enough. Do you really think you have the balls to kill me?"

Steve shot off two jets of fire. Melvyn dove to the ground a split second before the flames struck.

"Your jhorun has grown stronger since we last met," Melvyn was forced to admit, dusting himself off and picking up his hat.

"And yours has been stripped," Steve returned. "Again. That's gotta sting. To think all your hard work is now wasted."

"There's no way you've fixed everything, partner," Melvyn scoffed. "You could be searching for years and you'll always wonder if you've found everything I've done."

"Dwarf wars averted," Steve said, ticking off a finger. "That repairs the alliances with the griffins and dragons. Let's see, we snapped dozens of soldiers out of your grip, sparing the royals from an untimely death. No assassin, no usurpers to the throne. Let's see … the creeg, the twisted ruby, the underground lake. I'm so very not-sorry to tell you that it's back where it belongs, and the damage has been repaired. Need I go on?"

Melvyn's smug smile vanished.

"This ends here, right now."

"For once," Melvyn said, as he removed his flat-brimmed Boss of the Plains hat, "you and I are in total agreement, partner. Do you really think I'm surprised to see you here? That I wouldn't have taken precautions?"

Steve grinned. "Oh, I know you have. In fact, I'm counting on it. I just didn't know what you had in mind, so I had to find out for myself. You're becoming predictable in your old age."

"Predictable my ass," Melvyn growled, finally dropping the smug visage he had been wearing. "Let's see what you think about this!"

There was a bright flash of light. In less time that it takes to blink an eye, two daggers appeared out of thin air and flung themselves at Steve.

"Hah!" Melvyn shouted triumphantly. "There's no coming back from that, you miserable … what the hell?"

Both blades vanished into Steve's chest, passing harmlessly through him to strike the rock formation behind him. Steve smoothed out his clothes, as if the knives had wrinkled his shirt, and pretended to brush a few particles of dirt off his shoulder.

"Is that the best you can do?"

"Why won't you just die?" Melvyn complained. "You're the wart that won't go away!"

"How'd you get those spells?" Steve asked. "We both know that you couldn't summon a letter opener, even if your life depended on it."

"Wouldn't you like to know?" Melvyn sneered.

"The wizard," Emerion's voice said, from somewhere

behind him.

"What wizard?" Steve asked. In that exact moment, Melvyn thrust a hand into a pocket and scattered a handful of stones into the air. Each stone became a full-sized sword that hurled toward Steve. After the last one had passed harmlessly through him, Steve turned to give the sheriff a piteous look. "You're not the brightest bunny in the forest, are you?"

"What have you done to yourself?" Melvyn demanded.

"How were you able to conjure those knives?"

Melvyn held open his right hand and revealed four items: two stones, one cork, and the last looked like a small, polished piece of glass. Melvyn lifted his hand, as if he had uncovered the kingdom's deepest, darkest secrets.

"Turns out that useless wizard was good for something after all."

"Zevern? You stole spells from him? You're braver than I thought."

"The guy's a moron," Melvyn admitted, "but these are more than adequate. I knew that, sooner or later, my newfound jhorun was going to be taken from me. I took precautions long before that could happen, and that included forcing that numbskull to make me a few spells."

There was a commotion behind him. Sarah had returned, and this time, nearly a dozen fully armed dwarf soldiers were with her. Selwyn appeared and began barking orders.

"Flanking positions! Surround the intruder!"

"You'll never take me alive!" Melvyn cried. He took one of the stones and tossed it toward them in a high arc. "Have a little fun with this!"

The stone exploded in mid-air, sending fragments in all directions. The tiny chunks quickly shifted into iron barbed darts. All at once, every single dart froze in place, then dropped to the ground where they were.

Steve made eye contact with Sarah, who nodded. When he turned back, their fugitive had disappeared.

"Where is he?" Steve demanded. "Split up! Find him! We cannot let him get away, or he'll pull stunts like this again!"

"You heard him!" Selwyn bellowed. "Find the human!"

The dwarf soldiers quickly broke up into six groups of

two and headed in different directions.

"Here!" one soldier called, a few minutes later. He and his companion were pointing at the mouth of a nearby tunnel. "He's making for the surface!"

"After him!" Selwyn ordered.

Steve was ready to join the chase but Sarah was nudging his arm.

"I think it might be time to become that big bug again."

Steve groaned, but half a second later, he had adopted the huge centipede form—thirty feet long with more than two dozen segmented joints in his body. He sighed and twisted to look at Sarah.

She hopped onto the segment directly behind his head and gripped him tightly with her legs. "Em, hop on. Hurry, Steve—go!"

They were off. Steve covered the distance to the tunnel in less than four seconds. This form was built for speed, and for once, Steve knew how to use it.

Almost immediately, they passed the dwarf soldiers who recoiled with surprise, wondering how a kritada managed to find its way inside the tunnel, when Steve felt a strange sense of wrongness overwhelm him. He immediately came to a stop. The dwarves stopped too.

"What is it?" Sarah asked.

"Something's not right." Steve's head lifted "Sarah, we're on the wrong track. I'm sure of it!"

"He didn't come this way?" Sarah asked, bewildered. "How did he fool us?"

"He has at least two spells left," Steve said, "but that's not important right now. He came this way, but he's no longer here. We must've passed a side tunnel."

"We did," one of the soldiers confirmed. "There's an offshoot about twenty meters behind us."

Selwyn and the other dwarves caught up.

"Melvyn found a side tunnel. We have to go back."

Briefly wondering how to make his huge form turn around in the tight confines of the tunnel, his kritada body surprised him by practically coiling around itself and neatly looping through its own coils. He now faced the opposite direction. Selwyn and Sarah both pointed at the side tunnel opening as he approached.

Steve slipped inside, increasing speed as he investigated the area. After a few moments, the tunnel dead-ended into a smaller cavern. Stalactites and stalagmites were everywhere, affording hiding places galore.

Steve clicked his pincers, sampling the air. His vibrissae tingled. There was movement in this cavern; they had come to the right place.

"He's here," he announced. "Come out, come out, wherever you are!"

"That's definitely a good look for you, partner," Melvyn called, from somewhere within the depths of the cavern. "You'd better end this now, 'cause you know I'll never stop huntin' you. I'll never stop until I know you're either good and dead or else there's nothin' left of your future! You get that, you numbskull?"

"He wants you to kill him?" Sarah whispered, appalled. "What in the world for?"

"Maybe for the satisfaction of having his death on your hands?" Emerion suggested.

Steve nodded. He concentrated on his human form, and, once it was back, joined his wife and son behind a large stalagmite.

"Look out!" Emerion cried.

Without a glance, Sarah flung her hands outward and issued the command to *stop*. Tentatively, she and Steve peeked around the stone pillar and gasped with alarm.

The air was thick with hundreds of arrows, a dumfounding sight. Steve nervously cleared his throat.

"Where the hell did *they* come from? I'm beginning to think Zevern is not such an inexperienced nincompoop after all. That's impressive."

"I'll be sure to tell him," Sarah teased.

"And I'll deny it until the day I die. Now, allow me."

There was a brief blast of heat as every wooden arrow flared brightly before turning to ash.

"That's one down, and one left, Melvyn," Steve called. "Surely you know you won't be getting out of this by now.

You've lost. Again. Let it go, pal."

"You want me, partner?" Melvyn taunted. "Come and get me!"

Steve turned to Selwyn and pointed at Sarah. "Keep her safe. I need to end this."

Sarah took his hand. "Don't. Don't stoop to his level."

"My dear, if I don't do this, then we're always going to wonder what could happen. He's in the past, we're not. He'll always have the power to mess with us. I'm sorry, but this ends now. I will not jeopardize you, Em, or any of our friends from the current Lentari, ever."

"I don't like this," Sarah said. She turned to the griffin. "Em, follow him. Follow *and* protect."

Emerion's eyes widened. "You're trusting me with … his life?"

Sarah laid her hands on either side of Emerion's avian head and rested hers against his. "We've tried to protect you with the best of our abilities. I … *we* have only wanted what's best for you. Now, I'm asking you to do the one thing I swore I never would, and that's to put yourself in danger. Please, protect Steve."

Emerion bowed. "I am honored. That is the ultimate request. Rest assured, I'll protect him with my life."

"The rest of us will be waiting outside. Please be careful." She teleported the others out of the cavern.

Steve turned to Em. "Are you ready? And don't worry. I've got your back."

"And I've got yours," Emerion returned.

"Would the two of you like some time alone?" Melvyn scoffed. "You're makin' me sick."

Steve ignited his hands. He nodded at Emerion and stepped away from the pillar. Melvyn was nowhere in sight.

An ear-splitting roar ripped the air. Steve flinched and the hairs on his arms stood on end. The ground trembled beneath his feet as he felt something large, something *solid*, walking his way. Emerion appeared next to his side and immediately used a wing to push him back.

"I don't like this," the griffin was saying.

"But I do!" a raw, powerful voice bellowed. "Oh, this is

gonna be fun, paarrrrtttnneerr!"

Two pillars of stone, each at least five feet thick, broke apart as hands as large as manhole covers smashed their way through. The creature that emerged was twelve feet tall, heavily muscled, and covered in a dense, matted brown fur. Two red eyes leered evilly at him as it lumbered forward.

"What is it?" Emerion asked.

"It's a drakyr!" Steve exclaimed, stifling a curse. "Melvyn's last spell must have been a shifting spell. We haven't seen one of these demons since the queen was kidnapped!"

Emerion screeched a challenge. "What do I need to know about them?"

"They're big, ugly, strong as hell, and can spit fire, like a dragon. Don't stay too long in one place!"

As if to make his point, the hellish figure opened its maw and a jet of flames burst forth, angling for Emerion. The griffin nimbly leapt away, leaping from mound, to rock, to stalagmite with ease.

Steve looked at the monster Melvyn had become and nodded. "I have to give credit where credit is due."

The drakyr's mouth gaped open. "Thank you. It's the ..."

"It's an improvement in looks, that's for sure."

Melvyn growled. His mouth opened again and Steve knew he was ready to fire. But, before he could, Emerion appeared behind the brown figure, gave a vicious swipe with his front talons, and leapt away. The drakyr roared in pain. Thick black blood welled out from the cuts and dripped onto the floor.

"Ooo, that's gotta sting," Steve decided.

He threw several chasers and spun them around the cavern before targeting Melvyn's chest. He watched the weirdly twisted arms brush the fire off as if it was nothing more than a dusting of dirt.

"That was pathetic," Melvyn snarled. He took several steps forward. "Didn't feel a thing. I ... arrgghh!"

Emerion had lashed out again. More blood dripped to the ground.

"I will turn that pet of yours into a blasted rug, do you hear me?" Melvyn howled. "Then, I'll put his head on my wall, hanging it next to yours! You're dead! All of you!"

Steve bolted from one stalagmite to another. Fortune was not on his side. Melvyn caught sight of him and let loose a barrage of fiery blasts. Steve swatted them aside and noticed Emerion approaching in stealth. It was time for another distraction.

He hopped onto the boulder in front of him, and, getting the drakyr's attention, fired off twin blasts. Both jets blasted past the walking nightmare, which earned him a smirk from Melvyn, until Steve's two jets curved in mid-air and circled around.

"Don't see that every day, do you?" Steve taunted, as Melvyn howled with frustration.

On and on it went, and a pattern became apparent. They had reached a stalemate.

"I think we need to regroup," Steve told the griffin. Both of them were winded and Steve's jhorun was feeling the strain of its constant use. "I feel like I'm fighting Flinn again." Steve looked around. "Where is he now?"

Emerion crawled to the nearest stalagmite and continued *up*. Thirty seconds later, he was back.

"He's still in the same place, nestled among a group of the stone formations. At the moment, he's staring up."

"Up?" Steve repeated. "Why? What's he looking at?"

"I tried determining that myself. I didn't see anything other than a few small holes. There's no way he'd fit unless he reverted to his human form. I deduce he's trying to find a way to use them to his advantage."

"Holes? Em, how close are they to Melvyn's location?"

"There are four. Three are a few meters away, and the last is closer. Why?"

"Show me. How big are they?"

Emerion used his wings to answer the question. Steve grunted. His hands flared to life. He generated a dozen chasers and flung them up. One after another, the fireballs slammed into the dark openings, causing chunks of stone to break away and fall down.

"It's not going to work!" Melvyn taunted. "You think rocks are gonna hurt me? This new form is far superior to yours! Think I'm joking? Come on, right now! I challenge you to a round of bare-knuckle boxing. No weapons, no fire, just you against me!"

"Do you honestly think I'll agree to that?" Steve scowled at the ceiling. Nothing was happening. He generated another dozen chasers and tried again, but his jhorun was significantly weaker, less than half of normal by this point. "There's nothing fair about a hand-to-hand fight, Melly."

"Don't call me that!" Melvyn roared. "And you'll agree, partner, or else I'll rip that pretty wife of yours limb from limb. Think I'm kidding? Try me."

"I'm detecting movement," Emerion reported.

"I know, I know. Melvyn's heading for Sarah. Come on, we have to …"

Emerion extended a wing and prevented him from moving. "No, not him. There's something on the ceiling. Several somethings. More are emerging from the holes you've been targeting."

Hope flared. Steve looked up, but couldn't see anything in the dim light.

"Tell me," Steve implored, lowering his voice to almost a whisper. "Do they look like rocks with legs? Ten apiece?"

"I'm counting. Yes. How did you know?"

"Quick, Em. How many are there?"

"I count five. No, now there's eight. No, they keep coming. There's at least fifteen now, with more on the way."

"Okay, mission accomplished. We've got to go now! Melvyn? As much fun as this has been, and as much grief as this has caused, I do believe it's time for us to part ways. Good luck, pal."

"Coward! You're fleeing from me? Are you kidding? If you don't face me now, I'll haunt you the rest of your … what the …?"

The creatures, scuttling about on the ceiling, began dropping like stones.

"Get off me! Get away!"

Parts of the cavern flared with light as Melvyn blasted fire at this new threat.

It was the guur. Steve knew, better than anyone, what

lived in the dwarf tunnels of *this* particular time. It was a problem that he, himself, would deal with back in his own time, during his first excursion to Lentari. But, that wouldn't happen for years. In this time, the nightmares-on-legs were plentiful.

He had guessed—correctly—that those holes were guur tunnels, home to heavily armored, ten-legged insects with a thirst for meat and an attraction to fire.

"Arrghh!" Melvyn howled. More flames ensued. "You sumbitch, you bit me! You dare to take a bite out of me? Out of me?! You nasty son of a … get off me!"

"He is lost," Emerion told Steve. "He is now covered with the large insects. I will carry you. Get on my back. Hurry! More are approaching. We must flee!

Steve didn't argue. He leapt onto Emerion's back. "Go, Em! Get out of here!"

The griffin bunched his muscles and sprinted in the opposite direction. Emerion effortlessly leapt over large formations, banked off of stalagmites, and pounced into the tunnel. In moments, they encountered Sarah, nervously pacing. The dwarf soldiers had lined up on either side of her, silently watching, as most clutched their torches.

Sarah looked up. "You're back! Did you …?"

She let out a cry of alarm as Steve suddenly pulled her into an embrace. "All of you, get close! Hurry! Sarah, get ready to teleport us out of here!"

Sarah nodded. "Say when."

Steve generated an extra-large chaser and flung it at the tunnel's mouth. It detonated on impact.

"Now!"

The rumbling began, as tons of broken stone fell from the ceiling and walls, and sealed off the cavern. Then, the soft filtered light from Borahgg surrounded them. They were now standing in the plaza, in front of the large council chambers. Of the hundred or so dwarf citizens who were present, all cried out with alarm and jumped away.

"What happened?" Sarah demanded. "Where's Melvyn?"

"He was invited to lunch," Steve told her. He started looking at their dwarf companions. "Tell me everyone is accounted for."

Brunt nodded. "We're all here. What happened? Did you encounter guur?"

"A whole group of them," Steve confirmed. "As for our fugitive, well, I'm not sorry to say that he became their guest of honor."

"What a way to go," Sarah breathed. "Em, how are you?"

"I am good."

"He's better than good," Steve told her. "He's a fantastic companion to have by your side during a battle. He inflicted more damage on Melvyn than I did. Nicely done, buddy. You made me proud."

Emerion nodded his appreciation.

"Just tell me what happened to Melvyn."

"Let's just say he's guur spoor."

Chapter Sixteen–Unexpected Revelation

Bet you didn't think we'd be seeing that again, did you?" Steve challenged, as they walked up to an iron gate set inside two brick pillars. The gates were closed, and a chain looped through the two gates to make sure they stayed that way. "I hope they're home."

"It's not like it's common to go on road trips in 1884," Sarah told him.

"Wouldn't it be, what, 1890 now?"

"Oh. You're right, of course. What now? Should we ring the bell?"

Steve nodded. "Ordinarily, I'd be worried about someone spotting Emerion out in the open like this, but in this case, I think we're fine."

"That's what's different!" Sarah exclaimed. "There are no neighbors! There should be two, one on either side! What happened to their houses? I don't see anything!"

"I'm pretty sure you took care of that when you insinuated to the good folk of Coeur d'Alene that Luther and Cora's house was haunted."

Sarah shrugged. "A girl's gotta do whatever it takes to survive in this world."

Steve burst out laughing. He caught the end of the rope dangling next to the right pillar and gave it a good yank. A brass bell sounded from somewhere on the other side.

"Remind me, this is someone you're related to?" Emerion asked.

"Luther is my great-great-grandfather."

Emerion squawked with surprise.

"It's true," Sarah confirmed.

"Who's there?" a male voice asked.

"Someone who wants to say hello," Steve called back.

"Fine, you've said it. Unless you'd care to tell me who you are, then I will wish you good day."

"Watch this," he whispered to Emerion. "How about … it's your great-great-grandson?"

There was a lengthy pause.

"S-Steve? It cannot be you!"

A man came hurrying around the corner. He was the same size as Steve. Luther had his hair in a short ponytail, longer than Steve remembered. Suddenly, the gate couldn't be opened quickly enough.

"Wizards be damned! Sarah, you're here, too? What in the world are you doing back here?"

"It's a long story," Steve began. "We …"

"I'm sorry to say I'll need another jorii if I'm to return you back to your time again."

Steve shook his head. "Don't worry about it, Luther. We came prepared this time. A spell was created explicitly to bring us here, and then to take us home."

Luther slipped his arms through Steve and Sarah's, and started to pull them through the gate, when he noticed their third companion.

"By the maker! There's a griffin here! How …? What …?"

Steve clapped a friendly hand on his ancestor's shoulder. "Luther Miller, meet Emerion, our son."

As predicted, Luther fell silent as he digested that bit of news.

"Adopted son," Emerion clarified, trilling with laughter.

Luther shoved the gates open. "By all means, come! You're all welcome here. Wait until Cora sees what I'm bringing her! How long will you be here?"

"Not long, I'm afraid," Sarah said. "We are only here long enough to put our timeline back in order."

"I don't understand," Luther admitted.

They rounded the bend in the road and came within sight of the manor. Steve smiled. His future home had been finished, the carriage house moved and expanded. Did that mean Mina, Luther's sister whom he rescued during their last visit, had already burned down the garage?

The manor door opened and two women appeared. One was unmistakably Luther's wife, Cora. She was wearing a bright yellow dress and a white hat, and if Steve didn't know any better, he'd say she was dressed for a day in town. Her companion was garbed similarly, wearing a light blue dress with a yellow hat. Both were wearing white shawls draped delicately around their shoulders. Cora's eyes widened.

"Guess who I bumped into today?" Luther said, smiling, as the four of them approached the house. "Are you headed somewhere, love?"

"Oh my word! Is that …? Could it be …? Mina, do you remember who these people are?"

In response, the younger woman let out an exclamation of surprise and rushed forward to fling herself into Steve's arms.

"I remember you! You are Steve, and you are Sarah. You are my kin! Oh, what a wonderful day!"

Mina released her grip on Steve and pulled Sarah in for a hug.

"You're looking much better, Mina," Sarah said, wiping away a tear from the corner of her eye. "You look … happy! Happy and healthy!"

Their trip to town long forgotten, Cora and Luther invited them inside and for the next hour, they shared stories. Naturally, questions were asked about Emerion. Steve and Sarah learned Cecil and AnnaBelle had moved to California after Cecil had been given the chance to manage his own bank branch. Rosamund Jones, unfortunately, became a widow last year after her husband, Gerry, passed away of natural causes. She ended up selling the Silver Spike Saloon for a hefty profit and moved back east to live with her sister.

After they had finished recounting everything that had happened to them since their prior visit, talk turned to the purpose of *this* visit. Luther and Cora, understandably, were astounded to learn about Melvyn's dastardly deeds and the messed up timeline. That was about the time a sleepy, tousle-headed boy of five appeared in the doorway, clutching a blanket.

"Oh, look who's awake," Cora said, motioning for the boy to join her. "Come meet some of Mommy and Daddy's friends. Everyone, this is Stephen."

The boy's eyes widened as he noticed the griffin resting on the ground, next to the couch. He pointed at Emerion.

"Is that a horse?"

"He's as big as a horse," Steve chuckled, earning himself an elbow to the gut. "This is Emerion. We call him Em. He travels with us."

The child digested this news with a solemn nod.

Steve turned to his aunt. "Mina, if you don't mind me asking, how are you doing? How are you finding life in a world without jhorun?"

"I'm loving it here," Luther's sister said, offering him a smile. "Besides, it's not like I was using my jhorun that much in Lentari in the first place. The people are so very nice, we have a kind and caring sheriff to keep us all safe, and a beautiful house I can call home."

"You'll always be welcome here," Cora promised her.

"Did you know," Luther began, "that Mina is quite the talented tapissier?"

Cora noticed their blank expressions.

"Embroiderer. Mina makes the most wonderful tapestries! She has started up her own shop and does incredibly well for herself."

"Good for you!" Steve praised.

"I will make you one," Mina promised. "But, I don't know where to put it to verify you'll eventually find it?"

"Put it in the same spot where you put all of Sarah's clothes from the last time we were here," Steve suggested.

"How do you know about that?" Luther asked, puzzled.

"It was in your letter."

"Letter? I've been thinking about writing you a letter, but I haven't done so yet."

Steve smiled. "You will."

"What will you do now?" Luther asked. He was sitting companionably next to his wife, and had his arm protectively wrapped around her waist.

"We head home and verify the king and queen are okay," Sarah answered. "Visiting Lentari with a broken timeline had to be one of the most unpleasant experiences of my life. Everyone I knew, and everything that I loved was gone, with no explanation why."

"I can only imagine," Luther breathed. He and his wife both shuddered. "I truly wish you could stay longer."

Steve rose to his feet, prompting the others to do the same. "I'm sorry, I know you do. And I'd love to see how the town has changed after Sheriff Melvyn's influence was removed, but speaking for the others, we'd like to go home. It's been a long couple of days."

"There's no need to apologize," Cora's soft voice told them. "We are so grateful you visited. It was such an unexpected surprise."

Emerion approached and bowed. "Thank you for protecting my parents while they were here the first time."

Cora turned to Luther. "Parents? Did I hear that right?"

"I'll fill you in later," Luther promised. "Oh, the stories you must be able to tell."

Steve hooked an arm around Emerion's neck and pulled the griffin close. "You have no idea. This bundle of fur and feathers was unexpected, but I'm so very glad Sarah brought him home. Em? Ready to head outta here?"

"I am."

Steve produced the seashell he had been carrying with him ever since the beginning of this adventure and gazed at it with fascination. Luther and Cora both seemed unimpressed by the object, but once Steve held it in his open palm, the shell began glowing and their attitudes quickly changed.

Sarah slipped her arm through his. With both of his companions in close physical contact, Steve glanced briefly at the spell before making eye contact with Luther one final time.

"See you around, gramps."

Luther sighed. "You just had to say that, didn't you?"

Steve grinned and took a breath. "I *invoke* you."

One moment they were in their mansion, and the next, bright sunshine shone down from above, filtered through the forest canopy. Falling water sounded nearby, with the cheery chirps and whistles of a multitude of birds assailing their senses from all directions.

Emerion wandered a few steps away and studied their surroundings. "Are we back in Lentari?"

Steve shrugged. "No clue. I was waiting for a flash of light, or a sense of dizziness, or something to suggest the spell worked. I didn't feel a thing."

"Neither did I," Sarah admitted. "Wait. Honey, are you still holding the spell?"

Steve opened his fist and saw that, indeed, he was still clutching the small white seashell. "It would appear so. I wonder why it didn't disappear?"

Sarah shrugged. "We'll probably never know. I mean, if everything worked, the Balthor who created it no longer exists, and the one from this time will have no memory of what happened. You know, this almost looks like … come on, I want to check something."

Steve and Emerion followed along as Sarah carefully picked her way through the woods. From the ever-increasing sounds of splashing water, Steve figured they must be headed toward a waterfall, and based on the area, it must be the one where their cabin was located. Or should be located. Or …?

"This is it," Sarah exclaimed. "All right, everyone. Cross your fingers. Er, Em, cross your talons."

Emerion looked at his front avian legs, shrugged, and rested one over the other. Sarah looked at the empty space where their cabin should be and recited the specially-selected word that would nullify Shardwyn's concealment spell. For a few moments, nothing happened, and Steve was ready to start swearing, but just then, a small one-bedroom log cabin appeared, popping into existence as if it had been there all along.

"Oh, thank goodness," Sarah sighed. "We made it back. When do you think Balthor's spell returned us? Assuming time progressed the same here, it'd be, what, a few days from when we originally left?"

A disturbance in the water caught their attention. Speechless, the three of them watched the surface of the small lake bulge outward, as though something was pushing from underneath. The growing mass of water continued to rise until a column had formed nearly a dozen feet high. It rippled as the shape changed to something more recognizable. A head formed, followed by a torso, waist, and right before their eyes, legs. The figure stepped onto shore as more curves continued to appear. Steve finally put it together.

"Aeia!"

The figure nodded. The watery figure rippled once more before more detail appeared and they could see the Ancient's eyes open. Aeia faced Steve and held up a finger.

"A correction, fire thrower. Your friend Balthor did *not* bring you back here. *I* did."

"Wh-what?" Steve sputtered. "He didn't? I mean, we have this spell, and ..."

Aeia extended a shimmery arm. Her hand appeared, palm facing up.

"Give her the shell," Sarah told him. "I think she wants to see it."

Steve handed it over. Aeia only had to close her fingers around the shell before she grunted. "It's as I thought. The shealk wizard neglected to take into consideration the trickiness of the time barrier to you mortals. Humans are simply not equipped to move to different points in time. As such, had I allowed this spell to run its course, you three would have ended up hundreds of years from now."

Steve swallowed nervously. "In the past or the future?"

Aeia's torso rippled as she shrugged. "Does it matter? A hundred years in the past, or a thousand in the future, it matters not."

"Why did you step in to help us?" Sarah asked.

Aeia's head turned. "Because I think you two have suffered long enough. And ... well, I thought you would benefit from an ally."

"An ally," Steve repeated. "Whoa. You? You're actively helping us?"

"I have been, since the beginning." Aeia's water form rippled a few more times before she finally shrunk herself down to their size and stepped onto the grass-covered ground. "As I told you before, your actions resulted in the return of my stone. I then realized that not all humans are ignorant louts. Er, no offense."

Steve waved a dismissive hand. "None taken, I assure you."

"I have a question for you. Usol gifted his stone to you. Why?"

"I think it was more for his amusement. That damn thing has been giving me headaches ever since he gave it to me."

"Then why not simply give it away?" Aeia asked. "The stones can only be given, never taken. I know you know this."

"I do," Steve confirmed. "But, I know how powerful those things are, and in the wrong hands? Well, we saw what happened when Flinn got his hands on yours."

"You intrigue me, fire thrower. Go. Check in with your companions. I do believe you'll find a life-changing decision is about to be made."

There was a large splash of water as Aeia's form collapsed to the ground as nothing more than several gallons of water. Ignoring the Ancient's departure, Steve gave Sarah a querulous look.

"What did she mean by that? A life-changing decision?" Steve pointed at their cabin. "Hide that thing and let's head to the castle. I want to see for myself if the true king and queen are back, and if they're okay."

Steve?

Hello, Pryllan. Oh, I'm so glad to hear from you.

Are you all right? I sense you've dealt with much stress in the past couple of days.

You have no idea. Is everyone okay there?

Aye. Is there a problem?

Not anymore. I'll fill you in the next time I see you, my friend.

Very well. See that you do. Until then.

Once their cabin had been properly secured, Sarah jumped them to the castle, choosing the throne room as her safe zone. The forest winked out, replaced by the same corner in the Great Hall that they had departed from only yesterday. Or had it been earlier today?

Steve shook his head. Had it only been two days? His mind was still spinning with the possible repercussions to their timeline should they have failed. What if the dragon-dwarf alliance had stalled? What if Maelnar now took extra precautions, and that alone caused him to have an accident?

The possibilities were endless.

Husband and wife surveyed the room. Guards were chatting among themselves, the kitchen staff was wiping down tables, and three musicians were playing a cheery song near the hall's entrance. It certainly felt like everything was back to normal.

Steve's eyes sought out the thrones. They were gilded once more. Gone were the ugly, uncomfortable iron chairs that the previous versions of the monarchs had used. Gone was the heightened security, and the closed windows. Every window in the hall was wide open, allowing fresh air to breeze through. He sighed with relief.

"I'm liking this already," he announced, as they studied the room. Colorful pennants were hung on several walls, and there was a steady flow of people walking to—and from—the castle interior. "This is what it should've looked like the first time. No one is stopping us because they don't know us, and certainly no one is surprised to see you walking with us, Em."

"And if the impostors are still here?" Emerion asked. "What then?"

"I think everything has been restored," Sarah said.

"Where to?" Steve wanted to know.

"Maybe the Antechamber?" Sarah suggested.

Steve nodded and, together, the three of them made their

way through the Great Hall and past the kitchens. Coming to a stop before the king's private chambers, Steve held his breath while two guards he didn't recognize, one standing on either side of the doors, looked up at their approach. After a moment's hesitation, one of the guards nodded, knocked once, and entered the room, no doubt to announce their presence.

"I'm telling you, Entu," they heard the queen's voice say, "it's time. Don't you want to … hello, is there something I can help you with? I'm sorry? They're here? Well, of course! Send them in."

The doors were opened and they were beckoned inside. The king was seated at his desk, and was just replacing his crown, when he looked up to watch them enter. A smile appeared on his tired face.

Kri'Entu, the current king of Lentari, was near the same age as Steve, only he had considerably more gray in his hair. Steve figured it was the same with all kings and presidents. Being responsible for thousands of people, and their overall safety, inevitably takes its toll on the body. The king was slightly taller than Steve, much leaner, and had a gaze that Steve maintained could make the most hardened criminal crack in less than ten seconds. But, Steve had also gone on record several times, saying he had to be the most patient person he had ever encountered. Anyone else would have pulled their hair out after listening to numerous, *frivolous* complaints by the people, yet Kri'Entu had never lost his professional—and regal—demeanor. Ever.

Ny'Callé was wearing a long purple gown, had her brown hair woven into a single braid, and judging from her body language and the way she was standing next to her husband's desk, with her arms folded across her chest, had been in the midst of some type of argument with the king. The queen was slightly older than Sarah, was shorter by several inches, and was without a doubt, the kindest woman Steve had ever met. Would he ever admit that out loud?

Steve chuckled and gave a mental shake of his head. He'd been married too long to get caught in a situation like that.

"Sir Steve! Lady Sarah!" Ny'Callé exclaimed. "So good to

see you both. I didn't know you were here."

"Nor did I," Kri'Entu added, with a smile. "What can we do for you?"

"We're so very sorry to interrupt," Steve said, after hesitating for a moment to figure out how to best phrase his response. "Ah, er, is everything all right?"

Kri'Entu's face hardened. "Why? What's happened?"

Steve stretched his back and held out an arm, indicating the chairs set around the hearth. "Got a minute? Or an hour? There's something we need to tell you."

This time, since both husband and wife carefully considered what they were willing to tell the Kri'yans, it took nearly two hours to relay everything that had happened, starting from the time they noticed their keys were missing in their world, all the way to saying their farewells to Luther and Cora for a second time. Kri'Entu sat back in his chair and asked all the appropriate questions, while Ny'Callé listened to the tale, and their exploits, with sheer incredulity written on her face. As soon as Steve had finished, the queen turned angrily to her husband.

"See, Entu? This is a sign. *This* is telling us that it's time."

"It's time for what?" Steve wanted to know.

"Time for a change," Ny'Callé answered.

Kri'Entu removed his crown and set it on an end table near his chair.

"I cannot believe I'm going to say this, but I do believe you're right, my love. Life is too short. In fact …"

Kri'Entu trailed off as he rose to his feet, strode to his desk, and retrieved a piece of parchment. The room fell silent, so that the only thing they could hear was the soft scratching of the king's quill. He took the paper, folded it in half, and handed it to a nearby guard.

"Would you take care of this for me?"

The soldier bowed. "Of course, Your Majesty."

"What's going on?" Steve asked, as the king rejoined them at the hearth. "Did you just send a message to someone?"

"I did," Kri'Entu confirmed. "So, if we're going to do this, and I now know we are, then we will do it properly."

"What's going on?" Emerion asked.

Sarah laid a finger on the griffin's beak. "Hush. We'll know soon."

Ten minutes later, the Antechamber's door opened, admitting several people. Chief among them was Kre'Mikal, who was leading the way. Lissa followed close behind, cradling a young toddler on her hip. A very familiar face was behind them.

Steve rose to his feet. "Rhenyon! I'll be damned! It's good to see you, buddy. How's retirement treating you?"

The two friends clasped forearms.

"Sir Steve! You're looking well! And Lady Sarah. A pleasure to see you both."

Sarah gave the former commander a hug. "It's nice to see you, Rhenyon. Retirement suits you. What are you doing here? We had become accustomed to seeing you only on special occasions."

Rhenyon nodded toward the king. "This one qualifies. The king knew I was at the castle, visiting a friend. He asked that I stop by."

Heads turned. Kri'Entu nodded. "Aye, I asked for some advice, just like old times."

Lissa set her daughter down and hugged Sarah. Little Vivian wasted no time in scurrying over to Steve and holding her arms up. Grinning, Steve scooped the girl up.

"Hey there, princess! Your Majesty? You asked for advice? If you don't mind me asking, will you tell us why?"

The king made a signal to the guards. Within moments, several more chairs were added to the group. Once everyone was seated, Kri'Entu smiled warmly at his granddaughter before turning to his wife. "My darling dear, you're right. It's time."

Ny'Callé gasped with surprise. "You mean …?"

Entu turned to Mikal. "You've become a fine young man, my son. You will make a fine king."

"When the time is right," Kre'Mikal agreed, nodding. He clasped Lissa's hand in his own and was in the process of turning to check on his daughter when he caught sight of Lissa's face. She was staring at the king. "Is there something I missed, Father?"

"Effective in one month, your mother and I will step down from the throne. You and Lissa will become king and queen."

Steve's eyebrows shot up. This was the advice Kri'Entu was seeking from Rhenyon? He turned to Mikal, who was staring—slack-jawed—at his parents.

"You'll make a fantastic king," Steve told him, slapping the twenty-six-year-old prince on the back. "If you ask me, you've already proven yourself a very dependable one."

"Y-you're retiring?" Mikal sputtered. "Whatever for? You're not that old, Father."

"Life is short, son," Kri'Entu told him. "We've done our part. I think it's time to accept Sir Steve and Lady Sarah's offer and move to the kingdom of Idaho."

"I'm not ready!" Kre'Mikal protested.

"Yes, you are," Ny'Callé countered. "We both believe that … Entu? Where's Shardwyn?"

The king frowned as he realized the castle wizard wasn't in attendance. He rose and headed for his desk. "I'll summon him. It's not like him to …"

The Anteroom's doors opened, permitting a young man and woman, younger still than Mikal, to enter the room. The man was tall, had thick brown hair, and a tiny wisp of a beard. He was very lean, and his clothes practically hung off him. The girl had fiery red hair, was much shorter, and wore black spectacles. She locked eyes with Steve and nodded once.

"This is a private meeting," the closest guard said, as he moved to block the couple from coming any farther into the room. "You'll have to wait outside."

The strange man's nose lifted. "Lay one hand on me, or my wife, and I'll turn you into a troll."

Sarah gasped. "I would know that voice anywhere! Shardwyn, is that you?"

The entire room gasped with surprise. Kri'Entu and Ny'Callé quickly stood and approached the couple.

"Shardwyn?" Kri'Entu asked. "Is that really you?"

"It is, Your Majesty. I brewed a …"

"Your wife?" Steve interrupted. "She's your wife? Holy crap on a cracker. Andra? Miss Andra Alwyn, the head of the Archives?"

Surprisingly, the girl flashed a smile at Steve before slipping her arm through Shardwyn's.

"We married early this morning," Andra announced, as she proudly showed off her wedding band, a glowing teal ring. "I suggested to my new husband that it'd be nice if we could be young again, and experience a full life together. And look what he did! Isn't it amazing?"

Speechless, Kri'Entu looked at Ny'Callé, who could only nod.

"What about your work at the Archives?" Steve asked. "Everyone's afraid of you. If you look like that, you're going to lose your reputation as the castle's fiercest records keeper."

Andra actually blushed. "I, er, tendered my resignation. I've worked with books and scrolls my entire life. Now, I think I've earned my retirement. I apologize for giving you such little notice, Your Majesties."

"Think nothing of it," Ny'Callé assured her. "We can only hope to find a suitable replacement with *half* of your qualifications."

Steve looked at Andra. "Can I ask you something? Have you ever heard of a graeus?"

The former archivist stared at Steve for a few moments. "A very rare relative of the griffins. Gold, with four wings. There have been no reported sightings in years. Have you …?"

"Emerion and I saw one, yes. But, it was also over a hundred years ago. What was his name, Em?"

"Zieth."

"Fascinating," Andra breathed. "I could … no, I'm no longer in charge of the Archives. That is a habit that will be hard to break."

Ny'Callé suddenly straightened in her chair. "Wait. Andra, if you're retiring, does that mean …? Shardwyn, are you leaving us, too?"

The tall youth nodded eagerly. "I am, I am. I know it'll be difficult to find someone to replace me …"

"… it's not as hard as you might think," Steve mumbled, under his breath. The king overheard and snickered once.

"… but I do know you will be fine. Your Majesty, I have

never seen you fail at *anything*."

"We wish you nothing but happiness," the queen told them. "Go. Be happy."

Once the lovestruck couple—walking hand-in-hand—had left, Kri'Entu looked at Kre'Mikal and sighed. "I do believe I need to talk with your friend, Mister Gareth. He ... actually, I think this will be *your* first item of business."

Mikal nodded. "In that case, it'll be an easy one." He pulled a tiny figurine from his pocket and knocked it against the table three times. "Gareth."

Nothing happened for several seconds. Then appeared a brilliant flash of light. Gareth, Shardwyn's former apprentice, and wizard-extraordinaire, appeared, munching on an apple.

"Hey Mikal. Steve! Sarah!"

Steve nodded. "Hey, Gareth. It's good to see you. Listen, I just thought of something. When's the next time you're going to see your father?"

"In a couple of days. He and I will be going fishing, as shealk. How cool is that?"

"Very. Listen, tell him I have something for him. If he wants to know how I got it, then see if you can arrange a meeting, okay?"

"You have something of his? What is it?"

Steve passed the white seashell to Gareth. "This is his ..."

"... marisk shell! What are you doing with it? How'd you get it?"

Steve grinned. "That's a story for another time. Literally. Let him know, would you?"

"You got it. Hey, Emerion! I didn't notice you over there. What's everyone ...?"

"Lose the apple," Lissa quietly told him.

"Oh, yeah. Sorry. What's going on? What's the emergency?"

"You told me something a year ago that still resonates with me," Mikal formally began. "So, I'll simply say congratulations. You've been promoted."

"Promoted? The only way I could do that would be ... no! Did Shardwyn finally make that de-aging spell?"

"You knew he was going to do that?" Mikal asked.

"He talks to himself all the time," Gareth explained, shrugging. He turned to the king. "So, is it official? I'm being offered the position of castle wizard?"

"Do not look at me, Mister Gareth. You'll need to confirm with my son. The king."

"Your son, the … *what?*" Gareth repeated. His eyes widened. "You guys are retiring! You're moving to their world, aren't you? How cool is that!"

The former king and queen looked at Steve and Sarah.

"We are," Kri'Entu confirmed. "Provided, of course, your more than generous offer is still open?"

Steve took Sarah's hand and pulled her close. "Welcome to Idaho, Your Majesties."

Author's Note

Welcome back to Lentari! I have some people to thank for this return visit. First off, that'd be you, the reader. While never specifying that *These are Not the Stones You're Looking For* (ToL#9) was going to be the last fantasy set in Lentari, I kinda left it that way. But, my wife encouraged me to return to the kingdom and see if I could come up with any stories. Before I knew it, I had a plot sketched out and I was six chapters in. This one was in the works for a while, and I can definitely appreciate my wife's not-so-subtle pushes toward making it the final title in the Tales of Lentari. Yes, that's right. This story has wrapped up a lot of plot threads, and it is definitely the place to end the series. I hope you all like the way it ended. with the king's retirement, the bad guy vanquished, and new roles for the other characters.

If you enjoyed the story, please don't forget to leave a review. They really do help us authors by making us more "discoverable" in the big search engines at all the retailers. So, wherever you purchased the book, please consider telling others what you enjoyed about the book. Thank you!

Happy reading!

J.
July, 2023

ABOUT THE AUTHOR

Jeffrey M. Poole is a professional writer who writes in both the fantasy and mystery genres. He lives in picturesque Southern Oregon, with his wife, Giliane, and their Welsh Corgi, Kinsey. His interests include archery, astronomy, archaeology, scuba diving, collecting movies, collecting swords, and tinkering with any electronic gadget he can get his hands on.

In March, 2015, Jeffrey became a proud member of SFWA, the Science Fiction & Fantasy Writers of America! Jeffrey encourages readers to connect with him on Facebook (facebook.com/bakkianchronicles). Fans can also follow him online at: www.AuthorJMPoole.com where you can sign up for his newsletter and receive a free short story.

BOOKS BY JEFFREY POOLE

BAKKIAN CHRONICLES
The Prophecy
Insurrection
Amulet of Aria
Disneyland Debacle (short story)
Winter Wonderland (short story)

TALES OF LENTARI
Lost City
Something Wyverian This Way Comes
A Portal for Your Thoughts
Thoughts for A Portal
Wizard in the Woods
Close Encounters of the Magical Kind
The Hunt for Red Oskorlisk (short story)
May the Fang Be With You (Pirates trilogy #1)
The Hammer is Strong with This One (Pirates #2)
These are Not the Stones You're Looking For (Pirates #3)
Blast from the Past

DRAGONS OF ANDELA
Harness the Fire
Strike the Spark

Mystery
CORGI CASE FILES

Case of the One-Eyed Tiger
Case of the Fleet-Footed Mummy
Case of the Holiday Hijinks
Case of the Pilfered Pooches
Case of the Muffin Murders
Case of the Chatty Roadrunner
Case of the Highland House Haunting
Case of the Ostentatious Otters
Case of the Dysfunctional Daredevils
Case of the Abandoned Bones

Case of the Great Cranberry Caper
Case of the Shady Shamrock
Case of the Ragin' Cajun
Case of the Missing Marine
Case of the Stuttering Parrot
Case of the Rusty Sword
Case of the Unlucky Emperor
Case of the Ice Cream Crime
Case of the Hobbit Heist
Case of the Secret Staircase
(short story)